CAROUSEL

To my mother, Joyce, who, in those torturous early days, always kept asking.

SPRING

CHAPTER 1

LUKE

"That's how I looked?"

Luke smiled. This was the first time she'd seen herself on canvas and he was fully prepared for her reaction. "You don't like it."

"I'm all shadow," Emma told him. "Like a ghost. Like I'm not really there."

"You weren't really there. You were staring out of the window." He stepped behind her, slid his arms around her waist, relieved that she didn't pull away as he looked over her shoulder at the painting. He could feel her warmth against his body and smell shampoo in her loosely braided hair. "And you don't look like a ghost, you look beautiful."

"Well, at least you didn't paint me naked." Her voice became softer, more amenable. "Does this mean I'm your muse?"

"You've always been my muse." He leaned in further and nuzzled her neck.

She laughed. "Sure. We've been together six months and your brother told me you've been painting since you could crawl."

"He told you that, huh?"

"Yes, he did."

"Hmm." He fell silent, studied the picture and resolved not to show her the one he'd painted not long after they'd met where she was unequivocally naked, an altogether different play on light and shadow now hiding in the midst of a stack of canvases back at the apartment.

"Are you scared?" she asked after a moment.

"About tonight? Nope." Wrapped around her like this he felt at peace and content; he felt grounded and safe and he was determined to savor the moment. As for tonight's exhibition, only the second in his fledgling, not so illustrious career, was he scared about that? Hell, no, he was terrified.

He made an effort. He changed into unfamiliar clothes, forsaking his usual jeans and T-shirt for tailored black pants and a gray cashmere sweater Emma had bought for him, and for the better part of two hours he stood nursing a tiny plastic tumbler filled with cheap chardonnay, and stoically bore the companionship of strangers while they discussed their interpretation of his work and quizzed him about the bullshit artist's statement Emma had written for him. He tried to be polite, and he tried desperately to pretend the surrounding walls were not covered with pieces of his soul, ripped out and stretched painfully over canvas.

However, painful or not, his work had been beautifully presented and he had to give Rob, the gallery owner, his due, and each canvas had been hung in the order he'd requested and had been given the correct amount of light and space. Rob got it. Presented like this, the man had enthused, it's like a trip through a nightmare. Sure, just like being here was akin to standing naked on a street corner during rush hour, and Luke figured he would be glad when the evening was over, despite the real economic need to put a few sales under his belt and get his name out there.

Emma was nowhere in sight. She had already met up with a couple of friends from college and they were squirreled away in a corner somewhere, probably catching up on the latest gossip. The guy from the local press had already been and gone, and at the opposite side of the gallery the female artist— with whom he was sharing the exhibition— was surrounded by a gathering of nodding, smiling sycophants. He couldn't recall anyone smiling like that while they were looking at his work, but then he wasn't sure if that was a good or a bad thing. Their respective styles, dark and light, barely complemented one another.

A few more minutes and he made his excuses and found a quiet area where he could dial down the noise. He tried not to pace back and forth, or prowl as Emma called it. You're doing it again, she'd have said, prowling like a starving wolf. And so he attempted to relax. He nodded at two of the local matrons who'd already given his work a critical once over and had proved surprisingly erudite and quite shocked when he'd revealed he had none of the formal art education they'd expected. A natural they'd called him, and had smiled and chatted to him for quite a while and it felt mildly disingenuous now to wonder if they considered his lack of education a mark against him. Very likely his opposite number at the other end of the room had MFAs coming out of her ears.

So what? Don't be so fucking defensive. The voice of his elder brother was a demon perched on his inner shoulder. Typical that John always found a way in, despite being perpetually absent.

He began a slow march along the back wall, so busy pushing out all the unwelcome thoughts in his head that he didn't notice it at first. Just a small tag on the bottom corner of the title card and, once seen, his mind was about to write it off in disbelief until he did a double take.

Sold.

And now he had to fight hard to stop a goofy grin from splitting his face in two. He also wanted to punch the air, but that would have been undeniably gauche and so he reined it all in as best he could and looked around for Emma. He took a large swig of wine that was sour and warm after being held so long in plastic between nervous fingers. He stepped away from the painting to avoid becoming mesmerized by that little sold tag, and he spotted his girlfriend at the far side of the gallery, on the light side, talking animatedly to those friends she'd brought with her. He tried to attract her attention, but before he got the chance, someone stepped in front of him.

"I'm assuming she didn't sit for that."

Luke was tall, around 6 ft. 1 in., and yet he still had to look up at the man who had a slender build and hair the color of pale limestone. The air seemed cold all of a sudden, as if the guy had recently stepped inside and had brought the outside with him. "No, she didn't," he replied. His voice quickly assumed the practiced cadence he'd employed all evening. "I caught her unawares, just a couple of quick sketches before she saw me."

The man nodded. "You captured her beautifully."

"Thanks." Pity I can't sell it twice, he thought. He stood up tall and straight, as if it mattered.

The stranger glanced at the art on the surrounding walls. In this particular corner, along with Emma's painting, were a street scene and two variations on his doorway theme, all of them inviting the viewer to step further, beyond the canvas. "This is— impressive. Is this everything?"

"No. But I don't have any others for sale right now." The guy was beginning to get under his skin, like a splinter, and for no particular reason he could think of.

"I see. Well, I have to say I'm surprised you wanted to part with this one," the other man continued. "And I think you undercharged. Although I'm not complaining."

"You bought this?"

The man smiled. The expression softened his features and made him look pale, tired, as though he'd traveled a long way to get here. "Yes, and two others. I like the— how does it go— compelling arrangement of shadow—"

"That was Emma," Luke said, abruptly embarrassed.

"The girl in the portrait. The one doing an excellent job over there, of promoting your work this evening."

"She sold you on it?"

"Not exactly." The man was staring toward the painting— his painting now— his eyes as far away as the subject on canvas. "So. Can I call you Luke or would you prefer Mr. De Grasse?"

"Luke's fine." A warning bell was still ringing. Just a faint toll but enough to tell him something was coming, and his mind toyed with a variety of reasons, most of them drifting toward the abrupt chill and how the guy was giving him the creeps.

"Very well. So tell me, Luke, how are your grant applications coming along?"

He frowned, disappointed. He thought it would be something more profound than this and okay, I'm broke, and why don't you mind your own fucking business? He opened his mouth and hoped that last sentiment wouldn't come out while he wrestled with the composition of a polite, non-defensive reply.

The man held up a hand, stopped him short. "I know. An intrusive question. However, I have a proposition for you, a commission, not art on canvas I'm afraid, but it would pay well. Enough to keep you solvent until your grants came through."

"I see. What kind of commission?" Still hostile he wanted to say no, and knew he couldn't. Not really.

The man shrugged, gave him a smile laced with challenge. "Would it matter?" He made Luke an offer, one that had a big, shiny number attached to it.

Luke had to struggle to get the words out. "For that kind of money I'll do what the hell you want."

"Good, that's what I wanted to hear."

"Do I get to know what it is?" It came out mildly belligerent. He couldn't help it despite the offer, regardless that he was swimming in dollar signs. With the amount of money currently on the table he should have been down on his knees. And yet...

The stranger shrugged. "I'd rather you came at it with no preconceptions. It's a precursor, to a much larger project."

Luke gave him a flat grin. "Is it a test?"

"Yes. Are you up for it?"

"Like I said, for that kind of money. Look, if we're making a deal, I don't even know your name."

"Black, Elliot Black. You may call me Elliot." He held out a hand and they shook. The man's grip was so hard it soon became intolerable.

"Careful. I need that." Luke regarded his hand. He wanted to smile, to laugh off the crushed knuckles, but the laughter didn't arrive.

Elliot Black checked his watch. "I have a plane to catch. It's been good meeting you, Luke, I have your details and so I'll bid you farewell, and rest assured I'll be in touch."

Luke watched him go, saw him pause and talk to Rob for a little while. He saw them shake hands and this time he did smile when he saw Rob wince afterwards. He set off toward the gallery owner but after a pace or two he felt a hand slide into his own; delicate, decidedly more gentle fingers he recognized immediately.

"Who was that?" Emma was staring toward the entrance.

"The man who just bought your painting."

She stared at him, her mouth slightly ajar. "Oh. Wow." And when he didn't reply, "He had money, going off the suit he was wearing. Maybe he's a big shot collector and you're about to become famous."

Luke shrugged, began to wish he hadn't let Rob hang her picture and realized it was a sentiment he couldn't afford. "He had money enough to buy three pieces," he told her, "and he just offered me a shit load more."

Her face lit up. "Is he buying your entire collection?"

"No." He looked out beyond the main entrance, to the darkness outside. "Until he gets in touch I don't know what he wants."

"Are you okay?" she asked. "You look, I don't know— not how I'd expect a guy who'd sold three paintings to look."

"I'm fine," he lied.

And for the remainder of the evening he didn't trust himself to be in any way coherent, or polite, and so he stayed by Emma's side and let her do all the talking. He could feel her concern and uncertainty toward him via the occasional touch or glance. But he had no answers, only more questions. And not just about the stranger, either. His own behavior was rattling him, too. He should have been jumping for joy, thinking about paying off the rent he owed, and not having to beg Emma to let him sleep at her place when his landlord finally gave up and had him evicted.

The stranger had also said it was a precursor. But a precursor to what? He should have asked more questions, been more eloquent, more loquacious and inquisitive and all those other things that would have given him more clues about the guy and what his mysterious, extremely well paid project was, when instead he'd acted as if he were backed into a corner, defensive, uncomfortable; a rat with no other recourse than to bite its way out.

Had it been him offering the deal, he might have said screw it and walked out. Could be the guy was having second thoughts right now. And there, on that particularly dour note, his mood hung.

The gallery owner, in contrast, was over the moon.

"I guess three pieces isn't so bad," Luke admitted at the end of the night.

"Actually, it was five," Rob told him. "Those two ladies who'd been following you around all night bought one, and a couple passing through from Los Angeles bought the street corner piece. That's almost a third of the collection and I'm certain Gerard Helms at the Examiner is going to give you a good write up. He seemed particularly enamored."

Luke rubbed the bridge of his nose. "I guess I haven't been paying attention."

Emma and Rob were staring at him.

"What? It's just, that guy who came in—"

"Dr. Black?" Rob asked. "Did you know he went straight to your side of the gallery? And he hardly looked around at all. But he wanted to know all about you."

"And what did you—" He stopped himself, felt the bile rising, along with the inexplicable need to protect himself at all costs from his new benefactor.

"Don't worry. I just gave him your bio," Rob told him. "And I didn't mention your obsessive hanging requirements once." He followed it up with a wink that made Emma laugh. She squeezed Luke's hand. You're being an ass, the gesture said. It was enough for him to try out a smile and to his credit he almost succeeded.

"Sorry," he offered. "Tired, I guess."

"That's fine," the indefatigable Rob told him. "Go home. We can talk business tomorrow."

He nodded, felt a burden lift, as though he'd been carrying sacks of grain on his shoulders and they'd just landed with an almighty and rejoicing thud on the floor.

On the way home he sat silently in the passenger seat of Emma's battered car. He noticed with some relief they were heading for her place. In his current mood he suspected, had he been left alone, he would spend the entire night pacing and going over the events of the evening, and then the ground would open up, and then it would be a slow slide, all the way down—

"So, what is it, Luke? What's wrong?"

He shifted position slightly, so he could look at her. Her attention was on the road and her brow bore a slight frown of concern. "I don't know," he said. He watched her face grow pale for a moment, illuminated by lights from a passing car. She looked fragile and precious, his little goddess, and he felt undeserving. He reached across, placed his hand on her thigh, saw her break into a smile. And so he kept it there until they arrived at her apartment.

Inside he was even more tactile. He wanted to wipe away the uncomfortable feeling he'd had ever since he'd laid eyes on the strange Elliot Black and his lips and hands became hungry and he pushed her against the wall and slid his fingers beneath her shirt.

"Not here," she whispered. "Let's go to bed."

He let her go, let her take him, and hours later, still awake, he lay propped up on one elbow, playing with tendrils of her hair while he watched her sleep. It was a familiar ritual, an interlude before oblivion finally captured him, and usually he was content enough to let his mind roam across whatever landscape it pleased in the meantime. But on this occasion the foreboding he'd felt earlier was still with him, sliding along his nerve endings like a violin bow, and no matter how often he tried to divert his attention away it was back moments later.

It wasn't a question of *if* he should go ahead. He'd already picked up the gauntlet, accepted the challenge and felt confident enough that he could rise up and meet whatever Black threw at him; that part of the deal was fine. So instead he toyed with the consequences, which ran the gamut of an important shift in his career, all the way through to the notion that he'd just sold his soul to the devil. In the end he suspected it was more of the former, seeing as he didn't believe in the latter, and so persuaded, he scolded himself for being a wuss and finally drifted off to sleep.

Hours later, in the moments before awakening he dreamed of horses. They were screaming and it was a horrible, gut-wrenching sound. They were trapped, they were tied down, and they couldn't get out. And they were entirely engulfed in flame.

CHAPTER 2

EMMA

"And is he always so intense?"

"I guess." Emma leaned forward in her seat and wished she hadn't said anything. She tucked resolutely into the remains of her salad.

"Well, he's a looker, and extremely talented. Where did you find him?"

Luke had been the topic of conversation for the last twenty minutes, and for one reason or another they seemed to have worked backwards, starting with the awkwardly intimate subject of how he was in bed to the more polite 'where did you find him.' But that was Gillian, always straight to the point, always wanting the excruciating, personal details. It was part of the price Emma knew she would have to pay on getting her friend to go to the exhibition last week. The woman was gregarious and enthusiastic, would spread the word like wildfire around campus on how good Luke was, along with all the variables of their sex life. Sorry, baby. The price of fame.

"Remember I used to work at the art store?" And when her friend nodded, "He came in, we got talking." Presented like that, in two short sentences, it sounded ordinary and commonplace, and not at all like the actual heart stopping moment when she had set eyes on him— tall and lean, with dark hair and dark eyes that reeled her in like a fish. But she'd already given her friend more than enough.

Gillian nodded. "But six months, and you never said anything? Aren't you the dark horse." She laughed. "Does he have a brother?"

"Yes, he does. But I doubt you'd want to meet him." John— the surly, inevitable downside to her wonderful discovery. She'd met Luke's elder brother only twice, and on both occasions he'd acted with disdain and dislike and had given her no clue as to why.

"Not my type?"

"Not anyone's type. He's a felon for one thing." Ah, and now she was definitely giving away too much, not that the guy in question didn't deserve it.

Gillian held up her fork, brandished it like a wand. "No thanks. Life's complicated enough. So, where's he from? You met his parents, stuff like that?"

"His mom died when he was young. His father, I don't know. To be honest, I'm not pushing it." She left it at that. No need to go into past relationships and a desire for breathing space.

Her friend grinned. "I admire your restraint. Me, I like to know everything on the first date."

They lapsed into silence and finished their lunch, leaving Emma wondering if she'd been a little too forthcoming about Luke and that night after the exhibition, almost a week ago now, when she'd taken him home and they'd gone to bed, and at some point during the night he'd pinned her down like a butterfly under glass and his hand had been wrapped in her hair and he'd pulled slowly, relentlessly until her scalp was tingling. And she had felt his lips brush lightly against her flesh and he'd whispered. Tell me you want me. Tell me you love me. So needy and demanding and he hadn't let go until she'd said it. He'd made her repeat it, too, as if he was desperate for confirmation and the words were a magic spell that would calm whatever dark mood rode rampant and unchecked inside him.

"Hello? Are you in there?" Gillian was staring at her, another smile on her face. "Are you in love with him?"

Caught out, Emma felt her cheeks starting to glow. "I guess."

They both laughed.

"Hey, I'm happy for you. I hope it works out."

Emma nodded, her smile hopeful. "Yeah, me too."

After lunch, she said her farewells and set off for the library, and a few hours later her shoulders were sore and aching after being hunched over a multi-layered spread of opened books. However, it had been time well spent. Prior readings of Pirenne's and Hodges' conflicting theses on the origins of Europe had succeeded in pecking merciless holes in her Medieval History paper, but now she had further insight thanks to the discovery of two thick volumes published in the 1950s that had been languishing on the library shelves. Their attached bibliographies had also hinted at much more, until practicality had informed her she had less than a month before her assignment was due.

She leaned back in her seat and rubbed her eyes. Because of her lunch date she hadn't brought her laptop and the table was covered with scattered pages of notes. She stared at them, and figured by the time she'd compiled and typed them up her evening would be pretty much accounted for.

Her phone began to vibrate and slide across the table. It heralded a text from Luke. Come see what's been delivered. She stared at it. Dr. Elliot Black's mysterious project? They'd been talking about it for days.

She smiled, and quietly gathered up her papers. It

wasn't exactly busy in this particular hall, only two other people sitting at the tables, and a man standing by the door—imposing, hands behind his back, looking in her direction. A second glance and he was wearing knee breeches, and while she stuffed her notes into her bag she made the decision to ask him if there was an ongoing theatrical event. But by the time she had collected her belongings and was heading toward the door, he had gone.

Outside, she crossed the street to her vehicle, still on the lookout for people dressed in historical garb, but she saw nothing out of the ordinary and disappointed, she shook her head, slid into her car and set off toward Luke's apartment.

It was near dark by the time she arrived, all the closest parking spaces were taken up and so she had to park a block away and walk along an ill-lit sidewalk. The apartment wasn't in the best neighborhood and so she wore her game face and kept an eye out for trouble while trees rustled overhead, whispering in the breeze like a choir of ghosts, making her wish she had set off earlier while it was still light. The deepening twilight played with her eyes, confused her depth of field and allowed the journey to appear endless. Dark ivy clotted the ground on either side of the sidewalk and occasionally shifted as she walked past, as if something was hiding beneath them. Rats, she thought.

The light at the entrance to the apartment block was faulty and flashed intermittently on her approach. Almost there and she thought she saw someone waiting at the gate, a man in silhouette. The lack of detail made her wary; an inner alarm telling her he might be hiding there, waiting for anyone unsuspecting and she instinctively checked her pocket for her phone. Her eyes were away from the gate for maybe half a second, but when she looked back again the man was gone.

She stopped on the sidewalk, a mere ten paces away. Had he ducked out of sight? Was he waiting around the corner? Her heart hammered and she felt cold sweat emerging at the base of her spine and she cursed Luke for living at the shitty end of town. But in the end she scolded herself for being so jumpy. There was a liquor store at the end of the street, she had her phone, she was maybe fifty feet away from Luke's door and anyway it was probably someone smoking a cigarette. There were people hanging around outside buildings all the time for that very reason.

She kept wide of the gate, determined not to enter until she could see if there was anyone there, which of course there wasn't, and she began to wonder if she had imagined the whole thing, especially when she failed to detect the usual telltale smell of smoke.

As usual Luke's door was unlocked and so she let herself in, and had to squeeze past hillocks of plastic wrap, sheets of wood paneling, and wade through bundles of thin, knotted straw in order to get into a room that doubled as Luke's living area and studio.

He was crouched low, his hair fallen forward, partially covering his face while those long, adept fingers were carefully pulling away the remaining bundles of straw from the thing in the center of the room.

Still a little spooked, she had to clear her throat before she could talk. "Is that what I think it is?"

He looked up, grinned. "Yep. An old carousel horse. Come and take a look."

Emma stepped carefully over the tangle of packaging. "It looks ancient."

He stood up, put his arm around her and kissed the top of her forehead. "It's from our friend, Elliot Black." He raised his eyebrows conspiratorially and went back to his perusal of the carved horse.

The brightly lit room and the company of a lover melted

her earlier apprehension and she immediately forgot all about the shadow at the gate. "Your mystery project." She pointed. "What are those pieces of metal on the side?"

"They're to hang stirrups. I think."

He let her go and she crept forward, ran her fingers over the bare wood, and marveled over the shape of it. She saw places where tiny patches of filler had been applied then sanded smooth. "The musculature, the saddle, it's all beautifully carved. And someone has given it a new ear."

"Yeah." Luke had torn open an envelope and was examining a small sheaf of papers. "And it looks like he's given me carte blanche, as promised."

"So, what color are you going to paint it?"

He looked across at her and grinned. "What color do you think?"

She helped him clear up the mess of packaging materials, but once it was all stowed away the room still felt overcrowded. The carved horse appeared to have grown and commandeered all available space. Luke was oblivious, already sitting on the arm of the couch, sketchbook in hand, charcoal moving quickly over the page.

She left him to it, went into the kitchen and made some coffee, then took a seat and watched him. He was utterly engrossed, the hint of a lopsided smile on his face as he filled one page, and then another, his coffee getting cold alongside him. It was as if she didn't exist; just Luke and his subject and everything else had disappeared.

When they had first started dating, this particular behavior had annoyed the hell out of her. Suddenly he just seemed to focus on something, and a nuclear warhead could have gone off at the end of the street and it wouldn't have mattered because he just wasn't there anymore, like he'd flicked a switch and simply— gone.

And this, she realized, was going to be one of those times. She reached into her bag, brought out her notes and began to sift through and place them in some kind of order. She'd finish her coffee, and then —

"I'm doing it again, aren't I?" He was looking at her through the legs of the wooden beast that had garnered all of his attention, and he put down his sketchpad. "C'mon, let's go have dinner. My treat, while I can still afford it."

And just like that, the klieg light had shifted again and homed directly on her, and she wondered if this all or nothing attention span would ever evolve into a slightly more comfortable state of in between.

Outside, as they reached the gate, she remembered her earlier apprehension. "Is there a guy who hangs out here, sometimes?"

He shook his head. "Not that I know of. It's a shitty neighborhood but this block is always quiet." He gripped her hand and pulled her close. "Don't worry," he said, conspiratorial and teasing, "you won't have to put up with this area for much longer."

At the restaurant, he told her why.

She stared at him. "Luke, those are brand new apartments."

"Yeah." He had a rare, never quit grin on his face. "And when I called yesterday, they told me the lease had already been prepaid for six months."

"All this, so you can paint a wooden horse?"

He held up a hand. "I know, but I figure I've got nothing to lose. I was about to get thrown out of that shit hole anyway. And, I'll be just two blocks from where you're staying."

She nodded. It sounded wonderful. So, what's the catch,

she was about to say. Instead she kept silent. Perhaps this stranger was turning out to be more of a patron than a customer, and like Luke said, there appeared to be no downside right now.

Conversation lightened up, drifted toward a string of eclectic, everyday subjects. Luke made her laugh and she began to enjoy herself, and all thoughts of carousel horses, men who disappeared like ghosts and the mysterious figure of Elliot Black were forgotten.

And over the next few days she saw more of him than usual. She helped him pack up his belongings, and on some days he sat alongside her in the library while he researched his new subject.

"I could be wrong, but I think it's the lead horse," he said on one particular afternoon. He pushed aside her history texts and placed a heavy, illustrated book in front of her. "It has a lot of embellishment, like this one."

"I didn't realize a carousel had one of those."

He nodded. "Whole new subject, whole new world."

"What if he wants you to paint the whole thing?"

"A full carousel? Assuming he has one? I doubt it," he leered. "Not when he sees the result of this one."

Emma flicked through another book he'd pulled from one of the shelves, full of brightly colored, prancing horses, decorated with flowers and gold. And not just horses, there were rabbits, deer, ostrich, tigers. "Couldn't you just paint it like—"

"No, and— I don't think he wants me to."

She turned the pages until she found what she was looking for; a jet-black horse, its head facing skyward, a stargazer, the caption read. It had a gold mane and a gold, jewel encrusted saddle. "More like this?"

"Hmm, not gold— silver perhaps." He cocked his head, studied the photograph. "And it won't have that stupid, flat, fairground paintwork."

A woman sitting at the next table was glaring at them and so they stopped talking and carried on reading. And that's how it was for almost a week, until he'd moved in to his new apartment and made a start. And all of a sudden the act of them being together was torn apart as he became distant and more and more engrossed in his subject.

Two weeks, and finally she got to see the progress he'd made. For instead of walking over to her apartment, disheveled and exhausted, covered in primer dust and reeking of linseed oil which, to her eternal mortification she found a complete turn on, he actually invited her over to his place instead.

This was the first time she'd set foot in his new apartment since helping him move in and everything still looked the same; his belongings were still packed in boxes, his canvasses were lined up against the walls, and the horse had center stage in the living room.

But this time it was no longer a carved shape of gnarled, ancient wood. It was black, just as he'd suggested it would be, but the flanks and haunches were dappled with a dark gray, there was some discreet highlighting of the musculature; it looked alive, as if about to step off its temporary supports and start trotting around the room. But it was the head that ultimately drew the eye, its mane and forelock gray and silver tipped, a concave, elegant Arabian face, ferocious eyes and bared teeth and she stood mesmerized while it promised her a ride to some terrible, magnificent place.

"I haven't started on the saddle and tack yet," he began, "but—"

"Has he seen it?"

"Elliot? Yeah. I've been emailing pictures every day. He insisted."

"And?"

Luke shrugged. "I think he likes it."

"Is it dry? Can I— "

"No, not completely, and no, not yet." He pulled her away. "So, you approve?"

"It's beautiful."

He affected an accent. "Why thank you, ma'am."

"Seriously," she laughed. "It is."

"Well, I wanted your opinion before I went any further."

"But the horse is done. It's only the saddle—"

"No, not this." He glanced away for a moment. "What you said, about the carousel. You were right. He wants me to do the whole thing."

She stared at him. "And what does that mean?"

"He'll keep sending me pieces, for now, but it means moving to his place, for the summer."

"Oh, but I thought—" She shook her head. They'd already made tentative plans. They were going to travel, and she had hoped, despite what she had said to her friend Gillian, to discover a little more about him during that time, his family maybe, after all there had to be something more out there than that brooding, taciturn elder brother who, in all honesty she'd tried very hard to like.

"You could come with me."

"I don't know, Luke, this is sudden, and—"

"I know." He embraced her, ran his fingers through her hair. "It's a couple of months off yet."

"Does it pay well?"

He laughed. "You have no idea how much."

"I thought—"

"What?"

"I thought he gave you the creeps."

"I think I was just being over protective. Sounds stupid but it's hard sometimes, to see your work sold off like that. And he'd bought your portrait."

"It's just a painting." And when he stared at her, horrified, it became her turn to laugh. "Do I need to worry about the horse?"

"Maybe." He regarded his handiwork. "Nice haunches. I spent hours sanding those." He winked and she threw a pretend punch.

And right there she knew that whatever happened, come the summer they'd figure it out and everything would be okay. He could paint his horses and remain a mystery. No pressure, and perhaps that's how it should stay for a little while longer. Just the two of them, and everything would be fine.

CHAPTER 3

JOHN

Late afternoon and he tried to relax, sit back and let the vehicle eat up the miles. Occasionally he glanced at the occupant in the passenger seat but she remained asleep, out cold, dead to the world such as it was right now— a bleak strip of tarmac across flat and featureless land, the sky above it getting darker by the second. They were driving into a storm and John reckoned it would be touch and go on reaching the motel before they hit a wall of black cloud and torrential rain.

A show of lightning played in the distance, a beautiful sight providing one wasn't unlucky enough to be standing directly beneath it, and even then he figured the risks were worth it. Something about a storm that pushed everything else aside and revealed the true might of the world, its manner wholly indifferent to the lives it affected, whether it swept away everything in its path in one broad sweep, or merely chose to blast the occasional poor soul into oblivion purely on a whim. He wished he could master that indifference. The power, the storm could keep.

By the time they reached the motel, rain was hammering hard on the windshield and bouncing off the tarmac. He threw his coat over Rachel's head and tried to be gentle in getting her from the car and into the warm, dry confines of their room.

"I can manage," she snapped, at the threshold. And

so he let her go, let her stagger inside, watched her every move until she was sitting down on the bed and wasn't about to fall over and break something.

He stalked the room, switched on all the lights and checked the tiny bathroom. "Do you want something to eat? I saw a diner across the street."

"Coffee," she told him. She had thrown aside his coat and was crawling toward the headboard so she could lean on the pillows.

He filled the pot, poured coffee grounds into the filter and switched on the percolator. Only then did he enter the bathroom, close the door and remove his shirt. It proved difficult, and in the mirror he got his first look at the damage. There was a nasty scorch mark running across his right arm, his chest and abdomen were covered in bruises, his upper back looked about the same. He ran his fingers lightly across the skin and tried not to wince, when just the sight of himself made him want to whimper like a kicked dog.

He rolled his shoulders, twisted and flexed, hissed when the pain became too much. He'd had beatings worse than this, but it was small comfort right now. Back in the bedroom he poured coffee into two cups and took one to Rachel.

"Oh, John." She was staring at him, at the damage flowering like weeds on his skin.

"S'okay. No cuts, and nothing's broken."

"Still—"

"Don't worry about it."

"Come here. Sit."

"I'm fine." He sat anyway. "I'm hungry. I should go— " But she'd already touched him, and he was out like a light.

He opened his eyes and saw the vague shape of the ceiling fan above his head. He could hear her wheezing alongside him, slow and even, like a robust thousand year old. He shifted, listened for anything that might tell him they were in trouble, and after figuring they were okay for the moment he slowly rose into a sitting position. He ran a hand along his opposite arm, across his chest. The bruising, and the pain, was gone.

"Rachel—" He looked down. She was a tattered shape in the dark.

"You're my son. I couldn't bear to see you like that."

"And what about you?"

"I'll be fine." She coughed; the sound made him wince. "Just get me to the house in the morning."

He didn't turn on the light, for both their sakes. Her voice and rattling breath pattern told him enough. But he stayed awake, kept watch in the gloom. It was probably the main reason she'd fixed him up, despite her earlier sentiment and he had to face facts. He hadn't been in the best shape to protect her earlier, even though he'd already dealt with the threat and another was unlikely. They were not the only ones licking their wounds. He'd seen to that.

Five hours later and they were back on the road. The storm had dissipated, the road was dry and dawn was on the march. He'd taken as much coffee and doughnuts as he could get his hands on from the hotel reception, and Rachel was gorging on both.

"Do I look like the crypt keeper?" Her weak jaw made smacking noises while she chewed.

"Yep." He smiled. "And you're drooling."

"You'd drool too, if you looked like this."

"How are you feeling?"

"Better."

He nodded, kept his eyes on the road. He felt like a vampire, or a sick fetus still in the womb, fully satiated after feeding from his own mother. It hurt, it disgusted and shamed him, and yet, in her eyes it had been necessary. No point in ruminating, he let the countryside drift by as they continued their journey, until the horizon rose in the distance and they had to stop for gas.

She rolled the window down while he stood by the pump. But that was fine, she already looked human— old, frail, sure— but human nonetheless, and she was no doubt glad of the fresh air. He risked a trip to the store, bought more carbohydrates for her, an egg salad sandwich for him, and more coffee, and then they were back on the road. When it began to twist and turn through the foothills he turned off, took a lesser thoroughfare into the mountains until finally they arrived at their destination.

The house, as she called it, was more like a compound— four large connected dwellings behind a strong fence that hid most of everything from view. They were expected, and he spied a few familiar faces on the approach as they finally pulled up outside the main door.

He sat in the car, waited until Rachel had been helped outside and into the house. When there were less people around to stare and ask him things, he got out.

"So. How was the funeral?" Doc was standing by the door, his breath clouding in the cold air, his eyes not missing a trick.

He shrugged. "Getting in was fine. Getting out..."

The older man ushered him inside. John followed him through the entrance hall, down a narrow corridor lined with old photographs in heavy, dark wood frames, and into a cluttered study. When he was offered a seat he took it and pretended to relax. The debriefing was expected, and he was glad it was Doc and not one of the other Adepts; one who might dive in and take a more critical look at his psyche.

It was no easy task, saving the world from what came

crawling out of Hell and Bower's Fall, and for those rare souls able to navigate such bewitching habitats, seduction and insanity were omnipresent threats. The continual appraisal of peers was necessary, but it was also subjective and arbitrary, and John's acerbic nature did him no favors in the department of allies and friends.

"And how are you?" The man was standing behind his desk, staring at John as if he could see right down to the bones.

"I'm fine, now. Rachel fixed me up."

"Was it bad?"

He remembered the bulky nightmare that had squeezed through a breach in the tarmac. They'd wanted to get their hands on Rachel, of course, whereas he was expendable and so they'd damn near dropped the monster in his lap. "Nothing I couldn't handle," he replied. "And assuming it was Ralt's people, they're going to have to do better than that."

Doc smiled, shook his head. Now he took a seat in an ancient blood-red leather chair and leaned his forearms on the desktop. "You'll stay here for a few days. We'll have you checked out and you can get some rest."

"She's already given me another task."

"Oh?"

John nodded. "Luke. She wants me to look in on him."

"I sense ambivalence on your part."

He laughed. It came out hard and bitter. "Sure. And you know why. The more I see of him, the more vulnerable he'll be." Sentience was contagious, and no way did he want to expose his younger brother.

"Is he still painting?"

"Yes. It's a distraction, and he's good at it."

"And yet the danger is still there. You know, there was a time when we thought—"

"No. He needs to stay in isolation." He felt the edge in

his voice, realized he was flirting with insubordination. "Sorry," he muttered.

The older man let out a sigh, leaned back in his chair. "He could still find the path on his own. Perhaps I should have persuaded Rachel to have him brought here, right from the very beginning. If he gets into the wrong hands..."

"She wanted him to have a stab at a normal life, Doc." He wondered if any of the others were listening in. Screw it if they were. "And I can't say as I blame her."

"And what about this new girlfriend?"

"The bookworm? Still together, last time I looked."

"You've met her."

"A couple of times. She doesn't like me."

They both smiled. Doc stood up, went to an oak cabinet. "A drink?"

"Sure." Time to end the chitchat and start on the serious stuff. And with a tumbler of whisky in hand he started to talk, relieved now the subject had veered away from Luke. Rachel wasn't the only one who thought his brother didn't deserve any of this. He started talking, about the trip, the funeral, and what came after, and by the time he was done he felt like he'd been through some kind of catharsis. Doc understood all too well the creature that had manifested outside the mausoleum, and knew exactly what it had taken to get rid of it.

"You were lucky," the man told him afterwards.

He drained his glass. "Was I?" He stood up and placed the glass on the desk in front of him. "Look, I need to go talk to Jim. One of the guns jammed and—"

"You'll stay here tonight, John. At the very least." Doc finished his own drink, put his glass carefully, deliberately alongside the other one. "You're not invincible."

"That's an order, sir?"

"Yes. It is."

Sleep.

It was required, a necessity, it was even desired and yet it danced at arm's length, just beyond his reach and he had to be content with the next best thing. He'd long ago stopped fretting over his inability to drop easily into that temporary oblivion. Instead, during sleepless nights he found the act of simply lying there, acknowledging the fact he was still alive, brought him such an unadulterated and clear sense of joy that he was able to bear the pain of insomnia quite well.

Peace of mind was also reinforced knowing that Rachel was now in safe hands and that he was off the hook. Her insistence on traveling to his father's funeral had ruffled a lot of feathers, and despite her skills, fears for her safety had centered on him— apprehension, doubt, all of it chipping away at his resolve. But then, he'd been prepared. He'd been prepared from birth and he wouldn't have taken her if he didn't think he could protect her. Doc might have thought he was being cocky and dismissive, when in fact it was a simple case of knowing exactly what he was up against and knowing that he could beat it. In figuring out the odds, it didn't get much harder than that.

At some point he drifted off and sleep finally took him; it dragged him down and didn't let him resurface until way past dawn. And so it was around 9 a.m. that he finally got up, hit the gym, followed by the shower, and went in search of some breakfast, his mind already on the journey ahead of him; west this time, over the other side of the mountains and into central California. This time he suspected his most difficult task would be an emotional one, an altogether different battle and one he was bound to lose.

In the dining room he gathered a plate of sausage and scrambled eggs and poured a glass of grapefruit juice.

Others he knew well enough nodded politely as he sat at a table, but that was about as forthcoming as it got, until the arrival of Rhonda.

"This is a nice surprise." Her hand shook slightly as she placed her coffee cup on the table, and sitting opposite him involved some careful maneuvering of her lower limbs, but she managed well enough and he knew better than to offer help. She hooked her stick over the back of the chair alongside. "We didn't expect you back until later today."

He smiled at the one true friendly face he'd seen since he'd returned. "I figured it would be better for everyone if I got her back sooner rather than later." He poured ketchup on his plate and tucked in.

"And dare I ask?"

He nodded, but kept silent and continued eating. It wasn't a slight on his part, and she knew him well enough to drink her coffee and wait until he was done. Finally, "A few minor problems. You know how it goes sometimes."

She nodded, knew only too well. "And how is Luke?"

"He wasn't there. He doesn't know."

"Oh, John—"

"Come on, Rhonda. We knew there might be an incident. And Luke doesn't know shit about any of this." He stabbed his fork toward a table where a gaunt, vacant young man and his mentor sat. Even John's rudimentary insight was enough to tell him the guy was gone. He'd either been worked on by the others, and had been rendered safe, or he'd screamed until he'd finally cracked and broken. Lucky for everyone it had happened here. Had he lost it out there in the world... "Don't want him ending up like that."

Rhonda shook her head. "Some people can cope better than others."

"Sure. And what are the odds of that? Of being able to cope?"

"Okay, okay." She held up a hand, rolled her eyes.

He glanced at the other tables. People were staring. They might not have heard every word, but they'd have caught his tone and read his body language well enough, and knowing his reputation he was probably scaring them just as much as anything else they'd ever encountered. Which was stupid when you thought about it.

The fork landed with a clatter on his plate. "Sorry," he said. He took his napkin and placed it slowly, deliberately on the table, and folded his arms.

"Accepted," she told him. "Walk outside with me?" She leaned forward, braced herself.

And this time he did get up. He walked around the table, and he held out an arm that she used deftly to bring herself upright, and once she had collected her stick he matched her pace as they headed for the quadrangle doors.

"Seems like I'm getting slower every day."

He smiled. "You're doing okay, for a girl who had two of her limbs torn off."

"Thank you for reminding me." She jabbed him in the ribs. "How long are you staying again?"

"Tired of me already?"

Rhonda laughed and headed outside onto the concrete path. "Come on you son of a bitch, I can make it to the perimeter fence and back."

Outside, they encountered two of the Adepts, who nodded briefly and passed them by. Just one glance and John felt like he'd been stripped to bone and sinew. Both of them had exhibited that look, like they'd been all the way down into Hell and had stayed a while, and once again he counted his blessings. For his tasks rarely involved the long haul. If things came crawling out, he threw them back in, or, failing that he killed them. No need for him to linger in Hell or its equally deadly neighbor. Both places had a habit of sinking beneath the skin and showing up behind the eyes, and the others' exposure, whether in the name of altruism or research, hadn't done them any favors.

"So, who was it?" Rhonda tugged on his arm.

"They didn't leave a calling card, but I'm guessing it was Ralt."

She let out a sigh. "Still searching for Lucifer."

"Who's long gone. But I guess they figured if they had Rachel..." He gave up. It was a subject he found particularly distasteful, especially in present company. Ralt had attempted to kidnap their Adepts before, occasionally with disastrous results.

"Hey," she whispered. "Stop that."

"Stop what?"

"That. I can read you like a book and what happened to me wasn't your fault."

He grunted, felt a familiar argument coming on, dark and cloying, much like the storm of yesterday. Her grip softened.

"Let's just walk and enjoy the morning."

"Yes, ma'am." He acquiesced because she was right, as always. No point in going over his past failures, so he shoved it all into a mental closet, slammed the door shut, and tried for amiable. His companion let out a throaty chuckle and led him on, her stick thumping a slow rhythm on the concrete path.

Later in the day he commandeered another vehicle, an SUV this time rather than the big sedan his mother had preferred for the funeral trip. One of the caretakers, Jim, helped him stow his supplies. Two of his standard weapons a rifle and a pistol— were slid into a concealed rear compartment.

"Now, you go easy with those. Don't want to see you ending up in jail all over again."

John gave him a wolfish grin. “I was fine in jail.”

“I know, and that’s what worries me.”

He let it go. None of them had believed him when he told them that being inside, amidst that stubborn, solid wall of concrete and humanity, had given him nearly the same level of protection as the house did. It seemed incomprehensible to them, even though it was an easy enough equation to master as far as he was concerned. Brute force and ignorance being one hell of a barrier against all those things that went bump in the night and crept through the ether. Of course none of the people here had tried a stretch for themselves. Despite their own ordeals, in a lot of respects most of the Adepts led remarkably sheltered lives.

He figured by the time it had gotten dark he’d be on the road once more, but it was another full day before they let him go and he suspected it had been Rachel, ultimately, who’d kept him there, despite her urgency toward the welfare of his younger brother. And, he had to admit it had done him some good. He felt recharged, replenished within the confines of the house, where he wasn’t looking over his shoulder every other second. Just that state of awareness alone took its toll after a while, regardless of his conviction that he could deal with everything that was thrown at him. He was glad of the break, and now, back on the road, he felt that much stronger. And that made him wonder...

“What’s coming, Rachel?” He asked the question out loud, regardless that she wasn’t there to hear it, or answer it for that matter. Then he settled back, let the vehicle do the work of getting him to his destination, through switchbacks of dark stone and brooding cloud, while his mind got down to the what ifs and the wherefores, until he felt as prepared as he’d ever be, and attendant terrors and catastrophes be damned.

CHAPTER 4

LUKE

He'd been kidding with Emma about the horses, about ownership and being overprotective, and he'd laughed about the reluctance and sense of loss that came over him whenever one of his works flew the coop. And yet he stood biting his nails as the second carousel horse was crated up. He offered endless unwanted comments from the sidelines be careful, wait, can I suggest, maybe you should— on and on until he was sure the haulage guys were heartily sick of him. He hovered there like an overprotective mother on baby's first day of school while they built the crate around the horse, and it felt like a heavy wrench pulling his heart from his chest when he saw the truck disappear around the corner at the end of the street.

Gone.

Three weeks work. His baby.

Stupid, but he almost shed a tear, and immediately he got to work on unpacking the next one the guys had left in its place.

There hadn't been room to uncrate this next project, and although the men had offered, once they'd loaded up the finished horse, he'd waved them off and told them he'd take care of it. It was, he realized, becoming part of a new ritual.

He remembered the last time, when he'd caught the very first glimpse, how the ideas had begun to flow, his imagination inspired by those first encounters— a head peeping through straw, one reared fetlock and hoof tangled in brown paper and bubble wrap, the scent of wood and preservative. And how, by the time he'd uncovered everything, he'd known exactly how he was going to paint it.

However, on this occasion it appeared as if work had already been started. As he carefully prized out the nails and slid open the paneling he noticed the difference immediately. And on pulling away tufts of straw he saw that priming and sanding had already been completed. But despite the initial disappointment, that some other person had already laid their fingers on it, he continued the unpacking, carefully and reverently pulling away the straw until the creature was revealed.

This one was a galloper. All four legs off the ground and outstretched, as if leaping desperately over a fence. It was balanced on a temporary trestle, and there was a large hole running through its body, top to bottom, straight through the middle of a long, two-seater saddle. And this time the flanks were elaborately carved with rosettes, scrollwork, flowers, leaves and birds, leaving little room for the accompanying tack.

He circled it a few times, then stood and stared.

The phone rang. It was Elliot. And while they chit chatted regarding the delivery he noticed another marked difference to the last ones.

"The carvings are more significant on the left side."

"Yes. It's English. They ran their carousels clockwise as a hat tip to the military. If you're wearing your sword for a right hand draw, it's so much easier to mount from the left."

"I guess." He tried to imagine. "So, won't it—"

"It won't be the only irregular horse. They're all quite old, very rare, very hard to come by." Black's voice had taken on its familiar edge.

"I get it, and I'll be careful."

"I know."

"So what's with the prep?"

"I had someone else do that while you were working on the last one. That's how they'll arrive from now on. It'll move things along so much faster."

He couldn't argue with that. He reached out, stroked his fingers along the carved surface. "I'll make a start on this one tonight. Same M.O.?"

"Of course. I believe in giving the artist full rein, if you'll forgive the expression."

After the call, Luke remained standing and staring. The words English and military circled through his head once or twice but he quickly discounted them. The carving was far too romantic, far too evocative of nature and wildness to suggest anything so orderly. And as soon as he'd seen the face he'd known the colors had to be softer. "Female," he muttered.

He pulled off his shirt, and got to work.

Hours later, he didn't know how many, he stood bleary and narrow eyed in the gloom. He couldn't remember when he'd lit candles and turned the lights off. He couldn't remember starting on that bottle of cabernet Emma had left him, either, but the liquid line was in excess of three quarters of the way down, his glass was empty and he suspected he was feeling mildly tipsy.

And maybe it was the poor light, but wasn't he supposed to have painted the flowers and leaves a little brighter? After all, a glaze was going over the top that would really dampen it all down and— he took a step back, steadied himself. All around were pots, tins, tubes, bottles and, thankfully, stacks and rows of brushes that didn't show any signs of ill use and neglect. There was an order to it, to the initiated eye at least, and that suggested there had been some sense of order behind the results, too.

He looked to the window, noticed daylight coming through a crack in the blinds, and he almost tripped over one of the wrinkled drop cloths protecting the furniture as he walked around the room, blowing out all the candles before he opened the blinds and let the daylight in.

And when he did so —

She stood in the center, a picture of howling, glorious ruin. He still had hours of work ahead of him but already she looked as if she had emerged from some terrible aftermath of a nuclear war. The flowers adorning her throat appeared rotten, their colors dried up, faded hints of what they might have been. And although he'd covered her eyes with Vaseline they still appeared to be regarding him with a mixture of promise and reproach. Whatever dark hell he was consigning her to, that look told him she would make sure he was along for the ride.

He let out a chuckle. It sounded manic and high pitched, no doubt inspired by the wine. But— what a rush. And there were still hours of work ahead of him before she was perfected. Hours...

Despite the flush of alcohol and the sunlight coming through the window, he felt cold. He was done, he realized. Done for now. It was time to rest and eat. He sniffed his armpit, and yeah, get a shower before his girlfriend arrived. *If* she was due to arrive. In truth he had no idea what time of day it was, or even *what* day it was.

He decided on the shower, figuring it would sober him up and remove the black paint and solvent from beneath his fingernails. But as the water hammered down, plastering his hair to his skull, for a little while it only partially diluted the pigment on his hands. And for some reason he discovered he didn't want to wash it all away. Instead he smeared it across his forearms, and before the water swilled it down the drain he imagined being sat astride his mare of Armageddon, as black and gray and as full of ruin, his clothes in tatters, his face tarnished and bloody, while she bore them down toward a horizon he'd only ever seen in his very worst nightmares.

"Hey, are you okay?"

He blinked. He thought he'd been paying attention. "Sorry. Been up all night."

They were sitting outside a local cafe and everything appeared surreal— too clean, too bright, too much color. Three guys at the next table looked as if they were on a TV screen, two dimensional, behind glass, untouchable.

"So. Are you going to let me see it?"

I'll take her, I'll steal her away, the mare whispered, still with him, a thin line of black beneath his fingernails

"It's not really looking all that good right now. Maybe in a few days?"

Emma shrugged. "Okay. No pressure, Mr. Big Shot Artist."

He smiled, too tired to take the bait. Maybe he was hung over. That would explain a lot. He took a strong pull of his coffee, nearly drained the cup, and felt better for it immediately. Then he looked across at Emma and attempted to gauge her expression. They'd already had the 'I never see you these days' conversation, so at least that was over with. But, not to be outdone, there was another subject waiting in the wings, potentially more problematic. "So, about the summer..." Not far off now. Three, four weeks, if that.

"I checked with Mom and Dad, and providing I stay in touch, and go visit at some point," she shrugged, "we should be good to go."

Luke reached across the table and took her hand. The relief he felt was palpable, and right there he realized he truly hadn't wanted to go out there alone, despite the growing connection with his subject and a still belligerent but more bearable by the day rapport with Elliot Black.

They spent the rest of the day together, laughing, talking, and he began to feel more fleshed out, more human, and not at all like that scary, one foot in the beyond figure in the shower letting paint and water make pretty patterns on his skin. And after going back to her apartment in the evening, when they finally fell into an exhausted tangle of naked limbs he realized he actually felt happy, and at peace. Sentimental, trite, but screw it, he'd never felt better.

"So you were tired, huh?" she asked him, a smile on her face.

He laughed, rolled onto his stomach and slid a hand across her belly. "I am now." He felt gloriously dizzy, satiated. Her skin felt soft and warm and he stroked his fingers back and forth, reliving moments of the energetic, very physical dance they'd just completed.

"Well, maybe you should stay here and get some sleep."

"You don't want to throw me out, now you're done with me?"

"Sure I do, but—" Her expression shifted. "Luke, you need a break."

"All work and no play, huh?" Up on his elbows, his tongue slid forth and tormented her right breast until the nipple began to harden all over again. "Admit it," he whispered, "you're not finished with me yet."

"Luke—"

"Shh." He was becoming aroused again, a slow trickle of heat that gathered momentum as he went back and forth with his tongue. He heard her sigh, felt her skin tremble as his hand slipped up between her thighs. And after long minutes of teasing and caressing he entered her again and began the slow build toward climax, taking his time, reveling in the way she lay arched beneath him, her eyes closed, her expression a mixture of concentration and abandon, a look that suggested both pleasure and pain.

He began to lose himself, as he always did, and it was then perhaps that the dark mare slid in between them. He failed to notice until his surroundings became cloudy with lust and darkness, until her bared teeth and gray, fluttering mane obscured his vision.

The pillows, the sheets, the bed, it all disappeared and now they rode along a broad, endless plain of ash. He screwed his eyes shut, heard Emma cry out as he drove into her, harder and harder, not sure if he was trying to rid himself of that terrible vision or if he wanted to dive headlong into the depths of it and make it all the more real.

But in the end he couldn't see anything at all. He couldn't feel anything and he had no idea where he was.

Emma was gasping beneath him. "Oh God..."

His own breath came out long and deep, his lungs bellowed and drew in vast quantities of air. When he opened his eyes he felt disoriented and it took him a number of seconds to pull it all together. His girlfriend's face came into focus, her eyes were still closed, her features now relaxed, as if she had ridden along with him and was still somewhere out there in the dark.

"You okay?" he croaked. "Emma?" Her eyes flicked open and she let out a groan. He shifted alongside her and gathered her into his arms. "Hey," he whispered.

Her hand came up and rested clumsily on his forearm, and her head rolled gently against his chest. And there they both stayed, curled up together in a tangle of sheets while the physical certainties of the room gradually returned and eschewed all evidence of that pitiless landscape.

After a while she let him go and raised no objections to him pulling on his clothes, leaving her and getting back to work. His last sight of her, she was standing by the door. She was watching him leave but she had that look on her face, one he was wholly familiar with, the same one that now, in all probability, hung on a wall in Elliot Black's house.

He barely remembered the walk back to his own apartment other than it being the studious act of placing one foot in front of the other while attempting to avoid traffic as he crossed the street. He felt light headed and out of it; how he managed to get the key into his front door he truly didn't know.

When he turned on the light he was greeted by the mare, just a wooden horse, carved mid leap, her neck and flanks painted dark gray, the flowers and leaves garlanded around her neck a funereal wreath of dark purple and green. And right now it all looked flat, and harmless.

He stumbled into his bedroom and fell on his face into a disarray of crumpled pillows and sheets. He slept but had no idea for how long. But the daylight only seemed to linger for a short while on awakening, and as night came on again he threw all the lights on and got back to work.

He began with his usual methodical diligence, made sure everything he needed was prepped and to hand, and soon he forgot everything other than his tools and his subject, and he wasn't sure what time it was when he finally stopped, but when his awareness kicked in he was once again in candlelight and she had come alive again.

He was shirtless, as usual, and on his knees. Directly in front of him the mare's nostrils flared. She was staring right at him, her front hooves about to drive through his chest. She looked magnificent, the creature of his dreams, brimming with fury, much as she had done the night before at Emma's. Her expression was one of demand, and he wasn't sure if she wanted an apology for the indiscretion he'd shared with his girlfriend or merely a simple genuflection, a reverential acknowledgement.

In the end he bowed his head and closed his eyes, and for the very first time since he'd started work on her he wondered if he was going completely and utterly out of his mind.

CHAPTER 5

EMMA

The lasagna. It had to be. On the night of its ingestion she'd been insistent that he ate something and so they'd shared it between them and although it hadn't tasted bad at the time...

Thankfully she hadn't begun her first bout of vomiting until well after he'd gone. As for the hallucinations while they were in bed together, she didn't even want to try and make any sense of those. And after hours spent throwing up she'd called him in a panic thinking she might have poisoned him and he'd answered in that monotone that told her yes he was okay but he was working so could she please leave him alone... so, yeah. Now she was angry. And she was willing to bet he wouldn't remember she had called him, nor would he have any recall on what may or may not have happened the night before.

She let it stew for another night, and the following afternoon she was all set to storm round to his place and hammer on his door, were it not for the strange guy in the reenactment clothes standing outside her apartment. He was down on the street, alongside her car as plain as day and looking up at her window.

So now she was angry, and scared too.

It was an odd combination; it coursed through her and rattled her nerve endings until, tense and jittery as a foal, she pulled on her jacket, grabbed her bag, and figured she'd just dash out there and confront him —

And the doorbell rang.

Thinking it was Luke she hauled open the door and was about to launch into a well-rehearsed tirade until the sight of John De Grasse stopped her short and instead, frozen to the spot, she simply stood there like an idiot and stared.

"Where is he?" His eyes drew her in, exactly like Luke's but for the illusion they were set into the back of his skull; correction— bolted to the floor of a cavern 200 feet deep.

Emma let out a sigh and fought to stay polite. "Not here." She matched his stare as well as she was able, before stepping outside and shutting her door. "I'm on my way over to his place. Walk with me if you like."

"Walk?"

She was already approaching the stairwell. "He didn't tell you he'd moved?"

The smile he gave her was laced with sarcasm. "Why would he?"

Emma shook her head and set off down the stairs. Outside, she paused and looked toward her car. No sign of the strange man. Instead, John was alongside her, giving her an odd look. "I thought I saw someone over there," she explained, "just before you arrived."

"What did he look like?"

"How did you know it was a he?"

He shrugged. "I might have seen someone, too. Guy in a big shirt and short pants."

She began to walk across the street toward Luke's apartment. "That sounds like the guy."

He matched her pace easily. "Is there always some weird guy hanging outside your apartment?"

"With increasing regularity." She offered him a withering look he appeared to appreciate. His smile widened, lost its smirk.

They walked in silence the rest of the way. She felt

awkward alongside him, on edge, but at least her earlier sentiments had gone, his arrival significant enough to allay her fears and dissolve her anger. Instead she merely felt uncomfortable and by the time she'd juggled with the idea of small talk and dismissed it, they'd arrived at the main entrance of Luke's apartment complex.

John had stopped and was looking up at the building's facade. "Before we go in," he said. "I should warn you. I'm about to give him some bad news."

"Oh." A stupid response but it was all she could think of.

"Fancy place," he added.

"Yes. He has a new patron." And when he gave her a look that told her all of a sudden he was extremely interested in everything she had to say, she shrugged. "He'll tell you."

When Luke opened the door he had his jacket on, like he was about to go out, and he grabbed her hand, pulled her inside and hugged her while his brother waited on the threshold. Despite the strength of the embrace he felt frail in her arms, like he'd lost weight, which made her suspect she hadn't been the only one throwing up for the last day or so and now her guilt was kicking in again. She had poisoned them both. No wonder he didn't want to talk to her. And to make things worse, when he pulled away and looked down at her he had that strange look in his eye reminiscent of when she'd last seen him.

"Luke. We need to talk." John's voice came out soft behind them, but it was a command nonetheless.

Emma let him go. She walked further into the room, toward the kitchen in order to give them a little distance, past the latest project that looked about ready to leap straight through the living room window. Balanced on a rough wooden trestle, this horse appeared to have been caught mid-flight and frozen. However, the expert carving and Luke's paintwork had rendered her alive, as if all it would take was a flick of a switch, and she'd be off —

A she. She stared at it, hugged her arms close to her chest and remembered something Gillian said.

Aren't you the dark horse.

John had stepped inside and closed the door, and now he and Luke were standing there whispering, and to heck with being distracted by the carving because she'd missed overhearing what the bad news was. Instead she had to be content with body language and right now Luke had a puzzled look on his face, as if he didn't quite understand what his brother had just told him.

She didn't want to look at the horse any more and so she continued into the kitchen that proved to be, as expected, empty of provisions. Instead the sink was full of glass jars and bundles of drying paintbrushes and the room reeked of solvent. She shook her head, walked back out and rejoined the others.

Luke was now sitting on a couch that had been unceremoniously covered with a dustsheet. John was still standing; he had his hands in his pockets and was staring at the carousel horse. When they were together like this it was easy to see the resemblance between them, despite John's cropped hair, broader shoulders and eyes like mine shafts. They both had the same jaw, the same nose and hairline, and right now their expressions were identical.

For a moment she debated going back into the kitchen, but in the end she approached Luke, checked out the couch, prayed the dark spots on the dustsheet were dry, and sat carefully alongside him.

He didn't look at her but his hand reached across and rested on her knee. It felt heavy, like it was made of lead. "I don't know what I'm supposed to say." His voice sounded odd, distant; he was looking at his brother.

"What happened?" She placed her own hand on top of his, snaked her fingers in between.

"Our father died," John said.

"Oh." Her surroundings became disjointed, distant. Odd how news like that always seemed to make the rest of the world go away. A second earlier and she could have sworn she heard passing cars out on the street, and birds singing, but right now it had all disappeared. "So. There'll be a funeral," she began, clawing messily toward the practicalities of it all. She wanted to say she was so sorry, but the words were log jammed amidst the chaos inside her head.

"Already taken care of," John said.

Heat flared abruptly across her cheeks. Odd too, how anger was always able to cut through everything. "What? And you didn't—"

"It's okay." Luke squeezed her hand. She stared at him.

"Tell her if you like. It's up to you." John turned away and went back to examining the horse. He began to step carefully around it, as if he was afraid it might reach out and bite him.

Luke took his hand away for a moment and stared at the ceiling, and then he leaned back a little, and slowly began to roll up his shirt. There was a scar on his abdomen, old, faded, he'd told her that he'd got it at school way back when; they'd laughed about it. But now —

"I was eight years old," he said. "And Dad came after me and stabbed me with a kitchen knife." He cleared his throat, swallowed. "I think he was trying to kill me."

Emma drew in a breath and the world came rushing back in. "Oh my God I'm so sorry, I'm so sorry." She stared at the scar, mesmerized. But he was wrong, it was an accident, surely. A careless mistake. She couldn't even begin to imagine a father stabbing his own son.

"It's okay," he said again. "It's okay," and picked up her trembling hand.

But it wasn't.

They arranged to meet John for dinner, and headed for the campus cafeteria, and after a quick lunch they walked past the lecture halls and down toward the river. Luke held her hand with a strong grip, like his life depended on it. But she didn't care. She wanted the contact. It became an expression of how she felt, about the news, about him.

"So, after Mom died, I guess he just gradually flipped. If John hadn't stopped him—"

"He saved you?"

Luke smiled. "Oh yeah. He got cut, too, but not quite so bad. They had to haul me off to the hospital and—" He faltered. "I'm sorry, I guess this is..."

"Don't be sorry." She squeezed his arm.

"I should have told you, maybe. I just didn't want to scare you off. It's a lot of baggage."

"It's going to take a lot more than that, Mister." She tried to keep it light. In truth she was in shock. But this was good, she told herself. If she was going to spend the rest of her life with this man, and she was certainly beginning to think that way, then this was stuff she really needed to know, however awful it proved to be.

She let him talk it out, listened how, after his father had been locked away he'd ended up being looked after by an uncle and aunt, and how John had, from then on, been an intermittent presence in his life. And they discussed it and both agreed, providing he'd reached a decision that he wanted to at some point, that they'd go visit the gravesite.

"By the way," she said after they'd walked in silence for a short while. "I'm sorry about the lasagna the other night."

He stopped and gave her the strangest look when she explained. "Food poisoning?" He shook his head. "I mean, I didn't puke, but I thought I was losing my fucking mind."

He threw back his head. “Holy shit.”

Laughter arrived then. It came forth a little too nervous and easy, but as far as she was concerned it was more than welcome on such a strange day.

When the time came to meet for dinner she still felt at odds with her surroundings and flirted with the beginnings of a mild headache. She was hungry she reasoned, especially after feeling ill all day yesterday.

They met up with John at one of the local steakhouses Luke enjoyed. The interior was gloomy and full of shadow. I think it’s so you can’t see the blood, Luke had joked once about the dim lighting, and on that note, despite her hunger the place became oppressive and nauseating. The smell of cooked meat made her stomach lurch while they waited for a table and she was glad when they were finally led to a seat and she could drink a glass of water. When dinner arrived she kept her attention solidly on her plate of chicken while the guys tucked into their oozing medium rares and she was relieved, finally, when the dishes were taken away.

“You okay?” Luke asked alongside her. “You’re very quiet.” He’d been attentive and tactile all evening.

She nodded, and tried to avoid the silent analysis coming at her from the other side of the table. Perhaps John knew about the food poisoning and considered her yet another threat to his younger brother’s longevity. A petty, selfish thought, but she didn’t feel capable of much else while sitting in this house of blood and carnage, while all around her people laughed and talked and chewed and swallowed. She answered John’s scrutiny with a screw you stare that brought another, albeit brief, smile to his face.

Then his eyes shifted; he took the tiniest sip of wine. "So, this guy is paying you how much?"

"Eight grand plus expenses," Luke told him.

"For each figure?" John nodded in consideration. Unlike Luke he hadn't drunk very much at all and his fingers were sliding slowly up and down the stem of his glass. "You know, going off what I saw in your apartment today, that's going to be one hell of a carousel ride."

Luke shrugged. "It's what I do, and so far the guy hasn't complained."

"Not saying it's bad, it's just—"

Emma leaned back in her seat and let them talk, brother to brother. She was feeling a little better, her stomach had settled and maybe getting some food in there had done the trick after all.

At some point during the conversation she remembered the strange man, the one out on the street who'd been standing alongside her car, but right now the brothers were discussing the various merits of Luke's art on canvas as opposed to the carved horses he was painting and it didn't seem important any more, especially after the news regarding Luke's father earlier in the day. Slowly, gradually, she began to feel warm and safe in here with the two men, and the earlier atmosphere shifted, loosened, and became a dark protective cocoon.

However, a short while later, as Luke went to visit the restroom, John seemed hell bent on reacquainting her with her earlier disquiet. He pulled out a pen and wrote on a napkin. He pushed it across the table toward her. "Put this on your cell phone, and keep that somewhere you won't lose it."

She looked down at the number he'd given her.

He leaned slightly across the table. "Watch him. And if anything strange happens, call me."

"What do you mean by strange?"

He shrugged. "I'll trust your judgment." His eyes flitted briefly toward the aisle. "Oh, and that guy out on the street, today. I haven't forgotten. I'll look into it. Don't worry about him."

She opened her mouth to speak, but in the corner of her eye she saw Luke approaching. John was still staring at her, unnerving and unwavering as ever. *This is between us.* She frowned, nodded, slid her hand across the table and covered up the napkin.

After dinner, outside in the dark, they said their farewells. John told Luke he'd keep in touch. There was a will to be read, a few other things. Emma stayed close, hooked tight around Luke's elbow, felt him shudder slightly when he inhaled.

"You're staying with me tonight," she told him when they were alone.

"You sure?"

"I'm sure. This is no night to be on your own." She took his hand and pulled him along, thankful he wasn't protesting that he had to get back to work on that terrible, nightmare carousel horse.

Back at her apartment he appeared dazed and incoherent, as if she'd only managed to drag part of him home while the rest of him had tagged along with his brother. And she wondered, while pulling off his shirt as he sat on the edge of the bed and stared into space, if that wasn't partly true. She had seen another facet of him, one that to a larger extent included John, and now it seemed they'd all been pulled a little closer together.

"Come on, feet up," she muttered, and she pushed him backward onto the pillows and thought about the carefully folded napkin, still in her coat pocket. Watch him. It was understandable. A father who had tried to kill you was still a father, after all. She reached forward, stroked his hair.

"You okay?"

He nodded, pulled her toward him and kissed her. "Tired..."

"I know. Get some sleep."

He nodded, rolled over, and she curled in behind him, so close she could feel his chest expanding and contracting as he breathed. She stared over his shoulder into the dark, tried to think about tomorrow or the day after; tried looking forward to the summer months and the trip ahead of them. There was plenty to keep her occupied and distracted, and to steer her thoughts away from John's visit and its revelations and consequences. But in the end, when her dreams finally took her she went back to that awful place. Aware of his breathing and the heat from his body, her arms grew long and sprouted thorns, they coiled and penetrated him just below the ribcage while her narrow tongue slid forth and curled around his jaw, searching for any orifice it could find. Needy. Hungry. Blood and intestines first, and then would come the rest.

CHAPTER 6

JOHN

He followed them.

He was discreet and they didn't spot him, and when he saw their lights go out he stepped out from under the trees and walked toward her car. C'mon, he whispered, come on out, don't be shy. But he found no trace of the strange man and none of the usual residual evidence he'd expected to find, and after an hour or so, frustrated, he walked back to his vehicle and returned to his hotel.

He stood in the shower, his head directly beneath the hot spray and he kept it there, hoping it would wash away his misgivings. Alas they remained and grew. When he was toweled dry, he sat cross-legged on the bed, toyed with the idea of keeping it all to himself, and then picked up his cell phone.

He flicked through the surreptitious pictures he'd taken. Of the return address on the packing case stacked in the hall, and the letterheads of correspondence lying on the table in Luke's apartment, anything that would give him the whereabouts and some information on his brother's new benefactor. He checked the address against the house database, found no immediate red flags, and then he called Rhonda. Luke's patron he could deal with on his own, but that horrific carousel horse and the guy out on the street —

"It might have looked that way, John, but did you sense anything?"

"No. Nothing."

"Okay. So, maybe he just has dreams, you know? Given his heritage it would hardly be unusual."

"I know it's just—"

"Admit it, you were freaked out by a damned wooden horse." She was chuckling on the other end of the phone. It rankled, because she was right. That thing had scared the hell out of him.

He changed the subject, told her about the stranger outside Emma's apartment.

"In broad daylight? Now that *is* interesting."

"I thought so, too. Mind doing a little digging?"

"Not at all. And don't worry, I'll keep it on the down low."

"Good. Because we might have an additional problem, and not with Luke."

"Oh? With whom?"

"With his girlfriend. Turns out our little girl can see ghosts."

They kept the call short, so it was inevitable there were things he'd missed, maybe a piece of the puzzle Rhonda could make more sense of, that would allow the whole troubling scenario to come together. Because right now, other than the creepy carousel horse, and that ghost out there on a street completely devoid of shadow, he had nothing that made any damned sense.

He attempted to shut it all out and watch some TV. The news was coming to an end and Letterman was about to begin. He watched the opening monologue, even smiled a couple of times, but despite all attempts at temporary amnesia he kept on coming back to the ghost, standing there as bold as you please alongside Emma's car. "Ah, little brother," he whispered.

On the TV screen, the host and his guest began to laugh.

The following morning he rose early and ran five miles on the hotel treadmill, showered and had breakfast, then got to work on the guy who owned the carousel horses. The crates were being delivered to and from a small town in the mid-west, maybe seven hundred and fifty miles southwest of where Rachel had buried Dad. An initial search brought forth a loose sketch of a retired factory owner turned antique dealer. No pictures, and everything else appeared nondescript, excruciatingly average. He assumed the doctorate was philosophical rather than medical, but he couldn't find any details. Retired, bland, with a hard on for carousel nags painted like the four horses of the Apocalypse.

However, all the warning signs still pointed to Luke's side of the ball court as far as John could make out. Black's love for his brother's blind interpretation of Hell's antechamber didn't necessarily mean a psychic connection, nor indicate a card-carrying member of a group such as Ralt's.

Nevertheless, Luke was planning to go stay with the guy for the summer, and just maybe it was time for John to tag along. Not in any obvious manner, he was afraid of raising too many red flags. He'd be discreet, just keeping an eye on the younger sibling, their father having recently passed away and all.

He toyed with the idea, wondered how much attention it would draw, wondered if it was worth it. He wasn't kidding around with Rhonda about staying the hell away from his little brother under normal circumstances. Attention begot attention, and not only from the likes of Ralt and those other kooks. That's how this whole psychic nonsense seemed to develop, by association and gradual, collective awareness. Blind ignorance was bliss, literally. And yet, if there was a problem, and that antique guy turned out to be someone worth John's attention, then it was better to be safe than sorry.

"Shit." He closed up the laptop, unhappy about the entire situation.

An hour later he'd checked out of the hotel and was back on the road. He wanted to call Rhonda again but he knew he had to be patient. He'd also promised Luke some further information regarding their father, but he could do that during the journey and suddenly it became a matter of urgency to check out Elliot Black and cross the guy off the list. That way he could concentrate on the more viable threat regarding Luke's fragile platform of equilibrium— a solemn, marginally pretty young woman who could see ghosts.

He headed south to Los Angeles, battled through lunchtime traffic, parked the vehicle in a long stay at LAX, made a phone call, and picked up an American Airlines flight to Dallas. During the flight he waived away the Business Class lunch and prepped the info he'd send to Luke when he landed. And with any luck he'd be back in less than a week. Then the real trouble would start. Sorry, little brother, but your girlfriend is a bad influence. And trust me, I know all about bad influences.

He stowed his laptop, the flight attendant brought him a beer, and after he knocked back half the can he sat there and began to stew, and considered whether or not going after Black was merely a delaying tactic. After observing

Luke and Emma together he knew his brother was smitten, and she appeared pretty much the same. Prying them apart would take some work and he wouldn't exactly come out smelling like a rose at the end of it, and big, bad brother John would continue to live up to his reputation.

You've done worse.

Rachel's voice, reminding him of his redeeming qualities. Thanks, Mom.

The plane landed during the remnants of an early summer storm, with enough pitch and yaw to unnerve a few of his fellow passengers, and despite the rain he could still feel the returning heat drifting through the gap between the plane and the jet way. One of the first people off, he joined a fast paced stream of other travelers heading for the terminal exit, and after walking through security and looking for Henry's face in the crowd he eventually saw the old guy, neck craning above a jumble of people and luggage. They shook hands.

"Good to see you, John. Traveling light?"

"Yes, sir."

The man nodded, beckoned. And before long they were skirting around the Metroplex and heading north in Henry's red, early model F150. The surrounding terrain undulated in green, shallow folds, and compared to the choke of L.A. traffic, the roads here were deserted. Alongside him, his companion kept silent until they were a good half hour out of the city.

"This about Luke?"

He nodded. "He's doing business with some guy. I just wanted to check it out."

"And how is he? Don't get to hear much now he isn't staying with Matt and Lola."

"So far, so good."

The old man appeared to accept that and didn't ask him anything more. Another hour or so and they pulled off the highway, and shortly afterward took a left onto a track that curled over the low brow of a hill. It was getting dark and lights coming from the house in the valley up ahead beckoned them along.

"Make sure you go say hello to Helen," Henry said once they'd reached their destination and he'd brought the truck to a standstill. He smiled. "Won't be you who gets it, if you don't."

John slid out of the cab, just as a woman came out of the house, her arms outstretched. He was soon engulfed in a tight embrace. It felt good, and he welcomed it. Greetings like this were few and far between. No escaping her scrutiny, however. Man to man you could bluff it out, pretend it wasn't there; no such luck with a woman who knew exactly what she was looking at.

"Trouble at the funeral?" Her head was slightly cocked, her expression full of concern. He shrugged it off, what else was he supposed to do? "You're looking good, Helen."

"Flatterer." Suitably diffused, she began to pull him toward the brightly lit front door. "You're just in time for dinner."

He looked around. Henry had gone into the barn. "I'm sorry, I thought—"

"Dinner," she told him, and hauled him inside the house.

He acquiesced. No choice. And spent an hour enjoying what he imagined a normal family dinner get-together might be like. It was over too soon, but he relished it while it lasted. And afterwards it was Helen who handed him the Kimber and ammunition, while her husband brought out the vehicle he'd come to pick up.

"If it turns out to be something, you call for help, you hear?"

"Yes, ma'am."

Despite the urgency, when it came time to leave, regret balled in the back of his throat and he was glad when he couldn't see the lights of their house any longer. He turned north, found a country station on the radio and drove for three hours until he reached a truck stop. He found a bed for the night, managed four hours sleep, and then it was back on the road again.

Until finally he rolled into a small town with two stop lights and a charming, tree-lined main street full of cafes and antique stores. The largest building in town was the local Masonic lodge and the only place that had a vacant room was a converted Victorian mansion along a narrow, leafy lane about a quarter mile from the center. Not ideal, but he chose it. Otherwise it was back to the highway, another five miles and the good old Motel 6.

There was no wifi, but at least his cell phone worked, and he'd already checked out Black's place on Google Maps. All he needed to do was figure out a way to get in there and take a quick look around, and somehow come face to face with Dr. Elliot Black. Then he'd know for sure.

"Shouldn't be too hard," he muttered. From his new hotel room window he could see out onto the lane and across the treetops toward the other side of town. That's where Black's house was— big, going off the map, with outbuildings and a few acres of woodland.

His phone rang. It was Rhonda. "Anything?" he asked.

"It took me a while, but yes. John are you sure..."

"About what?"

"Luke's girlfriend. Let's not forget, your perception is damned near the level of Adept and you've attracted the dead before."

"Yes, I'm sure." And abruptly he had to fight to keep a

lid on his temper. "Tell me about the ghost. What about placement? And strength?"

"Well, he's old. We're talking mid-1700s. And his strength is off the charts. I did some research, based on what he was wearing. Right now, somewhere in northern Europe is all I've got."

"Think you could get him to talk? Assuming you can understand him."

"At the risk of scaring him off? Not sure. Want me to keep trying?"

"Yes. But be careful. Don't put yourself at risk."

"I won't," she laughed. "And hey, take it easy. Calling you Adept isn't an insult."

He knew better, but he dived in anyway. "You sure about that? When all it does is signify I'm a card-carrying member of the stupidity club? All that so-called research for the greater good. Why can't we just agree it's dangerous and shut the whole thing down?"

"But it's not just us, John."

"Ralt."

"Yes. And the others. We're not the only ones opening doors and letting the monsters out. And at least we have the ethics and—"

"Ethics? Jesus, Rhonda..." He rubbed the heel of his hand against his forehead. This was contentious, familiar territory, where he always ended up on the ropes. "Okay. Let's stay on topic."

After a moment of silence, "Sure. So, are you thinking what I'm thinking? To attract something of that caliber..."

"Yeah..."

"Are they serious? As a couple, I mean."

"I think so."

"What are you going to do?"

"Right now, I'm not sure."

"John, you need to be careful."

"I know."

He slid the phone in his pocket and returned to the view outside the window. Rhonda's confirmation had left a bitter taste in his mouth. So, his brother was involved with someone who could attract a two hundred and fifty year old ghost. The manifestation he'd witnessed had been exceptional. At-a-glance three-dimensional and usually it didn't get any better than that. It was looking more and more as if he'd have to play the asshole and split those two lovebirds up. And as a consequence Luke might spiral down and find his own way to Bower's Fall, or worse, all on his own.

He focused on the horizon above the trees, toward Black's house. Time to get this red herring over with and get back to where he was needed the most.

CHAPTER 7

LUKE

He awoke with a start. He pushed up on his elbows and blinked at the light coming in through the window. He'd left the blinds open on purpose, figuring dawn would rouse him early, enabling him to go get breakfast at the local McDonald's and then continue work on her saddle.

He staggered to the bathroom and stared at his reflection. He looked a wreck, like he'd been on a three-day bender, and the ritual of showering, shaving and getting dressed became hampered by incoherent limbs and a brain only half in gear. Maybe he was putting in too many hours. Once he started it became hard to stop, and in truth he didn't want to. Not with this one, especially not with this one.

He pulled on his sandals, walked into the living room. She was floating above his rags, paints and brushes and cans of solvent, balanced on her trestle, facing away from him as if in disdain. Maybe she was angry because he'd woken late, that it was well into the morning and not the 7 a.m. he'd promised.

"I'm sorry," he whispered. He stood there for a while, confused, not sure if he should go out or not. His stomach felt hollow, but he was feeling light headed rather than hungry. And he figured maybe he should make a start, and then take a break when he did feel like eating.

Decision made, he approached his subject. He reached

out, ran his fingers over the elaborately carved rear of the saddle, a two-seater that rose up at the back, protruded, and fanned out slightly. Beneath that protrusion were tiny little carved figures, grotesque, their faces only partially rendered; they had mouths and noses but there had been no provision made for the eyes, as if the carver had either forgotten them, or maybe he'd got the scale incorrect and assumed they could be painted on afterwards.

He remembered puzzling over this the night before, and he frowned. In the end he asked the Lady Armageddon. "Eyes, or no eyes?" She was still facing away from him and of course she didn't answer, but after a moment, "Okay, no eyes it is."

He pulled off his sandals, began to put together the colors and palettes he'd need, lined up his brushes and knives and placed his cloths and rags in a neat pile. He felt a little thirsty perhaps, but he'd rectify that when he took a break, maybe in an hour or two, and that settled, he got back to work.

After a while he forgot the time and he ignored his hunger and thirst. When he finished the saddle he worked on touching up the rear hooves, and then a few further embellishments on her rosettes, highlights that would show up through the glaze, until finally he checked the paintwork around her eyes. He cleaned off the Vaseline, examined her expression from all angles. She had a beautifully carved face, elegant, delicate, her head raised, her mane windswept. "What do you think?" he asked her. "A little more depth?" He smiled, saw the eyes slightly more elongated and reached for the appropriate brushes. He rummaged for one of his smaller pallets. A few minutes later, his colors prepared, he began. The daylight shifted, the room faded. The horizon was a thin line, miles distant. In his peripheral vision he saw trees and vines, and beneath his naked feet the floor felt like dust; like ash.

"Luke."

Ash. It was still there, he could taste it.

"Can you hear me? Luke. Shit..."

It coated his tongue and the roof of his mouth, it tasted like the entire world had been consumed and turned to ruin, and when he took in a breath he felt rocks in his throat and began to cough.

"Drink this. Can you drink? Oh, shit..."

Water. It slipped past his lips; it felt glorious. He let it trickle down his throat, even though it hurt to swallow. "More," he gasped. It energized him, made him greedy and he reached out and began to drink.

"Easy. Easy. Not all at once, just— oh God, I need to get you to the Emergency Room."

"No." He slowed down, stopped. "No. Emma, I'll be fine."

Fine. With dry, swollen lips and a tongue like sandpaper, he could barely say it. He reached out with one of his arms, searching desperately but he couldn't find her. But then he felt her hand take his own; it felt so warm and he wanted to curl up alongside her and go back to sleep.

Instead he let her bully him and haul him away from the wooden horse, and it took a while before he could think straight.

"You were dehydrated, you idiot." She'd made him drink small quantities, a little bit, then a little bit more. She'd wiped the vomit from his face, his hair; he'd been lying in a pool of it amongst his paints, rags and brushes at the foot of the Lady.

"I'm sorry," he croaked. He drank some more. "I guess I lost track of time. Do I get something to eat?"

"Not yet, you don't. Food needs liquid to digest."

He felt fragile, like paper. When she left him to run to the store for Gatorade, he crawled out of the living room. He didn't want to be like this in front of *her*. Not like this. And when Emma returned he was glad he'd moved; he felt more capable somehow, more able to do as he was told now he was out of range of that bitter scrutiny.

"I still think we should go to the Emergency Room. Get you checked out."

"No. No insurance. It's okay. I'll keep drinking, I'll be fine."

"Luke—"

"Shh." He rested his head on her shoulder, and there he stayed for as long as he dared, until it became a matter of urgency to get the hell out of the apartment— no, to get Emma out of the apartment. He was weak, he knew that, and his imagination was bringing everything to bear, its smoke and mirror vaudeville act difficult to ignore. But in the end he persuaded Emma he'd be better off outside, maybe getting something to eat, and he willingly let her dress him and lead him by the nose to her apartment, where she installed him on the couch with blankets and fed him bowls of soup.

In transition he realized it was daylight again and he tried to put the past couple of days into some kind of chronological order, but he soon gave up. Instead he kept silent and listened for clues.

He knew Emma was mad at him, that she'd tried calling, figuring he was busy, until it had got to the point where she'd gotten worried and come around and found him lying there in his own puke in a dark room and even though most of the candles had burned out there were still a few lit and left alone like that they could have...

Candles. How long was it, before he'd passed out, that he'd once more turned the room into an altar of worship?

He decided he didn't want to think about that anymore.

Decided also, now he was feeling stronger, that the Lady would have to go. He was more or less done with the paint but there was still the glaze to apply, and once done it could take more than a week before she was ready for transit. He checked his phone but the battery had run flat, and so he borrowed Emma's and called Elliot Black.

"When you say— not finished?"

"It's hard to explain but I'm on a roll and I need the next subject. If you could see her in the flesh then you'd understand. And I can finish the glaze while I'm out there."

"All right. As it happens the next one is already in transit, and so am I. And I'd like very much to see her."

"Sure."

"Tomorrow?"

"Perfect."

When he signed off, relief hit him so hard he barked out a laugh.

"He's coming here?" Emma asked.

"Yep."

"Feeling better?" She was sitting alongside him, curled up with her head in the crook of his shoulder.

He put his arm around her and drew her close. It felt so long since he'd touched her like this. So long since they'd had any physical contact whatsoever and he became convinced it was because of that stupid horse. He felt empowered now he knew she was leaving, and he shifted and pulled Emma on top of him with a strength he hadn't felt in days.

She was ginning at him, her hair falling softly over one shoulder. "You need a shower, you filthy animal," she told him. She reached forward, her fingers like probes sliding along his throat and chin. "And a shave, although I kind of like this."

He opened his mouth, sucked greedily on her fingers. "You do, huh?"

And for the next few hours he felt relaxed and free of the torment he had suffered earlier. And yeah, it was time to face facts. All this, it had been self-inflicted, hadn't it? That creature back in his apartment was just a carved, doweled and glued together inanimate object, despite the life he'd given it via his skilled hands. When he looked upon her, he was really looking back at himself. That's what this was all about. She was his reflection, in all her dark, fiendish glory. It made him remember the knife, how it had shone as it was thrust forward. There had been a reason for that knife. All those years ago, Daddy had come at him with a purpose because he was afraid. Luke had seen it in his eyes and had never forgotten.

But it was okay, because he had Emma, now. He had John, too, sometimes. But it was Emma who would save him. Save him from himself.

In the morning they returned to the apartment before Black arrived with the new crate, just so they could tidy up the mess Luke had left behind. It didn't take long, and with Emma alongside him the Lady Armageddon remained silent and inanimate on her trestle, just as a well-behaved carousel horse should. Nevertheless, when they were ready and waiting for the others to arrive, a harmless block of wood or not, he couldn't help stand and stare.

"She's beautiful," Emma said, now taken to calling the thing "she" like everyone else. "Frightening, sure— look at her eyes— but I still want to ride her."

He shook his head, told himself he was better off not dwelling on that particular image. "Thanks, although she's not quite finished yet."

"I can't wait to see the next one."

The next one. Could he handle another? He felt a wave of panic, and his gut rolled and tied itself in a double knot when Emma stepped toward the window.

"I think they're here."

He joined her and looked out into the street. He recognized the truck immediately. But there was a car pulling in behind it, a black 5-Series Beamer. A man got out of the driver's side and immediately looked up toward the window. Luke nodded. The man smiled.

Emma seemed excited; she was standing on tiptoe to get a better view. "Is that him? He's wearing a darker suit."

He'd forgotten she'd only seen him once before, and theoretically he could say the same, but after that initial conversation at the gallery and their subsequent phone calls and emails he felt as though he knew Black almost as much as his brother. "Yeah, that's him. What did you call him, my patron?"

She shrugged. "It's how they took care of their starving artists in the old days."

"Instead of Nike sponsorship, stuff like that?"

They laughed, and Luke tried to swallow the ball of anxiety hanging at the back of his throat that was doing an excellent job of trying to choke him.

The doorbell rang. And within minutes the apartment was full of people. Elliot squeezed his way through. They shook hands, the anxiety disappeared, and when Black took Emma's hand and raised it to his lips Luke experienced a brief return of the rancor he'd felt when they'd first met. The act made her blush, and Luke would have kidded her about it if tiny little goblins of jealousy weren't jumping up and down in his head and pointing accusing, goading fingers, and he was glad when the man excused himself and waded through a tangle of men and a half-assembled crate to look at the horse.

Luke stood back and watched him, took in every nuance on Black's face as he slowly circled the carousel horse and stopped directly in front of it. The man reached out to touch her face, but then appeared to think better of it.

"And you say it's not done?"

He stepped forth and let out an audible sigh. He began to explain how the glaze would bring out more features, by giving depth and shadow to all the indents and crevices.

"So. She'll actually look darker."

"It'll dampen down some of the color, and it might highlight one or two of her flaws. The joint here, see?" He swept his hand along her haunches. "But I think, from a short distance away you won't see that."

Elliot nodded. "I'm almost tempted to ask you to leave it as it is."

"You don't trust me."

"Oh, I trust you, it's just..." He trailed off, dropped into a momentary reverie that uncannily resembled Emma's faraway look. "All right, do what you need to in order to finish her." He herded Luke away from the carving. "Now, I'd like to take you both out to lunch."

"Oh, there's no—"

"I insist. It will get us out from under the feet of our haulage crew at the very least. Come."

Luke had no desire to go out to lunch with Elliot Black, but in the end obligation and Emma dragged him outside and pushed him into the passenger seat of Black's big German car. Once installed, his seat belt on, he looked over his shoulder and saw his girlfriend's fingers. Having scraped so erotically through the bristle on his chin yesterday, they were now sliding in very much the same manner across the plush leather upholstery. Her eyes were staring out of the window, but her entire body appeared to be soaking up the luxurious interior. He turned around, kept his mouth shut until Black asked him if he liked Italian, and before long they were walking through the doors of a restaurant Luke would never dream of eating at, despite his newly acquired income.

"I feel underdressed," Emma whispered, clinging to his hand.

When they were seated, with linen napkins lying graciously across their laps, and after the wine had been poured, Black offered a toast. "To the carousel," he said.

Luke mumbled through it, clinked his glass. A quick glance told him Emma thought he was being surly, and so he sat up and tried to put on a party face. When she rolled her eyes he smiled for real. But the smile gradually fell after they'd ordered and Elliot was asking her about college, and she went into a reasonable amount of detail about her Junior year and told him how she wanted to work at the Smithsonian. It was nothing new, but hearing it all delivered to Elliot brought forth a strong sense of proprietorship and, he had to admit, jealousy. His problem, of course, and thankfully it meant that he wasn't being quizzed about the horses, specifically the Lady, and so he sat back, listened and attempted to relax.

"So, will you be joining us for the whole summer?"

"No, I—" She glanced at Luke for a moment. "I have to go see my parents. So, we figured the first month, then I'll leave him in your hands."

Black nodded. "Of course. And you're welcome to stay as long as you like. I assume he told you about the accommodation?"

Now both of them were looking at him.

Luke nodded. "The hotel? Sure."

"He showed me the website. It looks charming," Emma added. "I just hope it's not too much trouble, me being there."

"No trouble at all," Elliot assured her, "Unless you stop him from working." He raised an eyebrow.

She laughed. "I don't think that's possible, especially now. He's—"

The food arrived, and Luke breathed a sigh of relief.

After lunch, they went back to Luke's apartment. The Lady had gone, and in her place was a new crate, contents waiting patiently to be revealed. Luke felt another lurch in his stomach as he tried to imagine what lay inside.

"I think you'll find this one is a little different," Black told him. "I hope it doesn't put you off your stroke." His face held the same challenge he'd offered at the art gallery at the beginning of this whole business.

Luke nodded, game face full on and solid as a rock. Not much he could say to that without being churlish and so he kept his mouth shut. They shook hands, exchanged mild pleasantries that amounted to 'See you in a few weeks', and Black took off in his big fancy car, leaving them alone and staring at the crate.

"You think I'm rude," he said.

"Honestly? I don't know how he puts up with you."

"It's because I'm a genius," he offered. He wrapped his arms around her. "You like him, don't you."

"Yes. He's charming; for an older guy he's good looking, too. Unfortunately I like you a whole lot more." She pulled away, grabbed his hand. "Come on, let's open the crate. I want to see what's inside."

Taken by surprise, he hesitated. Open the crate. This was his task and his alone, part of a ritual he'd insisted upon. Until he realized on this particular occasion, he didn't want to do it alone. Not at all. In fact the whole idea of opening up this crate had been nagging at him all through lunch. Because he was afraid of what he might find.

Emma found the crowbar and pushed it into his hands. “C’mon, open her up.”

It didn’t take long to get the lid off, and after they’d carried it into the hall, the act of unveiling Luke’s new subject became methodical and far more efficient now there were two of them, and when they were done –

Emma was on her knees alongside the creature’s large head, staring at the open mouth and enormous teeth. She was laughing. “Oh my God, it’s a tiger.”

Luke barely heard her. He felt so light headed with relief the room was spinning, and inside he had begun a litany. It’s not you again. It’s not you.

It’s not you.

CHAPTER 8

EMMA

Despite Luke's ebullient mood she was reluctant to leave him. But after his assurances, which she discounted, and his insistence that he needed to be alone so he could concentrate and visualize, which she could understand, along with his deliberate, vocalized acceptance that she wasn't about to let days go by without contact, she let it go, turned him loose, and returned to her own apartment.

Once there, she realized she was glad of the space. Sure, the sight of him lying there unconscious had frightened the hell out of her, but he was still an adult and had to take some responsibility for looking after himself.

She'd sworn, after one particular bad and thankfully short relationship, she wasn't about to become someone's momma all over again. No way. And yet, here she was, mopping up puke because some guy had sunk so deep into his work he'd forgotten to feed and hydrate.

And on that thought rested a few pangs of guilt. What if it had been more after-effects of the now notorious lasagna?

She sat down at her desk, tried to let it all go and concentrate on her own life, her own path, her own immediate future. She booted up her laptop, got online and checked the delivery status on books she had purchased to take along with her for the summer. Because following her boyfriend to some quaint little town out in the Midwest wasn't as selfless as it sounded.

Despite telling the distinguished Elliot Black that she'd enjoyed her Junior year and was looking forward to September, Junior year had been tough, Senior year was already promising to be a whole lot tougher, and she was determined to get a jump on it by doing as much reading and note taking as she could during the summer months. Out there, with Luke working, she'd be alone and could concentrate. A far better option than going home and being dragged into all kinds of family activities and, consequently, getting nothing done.

She checked Facebook, a few blogs and message boards, and by the time she was done her limbs felt leaden and she had a mild headache. She took an Excedrin and ran a bath, poured in far too much scented bubble bath and let herself soak for a while.

Eventually her mind drifted and she began to think of the summer trip, the weather, clothes she'd need to pack, shoes, makeup, sunblock, whether she'd need mosquito repellent, and gradually her thoughts led her once again to the mysterious Elliot Black.

She hadn't lied to Luke. She had found the guy very charming and had enjoyed his company at lunch. She'd noted that he wore cufflinks, that his hands were expressive and moved while he talked; that he had intense gray eyes and that try as she might, she couldn't pinpoint his accent or figure out exactly how old he was. However, she also had a strong impression it was a mask, a facade and there were things hidden behind those hard eyes that aroused her curiosity, way more than perhaps they should.

The heat made her drowsy and the room billowed with steam that eased past her throat and soaked her on the inside, and she tried to tell herself it really wasn't any of her business who he was, that everyone tended to wear one mask or another.

The haze shifted, grew dark just before she closed her eyes. Clouds of moisture became more tactile, like sheets of silk caressing her skin and beyond the bathtub steam drifted amongst branches clad with an array of broad fleshy leaves.

She reached out with languid fingers. The leaves twisted, shied away, and it became an important matter to stretch out and grasp, to expose and examine the underside of their glossy surfaces where the splay of veins were a pretty contrast to the gray green epidermis; they pulsed, bright red. They coursed with raw heat.

The only red is blood.

She came awake like someone had slapped her. The bathroom light glared down from the ceiling. The bath water was stone cold. She gasped, began to shiver, and with the sloppy grace of a stumbling drunk she reared up, clutched the sides of the tub and scrambled out. Her teeth began to chatter as she reached for a towel. The tufted fabric felt cold and damp, but she scrubbed herself dry, wrapped another towel tightly around herself and opened the bathroom door.

Outside, the hallway had disappeared. In its place— a landscape so dark it appeared as if she'd stepped inside one of Luke's paintings. And just for a moment there was a crowd of people standing there, shadowy and inanimate and she had to push through, toward a ruin like a pale old church, barely visible, its walls completely covered in flies...

She shook her head in disbelief and took another step forward. It should have been easy, but she was freezing cold and was still only half awake, and the clean lines of the hallway were barely evident and she stumbled hard into the wall.

In her bedroom, she saw a woman standing there in the dark, muscular and forbidding, her left shoulder adorned with a strange tattoo —

Terrified, Emma's fingers groped along her dresser and slid across the rough, shell-covered surface of her jewelry box. She picked it up, her heart hammering. She let out a yell and pitched –

The box hit the mirror hard, shattering the glass and bouncing away, coming open as it did so. And now lines of dust, carrying the same pattern as her rug were littered with broken glass and baubles and hairclips and a string of pearls and looked like sunken treasure strewn across a rippled ocean bed. It drew her eye and she stood there, mesmerized.

A knock on the door made her jump so violently she almost lost the grip on her towel. "Hey. You okay in there?"

Emma's chest began to rise and fall rapidly. She turned, staggered to the door and opened it.

"Are you— oh, my dear, what happened?" The lady from the next apartment was looking down. Emma followed her eyes and saw blood on her leg. It looked so bright, shiny like the underside of those leaves.

"I— I slipped," she began. "And the mirror—"

"It's okay." The woman, in her forties with short blonde hair, had put down her bags. "Let's get you inside and take a look at that cut."

And the next twenty minutes or so became an ordeal of embarrassment and an outpouring of relief as her neighbor sat her down, checked the cut on her leg and brought some blankets. Emma explained that she'd fallen asleep in the tub, had experienced a sharp, painful cramp in her left calf, and stumbled and fallen against her dresser.

"Charlie Horse, huh? Ye-ouch— those things hurt like hell." The woman smiled. "Well, your leg looks okay, see it's stopped bleeding already. But we're going to have to pick up all that glass."

"It's okay. I can do that. You've been kind enough already."

"You sure? I could go get my gloves, and—"

"No, really. I'll be fine."

The woman nodded. "All right. But you take care now, you hear? And don't be afraid to come knocking."

When the door closed and Emma was alone once more, she immediately regretted sending the woman away. She was afraid her apartment would disappear just as before, and so every subsequent step became slow and deliberate; she trusted nothing and double-checked every move she made.

Her bedroom floor glistened with an assortment of glass, her grandmother's pearls, and pieces of costume jewelry. She wanted to collapse and weep. Instead she gathered a swathe of blankets around her, crept carefully into her kitchen and switched on her electric kettle.

She thought about calling Luke but she was ashamed of how stupid it would sound. Hey, guess what, I fell asleep in the tub and when I woke up everything had turned weird and I threw my jewelry box at my own reflection.

Hours later she still felt as fragile as the mirror she'd broken, and despite the ingestion of mugs of hot chocolate and watching back to back re-runs of White Collar on the TV, the fear of her own reflection remained with her. And in the end, unable to face the task of picking up all that broken glass, she curled up on the couch and had one of the most miserable, sleepless nights she'd ever had.

Late morning, the day after, she came out of a meeting with one of her professors regarding grad school and headed for the campus restaurant. Her headache had returned and she wanted to scrub her face clean of all the concealer she'd daubed beneath her eyes.

The news, that she really needed to pick up on her extracurricular activities and volunteer work, in order to *demonstrate a genuine interest* in her field, had been a lecture she could have done without. It seemed more and more there were not enough hours in the day. Maybe if she gave up Luke...

She shivered despite the mild weather, and hugged her jacket close as she crossed the quad. Maybe she'd feel better if she had something to eat. It had been the last thing on her mind this morning and now her stomach was growling. Maybe a sandwich or –

He was at the other side of the fountain, walking in the opposite direction, his eyes looking straight ahead, his stride full of purpose. And maybe it was because she'd stopped in her tracks and was looking at him with such surprise that he noticed her; that feeling perhaps, of being under scrutiny.

He stopped and waved at her. He said something she couldn't hear, and she continued to stare like a fool while he walked over to join her.

They shook hands— a normal handshake this time. "Hello Elliot." It came out a little forced. Maybe she should have called him Dr. Black. Despite their chat in the restaurant yesterday 'Elliot' seemed terribly informal.

"What a nice surprise." He smiled down at her, and if he was offended by any impropriety he wasn't showing it. He was dressed casually; no tie, and instead of suit pants and polished black shoes he was wearing jeans and brown leather brogues. He looked very much like one of the university professors and seemed entirely at home on campus. "I thought you were done for the summer."

She smiled back, attempted to exude confidence and not look like some jittery freshman. "Not quite. I— I didn't expect to see you here."

He shrugged. "Just visiting a friend." His attention shifted for a moment, toward one of the administration buildings.

"Oh, well I shouldn't keep you."

"Heading for lunch?" And after she nodded. "Mind if I join you? My friend can wait."

Emma wondered if she should have made some kind of excuse. Already self-conscious about her appearance, convinced her makeup was visibly sliding off her face, it also felt strange standing in line in the cafeteria alongside her boyfriend's wealthy benefactor while a few of her acquaintances looked on, their eyebrows raised, their mouths starting to whisper.

She grabbed her choices, a chicken salad sandwich, an apple and a diet Coke.

"I'll get this," Elliot said.

She objected but he insisted, and when they were done at the counter she led him to a remote table by the window, away from the others. There was a minute or so of silence as they unwrapped their food and popped the tops of their drink cans, and after the meal yesterday it seemed a little too surreal and it brought smile to her face.

"What's so funny?"

She looked at him, came to a decision and pushed aside all politeness and formality. He might have looked like one of her professors, but he wasn't. "You," she said. "Sitting here with me, drinking out of a can and eating salad with a plastic fork."

He held the offending utensil in front of him for a moment and frowned. "What mean these masterless and gory swords?"

Her smile widened. "Romeo and Juliet."

He nodded. "I'm impressed." He tucked into his salad, and she followed suit and tried to relax. And a few minutes later, when they were both done eating, "Is Shakespeare part of your studies?"

Emma shook her head, piled the sandwich wrapper and her apple core neatly on her tray. "Not really. But he's one of the reasons I wanted to study history in the first place." She grew solemn. It was something she had to ask. "How long do you intend to keep Luke out there?"

Black drained his Coke can, leaned forward and rested his elbows on the table between them. "That depends on him."

"I see."

"Don't misunderstand. He's free to come and go as he pleases. But I'm confident he'll want to see the task through to the end."

"And is it just the horses?"

He shook his head. "There are rounding boards, a few other embellishments. You'll see for yourself this summer."

Emma sat back, gave herself a little distance. She was beginning to feel a little dizzy and light headed again. "And when it's all done, what then?"

"Then I give him back to you."

She stared at him.

"What are you afraid of, Emma?" He hadn't moved. He was still leaning forward, his expression telling her he could read every single word skipping through her head.

"I'm not afraid."

He nodded. "Good. I don't want you to be. And despite what's happening I want us to remain friends."

"What *is* happening?" Her voice sounded muffled, far away.

"Oh, he's changing you, my dear." His smile suggested a quiet delight.

"I don't understand." She glanced outside. The sun was shining and a slight breeze made the tops of the trees sway at the far side of the quad. She felt odd, as if her mind and body were in two different places. She grabbed her bag. "I guess I should be going."

Elliot Black was already standing. "I know." He came around to her side of the table and offered his hand. It seemed impolite not to take it, and so she did, and glided out of her seat. On their way out she felt his fingertips brushing against her shoulder, and outside, as they said their farewells he took her hand and once again raised it to his lips. She felt a jolt, like a belt of static that ran deep and resonated in her heart and lungs and there was a moment when his face appeared to gray out, but the illusion was gone in the blink of an eye.

He let her go. "We won't see one another again until your visit. Until then, take care Miss Vargo."

She mumbled, "You too," and watched him go. A few paces and he'd resumed that purposeful stride and moments after that he was gone.

She took in a deep breath and set off toward Luke's apartment. Every step improved her perception, brought more dimension to her surroundings, until she could feel the breeze on her face, and smell the warm, acrid scent of onions coming from a nearby hot dog stand. A pragmatic train of thought carried her back to the books she'd need, to the whereabouts of her luggage and power cables for various items, along with a hundred other mundane things pertaining to the trip, and she forgot all about the strangeness of the past hour and the evening before it.

She settled into her stride, thought about Luke, and a smile appeared on her face as she left the quadrangle and crossed the street. A few steps later and she'd completely forgotten about her lunch with Elliot Black.

CHAPTER 9

JOHN

Back on the road, well above the speed limit, while guilt, frustration and a cloud of unease flew in his wake like chittering harpies. It was hot and humid outside and the sun was high, casting short, pitch-black shadows and giving the surrounding landscape a sickly pallor, and despite the vehicle's air conditioning John's T-shirt hung slick and uncomfortable against his skin.

He'd done what he could, but it wasn't enough and now, after a clipped, urgent message on his cell phone he was being pulled away, task unfinished. The mysterious Dr. Black had eluded him, and after checking out the guy's store and house, John was still a long way from ascertaining whether or not he was a threat to Luke.

Yesterday he had stepped nonchalantly through the dark green doorway of Dr. Black's Antiquities. The store had been the first place he'd visited, and he'd been disappointed to discover that Black wasn't there. Too easy, he assumed. The old man tending the place told him Black was out of town, too.

"He's out west for the next few weeks. Not expecting him back until after then."

John had taken a look around the store. Polished Victorian furniture, trinkets and Tiffany lamps toward the front; old trunks, chairs and tables, collections of marionettes and Venetian masks at the rear, the latter staring down from the walls in an admonishing manner, as if they knew exactly what he was up to.

But it was what lay beyond the partially open rear door that really caught his interest. And he would have stepped through and gotten a much closer look if the old storekeeper hadn't been on his toes.

"Sorry. Can't let you through." The man had offered an apologetic shrug. "Don't want folk tripping up and hurting themselves is all."

John had nodded, like it was no big deal. "What are they working on? Looks like a giant bird."

The man had laughed. "Ostrich. It's part of a carousel menagerie. They're stripping it down, getting it ready for repainting."

"Wouldn't it hold more value with the original paint?"

"I guess it would, if Dr. Black had a mind to sell it."

"Not for sale, huh?"

"Nope."

He'd nodded again, decided to quit while he was ahead. He'd established two things perhaps, providing the old man was telling the truth— that Black wasn't in town, and Luke's handiwork wasn't being sold on. "Well, thank you for your time."

He'd felt the old guy's eyes on him all the way out of the front door, like he'd been made, although he wasn't getting any vibe that told him the man was anything other than a store owner. Maybe he'd thought John was the competition, another dealer perhaps.

As for the house in the trees at the other side of town, he'd had to climb a wall to get into Black's yard, and on the way out he'd scuffed his hands up pretty good.

Dobermans.

Three of them and they'd taken him unawares, chased him through the brush, and he'd had to take a flying leap at the wall and had only just managed to scramble over it. And those dogs hadn't barked once; they hadn't been the least bit interested in barking as a matter of fact and seemed entirely focused on chasing him down and tearing him limb from limb. And afterwards, once again he'd felt as if he was in the wrong place, chasing the wrong trail.

A quick glance at the speedometer told him how fast he was going and he slowed down, tried to attain some measure of calm and recall what he'd discovered before Black's dogs had arrived —

That the house was impressive, there were garages and a barn, a separate guesthouse and an indoor swimming pool. But it was all superfluous and ordinary and not what he was after. Black could be running a crack house for all he cared. Instead he was searching for anything of an esoteric nature— gateways primarily. Paths, temporary or permanent, stray, bewildered ghosts, any clumsy dabbling that left the usual residue. But in the end he'd got nothing and all that remained was what— intuition? Gut feeling?

Back at his hotel he'd rechecked the database in case he'd missed any obscure references, and had planned to hang out another couple of days, maybe circumnavigate those dogs and get a closer look, and he'd been part way through what amounted to Plan B, when he got the message. And now he was back in the car, eating up the miles, heading further east, further north.

It took him two and a half hours to reach his initial destination while uncertainty gnawed at him and made him wish he still had that vehicle with the rifle stowed in the back. He slowed and pulled in at a middle-of-nowhere truck stop and flicked open the lock on the passenger door. A woman in a gray sweatshirt and jeans and carrying a large shoulder bag slid inside, slammed the door shut and clipped on her seatbelt. John didn't say anything and he pulled out of the truck stop and back onto the highway. It was maybe five miles down the road before his passenger spoke.

"It's the next exit. Take a right and head south east."

And when he nodded, "Good to see you, John, despite the circumstances."

He glanced across. "Likewise."

Outside, everything had flattened out and agricultural land stretched for miles on either side. He saw the turn up ahead and slowed, took the ramp and then a right turn along a narrow but well surfaced stretch of tarmac.

"How far?"

"Another five miles and we're at ground zero."

"Is this guy on the list?"

"Yes he is. An individual. He dropped off the radar for a while. Always a bad sign."

Not a member of the group who'd tried to snatch Rachel, then.

He nodded. "Just the two of us?"

When she answered affirmatively he let out a sigh.

"I know, darlin'," she said. "But at least I didn't have to wait too long until someone got here. And hopefully we can nip this thing in the bud."

"Lucky for both of us, I just happened to be passing by." He looked at her and they both smiled. "You've got Doc or someone on speed dial though, right?"

"Yes I do, not that it'll do any good if things head south."

"Not going to happen, Charlene."

"If you say so."

"I do."

Conversation lapsed once more, and John used the silence to push away all things regarding Luke and get into the required frame of mind. Closer and he began to feel it, as if a solid barrier had softened, become a curtain, hinting at something beyond. No need to ask if Charlene had picked up on it. She was drumming her fingers on her thigh, in time to a rhythm he couldn't follow.

"This is..."

"I know." Her lips had thinned.

They passed by a house, and then another on the opposite side of the road. He saw a sign up ahead and reduced speed accordingly, and sure enough saw the sheriff's deputy parked discreetly at the side of the road.

Charlene snorted in disgust. "If he only knew."

"Better that he doesn't."

No need for any further direction, he could feel it pulling at him, like it had landed hooks in his shirt while he hadn't been paying attention. It would get worse. It always did. Other buildings were turning up with increasing regularity on either side of the road, their yards full of weeds for the most part, and more than one of them had a reasonable collection of rusty old vehicles in their front yards.

"There," Charlene said. "Dear, sweet Jesus, this is worse than I thought. I hope we're not too late."

John frowned and turned left through an open gate and into a pebbled front yard. Compared to some of its neighbors this place looked relatively well tended, but signs of the Fall were everywhere; the draining of color, like someone had taken a paintbrush to one side of the house, to the truck parked in the driveway, and the flower clad shrubs on either side of the front door and had spattered gray paint in streaks and blotches.

John knew not to look too close.

"Can you smell it?" his companion whispered.

"Not yet." But there was no doubt he would soon enough. He brought the vehicle to a halt, reached for the handgun Helen had given him, and on climbing out he stepped back toward the outer gate, checked the road, just in case that deputy had decided to follow the out-of-state plate. Couldn't be too careful these days, after all.

By the time he figured they were in the clear, Charlene was already climbing the porch steps. He cursed and broke into a run, and reached the front door after she had already knocked. They waited. She knocked again. The door crawled with veins of gray. This close he could see they were alive, that if he reached forward and touched —

"Okay, I think we've been polite enough," she said. She was already pulling at the contents of the bag on her shoulder.

He nodded, stepped back, and gave the door a hearty kick. It burst open and hit the wall with a solid thud. There was no one standing there, not even the few grayed-out, shambling figures that were usually in attendance at an event of this magnitude. He let out a sigh of relief. "Behind me," he told her.

"We're going to have to work fast."

"I know."

He entered a shallow, cluttered hallway that became thick with the scent of rotten food, sweat, and the underlying sweet aroma of Bower's Fall. Charlene had been right. It was worse. Someone had opened a gateway and that tactile, wholly indescribable scent was wafting through, as seductive and enticing as ever.

He kept the gun at shoulder height. No telling if there was anyone in the house, whether the guy had left in fright, or if he'd already gone through. He hoped it wasn't the latter. If he'd entered the Fall he was as good as dead; not a man any longer, more akin to a number of highly coveted, consumable pieces. As for whether or not anything had managed to escape in the other direction, he tried not to think about it.

To his left was a kitchen, and the play of twisted gray and black on its rear wall suggested all the good stuff was happening in the room further on. Nevertheless, he quickly checked the room at the other side of the passageway, a living room— the furniture inside scattered with newspapers and books. The TV was off, a good sign.

"Quickly," Charlene hissed.

He bit back a retort. Still no telling if there was someone

lying in wait, with a baseball bat, or a shotgun. There was a truck parked in the driveway after all. But he also knew she wanted to get inside and seal that breach, before it got any bigger and something did decide to try its luck and come on through. He tried not to think that far ahead. And stepped further into the house. Just before he reached the second doorway he stopped and took a deep breath. He knew what lay on the other side of the wall. He could feel it in his bones.

When he rounded the corner he let out an involuntary gasp, and that mental tug and pull became an abrupt, howling wind, buffeting and bruising his resolve. The room's sole occupant had closed the curtains, effectively shutting out most of the late afternoon sun. Whatever light remained was dampened further by the dark, yawning hole on the opposite wall.

It was a narrow room. A washer and dryer took up about a third of it, and alongside them a man stood, maybe in his fifties, early sixties— dressed in a vest and under shorts, his hair disheveled and stuck out at all angles. In the gloom his skin looked grimy and pale, like he hadn't washed or been outside for weeks.

John still had the gun held up in front of him and he kept his voice low and calm. "Step away from the wall, sir."

"No sign of the dead," Charlene whispered behind him. "We got lucky."

Good to know. He watched the man look at his weapon for a moment, and saw a crafty grin emerge when he finally looked John in the eye. I know what's going on, that face said. You can't hide it from me. And he moved closer toward the hole.

"Wait," John told him.

The man shook his head, glanced in the direction he was heading. The grin dropped.

"Don't risk yourself," Charlene said. She'd seen the look,

hungry, yearning. How long the guy had been staring at that wall was anyone's guess.

"Please. Step back," John continued, despite the fact he knew it was already too late. "I know how it feels, but you don't know what it does. It'll use you, turn you into—"

"Oh yeah?" The man laughed, sneered. *Liar*. He pitched forward, intent on dashing through before John could stop him.

"Shoot him!"

He hesitated. The man had one foot beyond the wall.

"John!"

He pulled the trigger, didn't wait to see if he'd hit, he pulled it again and again. He saw the man fall forward, and drop beyond the gray and black twisted hole in the wall. He lowered the weapon, knew he had to step back, that he was in danger himself.

"Get out," she said.

The room was starting to bend and he became disoriented and nauseous. One step back, then two. At the doorway he saw Charlene standing next to the washing machine with an object in her hand, her eyes closed, busy righting the crawling ill in the room. Nothing he could do now, and so he kept on going, until he was outside and leaning against the truck belonging to the guy he'd just murdered. He wanted to collapse right there against the front wheel, but his job wasn't done yet.

He checked his weapon and tucked it behind him. He walked toward the gate, saw no one out on the road— the mailman, or that sheriff's deputy— and breathed a sigh of relief. Nevertheless he kept vigilant. Someone may have heard the gunshots, and he knew they'd have to be on their way just as soon as Charlene was done.

When he looked back toward the house he could see the encroaching disfigurement had almost gone, and so he waited, until he could see nothing at all, then took the pistol back to his own vehicle and placed it in the glove compartment. Another minute and Charlene walked out of the front door, closing it behind her like she'd just paid the owner a friendly visit.

"You okay?" she asked.

"For a guy who just killed someone, yeah, sure."

Charlene held out her hand. "Keys. I'll get us out of here. And don't beat yourself up. This was about as bad as it gets."

John didn't argue, gave her the keys and climbed into the passenger seat. His companion reversed the vehicle, backed out of the drive, set off down the road and not back the way they'd arrived.

"We can re-join the main highway further on," she explained. "No need for that deputy to see us twice."

He kept silent, attempted to distract himself by watching the passing landscape, but he couldn't focus and it all slipped by as a blurred accompaniment to what lay in his mind's eye. He attempted to justify what he'd done, that some part of the guy, the sane part, would have thanked him for ending his life; better that than the exotic terrors that awaited him through that hole. Or, maybe not. Maybe he'd have welcomed them instead.

A few miles later, on their way back to the truck stop. "Just how the hell did he do that, Charlene? How the hell?"

She shook her head, kept her eyes on the road. "The heck if I know for sure, hon.' It was sloppy and homegrown, I could tell that much. But at least he was on his own. I got your bullet casings by the way. They're in my purse."

"Thanks." He looked toward her. She appeared steady as a rock, like fixing a weeping dark hole in the universe was something she did on a daily basis and he wondered if it took anything out of her physically at all. Charlene made saving the world look easy.

At the truck stop she refused to hand over the keys.

"Not until we've been inside, had a cup of coffee and sat a spell, young man."

He shrugged and gave in. And right now she was probably the better judge of his state of mind than he was. It was going dark and the lights were on under the gas pump canopies. Beneath them hundreds of fat insects danced. They reminded him of Bower's Fall and he had to look away. In the self-service cafe adjoining the store she made him sit down while she bought coffee and two slices of apple pie. Behind him two guys were talking the price of gas and the best way in and out of St. Louis. It felt surreal after everything he and Charlene had been through.

Thankfully he hadn't had to look at the guy's face for too long. You'll thank me later, buddy. Sure. That was the trouble. The guy would never know what John had saved him from.

His companion arrived. She placed food and drink on the table, took a seat and stared at him until he began to eat. He felt like he was twelve years old instead of thirty-eight. He grimaced, but tucked in and let the act of chewing and swallowing distract him.

"Better?" she asked, once he was done.

"I'm not sure. What if he could have survived?"

She shook her head. "You know the odds, and what had to be done," her voice had softened a little, two notches down from strict school ma'am, "and you know what would have happened." He nodded, took a sip of his coffee.

"So," she continued, "what is it, hon'? What's really bugging you?"

He'd known Charlene a long time, knew how perceptive she was. "Luke," he said finally.

She frowned. "Is he—?"

"No. Not yet."

"It might never happen. I wish you wouldn't keep torturing yourself over this."

"And if it does?"

"You're afraid you might have to shoot him, too?" She shook her head. "Oh, darlin'..."

He stared at her. A woman. So fucking practical. She had no idea what it meant. To be a man. In there.

"Actually, I do," she said, startling him in mid thought. "Just remember who pulled you out the last time. And it's no picnic for us, either."

"Sure," he retorted. "You become super-human. We're just— consumed." John sat back in his seat and immediately regretted his outburst. For a moment there he'd forgotten how far her perception ran and he ventured a guess that she'd known all along what was sticking in his craw, and this was her way of getting him to open up about it. He could have damned her and blessed her in equal measure. "I'm sorry," he said finally.

She shrugged, finished her coffee. "It's okay. I forgive you and I want you to remember something. You're not on your own, so if anything happens you don't go and be the gosh danged Lone Ranger."

"No ma'am." He held up his hands in mock surrender.

Outside on the truck stop forecourt she drew him into a tight hug. He welcomed it, wallowed in its warmth and honesty, and hated the moment when they finally split up and went their separate ways.

Back on the road in the dark, the vehicle's headlights cutting a path along the tarmac, he fought hard to push away the horror. Nevertheless it became so easy to allow the afternoon's events affect his judgment on what to do about Luke.

There was no doubt his brother's artwork was inspired by Bower's Fall. But right now it was two-dimensional and harmless, akin to looking at photographs of an atomic bomb blast. No way the illustrated heat and destruction would ever reach beyond the plane of the image.

However, Emma was sentient, whether she realized it or not, and that spelled trouble. John's face twisted. Could he shoot her? Oh, sure...

He handed over the weapon, watched Helen carefully unload it and place it on the table. She took his arm and led him to the window. Outside, her husband had the car in reverse and was putting it in the garage. "How long do you think Henry and I have been together?" she asked.

He frowned, knew exactly what was coming. "More than twenty years?"

"Thirty seven, all told."

He stared out of the window, watched the garage doors close. The red truck was waiting in the yard, its lights on, the engine running. "Helen, I know what you're trying to say—"

"Do you?" She tugged on his arm. "Fact of the matter is, Henry would be dead right now if it weren't for me."

He tried not to think about the look on that old guy's face before he realized John was going to shoot him. Pure madness, like all his reason and humanity had pushed out from shore a long time since and had left him alone with that yawning gap in the wall for company. No way baby brother was going to end up like that. "So, you're telling me to leave it alone; that she might actually be good for him."

"Or—" she let out a tiny groan of exasperation, "—you could step in, and offer to help her."

"She's not one of us."

"After what you've just told me?" Helen's voice took on an edge. "I don't believe I heard you say that, John De Grasse."

He looked at her. “We don’t exactly get along.”

“And whose fault is that?”

“Mine. Of course.” He tried not to grind his teeth over what she was suggesting. Henry had left the garage and was approaching the truck. It was time to go. Time to do the right thing, whatever that turned out to be.

SUMMER

CHAPTER 10

LUKE

He could hear Emma and Elliot talking outside, having left him alone to explore his new domain. A short while ago they'd arrived just in time to see the tiger delivered. He and Emma had laid bets on who would arrive first and she'd won by about fifteen minutes. They'd stood outside in the yard with Black, laughing about it before Luke had been introduced to his new workspace and then all of a sudden it wasn't about the carousel animal any longer, or if the journey had been pleasant, or how comfortable their hotel was.

He ran his fingers along the edge of a bench stacked with brushes, paints and solvents. He realized he had an idiotic, kid in a candy store smile on his face, but it didn't concern him in the slightest. And once he'd gotten a feel for the place he turned around and approached his next subject. Another horse had been brought in, a stander, and this time instead of flowers and curliques and strange creatures adorning its torso, this one had a military theme, with a bedroll carved under the saddle, brigandine armor, a knotted mane and a sword and scabbard carved on its right flank.

He crouched alongside, traced his fingers very, very carefully above the carvings, mindful not to transfer the oil from his hands onto the woodwork. He noted the scale, the precision and expertise, and vowed to match it with his own not so humble skills and he felt the tension in his fingers, knew they were dying to get started, and wondered if he should indeed roll up his sleeves and get to work.

Politeness curtailed his desires and instead he stepped back outside into the yard.

"Is it to your liking? Is there enough light and space?" Elliot Black was standing alongside Emma. Close, maybe a little too close.

Luke took her hand, pulled her away. "Yes," he said. "It's perfect. You were going to show me where the others were stored?"

Elliot nodded. "Good. And yes, follow me."

He led them across the courtyard, hauled open a large sliding door. Inside the barn Luke saw the tiger had been placed alongside the others he'd already worked on, most of them waiting to be glazed and varnished, a task that would probably take as long as the paintwork.

Emma had let go of his hand and was looking at another row of animals, all of them pale with primer. "Oh, a tail. What *is* that?" she said.

"It's a hippocampus," Elliot told her.

"Oh, so it is." She laughed, astonished.

Luke was barely paying attention. He'd spotted the Lady and already she was garnering all of his attention. He tore his eyes away, strode over to take a look at the creature his girlfriend was fawning over, ran his critical eye over a beast that looked part horse, part fish. "I thought it was a part of the brain."

"Yes," Elliot purred. "So called because it looks like a sea horse."

He nodded, ignored the man's condescension. Emma's fickle attention had moved on, to a carriage further along, its sides composed of two formidable dragons with curled tails. Luke kept his eyes on the sea horse. There were no scales carved into the tail, so he'd have to paint them in, interpret —

"The tiger is magnificent."

"Hmm?" He pulled away from a disturbing image of dark, slick, shimmering scales edged with just a hint of turquoise and gold that reminded him uncomfortably of the ocean during an oil clean up. "Oh. Thanks." Half-heartedly he tried to remember, until he saw the tiger a few paces away— black and gray stripes with touches of silver that once again reminded him of spilled crude. The creature seemed bigger than he remembered. More forbidding. "What about the carousel?" he asked.

Elliot grinned. "Ah." He beckoned.

Luke gathered up Emma and followed Elliot Black out of the barn and along to the side door of a building right alongside. It was the carriage house. He'd figured it was where Black kept his vehicles. He'd figured wrong.

The empty carousel took up most of the entire space, and it wasn't at all what Luke had expected. He'd imagined the typical fairground contraption, gaudily painted, all metal poles, light bulbs and wood paneling, with a concealed core that drove the thing, either by electricity or steam. But this —

It was set into the wooden floor, the only delineation between what was static and what would likely move being a dark painted circle on the floor. A magic circle, he thought. There were slender wooden poles erected just inside the circle, supporting an elaborate canopy that didn't appear to serve any purpose now it was under shelter. As for a central core, it was non-existent, he could see right across to the other side.

Emma was hanging back, pulling at his hand and so he let her go. He stepped across the circle, and a smile appeared when he didn't burst into flame or disappear in a puff of multi-colored smoke. "How does it run?"

Elliot pointed to the top of a stairwell at one side of the room. "Come, I'll show you."

He led them downstairs and Luke was startled for a moment when he discovered two men at the base of the steps, in a room not quite the same size as the one above. One of the men was half way up an aluminum stepladder while the other was at the bottom of it, holding a length of cable. Both men stopped for a moment, nodded, then continued with whatever they were doing.

Luke blinked in the gloom and saw Elliot stepping over toolboxes and pieces of wood toward the far side. He followed him and picked his way deftly through the obstacle course.

"It was built to be pushed manually," Elliot explained. "It was originally built in the 1700s, in the grounds of a grand schloss in Europe. I had it dismantled and imported. And as you can see, we've restored what we can." He pointed at the thick central core holding up the ceiling. There was another ring of columns, too, that ran along a similar circumference to those on the floor above. "I'm having it wired to run on electricity, there's a whole lot more going on below these floor panels, but— it's still capable of the manual option, too." He smiled. "More authentic."

Luke nodded, looked around. The ceiling was high enough for him to stand, nevertheless he felt like stooping and it became an effort not to. He saw Emma, still standing at the base of the stairs. He beckoned her over but she shook her head.

"They'd have plenty of servants in those days, of course," Elliot was continuing. "Able bodied men to push the thing around."

He tried to appear interested but most of his attention was on the ceiling. He could see various brackets and bolts. He supposed the whole thing could spin around the central axis, like a giant, horizontal wheel with the carousel balanced on top and it was easy to imagine people toiling away down here while others were having all the fun upstairs. Down here one could probably hear the muffled cries of spoiled children in fancy clothes, and he visualized the men, shoulders straining —

A shiver ran through him. "It's cold down here."

Elliot nodded. "Let's go back upstairs."

Emma was waiting for them at the top of the steps, her arms huddled across her body.

"Cold?" he asked her. She had an odd look on her face as he wrapped his arms around her and brushed hair away from her brow. "You okay?"

She nodded. "It was just a little chilly down there, that's all."

Behind her, Elliot was staring at the back of her head like he could read what lay on the inside. Luke frowned, annoyed. He couldn't imagine them coming to blows, but he realized the necessary detente was still fragile.

They left the building and he let Emma go, pushed aside his animosity and focused on work. "So," he said, "when do I start?" He looked back at the workshop. Its door lay open and the afternoon sun offered him a glimpse of the interior. Everything appeared to be waiting. Waiting for him.

Elliot shrugged. "As soon as you've settled in? Why don't you take this afternoon and have a look around town, make sure Emma knows where everything is?"

"I'd like that," she said.

"And perhaps make a start in the morning?"

Luke regarded her, a question on his face. Truth was, he was itching to begin, maybe set the place up in the evening, make sure he had everything he needed, sketch out a few color plans, apply some base coat. But going off the challenging arch in her eyebrow it was like she knew exactly what he was thinking and wholeheartedly disapproved.

"Tomorrow morning it is," he said.

They walked hand in hand back into town. It was an easy, five minute stroll along a narrow, tarmac road lined on either side by trees, their heavy bows extended overhead, creating a natural tunnel. Just ahead of them to the right lay the town's main street. He sensed something was coming, via the tense grip of her fingers.

"You really want to make a start tonight," she began.

He grinned at her. "I should..."

She gave him a sigh. "Well, I guess I could—"

"I'm kidding." He put his arm around her shoulder. "Let's check this place out. Find the liquor store, the bar and the strip joint." He deftly avoided the expected jab in the ribs and began to laugh. He was feeling a whole lot better, he realized, now he wasn't in the company of his employer.

They crossed the road, changed their pace and began a slow tour of the stores on Main Street. Their hotel, a two story Victorian with a huge, wraparound porch, was part way down, set back behind a tidy rose garden, and by the time they had completed a full circuit they'd spotted the post office, the fire station, a few restaurants they wanted to try, and a small supermarket and laundry on one of the side streets. They'd also discovered Elliot's retail antique store, just fifty yards or so from the hotel, at the opposite side of the thoroughfare. Emma had wanted to take a look inside, but by then it was late afternoon and the store was closed. Luke had taken a look around the back and peered over a high, red brick wall. Black had told him the carousel animals were being prepared here, but he couldn't see anything other than a couple of adjoining buildings, their doors resolutely shut, their windows opaque. It didn't concern him. He figured he'd get the chance to take a look around sooner or later, if he could summon up the required interest.

Back at the hotel he joined Emma in the large, claw-footed bathtub brimming with foam and afterwards they indulged further in a warm, take-your-time sexual ritual he knew she enjoyed. And afterwards, while she took a nap he lay alongside her, wide awake and staring at the bare skin on her shoulder, marveling how her hair swept back and rolled like a wave from the nape of her neck. He decided he'd paint her like that; he'd get her to sit this time, have her sweep her hair over one shoulder so that one side of her face and throat was completely exposed. It would be exquisite. She had beautiful, fragile cheekbones, offset by a strong jaw that was often thrust forward when he tried to bullshit her or attempt to duck out of something he'd promised.

Propped up on one elbow he got to work, raking his fingers carefully through strands of her hair, arranging it carefully on the pillow. Then he sat up and slowly peeled back some of the sheets. He began to arrange and fold them, exposing her breasts and upper torso, until they pooled around her lower abdomen. He slid out of bed, careful not to disturb her, and looked around for his sketchbook.

Two paces across the room, she moved, and rolled onto her back. He froze, and watched as her hand came to rest gently on her stomach. He waited for her eyes to flick open, and oh boy was he going to get it. But she didn't wake up, and in her current position he decided she looked damned near perfect.

Foregoing the sketchbook he reached for his small Olympus camera. She'd go crazy if she found out, but he had to capture the image before he lost it. He fumbled with the thing, knocked off the flash. Then he stepped forward and began taking pictures. When she didn't awaken he became bold, took some closer shots of her face in repose with her hair swept out along the pillow. He tugged gently at the sheets, exposed more and more of her flesh. And afterwards he tried hard to feel guilty when he finally slipped the camera into his jacket pocket. Instead a smile kept coming to his face. He'd never managed to capture her like that before, and providing he hadn't been a total klutz with the camera he now had material for maybe a dozen paintings, maybe more.

He covered her as gently as he could and wondered if he should simply crawl back into bed. But he decided on another course and reached for his sketchbook instead. And by the time she did wake up it was fully dark outside, he'd completed one fine pencil drawing and was a third of the way through another.

She sat up, drew up her knees and pulled the bed sheets up in front of her. "How long have you been doing that?"

He shrugged. "A while. Want to take a look?"

"I don't know." She looked uncomfortable. "I wish you wouldn't—" She didn't finish and let out a sigh. She emerged from the sheets and crawled alongside him.

He handed her his sketchbook, watched as she stared at the partly finished drawing before flicking over the page. She gave a soft, derisive gasp. "I don't look like *that*. She's pretty."

"Actually, you do look like that." When she stuck out her tongue, "Okay, I admit it. While you were asleep I climbed out of the window and sneaked into the next room. There was another girl there, and—" She launched herself at him and they ended up in a tangle, and the momentum carried them off the bed and they landed on the floor with a loud thud.

Luke burst out laughing.

"Shit." Emma scrambled to her feet. "They'll wonder what the hell is going on, downstairs." She marched toward the bathroom, stopped in the doorway and stabbed a finger toward him, a gesture he was entirely familiar with. "You get your pants on, Mister. You owe me dinner."

Neither of them felt the particular need to dress up or make a fuss, and so they ended up at a scruffy, incongruous diner just a few doors down that advertised meatloaf and spaghetti and meatballs as the specials on the chalkboard outside. They sat together, his arm around her shoulder while they ate lazily and talked about the next few weeks.

He ended up making a few promises he knew he wouldn't be able to keep, but as lies went, they were not so bad, and he justified them by not wanting to get into any negotiation that might spoil the mood. Right now he felt at ease, relaxed, and the burgeoning task ahead of him lay hidden behind a woolly veil of amnesia.

Even his attitude toward his current employer felt benign and harmless, and he began to imagine eventually that particular relationship would ease up, that they might even become friends. He looked out of the window, saw their reflection and he smiled, utterly content.

Emma shifted alongside him, bringing him out of his reverie. She had grown stiff and was pulling away. Someone was standing alongside the booth, casting a shadow over the table.

He looked up. And smiled.

CHAPTER 11

EMMA

She switched places with Luke, let him slide out of the booth then he could greet his brother, and that allowed her to sink a little further into the corner and assume a defensive position, in other words, as far away from John De Grasse as possible.

She still had his number on her cell phone; she'd spotted it on occasion when she'd gone through her list, but the thought of actually dialing it had brought a bitter taste to her mouth and luckily, so far, she hadn't needed to. Whatever he had alluded to a few weeks ago hadn't happened, Luke appeared to have been fine, was fully, happily absorbed in his work, and so their line of communication had stayed silent and that was how she liked it.

But now here he was, in the flesh, his eyes telling her he'd just crawled out of Hell, making her wonder exactly what he'd been up. It was typical. After an unsettling afternoon at Black's mansion she'd finally climbed down to a more relaxed and certainly more preferable state of mind, and now it was back up again— sirens howling, on red alert.

She placed her elbow on the table, rested her chin on her hand and tried to look as if she was listening politely, and wondered if it was a pose she'd have to get used to now that big brother had dropped in on them once more without warning. Luke appeared to be okay with the surprise visits; she suspected that's the way it had always been and, thankfully, John never seemed to stay for long. But his broody nature always bled into her, dragged her down, throwing her off kilter and on guard. Thankfully its influence disappeared at the same time as he did, and so she prayed this visit would be as short as the others.

"I couldn't afford that place, so I'm at a bed and breakfast around the corner."

"You're staying here?" Luke asked.

"For a little while. You mind? I wanted to make sure you were okay, with Dad, and everything."

Emma kept her face blank. So he was staying for a few days. It was okay. Not a problem. She'd cope.

"I'm fine," Luke said. "And I don't mind you being here. Thing is— I'm going to be working."

"I know." John shrugged. "Truth is, I guess you're the only family I have left. And with Dad..."

"Hey, it's okay."

Emma watched the brothers clasp hands across the table. Under normal circumstances she would have been touched. Instead she felt a brewing resentment, quickly followed up by a strong dose of guilt and contrition. She'd never once witnessed Luke grieving over his father, so perhaps some family time might do him good. And perhaps it was time to start looking on the bright side. If she got to know John a little better, then maybe things wouldn't be so bad between them, and so she swallowed her misgivings and attempted a smile.

Moments later, Luke threw an arm around her shoulder. "Guess we could put up with him for a little while, huh, Em?"

She nodded, and met John's odd, unsettling stare. "Sure."

The man smiled. There was no irony, or sarcasm delivered along with it, and while small talk began to flow she felt the beginnings of a truce.

At the end of the evening, the two brothers embraced, John offered her his hand, which she shook, and they went their separate ways. But on the walk back to the hotel –

"Something's wrong."

"With John? Is he in trouble?"

He shrugged. "I don't know. Not that I'm aware of. Maybe it's just personal. Dad, maybe."

"And maybe you both need to talk it over."

"I guess."

He was silent for the rest of the journey, and despite the cordiality in the diner, she could tell John's arrival had unsettled him. And when they finally climbed into bed he became that urgent, needy boy all over again, pinning her down and demanding all kinds of reassurances that left her cast adrift in a miserable pool of insomnia.

And in lying awake she couldn't help but revisit the events of the afternoon, and she discovered a well of rancor brewing in her innards. Sure, he'd been distracted by John's arrival and, truth be known, she hadn't really wanted to discuss it, but he hadn't asked her any more about the afternoon and why she didn't want to linger inside Elliot Black's carriage house. Maybe she should have said something. And there was her dilemma. For she could hardly blame Luke for not giving her any attention over something she hadn't wanted to talk about in the first place. And as for the idea of informing Elliot Black that he might have ghosts in his cellar –

It all came back to her, here in the dark, lying on her stomach, her lover's arm weighing heavy on her shoulder. The deepening chill as she descended those steps, the forbidding, heavy ceiling; drifting shapes and whispers that held the fragile solidity of dragonfly wings, and that man again.

Barely evident, and yet, she was still able to recognize him– the gathers of his shirt, the straw blond hair. And this time he seemed to be in some kind of trouble, for he was bound to one of the wooden poles in that basement, right next to the ladder where the electricians were working. And when he saw her he'd started to move, to struggle, to get free. His mouth had moved as if he was trying to tell her something and that was when she'd bolted, back up the steps while Luke hadn't noticed anything was amiss at all.

She wondered. Am I going crazy?

Determined to keep her awake the entire night, her memory stirred and reminded her of that day back in California, when Luke's brother had knocked on her door. He'd told her he'd seen the man, too. Maybe his collaboration should have brought her some relief, that she wasn't alone in this. But it didn't.

At the end of Main Street she had the choice of turning left, or right. She chose right, picked up her pace, and was soon running up a slow incline toward a copse of trees. It was approaching mid-morning and yet there was still a skin of mist clinging to the fields on either side of the road. It leant a soft, ethereal filter to the view and for a short while she forgot everything else and let the surroundings take her. She felt the jarring of her feet on tarmac, the roar of her breath escaping from her throat and the deep pounding of her heart and she let it flood her senses and push out every nagging thought that had kept her awake the night before.

Past the trees and out toward the main highway, there was a gas station at the junction ahead and so she headed for that and planned on doing an about turn once she'd reached it. Time enough then to figure out what she was going to do for the rest of the day.

Despite the pretense, that she was simply exploring the neighborhood, she had chosen this end of town to give herself some distance and perspective. Her second day and one sleepless night did not the entire summer make. She'd already forgiven Luke for his moodiness late last night, and out here on a pale summer morning all those stupid notions and fears seemed crazy and ridiculous. After all she'd had a plan when she arrived here, one that would keep her far too busy to be concerned with the likes of Elliot Black, fanciful ghosts and her boyfriend's brooding sibling.

She smiled as she reached the gas station. The prices were so much cheaper out here and yet the place was empty. In California there would be a constant stream of traffic, in and out, the drivers wandering over to the store only to return with drinks in their hands and surreptitiously stored packets of cigarettes.

Right on the corner of the junction she stopped and took in a few slow, deep breaths. Looking back toward town she could see distant buildings beyond the treetops and wondered if Luke was painting right now in one of them. Maybe she would drop by later and see how he was settling in. And so with a day's itinerary forming in her head, she started back. She had already called her parents, but she'd promised a few friends she'd either call or email to let them know she'd arrived. And there was work. Time to start going through her stack of books and figure out where to begin.

The mist had disappeared as she approached the outskirts of town, and traffic had increased; the sky was brighter and she wished she'd brought a hat. Back on Main Street she was about to cross the road toward the hotel and she saw John.

He was standing maybe thirty feet away on the sidewalk

and was staring into one of the stores, Elliot Black's store, in fact. Her face fell. Dislike him or not, she didn't particularly want to run into him all sweaty in her running gear with her hair bundled in an untidy ponytail.

But it was too late. He raised a hand, waved, and she became obliged to slow down and say hello.

"You run?" His lips curled into a smirk.

She fought desperately to come up with a suitable, witty retort, but had to make do with a nice mental image of her hands squeezing around his throat instead. "I was just heading back," she began, her cue to keep on going.

A familiar car pulled up at the curb and two men emerged. It was Elliot, accompanied by an older man. She let out a sigh. John was looking at the other men with the intensity of a cat watching a mouse, and more than ever she wanted to be anywhere rather than here.

"Emma." Elliot smiled broadly. "Good morning. May I present Robert, my store manager."

She shook the other man's hand and said hello. He had a friendly, easy going smile and twinkle in his eye. "This is—" she began, about to introduce John, but he preempted her and an awkward moment followed involving stiff handshakes and cautiously exchanged names.

"We've met before." John said.

"Have we?" Elliot asked him.

John appeared to be confused.

There's a first, she thought. She took the pause as her cue. "Guys, I'm sorry but I need to go and get changed."

"You're not taking a look at the store?" Elliot looked mildly disappointed.

"A little later?"

"Sure."

She said her farewells and crossed the street. She'd almost made it to the hotel entrance when she heard her name being called. John was striding toward her like a murderous cyborg. Apparently his meeting with Elliot had been brief, too.

"We need to talk."

"We do?"

"Yes. Lunch?"

She chewed her lip. "I was— okay. Where and when?"

He checked his watch. "Diner. One o' clock?"

"Sure." She didn't wait any longer, left him on the sidewalk and headed inside.

She took a shower, dressed, brushed her hair and put on some make up. She toyed with the books she'd brought then sat at the small table by the window, made notes, drew up a plan. And at the end of it she stared down at her notebook and couldn't remember a word she had written. Instead all she could think about was John De Grasse. What did he want? It rang like a bell in her head, over and over.

When it came time to leave and head off toward the diner, she hung back, hesitated, paced the room while the same litany continued, scattering her thoughts until disgust offered an even bigger question. Why should it matter? Trouble was brewing, sure; it was written boldly across the planes of his face and deep in those intolerable eyes. He'd brought along extra trouble, too. She'd put money on it, and it was going to be dumped straight into her lap.

She almost didn't go; she thought about calling that number and telling him no. But instead, at the very last minute, she bounded down the stairs, strode swiftly along the sidewalk, entered the diner and slid into the booth only two minutes late. She put her bag neatly alongside her, clasped her hands in front of her on the table, stuck out her jaw and looked right at him.

He stared at her for a moment then broke contact. A smile slipped briefly across his features and he let out a sigh, as if he was tired, weary. "Please. Don't," he said.

"Don't what?" She tried to stay polite, keep her voice light.

"Look at me like that."

"What do you want, John?"

"Let's get something to drink first. You might need it."

"Why, so I can pour it over your head?" There. Cards on the table, and screw being nice.

He surprised her by laughing. "Maybe." He held up his hands in mock surrender. "Hear me out? I'll try not to be too much of an asshole."

Emma sat back. "Okay." She tried to relax while they waited an interminable amount of time before one of the wait staff arrived and took their order.

"How's the hotel working out?" he asked.

"Still good. Yours?"

"It'll do."

More silence, awkward and unbearable, until their drinks arrived.

She thanked the waiter, leaned forward, squeezed the lemon into her iced tea then stabbed and swirled at the drink with her straw. She took a careful, deliberate sip, then looked at him again.

He didn't waste any more time. "I want to know if you've seen that guy again."

"What guy?"

"The guy wearing the big shirt."

For a moment he appeared to fade from view. "Yes," she said. He'd pushed her out onto a frozen lake, right out there where the ice was thin.

His voice came out flat and emotionless. "Give me the details."

Another slow sip of iced tea, she placed the palms of her hands on the table to stop them from shaking, and she told him about the room beneath the carousel. And throughout the explanation she watched him like a hawk. And just one indication of disbelief, one snort of sarcasm or a mocking gesture and swear to God she would punch him. When she was done her hands were shaking regardless. That frozen lake she'd been walking on— it had cracked and she'd fallen in.

He didn't mock. Instead he reached across the table, but before he could take her hand she snatched it away, nearly knocking over her drink as she did so.

"Hey, it's okay," he said. "I believe you."

She swallowed, wanted to cry and only just managed to hold it back. "Who is he? What does it mean?"

"You said he was trying to warn you?"

She nodded. And it became hard to talk, to carry on an approximation of a normal conversation. She was scared, she realized. Frightened out of her wits, because with John sitting here, talking about it, the strange man with the odd clothes who had stood waiting for her at the library, and alongside her car, and who was tied to one of the poles on that strange carousel— was real and she hadn't simply imagined him. Unless —

"I really hope you're not lying to me. That you're not just going along with this."

He narrowed his eyes. "If I asked you to trust me, would you?"

"I don't know," she said eventually. "After all, this is about Luke, isn't it? Otherwise you wouldn't give a shit."

"Well, you've got me there, darlin.'"

And now the old John had arrived. She let out a sigh, grabbed her purse, and stood up.

"Emma, sit down."

"Screw you, De Grasse."

She started to walk toward the exit.

"Emma, I'm sorry. Please. Come back."

People at the next table were staring. And now the tears were coming for real. She took a step back, and then another, and slid back into the booth. She felt lost and defeated and held her purse in front of her like a shield.

"Okay, look," John implored. "I keep forgetting this isn't normal, for you. I'm sorry. I was being a jackass."

"Normal?" He looked blurry in her vision. She grabbed a napkin, began to dab at her eyes.

"Ghosts," he said quietly.

"That's normal. For you."

"Yes. For me, and a few other people I know. And I wanted to tell you that I'd asked a friend of mine to check out the shirt guy."

"I see." A deep breath. And another. Now she didn't feel so much like crying her eyes out, or clawing out his. It was a start.

"She says he's old. Maybe 1700s. And what that means is—"

"Same era as the carousel. That's how old it is, so Elliot told us."

He looked surprised. "Those fairground things go back that far?"

"This one does."

"So, maybe they're connected. The point is, something that old can't usually manifest like that without a strong catalyst, a sentient. One like you."

"You saw him." She glared at him.

"Sure. But I didn't bring him here."

"And you're saying I did?"

"Yes."

"I don't understand. What turned me into a ghost magnet all of a sudden?" She stared resolutely at the tall glass of iced tea in front of her on the table, watched condensed water trickle slowly down the side.

"I don't know. Maybe you should ask the ghost."

She rolled her eyes, an easy retort already on the edge of her tongue, its delivery only interrupted by the waiter.

"You guys ready to order?"

John smiled at her. "You hungry?"

She nodded. True enough, despite every nerve ending feeling raw. She was ravenous, and it was making her feel lightheaded and weak and she knew she needed to be stronger than this in order to deal with the man at the other side of the table. She snatched up the menu and quickly ordered a turkey club sandwich.

"I'll have what she's having," John said.

And now they were back to an awkward silence again, until they both began talking at once. "You first," he conceded.

"Okay. If you think this has a connection to Luke, then let's talk about that." Her voice came out silky smooth, controlled, making her feel immensely proud of herself.

"All right. I think he's in trouble."

"Really? He said the same thing about you."

He shrugged. "I'm always in trouble. He isn't."

She leaned back, let out a sigh, tried to focus. It was hard not to keep on jabbing, even harder to pretend she didn't agree. "Okay look, he's completely engrossed in his work, maybe a little more so with this particular project, but—"

"Explain more so."

It felt disingenuous, like telling tales out of school and she knew Luke wouldn't appreciate it. Nevertheless she told him about finding Luke in a pool of vomit about a month ago. That day had worried her, it still worried her, and now maybe his brother might shed some light on whether she needed to be worried any further.

At the end of it, John was silent and staring out of the window. Eventually, "Does he tell you anything, about where his ideas come from, whether he has visions, stuff like that?"

She shook her head. "He never talks about that. He's

not really a talkative guy when it comes to his work."

"So, nothing about a dark landscape, dust, weird foliage, anything—"

She began to feel nauseous. Her scalp prickled and her spine felt coated in ice. What he'd just described... Her eyes blazed, a swift retort was on the edge of her tongue. But he wasn't there. It was the ghost who sat there, who reached out across the table and pushed her backward with the flat palm of his hand. She could see over his shoulder and the diner was crumbling, falling away in gray flakes as if it were burning to ash. Her back hit the booth hard, and when she tried to breathe she discovered she couldn't. And while she gasped like a fish everything spun and she sank into darkness.

CHAPTER 12

JOHN

"Can we get those to go?"

"Sure. Is she okay?"

"She'll be fine. She just needs some fresh air."

He was on Emma's side of the booth, had her head resting on his shoulder. He waited until the waiter had disappeared. "Breathe," he instructed. She murmured, lolled like a drunk. He tapped her on the cheek. "C'mon, just breathe. You'll be fine."

"Did— did you see him?" She gasped, coughed, as if he'd just pulled her from beneath a deep pool of water.

"Yes."

A quick glance at the other tables told him they were drawing too much attention. "How long has it been like this?" he hissed. "How long?"

The waiter came back and placed their lunch inside the boxes. John dropped some cash on the table, gathered everything up, including Emma and her purse, and headed for the exit. Outside, he took her around the corner and sat her on a low concrete wall that delineated the boundaries of the diner's car park.

"John—"

"How long?" He was crouched in front of her, holding her arms.

She lashed out with a foot and kicked him. "Stop it. Stop shaking me."

"I'm sorry." He let go, hadn't realized. He backed off and took a seat alongside.

"Just give me a minute."

He knotted his fingers together and tried to be patient. But God damn it, that thing had pushed her. It had appeared right in between them and shoved her hard into the back of her seat, then disappeared as if the act had taken up every scrap of its energy and while he waited it became more and more difficult to stop his own hands from trembling and he wondered who was the more shaken up.

"I'm losing my mind," she whispered.

"No," he urged. "And I can help you. But you need to start answering my questions."

She let her head fall. He watched her take two, three, slow, deep breaths. "Okay," she said finally.

"When did it start?"

"I'm not sure. Spring maybe. I can't remember anything before that."

"And what happened then? Do you remember anything in particular? An event."

"Like I had an accident and I hit my head. You mean like that?"

"Not necessarily." His words were coming out sharp. He was getting impatient again. He tried to dial it down and took a few deep breaths of his own. "Just— try and think back, and tell me what you remember."

Emma reached into her bag and took an interminable length of time gathering a tissue and blowing her nose. "I was in college," she began. "Nothing unusual happened, no accidents. Luke had an exhibition at one of the local galleries."

"Tell me about that."

She looked at him. "It was a good night. He was a little nervous, but there was no need. He sold a third of his exhibits."

"What about his paintings, what were they like?"

"Very monochromatic, mostly street scenes, although he'd included one he'd painted of me, sitting next to a window, and—"

"Tell me about that one. Describe it."

She frowned. "I don't see what that has to do with—"

"Just do it." He sighed. "Please?"

"It's just a painting. I'm sitting in a chair next to a window. You can only see my face via the reflection—"

"As if you were somewhere else, looking in."

She shrugged. "Or looking out."

"Where's the painting now?" he continued.

"I assume Elliot Black still has it."

"What?"

"He bought it, along with two others. That's when Luke first met him." She'd narrowed her eyes, and right there she reminded him of Rachel. "You don't think Elliot has anything—"

He shook his head. "No. I met the guy this morning. If he had anything to do with this, believe me, I'd know."

"Are you sure? You said you'd met him before."

"No. I must have been mistaken." Her frown pushed him, made him dig, and he went back to that short encounter out there on the sidewalk with Elliot Black and the other guy. But if he was missing something he had no idea what it was. He'd already dismissed Black, and so now he was back to the painting. Maybe he was too late, and Luke's awakening had already begun. The thought turned him cold.

She was still looking at him, as though she'd given him enough and now it was his turn, and he realized he didn't know what to say. He'd never been the best conversationalist, and this...

"That ghost didn't mean to harm me," she said, bringing him out of his blank, flailing state. "He's trying to warn me about something."

"You sure about that?"

"Yes. And if he's attached to that carousel, then maybe you're right and Luke *is* in trouble."

That much he knew already. "Think Black will allow us to go visit? I'd like to take a look at it."

"Don't see why not." She was staring now at the bag on the floor between them. "You rescued lunch?"

"Yep."

"Mind if I eat first?"

John reached into the bag and handed her one of the polystyrene boxes. He watched her take a few ravenous bites before he did likewise. She looked stronger, as if she'd gotten over her ordeal and he wondered how many episodes like this she'd already had. Most people would have hit the drugs, the bottle, or gone crazy by now. You just didn't get over multiple encounters like that. And he wondered if her strength would be a factor in their future, for better or worse.

When they were done she gathered up the trash. "Come on, we can dump this on the way."

"Yes, ma'am." He stood up, prayed her fortitude was real, that it wasn't simply a mask.

Together they walked to the far end of Main Street and all the while he kept his attention on her, hopefully without it looking too obvious. He was waiting for a relapse, a sign that she'd crumble. But if she *was* holding up a mask it was a good one, for he saw nothing of the kind.

As they began to climb the slight gradient toward Black's mansion, "Before that ghost, before he... you mentioned something about a place, a landscape."

"What about it?"

"I've seen it. In stupid nightmares, just like you described."

He nodded, wary. "Just dreams, and not for real?"

She let out a derisive gasp. "I hope not."

John weighed up the pros and cons, decided to push it. "It's called Bower's Fall."

"It has a name?" She was staring at him, incredulous. "What is it— Hell or something?"

"Not quite. It's a stop on the way."

"Like on a bus route?"

"Kind of." He'd never heard of it described like that before.

"And how does that place connect with Luke, and the ghost?"

"It's..." How the hell was he supposed to explain, just walking along a leafy lane, on a sunny afternoon—

"Complicated?" she asked.

They were approaching the gate. He said nothing, and frowned.

"You know, I think I've figured out why you don't like me very much," she continued. "You think this is my fault, that it'll hurt Luke somehow."

"Emma—" He stopped as she gave him a derisive laugh.

"Well, it certainly explains the shitty attitude." She strode up to the high, wrought iron gate and rang the bell.

John glared at the back of her head and then turned his attention to what lay beyond the gate. He was expecting the dogs. Instead a middle aged woman approached and he fully expected to be turned away. But instead the gate clicked open and the woman smiled and beckoned them in.

Once inside the confines of the gate there was still no sign of the dogs. Emma was walking alongside the other woman, chatting about Luke; both of them seemed oblivious. Maybe the animals were caged up somewhere he reasoned. He stayed vigilant as they continued around the side of the house and into the rear courtyard, and remembered the layout well enough from his previous foray and the maps he'd studied.

Emma appeared to know where she was going, and

moments later the other woman had re-entered the house and left them alone once more. He was about to ask where Luke was when he caught site of his brother emerging from one of the buildings at the far side of the courtyard.

"Hey." Luke had his sleeves rolled up. He strode forward and swept Emma into his arms, looked over her shoulder and grinned at him. "Hey, bro.'"

John nodded, let them finish their embrace before he approached. They clasped hands, and concern washed over him. No signs of danger, though. Not yet.

"Come look," Luke beckoned, and led them inside a building the size of a three-car garage. The latest subject stood in the center. It was already partially coated in black and gray and a hint of purple— Fall colors.

Emma made sure he saw her look of reproach before she wandered back outside.

He gave her a shrug by way of reply and switched his attention back toward his younger sibling. "So, how many of these things are there?"

"Forty four." Once again his younger brother beckoned and led him back outside, across the yard and into a larger building. "There. Cool, huh? They're not all here, yet. Some of them are still being prepped."

John stared at the regimented rows of carousel figures; those coated in primer looked like innocent ghosts. The others, the ones already having succumbed to Luke's mastery with a brush were jaw dropping, beautiful, seductive, as if they'd been pulled straight out of Bower's Fall and were now waiting to ride out on some terrible, horrific crusade, along that dusty road, toward the hills, toward Hell. His breath caught in his throat. He couldn't stop staring.

His brother slapped him on the shoulder. He had a grin on his face. "Creeped you out too, huh? You see, I'm *that* good."

He shrugged, offered a jovial retort, and then he looked around for Emma. He wanted to witness her reaction, but she hadn't joined them. There were voices outside and he heard a door slam.

"It's probably Elliot," Luke told him. "You met him yet?"

He nodded. "This morning, although—" He struggled to remember. He'd shaken hands with the guy, and then—

Luke was giving him a knowing look. "Yeah, I know, he takes some getting used to." He headed out, leaving John momentarily alone with the menagerie. It was a moment too long and he turned away and quickly followed.

Outside, Emma was standing alongside an expensive model BMW talking to the tall figure of Elliot Black. She had a smile on her face, she seemed oddly at ease, completely the opposite of when they had been together earlier. Something else he noticed; Luke's face had grown solemn and a slight frown had appeared. It took him a moment to figure out why and it made him smile. A wealthy guy like Black would have to beat women off with a stick and he'd hardly be interested in little Miss Bookworm, although John considered he might have to revisit that nickname at some point and come up with something slightly more fearsome.

He approached, and turned his attention to Black. Once again he got a feeling of deja vu, as if they'd met before, but for the life in him he couldn't place when or where.

The man smiled. "Hello, John. Are you here to take a look around?"

He swallowed, couldn't help it. That smile. It plucked at his memory, sought his attention, and he realized he didn't want to know. "Sure." He had to push the words out, and in the end they were not the words he wanted. "You mind?"

"Not at all. Perhaps you'd like to see the carousel?"

No. All of a sudden he didn't want to go anywhere near it. Nevertheless he nodded. He began to follow the other man toward the large carriage house. He heard Luke and

Emma talking behind him, their voices receding.

Inside he could hardly breathe. This strong he should have been able to sense it outside, to pick it up beyond the gate and maybe half way into town, and yet it wasn't until he'd stepped over the threshold that he became fully aware; that he'd been given the necessary *permission*.

He couldn't see or smell anything yet, but he could feel it. Bower's Fall was tactile and it slid against his flesh like liquid.

"Downstairs," Black whispered.

John felt the man's hand push gently at his lower back, guiding him toward the stairwell. He struggled to talk. His jaw felt heavy as lead. "Your name—"

"Shh, downstairs."

He obeyed. He grabbed the stair rail to steady himself and began to descend, one step, and then another, into a well of dread he remembered keenly. The lights were off at the base of the stairs but he didn't need them. Whispers and hints of that terrible other dimension were everywhere. He started to shiver.

Two more steps into the room and Black's hand shifted to the back of his neck, and forced him down on his knees. "Do you see it?" he whispered.

John nodded. He pushed back against Black's considerable grip, not wanting to be any closer to the ground than absolutely necessary. For his trouble, the pressure increased and he collapsed onto his stomach. Something hit him hard on his lower back and then stayed there, a boot perhaps. He could feel the man hovering close, becoming part of the ill that emanated from a thick pole in the center of the room and oozed up through the ground. It was like being back in that room with the crazy old guy in his under shorts, staring at that gaping hole, knowing he had to blow the guy's brains out when really all he wanted to do was join him. And right now part of him wanted to relax, soak it all up, let it seduce him and taint him inside and out.

"You're not armed, John? You're getting sloppy. Careless."

He tried to raise his head. "I— I know you."

"Of course you do. We've known one another a long time, you and I."

"Please."

"Begging so soon?"

"Luke..."

"Ah, Luke. He has no idea of what he is capable of, does he."

He tried to struggle. It was useless. Physically, he stood a good chance, he knew that. But he also knew that right now this conversation was going on inside his head; that the other man had a mental lock on him that he'd never break in a million years. And yet he still tried, as hard as he could, for the alternative was as unforgiving as it was deadly. "What are you going to do?" He imagined the words emerging through clenched teeth.

"Make you forget, of course. As for why you ask that question of me in the first place, I wonder if you're perhaps feeling a little guilty, wondering if some kind of retribution is heading your way."

The pressure disappeared. His boots scraped the floor, his limbs dangled like those of a rag doll as he was pulled upright. He felt the other man's hand stroking his hair, fingers sliding along the nape of his neck. It felt relaxing, seductive, like the touch of a lover. Sweet breath tickled his ear. They were back to the spoken word.

"Do you remember your part in consigning me to Hell, John?"

Yes. He remembered.

Fear attempted to galvanize him, tried desperately to fire up his muscles and impress upon him the need for escape, but no matter how it tried, it failed, while the voice continued, easy and conversational, just above a whisper.

"Don't worry. I'm not going to kill you. You still have your uses."

John's survival instinct wanted to babble with relief and demand that he fall at this man's feet and thank him. It made him sick and he cast aside the idea. In its place, dread arrived and promised something worse than death. The truth? He was helpless, and that made him more afraid than anything.

On an abstract level he discovered he was leaning back, fully supported, his head resting on the other man's shoulder. He felt his heartbeat. Once, twice, three times, and he was gone.

He was back in the diner, at a familiar table.

He was alone this time. It was twilight and the streetlights were already shining beyond the window. Pushed to one side on the table were an iced tea and a turkey club sandwich, a meal he was convinced he'd already eaten once today. He was staring at the laptop screen in front of him and he felt light headed and ill equipped to understand why huge chunks of his research were no longer in the relevant folders. He checked the recycle bin; it was clear, as if he'd recently emptied it, even though he didn't remember doing any such thing. It was as if he'd only imagined pulling up details of the mysterious Elliot Black, that in reality he hadn't done anything.

But when he thought about Luke he became convinced Black was simply a red herring and he resolved to forget about the guy. He didn't need to waste any more time speculating on what lay behind that wall and that gate. He'd been there, found nothing, and he'd be better off switching gears and concentrating on something else.

Emma, Emma, it all came back to Emma. And yet —

He picked up his phone and dialed, waited impatiently for the call to connect. At last—

"Rhonda?" He let out a sigh of relief. "Please, I need your help."

CHAPTER 13

LUKE

In the end he had to cut her loose.

After emerging from the carriage house, a surprisingly non-committal John had made his excuses and headed back into town, and Elliot had offered Emma a tour of the mansion. Luke knew he'd be labeled an ass if he objected, and so he stewed for about half an hour while he did some dappling on the horse's flank, until she returned, kissed him on the cheek and told him she had to return to the hotel and continue her studies.

They arranged to meet for dinner, and Luke breathed a sigh of relief and returned to his work. Now he was no longer thinking about his girlfriend in Elliot's clutches he was able to work faster, better, and pretty soon his surroundings faded and all attention was on his subject.

Sometime later Black entered the workshop, and after a keen examination of the carousel horse, "It's getting late."

Luke regarded him, puzzled. He looked around. At some point he must have turned on the lights but for the life in him he couldn't remember when.

"Emma?" the man said. "I overhead you were meeting her for dinner?"

He checked his watch, realized he'd taken it off and placed it on the bench by the window, and when he saw what time it was, a few minutes before eight, "Shit."

Black laughed. "You've done enough for today." He

joined Luke at the bench, picked up a piece of paper, a hastily prepared shopping list. “Canvasses?”

Luke nodded. “The other stuff I need for the horses, but those I’ll pay for. Sometimes I need to switch gears, do something different. It keeps me sharp.”

“Then put them on the tab.” Black shrugged. “Like I already told you. Whatever it takes.”

“Okay.” Luke fiddled with his watchstrap, and felt a stab of regret on having to leave a pallet and a few of his brushes still clogged with paint.

“You know, if you ever want to work late, I can have dinner arranged here for you both.”

“I’m not sure if—”

“It’s just a suggestion.”

Luke grabbed his jacket. He found the way out barred by Elliot’s outstretched hand. There was a white card held between his fingers. “What is that?” he asked.

“The combination for the gate. So you can get in any time you like.”

“You trust me?”

“Any reason why I shouldn’t?”

He took the card, placed it in his pocket. “No. It’s a good idea. That way I won’t need to disturb Grace.” Elliot’s housekeeper, he’d discovered. An efficient, never take no for an answer woman who’d supplied a steady stream of snacks and drinks throughout the day. No way he’d collapse through lack of sustenance here. He made a note to tell Emma about that. He figured she’d be pleased. He knew he’d scared her on that occasion back in his apartment, something he truly regretted.

On his way across the yard he saw the door to the carriage house was slightly open. Elliot had already re-entered the main house, and he was now alone. He paused, stared at the open door and then headed toward it. Later he might consider that something profound had drawn him there, but right now the reason for his detour was simply because the door was ajar.

Inside, he saw the room was empty but the lights were on. He ventured in further until he was standing at the edge of what he fancifully considered as the magic circle. And there, just for a moment he hesitated, before stepping beyond until he was in the middle of the room, directly in the center of the empty carousel.

He smiled, closed his eyes, and he imagined being surrounded by all the creatures he had painted. After a moment it felt a little odd, as if the air had thickened. It felt comforting, too, and when he moved his hands it felt as if fine strands of silk were brushing past his fingers. The floor began to move and he experienced a slight disorientation but it was okay. It was just his imagination.

He saw the tiger, and the Lady; behind him were some of the other horses and Emma's hippocampus. He'd already envisioned its paint scheme, had sketched out its dark scaled magnificence in the workshop before he'd had chance to forget, and now he could see her astride it, her flesh covered in the same body paint, a fearsome, trident bearing warrior woman with thick strands of hair that flew behind her as the carousel moved.

His surroundings darkened, but caught up in his own nets of make believe the dimming light failed to register an alarm. He turned slightly, gave himself another inner view; the dragon carriage, the beasts on either side of the bench seemed alive, their tails tightening and curling as the carousel spun faster.

He felt something— a tiny, internal snap. It made him open his eyes and when he did so he discovered the lights were impossibly bright and that he'd dropped to one knee and both of his palms were flat on the floor. He'd lost his balance, obviously, and he chuckled, embarrassed. His outpouring of breath formed clouds that drifted and dissipated and he shivered, so damned cold all of a sudden.

As he looked down, something fell from him, crimson; it landed as a tiny blot on the wooden floor. It was followed by another, and another. He cursed, stood up, brushed his fingers against warm, wet nostrils.

"Ah, shit," he muttered.

He had no tissue in his pocket to stem the tide and so he had to make do with the sleeve of his shirt. His entire body felt numb, and the first step he took almost pitched him to the ground. His breath still flew out in clouds. It was so cold in the room, a complete contrast to what it had been only moments ago and it scared him enough to try out those legs once more and get the hell out of there.

Out in the yard, the temperature was markedly different— warm, balmy, and he could see the lights from the main house, a reassuring, familiar anchor on reality. He checked his bleeding nose. At least it had stopped dripping, but he felt the beginnings of a sinus headache, like something had swelled and burst open inside.

A few deep breaths and he began to feel a little better. He looked over his shoulder. The carriage house door was fully open and he could see directly inside. The lights were still on, he could see the wooden floor; someone's toolbox was still in there lying next to a few planks of wood and he could smell shavings and oil.

Feeling like a complete fool he headed toward the main gate, amazed his imagination had got the better of him. As for what caused the nosebleed he could only guess. Outside, on the road that led to Main Street he attempted to check his watch, but it was too dark. He approached a street lamp. Fat moths were dancing beneath it, daring to play Icarus, and beneath the light he drew back his bloody sleeve and checked the time.

It was nine thirty.

He stood there for a moment, and checked it again.

"Shit," he repeated, with more urgency this time. He fumbled in his pocket, brought out his phone with trembling fingers. It was dead, completely and utterly lifeless. He broke into a run, and as he dashed around the corner toward the hotel, he wondered how he'd managed to lose almost an hour and a half.

"I figured you might be late, but I was about to come and look for you. I called you, I called the house, and no one answered."

He sat on the edge of the bed, shirtless and shivering while Emma cleaned up his face. "I could have sworn I'd left just after eight," he told her. Maybe he'd got the time wrong, he considered. He would ask Elliot tomorrow—was it eight, or after nine when you reminded me?

"There's a lot of blood on your shirt. I put it to soak in the bathtub." She finished daubing him with a damp cloth, rummaged in one of the drawers, brought out one of his sweaters and tossed it toward him. "Luke, don't you think—"

"It's okay. Really." He pulled the sweater over his head.

"Have you had nosebleeds like this before?" She sat alongside him, concern still written on her face.

"No." He put his arm around her, leaned back and pulled her on top of him. "Keep me warm," he pleaded. He could feel she was tense, maybe a little angry with him. "Please," he whispered. He rose slightly, nibbled her ear, heard her let out a sigh.

She shifted until she was looking down at him. "I'm worried about you."

"I'm fine." He stroked her hair, reached up and kissed

her, waited for her to respond, paused when she didn't.

"I'm worried about me, too," she said. "I keep— seeing things."

He frowned, concerned. "Like what?"

"It's hard to explain. I can't remember. But then it keeps coming back. It's those stupid horses, that stupid carousel, and John."

"Stupid," he mimicked.

"I didn't mean—"

"Shh, it's okay." He kissed her again. "What about John, is he being a pain in the ass?"

She let out a sigh. "Maybe. I don't know."

"Hey, he freaks me out sometimes, too, and he's my brother. But if he's acting like a dick, I'll talk to him."

"No, it's okay."

"You sure?"

She nodded.

"I'm going to talk to him anyway." He wrapped his arms around her. "I need you, I love you, and I don't want anything to make you unhappy."

"I'm not unhappy, just... unsettled."

"Shh," he whispered. "Just stay here with me." He smiled as she wriggled alongside him, made herself comfortable and rested her head on his shoulder. "Diner's still open," he said after a moment. "You want to go get something to eat?"

"Not hungry," she said. And no, neither was he.

The following morning, his hunger reappeared and wouldn't allow him to leave the hotel until he'd eaten breakfast. And soon after, work pulled him away, leaving him a little concerned over Emma who'd sat at the table in the hotel dining room and had barely eaten. He made her promise that she'd come up to the house at lunchtime, and once out on Main Street he took out his cell phone, called John and arranged to meet.

His brother's hotel was along a narrow street lined with brick walls covered in dark green ivy. At first glance the bed and breakfast didn't look dissimilar to the place he was staying at, but as he walked up the front path he noticed the grounds were smaller, and he guessed the building didn't go as far back.

John was emerging from the front door; he'd obviously been waiting for him. "What's up?"

They began to walk back down the path toward the road. "I wanted to talk to you about Emma."

His brother looked surprised and oddly relieved, as though he'd been expecting a different, more contentious subject. "What about her?"

"I want to know what you said to her."

"What I *said*?"

"Yep. What you said."

"I don't—" John stopped and shrugged. And right there, that look— hooded, secretive— it emerged and confirmed Luke's suspicions.

"What is it," he snapped. "Are you jealous?"

John thrust his hands in his pockets. "Oh, little brother..."

"Don't give me any of that condescension shit." He felt a flash fire of anger course through him. His fingers jumped, curled into fists.

"Hey. Calm down. You want to blow off some steam, we take a walk."

Luke narrowed his eyes, followed John as he set off along the road. "What is it you have against her, anyway?"

"You really want to know? Some people aren't good to

have around. They're disruptive."

He matched his brother's stride and snorted in disgust. "You hardly know her. And if anyone could be called disruptive, it's you."

"Look," John let out a sigh. "I'm just trying to save you some pain and heartache, that's all."

"She's the best thing that ever happened to me."

"Oh yeah? Have you seen the way she looks at your current employer?"

Luke burst out laughing. "Is that all you've got?" He stopped walking.

His brother turned around to face him. "She's no good for you, Luke."

"She loves me, which is more than you, or Dad, or anyone else ever did. So fuck you and leave her alone." He turned his back and started walking. He half expected a bitter retort, a hand on his shoulder, maybe something worse, and he was relieved when it didn't come. He didn't look back, but he imagined John standing there, giving him that dead stare. The only family he had.

He swallowed, and kept on walking.

On reaching Black's house he tried out the combination on the panel alongside the wrought iron gate and was rewarded by the sight of the gate swinging open, silent and smooth on its hinges. He strode up the path and across the courtyard, waved at Grace, whom he could see through the kitchen window, and in his workshop he rolled up his sleeves, forgot about the fight and got to work, cleaning up the mess he'd left the night before and starting all over, applying color to the bedroll at the rear of the horse's saddle. After that came some fine detail along the length of the sword's scabbard, and some wet on wet color blends on the horse's tack.

It was after midday when he finally checked his watch, and a few minutes later both Emma and Grace arrived simultaneously, the latter with a tray of chicken salad sandwiches and a pitcher of iced lemonade. When the housekeeper had gone, a grin appeared on his face, he grabbed Emma and lifted her onto one of the benches lining the room. His teeth nibbled playfully at her ear while one of his hands slid up her torso and landed on her left breast.

"I could do you right here," he growled.

She was laughing and pushing him away. "But you're not going to. What if someone sees us?"

After her shadowy appearance at breakfast it warmed him to see a smile on her face and he joined her in laughter. "Hey, they might get a kick out of it, I know I would."

"Pervert." She pecked him on the cheek, slid off the bench and her eyes moved to the plate of sandwiches. She seemed a little more like her old self and for that he was profoundly glad. He let her go, and for the next few minutes he joined her in demolishing Grace's provided lunch. He felt happy, relieved that Emma appeared to have snapped back into her old self.

"I've brought my swimsuit," she said afterwards. "I was planning on staying for the afternoon. Elliot said I could use the pool, and I've brought some reading with me."

He looked out of the window. Directly across the other side of the courtyard lay the partially glazed building that held the indoor pool. He couldn't see the pool itself through the windows, but the thought of her being close by gave him a strong sense of relief and he readily agreed. Especially as he figured Elliot wasn't on the premises. That shopping list on the bench the night before had gone, and there had been no sign of his employer when he arrived this morning.

When they were done with lunch he watched her walk across the yard, and kept his eyes on her until she disappeared. Only then did he turn his attention back to work, and he smiled.

Just being close, touching her, listening to her voice,

and now he was planning the first painting. That vision he'd had of her the night before, astride the carousel, it continued to develop as he worked on the tack that ran across the horse's brow. Of course he'd have to keep it on the down low. What he'd told Elliot was perfectly true, of course. Switching to canvas would clear the palate, allow him to shift gears, but ultimately he realized there was some kind of connection between the two projects. They appeared to slide together, interlock like a jigsaw, as if both were required and were a necessary part of one another.

That settled and accepted, he sank back into the task at hand, and once again his surroundings disappeared and time became meaningless.

CHAPTER 14

EMMA

"No, I think you're just worried about him, that's all. And it's manifesting itself into— well— whatever it was you thought you saw."

"No ghosts?"

Laughter. "C'mon, Emma. This isn't like you. As for that brother of his, has he made a move on you yet?"

"Oh, God, no."

"Well, don't be surprised if he does. Believe me, some guys are manipulative, and this could be just some kind of far out, competitive sibling crap he's pulling on you."

The water flowed buoyant and warm against her skin as she performed a steady crawl, back and forth along the length of the pool. She'd always been a strong swimmer, and right now the very action of plowing slow and smooth through the water felt comfortable and enabled her to focus and build on her resolve after the conversation she'd had with Gillian a few hours ago. Men. Were they worth the trouble? Both women had finally agreed they were, but that any involvement always came with a hefty price tag.

She was glad she had called. After the frightening events of yesterday, despite repeated attempts to pull it together, her memory had continued to play tricks on her and she had become fractured and lost. Thankfully a long chat with a friend had gradually brought her out of her well of confusion. Why? Because what Gillian had suggested made sense.

There was a counter argument, of course, about how a blunt dismissal of her misgivings might well prove dangerous— to her, to Luke. But common sense told her she was simply being manipulated and it all came back to John. Gillian had gone as far as to suggest he might have put something in her drink at the diner. So, from now on there'd be no reaching out, no more attempts at friendship, and the sooner John was gone the better. It was funny how happy she felt, just by thinking of the man climbing into his vehicle and driving off, never to return.

After a hundred or so laps she climbed out and towel-dried her hair. It was hot in the pool house and so she sat on one of the nearby recliners with the intention of drying off, cracked open a bottle of iced tea and picked up one of the books she'd brought with her.

It began as a tough read, chock full of dates and methodical detail. But gradually it gave way to an ancient prince on his way home from a fruitless crusade, heading toward a dead father and a vacant crown. He seemed reluctant to reach out and claim what was his, as if he could see what lay ahead, the years of war and strife until an entire country lay beneath his iron grip, and she wondered how many nights he'd sat there by his campfire, staring into the dark, while destiny hung there like a wraith, becoming more tactile and grasping until there was no other way forward. She could see him via the light of the dying embers, his sword alongside and well within reach, the night swirling around him like an autumn dance of rotting black leaves —

A sound— a car door slamming shut. Footsteps.

She blinked in the light, realized she had closed her eyes, had drifted. The book lay open in her lap; her swimsuit and her hair were completely dry. There was movement by the door. It was Elliot. His own house, nevertheless he knocked before entering.

"I hope I'm not disturbing you."

Emma scrambled into a sitting position and closed the book, slightly embarrassed at showing so much skin. "No, not at all."

He smiled. "Did you swim?" And after she nodded, "Good. This pool is little used." He looked away for a moment. "I need to talk to you."

She grabbed her towel, wrapped it around herself. "Can I get dressed first?"

"Of course. The library in fifteen minutes?"

"Sure." And as soon as he left she rushed to the tiny bathroom at the far end of the room. There she dressed hastily and brushed her hair. As for what he wanted to talk to her about she could only imagine, and that was the trouble. When considering the subject of Elliot Black her imagination traveled to some odd places.

A quick reappraisal in the bathroom mirror, and she headed toward the main house and entered through a side door adjacent to the kitchen. At the end of a wide passageway, she took a right, through a beautifully furnished reception room, and then through a set of partially open doors and into the library.

Yesterday she had only caught a glimpse during Elliot's whirlwind tour, but now, standing inside, surrounded by shelves of books, polished tables and leather Chesterfields, she became awestruck and imagined a room of her own, just like this, crammed floor to ceiling with history books.

Shadows shifted in her peripheral vision and she gave an audible gasp as Black appeared out of nowhere. And right there she discovered the room was actually L-shaped and that he had been standing around the corner.

"I'm sorry I startled you."

"No, it's okay." Her cheeks flushed, embarrassed once more. "There's more to this room than I thought."

"Indeed there is." He beckoned. "There's something I want to show you."

Emma followed him around the corner into the rear part of the library and there, in a large alcove, hung the three paintings he'd bought from Luke at the exhibition those few months ago.

"Oh," she said, abruptly confronted by her own image. Her portrait was hung in the center, flanked by the street scenes on either side.

The paintings commandeered the entire wall, drawing the eye, the light; they seemed three dimensional, like she could step inside them, or reach forward and shake hands with herself. The effect drew her in so thoroughly she forgot to feel self-conscious about the young woman gazing out of the window in the center portrait. Nevertheless, after a moment she realized Elliot was looking at her.

"What did you want to talk about?" she asked. Better get this over with.

"Luke," he said, "and you."

Emma frowned. Abruptly she wanted to back away, get out from under his intense gaze, and considered for a moment that she'd walked into a trap.

"Don't be afraid," he whispered. He appeared closer, even though she hadn't seen him take the actual step to reduce the distance between them.

"I don't—" She faltered. He was directly behind her. His hand alighted on her shoulder. His other hand slipped around her waist. It felt easy, natural, like it belonged there.

She stared at one of the paintings, one of her favorites—a tree-lined avenue at night. There were parked cars and street lamps, but it had a night sky specked with a single star and right now she could see that star winking at her. It was like staring out of an open window, so real she began to feel the chill.

"You know, Emma, I wonder if it's you I need to be concerned with most of all. You're proving quite resistant."

"Elliot—"

"Look at the painting." His grip on her waist tightened a little.

His proximity should have sounded an alarm but somehow it didn't matter. She was captivated, and his body was an anchor, and the scene before her began to move as if she was walking along that avenue out there in the dark. She passed by the cars, and the trees, and headed toward open ground covered in dust.

"I've seen this before." She froze. This was a nightmare she had forgotten. Off to her left, a huge, muscular vine stretched forth, its tendrils reached out —

"You have nothing to be afraid of," he whispered.

"What is this place?"

"It is the road to Hell, my dear. But don't worry, that particular destination is many miles distant and we are quite safe here." He adjusted his grip slightly. "Now, show me what you can see."

She turned her head. The vine. It had caught something. She strained to look. The foliage became agitated. She saw a mouth in the shape of a perfect O before it was covered up and the thrashing lessened. Red rope dangled, then dropped with a faint plop. Her scalp prickled, informing her that she had just witnessed something horrific. She began to pull away.

"Shh," he soothed. "What else?"

Her anxiety receded, like a wave sinking back into the ocean. He felt solid behind her and she let her head fall back and rest on his shoulder. And right there she felt the presence of another. A female. "I can't see her," she whispered.

"But you can feel her?"

"Yes. And she flies."

"Then you're already there. It has begun."

"I don't understand." There was a strange scent filling her nostrils, sweet, floral, but nothing she could place, and when she looked down, still circling her waist, Elliot's arm had taken on a strange hue, like it wasn't his arm and more akin to the vegetation still shivering and rustling off to her left.

I know you...

She saw a street lamp to the right of her, and then another. The scene was beginning to recede. With a free hand she stretched out and ran her fingers along the side of a parked car, and all of a sudden it became difficult to recall what she had just witnessed. Everything had gone, and Elliot was standing alongside her, his hands clasped in front of him. "Do you think I placed them correctly?"

She blinked, stared at him. Her mind was fogged, the result of falling asleep back there in the poolroom she surmised. "They seem fine. To me, that is." She gave him an apologetic shrug, and she looked down at fingertips that still resonated with the flat, shiny, polished metal of the car.

Elliot's attention seemed far off, despite the conversation. When he spoke his words came out with only the slightest cadence. "Don't worry, the shift in your perception is inevitable."

Emma stared at him.

"Luke is a Rook," he continued. "They're exceedingly rare. Do you know they can open doors?" Black's voice abruptly became louder, harder, he looked at her and smiled. "Maybe I should consult him, with regard to the hanging."

She nodded. Her head felt stuffed full of garish cotton candy, until abruptly it dissolved.

"Yes, he'd appreciate that." She smiled. There. Maybe it was a change of pressure in her ears, or maybe she'd got water in them and they had finally cleared. "He's very possessive of his paintings."

"I can imagine." He beckoned. "I'm sorry for taking up

your time, but I wanted your opinion." And as he led her toward the door, "You know you're both welcome to stay for dinner."

"I'll ask him," she said, and the idea became agreeable the more she thought on it.

She discovered Luke on his knees alongside the horse, brush and palette in hand, and with the exception of the mane, the creature looked done. She watched him work, observed the mask of concentration on his face, saw how the brush did a slow, sensual dance across the surface of the carving.

Eventually he stood up, winced, rolled his shoulders and broke into a grin. He gestured toward the horse. "You like?"

She stepped through a maze of rags, pots and tubes, and kissed him on the cheek. "It's beautiful."

There was a smudge of black paint at the corner of his lip, his hair had fallen partially over his eyes and he looked utterly adorable. "Elliot wants to know if we're staying for dinner."

He shrugged, used his forearm to push back his hair. "Whatever you want."

"Okay. I'll go tell Grace."

Dinner was a surprisingly low-key affair, held in the large kitchen in the company of Elliot and Grace, and Emma soon found herself at ease. Her male dinner companions in particular had laid down their swords of contention while all manner of subjects were discussed, the carousel thankfully being only one of them.

Afterwards, she helped Grace load the dishwasher

while Elliot hauled Luke off to the library to look at the paintings.

"That was a lovely dinner."

The older woman smiled. "Thank you." She slammed the door and twisted the necessary dials. "You know, I'm surprised he hasn't asked you both to stay at the guest house."

Emma was taken aback for a moment. It hadn't really crossed her mind, even though Elliot had mentioned the place in passing during the tour the day before. She remembered a tiny, standalone clapboard house that stood on the further side of the rear lawn. They hadn't gone inside on that occasion. Elliot seemed more about showing her the features of the yard; he sounded like her mother and rhymed off dozens of plant names she'd never heard of.

She frowned, imagined Luke waking up in the middle of the night and stumbling across that huge, green expanse, drawn inexorably by his work, and she chewed on the corner of her lip. "Maybe a little distance isn't a bad idea," she offered.

Grace nodded. "He seems very dedicated, immersed in his art."

"He is." A little too much, sometimes, she wanted to add. And then it hit her, how selfish she sounded. "Of course if it was better financially—"

The other woman waved a dismissive hand toward her. "Oh, that isn't a problem," she said. "Money would never be an issue with Elliot."

Emma let out a sigh of relief. "Okay. I just didn't want you to think we were taking advantage."

"Not at all. And perhaps you're right, about distance. There's a fine line between dedication and obsession, wouldn't you say?"

She nodded, agreed readily.

Voices heralded the return of the two men, and soon afterward Luke and Emma were heading back into town, along the narrow leafy lane canopied so thick with foliage that it plucked at her memory.

Luke was holding her hand. "Did you know there's a guesthouse back there?"

Part way through trying to figure out what she'd forgotten and all of a sudden she knew what was coming. It made her wonder if Grace had broached the subject back there in the kitchen on purpose after Elliot's prompting. "Let me guess. He's offered to put us up there instead of the hotel."

He shrugged. "Well, it would make more sense, but he also insisted that it had to be your choice, and not mine."

"Terrific. "Why me?"

"Not sure."

A long exasperated sigh escaped her. "Well, what would you like to do?"

"Are you kidding? After that meal we had tonight, I'd be there in a heartbeat."

"And what if it's just a ploy? Once we're in there he might chain you to the workshop floor, make you sleep on a bed of straw and feed you bowls of gruel and make you drink from—"

He'd started to laugh, so hard his shoulders were shaking. "Gruel? What the hell is gruel?"

"It's like oatmeal, only thinner. It was a staple, when people didn't— will you stop that?" A smile appeared on her face. She couldn't help it.

Still laughing, he gathered her up, began to dance with her toward the lights at the end of Main Street. "You could chain me to the floor any time you want." And so began a barrage of teasing and laughing until, by the time they reached the hotel's front gate, she knew their mind had been made up and an agreement had been reached, and despite her misgivings they were about to grow closer to that strange tall man with his big house and his carousel monsters.

On a practical level it simply made too much sense to

ignore. She was already beginning to feel a little awkward about studying back at the hotel, and as for her worries about Luke, sure— he'd very likely sink into that obsessive all-hours state, but the difference was, she'd be there, she could watch him, make sure that beautiful face didn't get too thin and those eyes didn't get so haunted that he began to look like his brother. And speaking of whom, Elliot Black's wrought iron gate would provide yet another barrier between them, and amen to that.

CHAPTER 15

JOHN

Rhonda had reminded him to be patient. "Try and be nice for a change," she'd semi-scolded. And begrudgingly he'd agreed, yet again, despite his brother's girlfriend taking on the cruel visage of villainess, a caricature fully intent on his brother's ruin. But when Luke had confronted him that morning it was back to the same old argument; he was convinced he was right and he'd stuck to his guns, and in all probability had alienated Luke in the process.

But in the end he pushed his guilt aside, found a wifi spot and got down to some research on the girl's family. If he could just dig up something... but all he got was hard-working, lower-middle-class American— Spanish on her father's side, English on the mother's, courtesy of a genealogy group Emma's mother belonged to. The girl was second-generation white-collar, the family appeared humble in means and were registering none of the usual alarm bells. No murders, jail time or disappearances; nobody institutionalized, none of the usual markers. She was solid, perfect, and it didn't make any damned sense.

On a whim he began another search on Black, simply because of a stubborn recollection that he'd already compiled some research despite the lack of evidence, and he'd just arrived at details of the guy's business when the phone rang. He was expecting Rhonda once more, or maybe Luke, but it was neither. It was Doc.

"We've got trouble. You'd better get over here, right away."

"Yes, sir."

And that was that. It was time to pack up and leave.

After reassuring the hotel owner he'd be back in a few days, and after sending Luke a text message, he threw his bag in the vehicle and headed out of town. He got lucky at the airport and managed to catch an afternoon flight to Sacramento via Salt Lake City. Thoughts of Luke and Emma trailed after him and sat alongside him on both flights, and more and more he became convinced he was missing something, a key piece to what should have been a very simple puzzle.

It was late when he arrived in the state capital, and by the time he'd acquired a rental and had driven to his rendezvous point with Doc it was after midnight. He also found the road leading to his destination choked with emergency vehicles and had to park a full two blocks away and close the distance on foot.

As he approached the boundary the cops had set up, he reasoned the fire was a coincidence, a sideshow; someone had left a space heater on a few doors down, newspapers had caught fire and set the entire dwelling ablaze. He heard a woman crying, a man telling others there were people still in the burning house.

He saw Doc standing with his hands in his pockets, relaxed, a spectator, simply there for the show, and right there he knew the blaze, still bright orange and kicking up smoke and embers despite the firemen's efforts, was part of a cleanup. Was he too late? He looked around for some of the others and saw no familiar faces.

"I'm sorry," he said, as soon as he was alongside. "I got here as fast as I could. Is it sealed?" The Fall. It had to be. Anywhere else and Doc wouldn't have been standing there looking so casual.

The Adept nodded, his eyes still on the blaze. "Yes. And I managed to round up any stray ghosts. But something escaped. A harvester pod. We need to track it down."

John ducked his head. It didn't need to be said. Had he got here earlier... "Not going to be easy with all these cops and firemen around." Not to mention it was dark, they'd need guns, and John was extremely familiar with the authorities' view of guys running around brandishing unlicensed weaponry. "How big?" he added.

"Fifteen, twenty feet. It slipped into a drainage channel behind the house."

He looked around. "Who else is here?"

Doc shook his head. "You're it. I need to keep this quiet. I'll explain why afterwards."

John blinked, failed to comprehend what the other man had said. An escape was a major emergency. Half the entire house should have been here. Not to mention this was the second breach in as many months, which was highly unusual. "How did— I guess we don't have time. Where's the channel?"

Doc beckoned, led him away from the perimeter and down the street to a black Crown Victoria carrying a government plate. He popped the trunk, and John raised his eyebrows. "Don't worry," Doc told him, "You're under my protection, here."

He nodded, put that on trust, and pulled out a short barrel H&K MP5 and two 9mm. Glocks, along with whatever spare ammunition he could carry.

"Channel is across the street. See the fence? Gate's already open."

"And if it's still close to the house and I have to open fire?" He stared at the man, couldn't see much of his face in the dark.

"Like I said, you're under my protection."

John didn't waste any more time, he broke into a run,

keeping the assault weapon close against his body until he'd reached the fence. It was dark beyond, but that didn't worry him too much. Too many drops into Bower's Fall had left him with a comfortable affinity with the dark. It was the sunlight he couldn't stand too much of these days.

He shouldered open the chain link gate and slipped through. Ahead lay a shallow patch of weeds that ended abruptly at the edge of the concrete flood channel. He looked down. An immediate seven-foot drop and the channel looked bone dry at the bottom.

He sniffed the air, tried to get a bead on which direction the escapee had slithered off to. He smiled, recognized the familiar scent of terror and tried to forget he was on his own. No movement, and so he stepped off the edge, landed with a soft grunt, allowing his leg muscles to absorb the drop.

High concrete on either side. He brought the weapon to bear and began to move along the outer edge of a long, easy curve. Above him he could hear the noise of the fire and people shouting, trying to get the blaze under control. Closer, now. Louder. But he didn't need his ears. Not for this. Gut feeling and the scent of Bower's Fall drew him onward, past the far side of the burning house, through an atmosphere of hanging wet mist and the reek of sodden embers, until he knew he was getting close.

"C'mere, baby," he whispered... Let's get this over with." He could feel it, afraid in the dark having crawled into an entirely alien environment. But it would adapt soon enough.

There was a fork up ahead, a steep, narrow expanse that led up to a sewer pipe. He hoped and prayed it hadn't headed up into that. But no, it had chosen the wider channel. He tried to get inside its head, figure out its reasoning. Maybe it didn't like the idea of enclosed spaces. And maybe it knew he was coming and was getting ready to entice him, pick him up, and take him home to Momma. No reason to think its mindset had changed all that much.

He paused for a moment, felt for the selector on the gun. He'd have maybe one chance to slam all thirty rounds into its hide before it leapt at him. After that –

The dark shifted and coalesced ahead in a section of the channel he could have sworn was empty only a moment ago. He muttered a curse. By his reckoning, unless it had found time to eat in the meantime, Doc had underestimated. Another few paces. He had to be sure, had to be certain of his aim.

There was a hissing sound directly ahead, and the creature started to sing. John gritted his teeth and opened fire before it could get its aural hooks into him. The noise was deafening, amplified by the surrounding concrete, bound to bring any cop for miles, but he couldn't think about that right now. He emptied the full magazine, way too fast for his own comfort. The thing was on the move and he had no time to reload, and so he dropped the sub machine gun and brought out one of the pistols.

When it came out of the shadows he hoped he'd at least slowed it down. It reared up and he began to pump bullets into it from the 9 mm. He saw it slump and deflate. He lowered the weapon. He couldn't hear a damned thing any more but he smelled jasmine, rich and cloying. And courtesy of the distant firelight he saw the creature's skin glimmer, slick and smooth as though covered in oil.

His hands were shaking, his fingers fat and stupid with adrenalin, but he adjusted his grip and maintained his posture, ready to fire, while his eyes ran back and forth, looking for any signs of movement, anything at all. But it was too big, and right below his feet, something snapped forward like a whip; thin and cruel as piano wire it curled around his ankle and pulled hard.

He let out a yell, landed on his back, and pulled the

trigger, firing again and again while the thing dragged him inexorably forward. He saw the beginnings of its maw, feathered at the edges, spreading out. It was a carrier. And it was going to swallow him. He ran out of ammunition, started kicking with his free foot. Until, abruptly, the thing gave up.

For a moment he didn't dare move, he was completely immobile, like a frightened deer, and it took an immense effort to start dragging himself out of harm's way, terrified that the slightest movement would awaken the thing all over again. But after a few inches of retreat, pain shot up his leg like a bolt of lightning and made his breath hiss between clenched teeth. Its tendril was still wrapped around his ankle, and it had gone through his jeans, his socks, had dug deep into his flesh.

Slowly he sat up, leaned forward. The idea of touching the thing repulsed him but he had no choice, and while pain clouded his vision, he slowly, carefully, pulled the tendril out of the cruel channels it had dug into his lower leg. It seemed to take hours until he was loose, and during that time the light from the fire dwindled, leaving him alone in a pit of absolute blackness.

Once free he rolled onto his stomach and began to crawl forward on his elbows. Was it dead? The scent of jasmine was a definite giveaway, but it might still have some life in it, and so he crawled as far away as he dared, then brought out his remaining pistol, propped himself up against the concrete wall, and waited.

Pain swam back and forth, hindering his concentration, making his head spin. A few moments later and he leaned to one side and puked. His entire leg felt hot, as if it was burning up like the house somewhere above him. His hearing came back; there were noises, people talking. He fully expected flashlights to shine down, for angry commands to be delivered— hands up put the gun down on your knees hands behind your head lay down on the ground spread your feet— his surroundings spun and he threw up again, knew he was in shock, and that he wouldn't lay down the gun in time and they'd probably shoot him, just to be sure.

But instead he lay there unmolested, surrounded by darkness. Maybe he'd simply bleed to death, he considered, and that thought brought him out of his stupor. He put the gun down and began to unfasten his belt. He heard a noise, scrambled for the weapon but his hands were shaking so bad he couldn't pick it up. There was a whisper in the dark and he emptied the entire pent up contents of his lungs in an extended sigh of relief.

"Doc—"

"Shh, stay still, John."

"Left ankle," he croaked. He could barely get the words out, his teeth were chattering so much.

"Yes, and poison, too. We need to get you back to the car."

Poison. When Doc pulled him to his feet he let out a high-pitched whine. His entire left leg felt like it was on fire. "I think— I killed it."

"You did, it's already starting to dissolve. Now, no more talk."

He wanted to scream the pain was so bad, but he managed to dial it down to a few grunts and groans as Doc pulled him over to the slope holding the sewer drain and began to tug and haul him up the steep incline. At the top, emergency lights were dancing red and white, bouncing off the street and the cars and the ruined house and he could see silhouettes of people standing around, still miraculously oblivious to what had taken place down in the flood channel. But then Doc had always been good at that. Oblivion; he could bestow it like a blessing, throw it over a crowd like a blanket, and John wished he could make him forget about the screaming pain in his leg, not to mention the encounter with that dark, slick, skin-crawling horror they'd left back there.

"Not far now," the man reminded him.

He muttered something by way of reply, but his mouth wouldn't fully cooperate; he'd been reduced to the language of animals. When they reached the car, Doc slid him into the rear seat and John lay down across the length of it. What followed, the door slamming, the movement, it all came through a heady buzz of pain until that's all he could feel. All of his other senses had shut down. And after a while even the pain went away and he was back to the darkness again, lying there with that thing for company, daring him to believe it was dead and that it wouldn't just lash out and draw him into its hideous maw.

"John."

He was in Bower's Fall, lying on the ground after the creature had spat him out after deciding he was either unsuitable for collection or, alternatively he was simply the remaining husk after all the nourishment had been taken. It felt— painless, easy, the ground yielding beneath him, loosely packed dust, a gentle cradle for his head. And here he would stay, until he crumbled —

"John."

He snapped open his eyes. Now he could hear a TV. But there was no TV in Bower's Fall. And in the midst of that inexplicable puzzle, Doc appeared in front of him, or at least a guy who would look like Doc in another twenty years. He wanted to rise but he knew one of his legs had gone. Confused, he wriggled his toes, and slowly rose up on his elbows and into a sitting position.

"Welcome back," the ancient man said.

John looked down, he was stripped down to his underwear, both legs stretched out on the bed canopy. His left ankle bore some ugly marks, but the skin wasn't broken, and nothing appeared swollen. He bent the knee. It bent just fine. He was healed. "I'm sorry," he said. That parchment skin and mottled flesh on the other man was his fault. He hadn't been quick enough. He'd let the pod get its hooks on him.

Doc waved a dismissive hand. "You did well tonight. Unfortunately it isn't over."

He swung his feet over the edge of the bed, stood up nice and slow, tested his balance, shifted his weight quickly onto his right foot. Not one hundred percent yet, but it would suffice. "Another breach?" he asked.

"No. It's about that house back there."

John looked around for some clothes, spied his jeans hanging over the back of a chair. The legs looked stained and when he picked them up, one of them was all torn up and the fabric felt stiff and reeked of flowers. "Whom did it belong to?"

"Two women; they bought one of your brother's paintings."

He closed his eyes for a moment, thought his heart would stop. Dread wrapped its arms around him, constricted his chest.

"It's the reason I wanted it kept quiet," Doc continued, "why this operation was down to just the two of us."

"The women. I guess we need to—"

"They're dead, John. They died in the fire along with the painting. I made it look like an accident. Scented candles, nearby drapes." He shrugged. "It happens." The Adept's tone was mild, conversational.

The women were dead. Murdered. Because one of Luke's paintings had opened the way, created a breach. It resonated deep, despite years of skating over dark ponds of morality and guilt. Sure, people had died before. Like that guy standing in his laundry room in stained underwear and that had been bad enough. But this –

"How many more are there?"

"One more sale, and there are more pictures stored at a nearby gallery, and I'll deal with all that. But you have to understand, I can only keep this quiet for so long. If the other Adepts even suspect what Luke is capable of, that he's no longer latent, they'll insist he comes in and I'm sure you can imagine Rachel's reaction if that happens."

John nodded, accepted that Doc wasn't doing this for Luke's benefit. This was a peacekeeping mission. Rachel would rather see her youngest son dead than brought in and mentally neutered. And seeing as a dead son wasn't on the cards either...

"Not to mention what will happen if the likes of Ralt gets his hands on him. You have to stop him," Doc continued. "Whatever it takes. Do you understand?"

"Yes, sir."

The man approached, put a hand on his shoulder. "I'm sorry. Like you I was hoping this would happen later, rather than sooner."

There was a lump in his throat, making it hard to swallow. "I swear it, Doc, he still doesn't know."

"Hmm, I'm assuming his art is the stimulus. If you can separate him from that..."

He let out a sigh. Confession time. "He has a girlfriend. I'm pretty sure she's sentient."

"Ah." Doc walked over to the hotel room's single armchair, picked up his jacket and began to put it on. "Get rid of her." He shrugged the garment over his shoulders and pulled sharply on the lapels. "That way you might be in with a chance, and he might regress. Does anyone else know what she is?"

"No. At least, I don't think so."

The other man nodded. "Good." He gestured toward the bed. "Now, rest up, get your pants laundered. The room's paid up for another night."

"Sir." He inclined his head. He'd been given another twenty four hours grace, and then...

He stood in the center of the room, staring at the door after Doc had left him alone. He'd screwed up. He should have stayed closer, kept a more vigilant eye on his brother's choice of partners, paid more attention to the art. Two women dead, and a giant harvester pod deciding on a vacation. He supposed he should feel some relief that the retired pharmaceutical guy had Luke working on dumb carousel horses, and wasn't having him slap more paint on canvas.

He walked back to the bed, his left foot still a little tender, and sat down hard.

Get rid of her, Doc had said. And what had he meant by that? And why had John chosen to lie about Emma, and hidden the fact that he'd already talked it over with Rhonda?

Maybe he'd figure it out if he just sat and thought about it for a while.

CHAPTER 16

LUKE

It was mid-afternoon. He'd finished the horse, given it a frothy gray, silver and white mane; so much lighter than the others he'd already painted, but it was a necessary contrast to this particular creature's eyes— they were John's eyes, so shadowy and wretched, and now that was done a new subject stood pale and colorless in the center of the workshop waiting for him to begin. It was the twin dragon carriage, slightly asymmetrical he had discovered, the inner dragon fractionally smaller, her head and tail given less detail by the carver. Not that it mattered, he knew he could rectify that and make her the equal of her partner. He stood alongside with his sketchpad, his hair falling down over his face, his fingers moving rapidly back and forth with charcoal and pastels.

When he was happy with the sketch, he looked out of the window. The courtyard was empty of vehicles, Emma and Grace still had to get back from town, and so he put aside his current project and retrieved a canvas from the far corner of the room. He placed it on his easel and powered up his computer, and for a good few minutes he stood motionless and watch a looped slideshow of the pictures he'd taken of Emma while she was sleeping.

Eventually a smile crept over his face, he closed up the laptop and he got to work. He switched mediums, to the faster drying acrylics, their colors more hard edged, less subtle; it made him work faster, think differently about his blending techniques and color mixing, so the resulting color palette was slightly different to that of the carousel but was essentially the same interpretation of that bitter world that existed inside his head.

He'd already made a start, just an outline and some background shading at the line of horizon. And he stared at it for a moment, wondering if Emma truly belonged in that dark world. He'd taken a few tentative steps in that direction with the portrait now hanging in Black's library, and seeing it there, hung in the alcove, his reaction one of unexpected approval, it was simply another sign that he was on the right track. And so he loaded his brush with paint, pushed all doubt aside and continued, beginning the long, painstaking task of breathing life into each brush-stroke, embodying tiny fractions of Emma's spirit onto the course weave of stretched canvas.

He had no idea of the time but was fully prepared when he heard a vehicle arriving in the courtyard. A subconscious defense mechanism kicked in, urging his hands to throw a light cloth over the canvas, to put down his acrylic palette and pick up the sketchbook. When Emma entered and began to speak of her shopping trip with Grace, he nodded dutifully, made the appropriate noises, while on the inside his focus, his slave-like dedication to the canvas, hung there like a film on pause, just waiting for him to hit play.

He heard her scold him gently, because he appeared distracted, that she had some studying to do and she'd see him at dinner; she smiled, kissed him, and left him alone.

Click. Play.

So easy to slip back into it, and this time with an added dimension, for when she kissed him he had caught the smell of her perfume, something light and floral that danced inside his head and threw him further into that gray landscape, and as she began to take shape on canvas it became oh so easy to see just how much she belonged there. Another glance, just past the slope of her shoulder and he realized that dark, barren background was nothing of the kind. Life seethed out there, just beyond his vision.

"Show me," he whispered, so intent on the portrait he failed to notice his exhaled breath clouding in front of him.

It was just the three of them for dinner. No sign of Elliot and no excuse given. Luke didn't care. His eyes were on Emma, her hand gestures, the line and movement of her jaw while she talked, the way her hair shifted and changed color ever so slightly under the kitchen lights. It had to go on the canvas and he couldn't afford to miss anything. Eventually –

"Luke?" She was leaning forward a little, staring at him.

He became aware of Grace wearing a similar expression and he shrugged, and smiled. "What?"

Emma shook her head, she was now looking toward Grace but her fork was stabbing vaguely in his direction. She made some kind of quip about never getting involved with an artist, and while both women laughed he watched her hand on the fork, the way it moved between her fingers, a length of profound, shining silver. He stored it away, tried to pay attention, realized he'd hardly eaten anything and so began to stuff fork loads of chicken and broccoli into his mouth. He chewed mechanically, could barely taste anything, but he ate it anyway. He attempted a few lines of small talk and asked where Elliot was.

"He had a call from a seller, about an item for the store. I think he wanted to snatch it up before someone else got to it."

"I saw a documentary about antiques once," Emma said. "It seems a very cut throat business."

Grace smiled. "You have no idea."

Luke returned to his well of silence, and after dinner he made the appropriate promises and got back to work. And by the time he took a step back and checked his watch, it was just after midnight. He wanted to continue. He was still in the zone and not in the least bit tired, and yet he'd promised.

Reluctantly, he put down his tools and began the ritual of cleaning up. Another twenty minutes or so and his brushes and palettes were clean, the painting was stowed out of sight, and he had at least one foot back in the real world. Nevertheless he was reluctant to leave and felt a little disjointed as he left his workshop and headed toward the guesthouse; his mind hadn't given up yet, didn't want to let go of the creative process. And for the first time he noticed how warm it was outside.

As he entered their new temporary home he found no immediate sign of Emma but he saw a light on in the bedroom along the passageway. And so he turned off the lamps in the living room and crept along the corridor to join her.

He found her sitting before the dressing table mirror, brushing her hair, and for a moment he just stood in the doorway and watched her, until her eyes narrowed in the mirror and regarded him with reproach. He closed the door behind him and stepped closer; that look had lit a fire under him, and he felt his flesh tingle.

"You're mad at me," he whispered. He pulled off his boots and socks, flexed his bare toes on the rug.

"You're late."

He stepped behind her, looked at her reflection. She'd stripped her face of makeup and was wearing a thin, cream satin robe that was wrapped tightly across her body. Slowly, he lowered himself onto his knees behind her. He took in a breath and saw the light in the mirror dim. He slid an arm loosely around her waist. "I'm sorry," he muttered. His other hand caressed her hair, slowly drew it away from her throat. "Tell me—" he leaned in, kissed the tender flesh below her ear "—what I should do to make amends."

She let out a sigh. "Oh, Luke, I just wish..." She leaned back her head until it rested on his shoulder. "You can be so distant. It's like I'm not there at all."

He kissed her again in the same spot, let his teeth gently rake against her skin, and then he matched her gaze in the mirror. "You're always there. Inside me, tormenting me."

"Even at dinner tonight?"

"Yes, even at dinner." He wrapped his other arm around her, paying attention to her reaction. She didn't stiffen, or try to ward him off and so he became bold and slipped his hand inside her robe. Her skin felt warm and smooth and he breathed in more of the scent on her skin. He loosened the tie at her waist and began to slide the robe over her shoulders, all the while keeping his eyes locked on hers. "See how beautiful you are," he whispered.

The garment pooled around her hips; she was utterly naked beneath and he broke into a smile when her eyes narrowed once more. She'd thrown down the gauntlet, issued a challenge— no kidding around, no teasing, not now. And duly noted he leaned in for a kiss, waited until she'd turned her head toward him before brushing her lips softly with his own, and gradually he moved in, tested her hunger, waited until she had fully reciprocated before his hands got slowly to work, sliding her robe off completely, searching for her most sensitive spots, so that by the time they came up for air the fingers of one hand were teasing and tugging, exploring the means to arouse her further.

Her eyes snapped toward him once more through the mirror and she gasped. He watched her skin flush slightly as he stroked and teased, and in the meantime his own arousal demanded attention. His erection was pushing angrily against the zip of his jeans, insisting on release. He ignored it on purpose, let it grow harder within its confines while he continued to work on Emma, while he listened to her breathing, and waited until he could hear those familiar, shallow little gasps.

He slowed down, stopped. He rose, picked her up. Her head lolled and he could feel her skin trembling as if electrified. He carried her over to the bed and dumped her roughly on top of the bed cover. Immediately she came up on her elbows and bared her teeth, snarling like an angry cat. He grinned and slowly began to peel off his clothes, and once he was done he crawled forward, scooped her up once more and got to work on her all over again. He couldn't get enough, of her skin, and those sharp little intakes of breath. It became a hallowed ritual, an act of worship that made his balls ache and his engorged cock quiver unbearably. Until finally he entered her, pushing, determined and resolute, sinking further and further until he was fully inside her.

He felt her legs come up and wrap around his hips, effectively locking them together. Up on his elbows he stared down at her face. In the low light her eyes were as black as night. He gave in to them, acceded command.

"Slow," she said, relaxing her grip.

And so he began, the tortured back and forth, while he gripped her hair and pulled back her head. He was utterly enslaved, he realized. There were three of them, a triumvirate— the Lady Armageddon, ruler of the carousel, the woman on canvas, who drove him mercilessly to imbue her spirit and bring her alive, and Emma beneath him, flesh and blood, his beacon, his life raft in a dark, crumbling hell. And as he moved, and let Emma guide him with her strong slender legs, all three became as one inside his head, and the slavery, so glorious and absolute and so undeniable, he welcomed wholeheartedly. And once he'd satisfied her, and when he'd come in wretched, shuddering spasms that left him utterly spent, he lay awake, as usual, and he felt at peace in these shackles and chains, until he finally drifted off to sleep near dawn.

She'd left him a note 'Gone into town', and bleary eyed he'd staggered into the kitchen where Grace had supplied him with a much needed cup of strong coffee, and then it was back to work. He started on the carriage, decided on a base of black— and the act of applying the paint, methodically covering every nook and cranny, had a soothing effect and let him forget about the night before and its heady, ritualistic fervor.

He felt empty and lightheaded, and was grateful that the initial task was a simple one. And it was almost two hours before he finally got in the correct mindset to consider his next step, whether he could apply some wet on wet color before the base color had dried, and when he consulted his sketchbook he saw the word 'red' and a question mark alongside it.

He stood alongside the carriage and considered the slight shift in his, up to now, mostly monochromatic color palette.

The only red is blood, the Lady whispered.

He frowned, thought about that statement, stared at the creatures' flanks. There were no flowers or tack or any other ornamental features he could apply the color to legitimately. Instead it was all down to scales, claws, eyes and teeth. Until he took into account the landscape.

He re-checked his sketchbook. The word red and the question mark had been written at the bottom of the page, and so he attempted to back track and remember what lay in his mind's eye before the evening's obsession with Emma had swept everything aside.

Eventually he remembered the dark red bellies, the color a reflection of a fictitious lava-like glow on the ground beneath them. It just seemed to fit, and after a few moments of reconsideration, he decided to run with it and started mixing.

Movement in his peripheral vision gave him a start. When he looked toward the door he saw Elliot Black standing there, his hands in his pockets, his eyes on the carriage. Luke had just begun to blend streaks of carmine into the flat pads of underbelly on the smaller creature. He noted the slight frown, but kept on working.

"You disagree?" he said eventually.

Elliot shook his head. "Quite the reverse. I just wondered how you..." He trailed off and stepped forward into the room. "Where is Emma?"

Good question. "Must still be in town." He stood up. Should he be concerned? Perhaps he should. He looked for his watch on the bench, was surprised when he saw it was five after twelve. He stared at the timepiece and frowned, tried to get it together. He'd been spaced out all morning. What if she *was* in trouble? "Maybe I should—"

Elliot had brought out his cell phone and was reading something on the screen. "She's at the store." Luke put down his palette and brush, but Elliot held up a hand. "I'll pick her up."

"Is everything okay?" Now he was starting to worry. Why would she need picking up? Maybe she'd tried to call him. But his phone was back at the guesthouse, and he couldn't remember when he'd last put it on charge.

Black nodded. "Continue. We won't be long."

Luke's eyes moved to the door and he considered just taking off and making a run for Main Street. But that would look pretty stupid wouldn't it. There'd be issues of trust, his lack of in this case, and Emma would be so... He picked up his palette and brush, gave the guy a nonchalant shrug. "Whatever," he said.

When Elliot had gone he got back to work, attempted to calm down lest his brush strokes became stabbing, stippling affairs, hardly the result he was looking for. Emma was fine. He'd know if there was anything wrong. He'd know it in his bones.

CHAPTER 17

EMMA

Earlier that morning she had woken from a dream of trees and gray fog. She had left Luke face down and sprawled on the bed, and she'd pulled on her running gear and set off, with the full intention of clearing her head and reminding herself she had a full day ahead of her and that she really needed to get settled into that studious routine and the sooner the better.

And so, she found a street that ran parallel with the main thoroughfare and then followed the route she'd taken before, out of town and toward the highway. The sun had risen but mists still drifted in the remaining shady spots, reminding her of the dreams she'd had in the night. The roads were quiet and she heard nothing but the birds as she pounded toward the gas station on the corner and on arrival she hung out there for a minute or two before setting off on the return journey.

And while she stood and caught her breath and basked in the sunlight, she remembered something and pulled on the neck of her T-shirt until her left shoulder was exposed. There was a dark smudge still there, like the petals of a strange flower hidden partially beneath her bra strap. She frowned; paint, she assumed, left behind after her lover's amorous but stained hands from the night before. It had proved fairly impossible to clean off and it made her wonder if there was anything similar on other parts of her body that she hadn't noticed yet.

She shook her head, resolved to scrub it clean once again in the shower, and set off back toward town. This time she returned via the pretty, tree-lined Main Street, and part way along she spied Elliot's shop manager Robert wheeling a hand truck backwards across the sidewalk. It was stacked with half a dozen or more tall canvasses and the load appeared to be quite unwieldy.

Emma crossed the street and approached. "Need any help?"

He smiled. "Would you mind? The door."

It was already ajar, but not quite enough, and so she pulled it all the way open and tried to stay out of the way as he maneuvered the cart into the store. The paintings were covered in brown paper and bubble wrap so she was unable to see anything. Luke would no doubt have asked if he could take a look, especially if they were old, and she had no reason to doubt they would be. "That's quite a haul."

The older man nodded. "An estate sale." He winked. "We got lucky." He rested the cart on its wheels and stubby legs and let out a gasp.

"Do you want me to—" she began.

He waved her off. "No, my dear, I'll be fine. The difficult part has been done. I would have taken them around back, but I mislaid my key."

She looked around. "I've never been in here before." From her position by the door she could see polished tables, lace, and a number of clocks. They beckoned her in, whispering their secrets.

"You're more than welcome to take a look around," he said.

She was about to take him up on his offer when she realized she was in her sweaty running clothes. "Some time later this morning? I need to get cleaned up."

"Of course. We don't open until the afternoon, but come

knock, and I'll give you the guided tour."

"Hey, thanks." She grinned, said her farewells, and then continued her journey, hoping another encounter wasn't on the cards, this time with Luke's brother. Thankfully there was no sign of him and she made it back to the mansion without interruption.

Luke was still asleep when she poked her head around the bedroom door, and he was still out of it after she had scrubbed and scrubbed at not one, but three separate stains on her skin which point blank refused to wash away. Resigned to the possibility they were going to need the application of nasty smelling solvent before they'd come off, and that at least they were not currently staining her clothes or in any particularly visible spots, she got dressed, left Sleeping Beauty a note and walked across the yard to the kitchen.

Grace was already pouring coffee. "Is Luke joining us?"

Emma grabbed some cold oatmeal and fruit and sat at the table. "Still asleep. He didn't come in until after midnight last night."

The other woman joined her with the coffee cups. "Does he often work late?"

She nodded. "And he doesn't sleep too good, so..."

"Better to let him sleep while he can. So, what are your plans for the day."

Emma tucked into breakfast and mentioned Robert's offer about the store. "I figured I might walk down there fairly early, then settle into some study for the rest of the day."

"Robert will be glad of the company, I'm sure."

"I don't know. He seemed pretty busy, taking in a new delivery."

"Really?"

"Paintings. He had a whole stack of them."

"So, Elliot's journey must have been successful."

"I guess."

Grace seemed distracted for a moment, and a mild frown appeared on her face.

"Is anything wrong?" Emma asked.

"No, not at all." The woman snapped out of it and smiled. "Perhaps it means he's on his way back."

The door was locked and the closed sign was prominently displayed in the window alongside. She looked for a bell or a doorknocker, and after being unable to find anything of the kind she rapped carefully on the glass and waited. A few moments later she saw Robert on the approach from the interior of the store.

"Come in," he said, beckoning her with a wave of his hand.

She stepped inside and the door jangled as it closed behind her. No sign of the stack of paintings, the entryway was clear. The lights were lit but compared to the sunny sidewalk the surroundings appeared gloomy and claustrophobic until her eyes had adjusted, and gradually it became a treasure cave. She could smell furniture polish and lavender and the floor creaked slightly beneath her feet. She followed Robert past a mahogany dining table carrying an embroidered table cloth and two candelabras; beyond lay two ponderous, ticking grandfather clocks, an assortment of side tables and apothecary cabinets, lace drapes and displays of silver cutlery, pocket watches, cups and saucers and miniature portraits. She counted four Tiffany lamps, three chandeliers, and in the middle of the store hung a huge, dark metal Turkish lantern. Various tapestries, works of art and oval gilded mirrors adorned the walls.

"Wow," she said. "It looks so beautiful."

Robert nodded. "It's all very pretty, but the rare items are at the back." He beckoned. "Come, I'll show you."

Emma followed the man along a meandering path through the furniture and displays, and once they'd passed by the giant lantern, which seemed to indicate a barrier of sorts, she noticed the displays of small items were less prominent. Here most of the tables were bare, the cabinets unadorned, the upholstery was frayed; immediately ahead was a line of dining chairs, each one of them decidedly different to the other, their polished curves inviting the eye to roam.

"A Queen Anne is easy enough to recognize," her companion said as he caught her staring at them, "because of the legs; this next one is Dutch, a little heavy and overwrought, but in the right setting— and this one—"

"I like this. It's elegant."

His smiled broadened. "Good choice. Early nineteenth century, it's a Hepplewhite. The slenderness, and you see the shield back? Very characteristic. We also have—"

She let him continue, content to listen as they wove back and forth between various items, while she tried to imagine the houses they'd originally been a part of, and the people who'd used them. Early nineteenth century in particular struck a chord, a period that contained everything from the Louisiana Purchase to the Napoleonic Wars. She let her fingers trail lightly across one surface after another. What stories they could tell, if only they could speak. She was mesmerized, in her element, and completely lost all track of time.

Eventually, at the very far end of the store, were a collection of oddities— a slightly rusty fairground ball toss game, an ancient soda fountain, a line of old, wooden marionettes, and a collection of strange hand puppets that included a crocodile and a string of sausages. Here the edges of the room were lined with old, battered storage trunks bound by worn leather straps and above them the walls were covered in old fabric circus banners frayed at their edges.

"Ooh. What's this?" Looming large, directly in front of her was a strange wooden statue. It bore a carved, pointy hat and although the paint was worn, it suggested a depiction of tight, striped trousers. The face was odd, very large, and stared right at her with accusing eyes.

Robert was grinning. "That's our Mr. Punch. In a previous life he stood outside a tobacconists, advertising cigars. Do you like him?"

She winced. "He's a little scary. I'm glad I don't smoke." Her eyes shifted quickly to a display on a nearby wall. She stepped closer and a smile crept over her face as she examined an artful array of Venetian masks. "What about these?"

He shrugged. "Not particularly old, but they come from an estate belonging to a silent film actress. Beautiful aren't they?"

Emma nodded. "Did they appear in her films?"

"All except for this one—" he pointed at a plain red mask with a pointed chin, "—and this."

"A plague doctor mask. I read about those." She cocked her head, stared at the pale, long, narrow beak. It looked like a giant crow skull. And then her eyes skipped back to the red mask.

"This one is called a bauta. Not particularly feminine, but very practical," Robert said. "It enables you to eat and drink without taking it off. Masks like these were supposedly used as early as the thirteenth century."

"It looks... sinister." She laughed.

"Perhaps." He beckoned. "Shall we?"

There were two doors on the rear wall and the one he opened led out into a walled yard bathed in bright sunlight. There were two men out there, one quite old, the other very young; they looked like grandfather and grandson. And they were busy working on one of Luke's carousel horses.

"It's the very last one," Robert told her.

The men had stopped and were looking at her, and so she raised a hand. The younger man smiled. She thought she might have seen him up at the mansion, down in that room under the carousel, holding the ladder. The older man simply nodded and continued running a small buffing tool across the carved horse's mane.

"How many are there?" she asked.

"On the carousel? Forty four, I seem to remember."

She thought about that for a moment. That meant Luke was barely a quarter done. There was no way he'd be finished by the end of summer. But they'd already discussed that, hadn't they? Made plans? Still, she felt disappointed, knowing they were likely to be separated for months before he was finally finished, and abruptly she felt a stab of jealousy. She covered it up, kept the smile on her face.

Robert led her along the perimeter of the yard and slid open a floor-to-ceiling door that squeaked and protested on its rails. Inside was a storage space that looked larger than it did on the outside. It was well lit from the above skylights, and was packed tight with objects, their identities hidden by pale tarpaulins, although she caught glimpses of a chair leg here and there, presumably companions to those inside the store. She saw the tall, flat stack of paintings, too, leaning against the wall, still in their wrappings.

"Not much to see in here," he said. "Including the one out in the yard, there are four carousel animals to deliver to the mansion, everything else here is moved in and out of the store, dependent on Elliot's wishes."

Emma nodded. It was warm in this particular building. The skylight had a semi-opaque wash over the glass, nevertheless a mild greenhouse effect was still evident.

"It's almost time to open, but I can certainly make you a coffee before you go."

Emma looked at her watch, startled. It was almost noon. "Oh wow, I'm supposed to be working. Mind if I pass? And you've been so kind, I really can't trouble you any more."

The man smiled. "Of course. Come, I'll lead you back through the labyrinth."

She followed him back into the store and the contrast between the light in the yard and the store's darker interior, especially at the rear, made her momentarily blind. And like an idiot, instead of pausing for a moment, she continued in Robert's wake and walked into the corner of one of the battered trunks lying just beyond the door. Its edge was sharp, it bit hard into her knee and the impact caused her to overbalance and stretch out an arm in an attempt to correct herself.

The palm of her hand slapped hard against the flat, leather lid of the trunk. She winced, felt her hand tingle after the impact, and pain blossom on her knee. "I'm sorry," she began, attempting to stand upright. Instead, her other leg gave way and she dropped onto both knees, the injured one registering its displeasure acutely, and from there she landed hard, face down on the wooden floor.

The only red is blood.

She coughed, her limbs felt weightless. Directly ahead of her the floor had been replaced by an expanse of fine white sand, but when her fingers dug in it didn't feel like sand at all. Confused, she struggled. "Robert—" She reached out, felt his hands on her upper arm. He was saying something to her but she could barely hear him. The sand was starting to give way, pour down the cracks in the floorboards.

The only red is blood.

She looked down. Her nose was bleeding. It was dripping onto the floor in tiny little drops. But at least the sand had gone. Robert was making concerned noises and she started to feel extremely foolish. With his help she managed to stand but it became painfully obvious, if left to her own devices, she wouldn't remain upright for long. She saw the trunk alongside her and tried to sit down on it, but Robert pulled her away and sat her down in a nearby chair, instead.

The immediate vicinity became crowded as the two men who had been working outside arrived.

"Lean forward a little, don't swallow it," said the older man. "Does it hurt? Have you broken it? No? Then pinch there, that's it." The younger man handed over a bundle of ice wrapped in a thin towel.

Robert was on the phone.

"I'm fine," she said, her words nasally and muffled. She took the offered ice and placed it on the bridge of her nose. A few deep breaths, she figured. Maybe she'd hit her head when she'd gone down but right now that eerie landscape had returned. It kept switching out, back and forth, until it became hard to tell what was real. Shock, concussion maybe; it was okay, she'd deal with it, just relax, she was in an antiques store. But she wasn't.

A breeze had risen, and it lifted the top layer of dust and sent it skittering forth. Dust, not sand. Her hands, forearms and elbows were covered in it, and where blood had dripped from her nose onto the floorboards, a tiny little seedling grew...

Emma.

But the strangest part of all was the smell.

"Emma."

"It's like flowers," she murmured, and looked down again. The seedling had grown a little, and had sprouted a snapping, nasty little mouth full of needle teeth. The sight of it made her gasp in horror, and it became tantamount now, to stand up then she could stomp it, kill it, smear its remains into the ground.

As she flailed she felt arms around her. They felt restrictive, she feared they would delay her purpose, and so she pulled, and used her elbows to push whomever it was away. She had to stamp it out of existence, this thing that her blood had given birth to, before it grew —

"Emma, it's all right. Shh, it's all right."

The voice cut through. It had grown in volume, assumed a timbre of persuasion that cut through the living nightmare she was having. The dust, the plant, both faded quickly. She was on her feet, there was an arm around her waist, a hand threaded through her hair, gripping, pulling her head back.

"It's nothing. Just a silly dream."

She recognized the voice. "The trunk," she said. "What's in it?"

"Nothing," he whispered. "Nothing at all."

"No," she insisted. "It's full of dust." Breath caught in the back of her throat and the room spun. She didn't dare look down in case that nasty little flytrap was still there, snapping at her heels and growing bigger by the second. Just thinking on it made her skin crawl and so she slammed her eyes shut.

When she opened them once more she was beneath the painted skylight. Elliot Black's head and shoulders hovered above her, his face registering concern. She was laid partially across his lap, and her head was resting on the arm of an ancient couch. She offered him a wide, lazy grin, as if she were intoxicated. "Llennendhrad," she said.

"Shh," he crooned. "You need to rest now."

She spied Luke through the open door of his workshop and as soon as she had gotten out of the car he bounded over.

"Are you okay?"

"I tripped over a box at the antique store." She felt stupid and it became a struggle to recall exactly how it happened, but the pain on her knee was proof enough. “But I’m okay. Really.”

He let out a sigh of relief and embraced her. “I figured you would be, but after he’d gone I began to worry.” Elliot was out of the car now and there was some kind of silent standoff going on between the two men. Luke’s expression appeared mildly accusatory.

“She’s fine,” Elliot told him.

Lightheaded, still slightly dizzy and in no mood for confrontation, Emma took Luke’s hand and pulled him away. There was something she wanted to tease him, to scold him about, but she discovered she couldn’t remember what it was. Maybe after lunch she’d take a nap, her earlier blundering had obviously taken more out of her than she thought. And at the kitchen table she continued to make little of the incident, and was grateful when talk moved on to what creature Luke would start on when he’d finished the carriage. The hippocampus met with general approval; everyone appeared to want to see what he’d make of it.

Half an hour later, back at the guesthouse, she sat in front of the mirror and pulled off her jeans and her shirt. There was a dressing on her knee, which was odd because she couldn’t remember how it got there, but even more disconcerting was the stain on her shoulder. She thought it might have started to fade. Instead it looked worse, more prominent. If anything it looked to have grown.

CHAPTER 18

JOHN

On his return, it hadn't occurred to John that they might have moved out of their hotel, and after a call that didn't connect, and a text that still had to be answered, he was left cooling his heels in a tiny coffee shop on Main Street. He had considered paying a visit to that grandiose house, home of the antique dealer and Luke's current taskmaster, but in the end he held off. He had to think things through, get everything straight in his head, because it was all well and good for Doc to say 'Get rid of her', and quite another to do the ridding.

Back in Sacramento he had made full use of the motel room, and after two days, although the poison-inspired jitters had gone, and he could almost carry his full weight on his left leg, he still hadn't any answers regarding Luke. In fact if anything there were more questions. He was still convinced there were pieces missing. Even Doc's behavior was casting odd shadows over his hitherto beliefs and assumptions. Get rid of her. It made Doc sound like a TV gangster and not like the Doc he knew at all. It was a train of thought that led him back to his original fear that something big was coming, that it was affecting everyone around him while throwing up barriers of amnesia and confusion.

At least the hotel had kept his room open and he'd only been away for three days. And whereas he had no answers yet on how to deal with the Emma problem, chances were those two hadn't had time to do anything crazy. The clock was ticking, sure, and Luke's abilities were beginning to awaken, but another three days of painting wooden horses wasn't going to bring about the apocalypse. Not yet. Not unless, the way Doc had it figured, he was also painting on canvas.

John sipped his too expensive cappuccino and winced. While he'd been brooding it had gone cold and he wished he'd returned to the diner instead. They had free refills and, providing he could have gotten a seat by the window, a better view of Elliot Black's store. However, here the wifi was good, and he was back to his research. He'd attempted to regain all his info on Black, but after a while he realized his heart wasn't in it. He was delaying the inevitable, compiling dossiers he'd never need, and after a few more minutes he gave up.

He had to get to the girl, give her some explanation that would make sense. Hell, maybe even tell her the truth. He rubbed the bridge of his nose, wondered how that would pan out, and he tried to recall their last conversation and right there he was hit by a very strong sense of deja vu. But the more he thought on it, the more confused he became, and it took him a while before he finally figured out it was something about Luke's paintings. About Black having bought some of them. But that didn't make any sense because Doc told him there was only one painting to deal with back in California, plus those in gallery storage. Had Doc got to Black's acquisitions already? Was he even aware of their existence?

He picked up his laptop, paid the bill and left. All of a sudden there were far too many things not adding up. And as he walked back to his hotel he attempted to pull everything together, all those scenarios where pieces were missing, the paintings Black had acquired, and the research he was convinced he'd already done. Odd, how it always came back to Black.

He dropped the laptop off in his room then immediately headed back out onto Main Street, crossed the road and walked toward the antique store. Maybe he'd get lucky and this time he'd find Luke's art hung there on the wall and he could call Doc and tie up a few loose ends. The paintings were not exactly antiques as such, but he figured he had to start somewhere.

It was two in the afternoon. The store was open. The door was ajar, held open by a black, ancient smoothing iron, and so he slipped inside, pleased to see a few customers who would offer distraction while he scouted the place.

He looked around, spied the manager guy, his back partially turned, talking to a couple about midway through, and so John did his best to stick to the opposite side of the store while he wove his way through more people and furniture, keeping his eyes on the walls. Still no sign of Luke's paintings but the journey stoked his memory. He'd been here before.

At the very far end of the store, once again he discovered the open door, and this time there was no one to stop him. He made his way casually, slowly to the doorway and peered into the yard beyond. It was empty, and from his current vantage point he could see another open doorway that led into a small warehouse.

With no one behind him raising any objections, he slipped into the yard and approached the second building. He kept his hands in his pockets, assumed the gait of a curious customer and entered a concrete floored room stacked with items covered in tarpaulin. Above his head, light shone down from a partially covered skylight. He began to work his way around the room and eventually he came across a stack of panels covered in brown paper and bubble wrap.

He ran his fingers lightly along the paper. He wasn't getting any particular vibe and so he pulled out a small knife from his pocket and sliced along the edge. Another cut crosswise and he was able to lift some of the packaging and take a peek, still a curious customer if anyone asked.

He slid his fingers past the frame, enabling him to touch the canvas. He caught a glimpse of gray and a depiction of a tree limb, but he no longer needed a visual. He stepped back and counted them. “Ah, Luke,” he whispered.

His exclamation was followed up with a sigh of relief. These paintings were wrapped up, out of sight and therefore out of harm’s way. He’d have to destroy them, of course, and with any luck he’d be able to do that anonymously. All he needed was –

He heard a sound, a footstep behind him, and when he turned there were two men standing by the door, blocking his exit. He smiled, and was about to come up with a valid excuse for being here, until they were abruptly joined by another figure.

It was Elliot Black. Only it wasn’t.

It was as if he’d been wearing sunglasses in a dark room, and they’d just been snatched away. Now he could see, and the memory of their last encounter began to unfold and he was granted maybe half a second to orchestrate some kind of escape plan, before the will to do so left him altogether.

“Hello, John.”

A wave of defeat washed over him, and it took an enormous amount of effort not to fall to his knees. “Llennendhrad.” The name was a death knell. And right there he knew his life was over.

The man disguised as Elliot Black approached. “We can drop all pretenses now, I think. And I apologize for the subterfuge and any confusion I may have caused you, but I had to be sure a deal had been struck.”

Despite the heavy cluster of dread in his innards, John’s lips twisted with bravado. “An apology? From you?”

Black smiled. “I can do that much for Rachel’s least valuable son.”

"Before you kill me."

He received a noncommittal shrug by way of reply that did nothing whatsoever to calm his fears. Nevertheless he ploughed on. "What deal? With whom?"

The other man reached forward, grabbed the hair at the back of his head and pulled until John was staring at the ceiling. In his peripheral vision he saw the other hand, two fingernails extending like cruel stilettos. He can still do that trick, John thought, even here. The tips of the spines hovered, right before his eyes.

"Do you really think I'd tell you?" Black whispered.

He fought for control, of his muscles, of his bowels. Any second now and those points would pop his eyeballs. Get it over with, he willed, just get it over with. But instead, the blades retracted and Black let him go.

"Take off his clothes."

The other two men approached and stood either side of him. They pulled his jacket over his shoulders while he tried to summon the will to fight them off, but Black wasn't having any of it. In exchange for revelation, for handing him the truth at last, the man had picked up the reins of physical control and John could barely move. He tried not to shiver while his mind conjured all kinds of cruel demises that required him to be naked. Maybe if he kept talking. "What are you going to do with Luke?"

Black seemed to toy with the idea for a moment. "*I* have no intention of harming your brother." He cocked his head, broke into an incredulous smile. "He's a Rook; a guide between planes. Are you even remotely aware of his value?"

"I know what a Rook is," he snapped. His heart skipped in his chest. He'd been so short sighted, so fucking blind. It wasn't just the art. It wasn't a question of simply creating a breach. If Black was correct, and Luke was able to eschew his latency completely, he would be able to create a conduit of immense size and strength, and not just into the Fall. He could get in and out of Hell itself if he wanted to. And father had wanted to kill him when he was only eight years old. He must have known.

One of the men stripping him, the younger one, was ripping apart his seventy-dollar T-shirt with a box cutter. He imagined punching the guy in the face while lamenting on how badly his brother was about to be used. The conflict of emotion made his mouth dry and his flesh twitch.

When it was done, Black— he still wanted to call him Black while he looked so deceptively human— appraised him as though he were a newly arrived item for the store. "You have a lot of scar tissue, and recent damage, I see."

"So? Were you thinking of having me stuffed and displayed in the window?"

The man laughed before turning his attention to the two men who'd stripped him. "Bring the box."

John swallowed. His throat felt tight; no doubt partially under wraps so he couldn't bellow for help. His only hope now was that some stray customer would wander into the rear yard and see a naked man through the warehouse doorway. And maybe, just maybe, they'd call the cops. In the meantime—

"If Rachel finds out—"

"Rachel knows more than you think. And this isn't the first time her sons have been put in play."

Like it was a game. "I don't believe you. She isn't behind this."

"In this particular instance, no, she isn't. But don't be naive." Black took a step forward, reached out and let his hand glide slowly over John's shoulder. Fingers traced a diagonal scar across his back, and explored another running parallel below it. John let out a soft gasp. The touch was so intimate it made his nerves jump as if they were electrified; repulsed, or God forbid —

"Hell's denizens and the Fall didn't give you these," Black continued, his voice light, pretending to be unaware of the effect he was having. "Your father did this; I'm guessing, trying to beat it out of you."

"Leave Dad out of this."

"You shouldn't be so angry with him. He made you into one tough little son of a bitch. That you've managed to survive Bower's Fall on more than one occasion is testament to that." The hand had moved, was now stroking through his hair. "And it would be quite an admission of Rachel's, would it not, if she were to confess to standing by and letting him beat you for that sole purpose."

John opened his mouth to offer another bitter retort. He didn't believe it. He couldn't believe it.

"Silence. You might be just a soldier, John, but you've lasted longer than most, and despite your ignorance you know more about Fall politics than you've a right to. And like I told you some weeks ago, you might still be of use. No doubt we shall see."

Did that mean he was going to stay alive? Hope quelled his anger and leapt so hard into the back of his throat he nearly choked. Black's caresses had ceased and he saw movement outside. The men were returning and this time they carried a large oblong trunk between them. John looked on in horror. Were they going to put him in it?

He watched as they set the trunk down on the ground and tried not to wince as their fingers went to work on the leather straps that held down the lid. Did Black know how claustrophobic he was? Of course he did. But in the end it wasn't the fear of confinement that started him begging, it was immediately after he'd caught the telltale scent, when one of the men had popped the latch and a small crack had appeared between lid and base.

"No, no, no, please—"

The lid opened to reveal an empty trunk save for a sparse layer of fine white dust covering the bottom, and immediately, thin gray veins began to explore the exterior and spread tentatively across the concrete floor.

"Put him in."

"Llennendhrad, no. Please don't." He tried to struggle. It was useless. One of the men took his shoulders, the other his legs, they picked him up and with a little maneuvering back and forth they laid him in the trunk on top of the bed of dust. Contact with the white powder made his skin crawl, made him want to scream. Only Black's mental grip on him kept him silent. Not to be outdone, his breath emerged in short, desperate gasps.

Black was crouched alongside the trunk. "This should be an easy passage for you, because you know exactly where this leads." The man flashed him a grin. "Most don't make it. They asphyxiate or die of thirst."

"Please," he whimpered. "Not this." He didn't have a weapon, or a female companion, and where he was going, that meant he was as good as dead. Only death would be slow, and agonizing. Better Black had followed through on his threat and stabbed him through the eye sockets.

"Shh," Black admonished. "Time to see what you're made of. Use your wits, boy." He stood up. "All right, replace the lid. Close it up tight."

The few seconds it took to close the lid on top of him seemed endless, and he watched the light gradually, slowly disappear until finally he was encased in darkness. He wanted to howl in terror and despair. He heard the latch click shut, and the creaking of the straps as they were buckled and tightened above his head. Black had released control of him. He discovered he could move, not that it would do any good.

He heard voices, but they faded after a few seconds. He was alone now, shut down in the dark, a thin bed of the Fall's pale dust beneath his trembling limbs. In such a close space the scent was overpowering and immediately it began to sow the seeds of memory. He'd felt this before on a number of occasions, this exact same thing, lying in the dark on a soft dusty bed. It was the usual aftermath of a fight, or after an endless trek through the wasteland between Bower's Fall and its undoubtedly more dangerous neighbor that had rendered him utterly exhausted. He also knew just lying there made him easy meat, that any spilled blood would cause all manner of things to germinate beneath him; that he had to move, he had to get up, and keep walking.

Around him the darkness began to move. He was in that in-between place, where the stray dead lurked, those who had lost their way. They couldn't hurt him, couldn't touch him. Belief. It was his only shield.

He felt the dust shift beneath him. He was sinking. It didn't seem possible though such a thin layer, but it didn't take long to realize that slowly, ever so slowly, the surface was shifting and it was beginning to swallow him.

This time he did cry out. He struggled, but all that did was kick dust into what little air he had left and instead of screaming in terror he ended up nearly coughing up a lung while a small congregation of ghosts had gathered to watch. Black hadn't been kidding about the other victims. He wouldn't last too long in the trunk, not like this. And so he worked hard and he calmed himself and it took a while but in the end he began to draw breath, slow and even, and he thought of the Fall. There was no other choice.

The dust shifted further. It was attracting him, pulling him in, part of him willing. His legs were already buried. Not long now and he would sink completely and be gone. "I'm sorry, little brother," he said, before his head finally disappeared beneath the folding layer, and he tried not to think of his failure to protect Luke, and tried desperately to forget what Llennendhrad had said, about Rachel, his mother, and how she'd stood by and let his father so mercilessly beat him.

CHAPTER 19

LUKE

He shook his phone. "I don't know Emma, I thought it was on charge." She held out her hand and he gave it to her. "I'm sorry," he added. "So, how did it go?"

"They don't think it's septicemia, I'm not running a fever and my heart rate is normal. But they took some blood." She plugged his phone into the charger. "And they gave me antibiotics just in case. It cost me two hundred and fifty bucks and I have to call in about the blood test next week."

He nodded. "You told them I don't use lead based paint?"

"It was the first thing they asked, as soon as I mentioned paint." She let out a sigh. "Other than that, they have no clue what it is. They suggested it might be like henna, and simply wear off. Or, if it doesn't they gave me the number for a dermatologist."

"Wow." He raked fingers through his hair, and although he didn't say as much he felt relieved and somewhat vindicated. Because he always cleaned his hands, cleaned them thoroughly, and there was no way –

His re-energized phone began to beep and he picked it up. An old text message. "It's from John," he said. "He wants to know where we are."

"Oh." She turned toward their bedroom.

He grinned at her poor attempt at hiding her disapproval

and he keyed in a return message. "We're right here, bro'" he muttered.

It was early evening, just before dinner. Once he'd hit send he bounded after her, began a playful wrestle, picked her up and tossed her on the bed. He climbed on top until he was hovering over her. "Let me see," he begged.

"Luke, I don't—"

"Please? Pretty, pretty please with a cherry— ow."

She'd slapped him gently across the chin, and followed it up with a sigh of exasperation. "Just the one on my shoulder." She started to unbutton her blouse while he hung there curious, impatient. Until she pulled the fabric away and he reached forward, gently slid down the strap of her bra, and stared.

She was right, the stain was getting bigger, even he could tell the difference from this morning. He leaned forward and gently kissed the discolored flesh. "It's beautiful." To his eye it looked like an abstract rendition of leaves and flowers, and he said so.

"You *would* say that." She was still worried, despite the trip to the doctor. He could see it in her eyes, feel it in her tensed shoulders.

He gathered her up, kissed her gently. "It'll disappear, you'll see."

"I hope so, otherwise you're going to end up with one weird looking girlfriend."

"Well, I wouldn't mind—"

A car door slammed shut, out in the courtyard. Elliot, he presumed. He sat up. "Guess it's time for dinner, huh?"

She pushed him away. "Let me change my shirt."

Dinner was soup, beef bourguignon, and ice cream for dessert. Luke was hungry; he felt charged, ravenous, and he ended up eating half of Emma's meal when she pushed her plate aside. Conversation revolved around his latest subject and he told everyone how far he'd got with the hippocampus. What he failed to mention was that he'd also finished Emma's acrylic portrait and was about to begin another one and both canvas and carousel creature hung there in his mind's eye, waiting. They were the reason he was sitting on the edge of his seat, that he was so hungry, that his speech came out staccato and urgent. He wanted, needed, to get started.

"You mind?" he whispered to Emma, holding her hand under the table at the end of the meal. "Just for a few hours?"

She shook her head. "I need to catch up, make some notes."

"Still reading about Edward Longshanks?" Elliot asked.

"Yes, and Welsh longbowmen."

"Ah, the Gatling gun of the middle ages. You could write a book on that subject alone."

Luke glanced across at Grace, who smiled and began to gather the plates. He stood up, gave her a hand, and helped her load the dishwasher. And following a quick glance at the table, where Emma and his employer were still engaged in conversation, he took his cue and left.

Outside, dusk hung heavy in the yard. It was unusually quiet; the expected cacophony of insects was non-existent as if, at that particular moment they'd all chosen to hold their breath. As he reached his workshop door he paused. He thought he'd spied movement over by the carriage house, but when he focused on that particular direction he saw nothing. He took a step, then another, back out into the yard. "John?" he whispered. He had no idea why he'd called his brother's name. There was no one there as far as he could tell.

He pulled his phone out of his pocket and pulled it off stand by. No messages, no voicemail. He keyed his brother's number, no particular reason other than a peculiar moment of anxiety. Was he in trouble? It was impossible to tell. Luke had no idea what his brother did, and that was the way John seemed to like it. Luke suspected some kind of criminal activity. As if one day he'd receive a call and it would be from jail, or prison, or worse...

His own call went straight to voicemail. He left a short message— wondering if you got my text, give me a call then he put the phone back in his pocket, entered the workshop and switched on the lights. A few moments staring at the primed hippocampus and John was forgotten.

The evening was warm and so he pulled off his shirt. He studied the notes on his sketchbook and after a minute or so he broke into a smile and got to work on the base coat. Each brush stroke brought him closer to the elaborate carving and caused him to marvel at the subtle shift between horse and fish.

The front legs were reared up, the head tossed, pointing up at an angle of almost forty-five degrees. The transformation had already begun at the mane, where the carver had cleverly intermingled bundles of kelp within strands of hair. Lower down, alongside the shoulders were a pair of elegant veined fins, and once again the saddle incorporated wide strands of seaweed that gradually overlaid the falling tail at the rear. And at the base, the tailfins curled and flared dramatically.

There was no other tack carved on this particular creature, no bridle. You took your chances, he supposed. Ride if you dare. Every once in a while he came across circular indentations in the wood— some of them in amongst the seaweed in the mane, others on the saddle and on the breast of the creature. There was a box on the workbench containing a set of cut glass jewels. He'd need to go through them afterwards, maybe replace some of them. Perhaps Emma could help him choose some crystals in variants of black, green and silver.

Thoughts of Emma made his eyes shift temporarily toward the stack of canvasses in the corner. He already had the basis for his next portrait very clearly worked out in his head. But as his brush caressed and followed the curves on the creature the mental image shifted, evolved, until his beautiful Emma had become a mythical figure; fearsome, her hair floating around her as if alive, her skin partially covered in a swirl of dark green and black; kelp, or fish scales, it would come to him sooner or later.

An hour into his work and everything else lay discarded and forgotten. He was completely immersed in the task in front of him and as the minutes continued to tick by he was neither aware of, nor concerned about, the time. At some point he realized Grace had entered and left, but he had no idea why until much later when he walked up to the bench and saw a can of Budweiser and a sandwich alongside his sketchbook.

The beer was beginning to feel warm, despite its sides still slippery with condensation. He checked his wristwatch and saw that it was nearly a half hour past midnight. He cracked the can, drank nearly half of it in one slug, and took a bite out of the sandwich. Then he had a peek outside. There was a light on in one of the rooms upstairs in the main house, but the guesthouse was in total darkness.

That brought a smile to his face.

Back inside, he finished off both sandwich and beer, then tidied away his paint and equipment surrounding the seahorse. When it was done, he walked to the corner, picked up a fresh canvas and placed it on the nearby easel. The dead of night, everyone was asleep, and it was time to begin anew.

He was alone.

The bedroom curtains were closed, and light poured in at their edges, bright enough to suggest it was pretty late in the day. He couldn't remember what time he'd finally got to bed in the night, his only clue that it was still dark outside, and when he'd crept into their bedroom he'd discovered Emma talking in her sleep and she had been talking about John.

He sat up, scraped his hair away from his forehead, swung his legs over the side of the bed and staggered to the bathroom. His face looked gray in the mirror, a landscape of stubble and exhaustion. Even his eyes appeared more the color of gray than their usual dark brown; he looked like he'd been dead for a week and then dug up and only partially reanimated.

He did what he had to do, cleaned himself up as much as he was able, pulled on some clothes and then went in search of his girlfriend. He tried to remember what she had been murmuring about in the night, but apart from an uneasy feeling, partly borne of jealousy, he discovered he couldn't remember much at all.

She wasn't in the kitchen, and there was no sign of Grace, but there was coffee in the pot, and so he poured himself a cup and continued his search, finding her eventually in the pool house. Her laptop was closed, there was a pile of books on the small table next to the recliner, her towel was in a heap at the pool's edge, and for a moment he couldn't see her, until she burst from beneath the surface of the water and gave him a start.

"Holy shit, Em."

He watched her climb out, a smooth, athletic motion. She walked up to him dripping wet and planted a kiss on his lips. "Did I scare you?" She smelled faintly of chlorine. And he discovered his reply, his exhaustion, and his brewing resentment over her dreaming about his brother disappeared when he caught sight of the patch of stained flesh on her shoulder.

It had shifted slightly, elongated; what had begun as a dirty gray smudge that barely intimated the shape of foliage, it had now grown into a much bolder suggestion of such. It was like a branch, partially covered by a tumble of wide, flat leaves, and it trailed from the shoulder joint, partially hidden by her swimsuit and was now beginning to climb up and over her shoulder. He stared at it. He couldn't help it.

"Hey," she whispered.

"I'm sorry, I just—" He broke into a smile and dropped to his knees. His eyes roamed over her right hip, where a similar stain flowed from the groin. That one had grown slightly too, and appeared to be making a slow, resolute journey toward her ass. He brushed the tainted skin with his fingers.

"Luke. Stop that." She pulled away. "You're starting to creep me out."

He stood up. "I'm sorry. Does it hurt?"

"Nope." She turned around so he could see the remaining discoloration at the rear of her left ankle. "I think this one has grown, too."

He nodded. "It looks like a delicate tattoo. They all do."

Emma picked up her towel and began to dry herself. "Sure you're not working on me in the dead of night with a needle?"

"No ma'am. Here, let me do that." He took the towel and continued to soak up the moisture on her skin. Did he dare tell her he found the markings a turn on? He guessed not. She was obviously worried over them despite her attempts to remain nonchalant and he figured his best course was to try and sympathize. "Maybe they're developing while you sleep," he offered. "Just... moving around while you're lying there. Like a bruise."

She looked down at the one splayed across her shoulder and shrugged. "I just want it to disappear." She gave him a look. She wasn't worried. She was afraid. And right there he didn't know what else to say. "What time did you come in last night?" She was changing the subject.

"I'm not sure. But you were asleep." It came to him then, that tiny drop of bitterness, like bile in the back of his throat. "You were talking, too."

Emma looked genuinely surprised. "Really?" She grinned. "What did I say?"

It was about John.

"I don't know," he lied. "I couldn't make it out."

"Well, I don't remember anything, I was out cold." She grabbed the towel. "I'm going to get changed."

He watched her go. Was she lying? He felt his earlier sympathy slipping through his fingers. What if there was another reason for John paying them a visit? What if— he shook his head in disgust, and turned to see Elliot Black in the doorway, leaning on the doorframe, hands in his pockets and giving him a very strange look.

"Everything okay, Luke?" He stepped into the room. He was wearing his usual dark gray business suit, pale gray hair combed back as immaculately as always, an eerie contrast to the smooth skin on his face.

"I'm not sure," he answered. "Emma..."

"I don't want you to worry about Emma," Black said.

"But—"

"She's fine, Luke." The voice was soft, conversational. "Look at me."

He did. He stared the man right in the eye, and for a moment he felt confused. There were questions he wanted to ask, but right now... "Do you want to see what I've done so far on the hippocampus?"

Black's face broke into a beatific smile. "I'd very much like to see that."

There. Back to work. Whatever was troubling him a moment ago slipped off his shoulders like a silk lined jacket, and truth be known he couldn't remember what was sticking in his craw anyway. And so he led Black outside, across the yard, and into the workshop, and soon they were both staring at the carousel animal.

"Careful, paint's still a little tacky, but I'm going to start overlaying scales," he pointed, "about here."

"What about the jewels?"

Luke frowned. "I want to switch some of them out. To get the colors right. Might cost some, though."

"I've no objection. Let me know what you need. Now, about the other piece you're working on."

Luke stared at him. There was a moment of covetousness, of resentment. But then it became perfectly okay to show the guy his portrait of Emma. He walked over to the far corner of the room, carefully pulled out the still wet canvas he'd hidden and placed it reverently on its easel. There wasn't all that much to see regarding his subject, her position on the canvas was to one side of the foreground, her features currently non-existent.

"Ah," Black whispered. "The colors..."

"It's mostly the underpainting, but some elements will show through to one degree or another."

"I understand. But I know where this is. Do you?"

"Are you talking about the background?" He frowned, puzzled. "It's— just a background."

"Is it?" The other man smiled, his eyes still regarding a sky the color of a deep bruise. "That's the horizon, am I correct?" He pointed, and Luke nodded. "That— color distribution, it's always the same, it never changes, and you've already captured it. And this..."

"Sounds like you've already been there." He meant to sound sarcastic, but it didn't come out that way at all.

The other man laughed softly. "Which is impossible, because it's a fiction; entirely crafted by your imagination."

"What are you trying to say?"

Black stared at him. "Oh, nothing. But I'd like you to continue. I'm intrigued."

He nodded, still a little confounded that he was involved in such an even, mild-tempered discussion on the subject; that he might need *permission*, or approval to continue. He wanted to say something about that, because up until now he considered himself on even ground with the guy, despite that fact that Elliot was paying the bills. Whereas now— he almost looked down, just to make sure he wasn't on his knees.

"As for the horses," Black continued, "I think we're making good progress, but I'm wondering if we can move a little faster."

He considered it. "Unless I switch mediums it'll mean longer hours. I don't mind but Emma—"

"—will be fine. She has her studying to do and is quite content to let you do your work here unhindered."

Luke nodded, couldn't think of any more objections or obstacles. "I'll get on it," he said. And all of a sudden his world became a profoundly simple affair.

The work, the art, the carousel. Nothing else mattered.

CHAPTER 20

EMMA

It was only two days after the doctor's appointment and yet it felt weeks ago when she'd sat in a small, antiseptic room and let them poke and prod and draw blood and fill her with innocent sounding maybes. But despite the reassurance and feeling no ill effects, the stain on her skin was stubbornly refusing to wear off and continued its slow but resolute crawl.

Disquiet grew from her own ambivalence. An examination in the bathroom mirror this morning, while Luke was still asleep, had revealed slight traces of green in amongst the wisps of gray that traveled across her flesh, and her reaction had been more akin to fascination than horror. And that was the problem. Why was she not freaking out? Why wasn't she calling that dermatologist's number with shaking hands and a tremor in her voice?

Even now, twenty minutes into her run, determined at the outset to drum up a little concern, instead she was pushing it all away, letting her body relax into the rhythm, while her lungs bellowed, deep and efficient, pushing and pulling at the surrounding air.

It was a beautiful morning, she was on a different route, a narrow, tarmac ribbon bereft of gas stations that threaded its way through gently rising sweeps of pasture. She felt soaked up, a part of her surroundings, just another tiny piece in a huge, glorious collage. The effect was soporific, restful, giving her some respite from the tempest that nighttime had become.

And there, she decided, lay the root of the problem. For the shifting design on her skin had taken second fiddle to a deeper trouble, one that had haunted her dreams for the last two nights; crafty, insidious, creeping up on her until it chose to flash gaudy images of horror, of a nightmare world she had no previous knowledge of, and at the center of it

John De Grasse.

She had lied yesterday when Luke had asked, and in doing so had made matters so much worse. Subsequently her thoughts were now curdled with guilt and so it was no wonder her mysterious, rampant tattoo was low on the shopping list of concerns. Why couldn't she have said hey, I dreamed of your brother last night? Because she knew Luke was the jealous type?

Back at the mansion gate, she keyed in the number and waited for the gate to swing open, and became agitated when the mechanism didn't immediately engage. She checked her watch; she'd been out longer than she thought, certainly more than an hour, and looking down she saw her T-shirt was dark with sweat. She could taste salt on her lips and she felt hungry, although the thought of eating abruptly led her back to an image of her nightmares of sweet honey and bees dancing from bloom to bloom, and amidst a beautiful tumble of flowers, the tiny figure of John, lashed to the vine. Help me, he'd said.

"Stop that," she muttered aloud. "Just leave me alone."

Once inside the gate she lowered her head like a bull, and was about to set off with dogged determination when she saw movement off to her right. She didn't want to look. To her right was the carriage house and she didn't want to look in that direction because —

"Emma."

It sounded like a whisper but it must have been so much more than that; he must have called it out loud, otherwise how could she have heard it? She turned and saw Elliot standing by the side door of the carriage house. He was jacketless, he had his shirtsleeves rolled up and he was smiling at her. And now he was beckoning. But that was okay. She had an excuse all ready, poised on the tip of her tongue; it had its roots in honesty, too. Tired, hungry, thirsty, she looked a mess, give me half an hour? There was no need to mention her current state of mind, nor the sudden feeling of revulsion that had arrived snapping at its heels.

But the words never came. Instead she approached him and became astonished at her own compliance, at how she simply let him take her hand and lead her inside, out of the sunlight, into that big, malevolent room where Luke's carousel would eventually take shape. It took a few more steps before she summoned the will, discovered some backbone and began to pull away. "I can't," she began.

"Shh." He smiled and talked as if she was a frightened foal. "Don't be afraid." He held firm, began to draw her toward the staircase that led down to the lower level. It looked dark there, a deep hole that led to some terrible place she would never, ever escape from.

And yet— she followed him. Down one step, and then another. And there was light, she discovered, once they'd reached the bottom. It was coming from the rudely installed electric lamps that lined the walls, enabling her to see the silhouette of columns, and the rotunda and thick pole at the center. She shivered. The room was as cold as she remembered.

"There, you see?" Elliot's voice held a gentle lilt. "Nothing to be afraid of." His words counteracted the chill and offered solace.

A second or two and her eyes became adjusted. The

lights couldn't quite reach every part of the room; there were pools of shadow on the floor and areas where shade hung like rotten drapes. Another look at the complex scaffolding of the rotunda, and the hitherto sharp pattern of wood across the ceiling softened, until every length of wood had assumed the mild, organic curves of the tree it had come from; until the center pole had taken on a similar guise, becoming a thick, squat trunk, its branches stretched out, cradling what lay above.

The illusion darkened the room and made her spine shiver. It brought her alive and she began her tug of war once more. "Let me go."

Elliot's fingers curled tight about her wrist. He pulled hard, swung her into the wall and was on her in moments, pinning her there so she could barely move. His hand loomed over her mouth and clamped down like a vise. Emma pushed back as hard as she could; she drew back her lips and attempted to bite him, but eventually it became obvious she couldn't escape. In her frustration she let out a muffled snarl. So close to Luke, to Grace, to that sunny yard upstairs, she wasn't afraid of him— yet. It was the room that terrified her.

The smile had returned to his face. "Make a sound and I'll hurt him. Do you understand? I'll hurt him in ways you couldn't imagine."

She glared at him.

He pushed her harder against the wall, squeezed the breath out of her lungs. "Understand?"

Emma nodded as much as she was able, and gradually, slowly, he relinquished his grip.

"Good girl," he said. "Now, we appear to have a problem."

"What problem?" she hissed. Fear had clenched her jaw.

Elliot lifted her chin. "You're more sentient than I thought, and you appear to be getting stronger."

Sentient. She remembered; John had used that word.

"I don't know what you mean."

"Count yourself fortunate. But I need to take away your memories, Emma."

She tried to push him away. "Why?" But he was still too close, and still held her in his formidable grip.

"Shh," he said. He reached up, stroked her hair. "I'm not going to hurt you, and you're going to do this for Luke. Just relax. Don't fight me." A few moments later and Elliot had drawn her into a loose embrace, his arms draped easy about her shoulders, a deception that didn't fool her in the slightest.

"What do you want me to do?" The words floated in front of her, each one encased in a bubble of glass— ineffectual, abstract. In her peripheral vision the world was already becoming flat and pale gray.

"I want you to feel safe, and then I want you to forget everything. After all, you need to study, get ready for this next semester, remember?"

"Luke—" Her eyes were heavy-lidded and she felt dizzy.

"Luke's fine. This we already know. In fact, he needs to be left alone. That way he can work, and he'll return to you so much sooner." He gathered her up, brought her to the stairs.

She nodded, listened to the rhythm of his voice and she could feel the heat from his arms and body, so welcome in this chilly room. His words continued, flowed through her like soft ribbons of gauze that soaked up any further objection, and drew away the poison of truth, and left her with the bland logic of summer; she'd study, then go home and visit her family, and then return to college, and Luke would be fine.

The next three days were pedestrian and ordinary, captured by inertia, all outside influences kept at bay. She had stopped her morning run, and safe behind those wrought iron gates she swam in the pool instead. She read about Edward the First's war with the Scots; she ate her meals and listened to conversation; she slept, showered and cuddled up against the exhausted form of her boyfriend, who appeared like magic while she slept dreamless through the night.

And all the while the stains on her skin crept forward, cresting her shoulder, wrapping one full circuit of her ankle, tentatively advancing across the flesh of her rear.

As for John, a mild unease remained, like a scant layer of oil floating on the surface of water. It moved with her through the day, offered an occasional glimmer that made her glad he'd disappeared, that he'd simply left, like he always did.

Then, on the fourth day, just as she was heading toward the kitchen for lunch, she received a call on her cell phone. When it was over she ran the remaining distance, bursting in on Grace and Luke, startling them both. Luke looked pale, gaunt, like he'd barely slept, but now there were urgent reasons why his plight failed to register.

"It's my dad," she told them. "He's in the hospital. He's had a heart attack."

Grace immediately went in search of Elliot while Luke took her in his arms. "What do we need to do?" he asked. The "we" made her want to cry. She wasn't expecting it, the suggestion that he'd drop everything and support her.

She felt cold, confused as if everything was abruptly ripped sideways and more than anything she wanted him by her side. But when the time arrived to leave they decided it would be better if she went home alone. There was no argument; both nodded their heads like metronomes while Grace and Elliot looked on.

It was Elliot who took her to the airport. She sat in the front passenger seat of his car and he held her hand for most of the way. The contact, she welcomed wholeheartedly. It kept her calm, stopped her from imagining the worst, and it wasn't until she entered the line to go through security that her anxiety began to kick in.

"Goodbye, Emma," he told her. It sounded so final.

CHAPTER 21

JOHN

The scent pushed him toward consciousness, sickly sweet, like warm honey, tempting and seductive, and it poked and prodded and tickled his olfactory senses until his mind became flooded with the memory of Bower's Fall, registering dread, then panic, making his head jerk upward and his heart begin a rapid, punishing beat.

He couldn't breathe - his mouth was blocked. He attempted to pull back and escape but he couldn't and fear told him he was gagging, choking, and it was only after a number of terrifying seconds that common sense kicked in and told him he'd be okay, just so long as he calmed down and breathed through his nose. He'd be able to breathe. He would. He just had to slow it down, and get a grip.

That done, he had to wait a little while longer until the fog of terror cleared, enough to allow him a rough self-assessment, a broad brush reminder of his predicament. The thick, stubby little vine in his mouth was feeding and hydrating him; a slow trickle of nectar, keeping him nourished in his moment of respite. His host was being polite, exhibiting patience; letting him rest before it recalibrated its scent and got to work on him all over again. And while he fought distress and brought his breathing under control he kept his eyes clamped shut, determined for now to keep them that way, as a gut level alarm told him right now he'd be better off blind.

He could feel a slight breeze caress his flesh, hear the rustling of leaves and a faint rattling sound, and through the befuddlement of intoxication he tried to remember how long he'd been here, strung up and dangling from the boughs of a harvester.

He struggled to recall the moment of arrival, couldn't remember the chase, or any attempt to escape. There had been a moment of suffocation, of being closed in; sand and dust brushing against his skin before he was conveniently dropped into the voracious plant's clutches, way too fast and easy. There. That neat trick-box of folding sand; it had delivered him right here so there'd be no hope of escape. But then, Llennendhrad had promised him some form of retribution, hadn't he?

He became aware of his arms, outstretched, bound and aching, his wrists free, fingers able to wriggle and twitch; likewise, the vines that wrapped, chafed and held up his torso, effectively crucifying him, leaving his legs to hang loose below. How long had he been like this? Dull pain told him it had been hours at least, maybe days, and a further riff through recent memory gave him nothing but the images and sensations plucked forth from his mind by the tree and he really didn't want to dwell on those.

One thing he did know for sure. He was screwed. Dead but for the coup de grace. And on that thought his brain lingered; it became all practical and rational and wondered how long it would be before the tree considered it had taken enough of the appetizer and decided it was time to move on to the entree.

He felt it stir. It had caught on that he was truly awake, and now all the relevant appendages were beginning to rally and begin on him anew. The thing on his groin tightened a little, wrapped so languorously around his cock it began to awaken and ever so slowly it began to tighten, to stroke and pulsate. The stubby protrusion it had jammed in his mouth began to thicken, same with the one it had pushed gently but resolutely into his anus and wriggled further into his rectum. The air became heady with pheromones and other stimulants and the tree crept silently into his head, searching for whatever might help the arousal, examining every sexual thought he'd ever had, from the mundane to the downright deviant; anything and everything that would prompt him to ejaculate and let it steal away his reproductive seed.

Pleasure, pain, whatever he desired, it created the necessary props, and the thin tendril wrapped around his throat, all set and ready to partially asphyxiate, was testament to the depths it had plunged and the lengths it would go to. It overturned every rock, pulled out every beautiful, pleasurable, embarrassing, shameful thought he'd ever had. It spared him nothing. On and on and on, until it was done, until he was spent, then it let him rest— mortified and barely conscious— until it considered he was recuperated, and then it began all over again.

It played him like a harp. It had created, or recreated longings he never realized he was capable of; sick things both masochistic and sadistic; the abstract and the disjointed. It brought forth the scent of vanilla and caramel, the touch of fur and velvet; it had specifically bound him— in a manner so obviously sacrificial it brought forth a keen recollection of the pain his father had inflicted on him but better it was him and not his tiny little brother while his mother stood back and let it all happen and Mother how could you and how the fuck could he get turned on by something so cruel and twisted as that and oh, of course there was Emma. Of all the thoughts and recollections and dreams, it kept coming back to her, his brother's girlfriend whom he'd convinced himself he did not covet.

His host and tormentor begged to differ. It brought forth that day when she'd slid into the booth at the diner, so vulnerable and yet still giving him that look, the one that told him she wasn't going to break despite how much truth or bullshit he plied her way and no matter how upset she was. It was honest, it was brave, and it had stirred thoughts he should not have entertained. Truth be told, he could have pushed aside all the drinks and plates and utensils and nailed her right there on the table in front of the window.

He remembered his recent journey to California when he'd been particularly envious of Luke, and he'd let his mind wander, taken his brother's place and imagined being cocooned with her in first class - the seat reclined, the curtains fully drawn and claustrophobia be damned. He'd stared down at her, watched her eyes close and her lips part as he drove into her, again and again...

He was becoming aroused. The vines shifted their grip slightly in anticipation, their movement like snakes, smooth, sensuous and muscular. He let out a stifled moan— self-pity or a reflection of his aroused state, it was probably a result of both. Or maybe it was because of the absurdity of it all.

He was, systematically, methodically, being raped by a tree.

He started to giggle but then had to stop; with his mouth plugged it sounded wrong, too close to a sob and it constricted his breathing. He could do nothing but hang there and suffer in silence, and wait until it decided to move on to its primary crop - blood, then flesh. It would drink every drop of liquid, eviscerate him, strip him of his skin and in the end leave nothing but the bones.

And so he fought the sensory overload, figured his best bet was to stall the inevitable and give himself a few more minutes, a few more hours to wallow in regret and maybe drum up a little outrage at his current predicament. He brought to mind the man who had committed him to his doom, and now he knew the true identity of his assailant, he realized this end result had been unavoidable.

Llennendhrad.

Given a choice, the entire group of Adepts wouldn't have taken him on. As for what he was up to, out there in the world, building a carousel —

But that wasn't John's problem. His problem right now was staying alive while hanging helplessly from the boughs of a harvester as it sought to strip him of one essential half of the human reproductive miracle. Then it would drink up all his blood, slit his guts and let them splatter on the ground near the hungry roots, and that would be that. Life was over, unless he could figure a way out.

He continued to fight the bombardment of pheromones and mental imagery, knew at some point he would have to open his eyes and lay his final card, terror, on the table as a last ditch effort to hold off the inevitable. And after a few more minutes he had no other choice.

Light was never akin to the harsh glare of the sun in the Fall; it was always gentle, diffuse, easy on the eye; tints of purple, lavender and green amongst an otherwise black and gray world. So there was no need to blink, or squint, no need to raise a hand or shield his eyes, not that he could. Instead the vista before him played havoc with his sense of balance. He was way up, strung up high on the edge of Bower's Fall's voracious jungle, enabling him to see right along a narrow valley that didn't stop until it's integrity began to falter and the fractured ground revealed a red glow. Hell lay at the extent of that long march, along a valley he had traversed more than once.

A slight inclination of the head allowed him a glimpse of the ground, a gray, featureless mass far below his bound chest and closer still, the cluster of vines that resolutely tended his groin. He swallowed in revulsion, nearly choked on the protrusion in his throat. A slight shift of his head, to left and right revealed his outstretched arms, very firmly tethered to the thick, succulent boughs, and beyond them —

The gentle rattling sound of bones. Strings of them, rearranged and reconnected via small thin tendrils, they hung from the branches, artfully displayed, like necklaces, or occasionally like a giant beaded curtain that shifted gently on the breeze.

The bones were human; skulls, femurs, ribcages, and their numbers were beyond counting. He remembered what Llennendhrad had said, about that deadly trunk back at the store and how others had fared within it. And once again revulsion rippled through him. This wasn't simply a harvester. It was a tree of execution.

He risked another glance at the array of bones, noted how they had been strung with careful, meticulous precision. As if some thought had been given to the arrangement.

Use your wits.

Llennendhrad's final words.

He let out a muffled grunt. The tree had had enough of his attempts at distraction and was burrowing deeper inside him, determined to get his attention. Or maybe it was time. Maybe it was too late and this was the end and it was about to gut him from the inside.

John steeled himself, prepared for the worst.

AUTUMN

CHAPTER 22

LUKE

Luke was on his knees, leaning forward. There was a Sharpie in his left hand that moved quickly over the large sheet of paper spread out on the floor of the carousel, and after a few more notes he stood up and appraised the diagram as a whole.

"You sure she goes on the outside?" Elliot was standing nearby, his head cocked, a slight frown on his face. "She's smaller than some of the others, she belongs on an inside row."

Luke shook his head. "No, and I know the carving is on the wrong side, but she's your lead horse. Trust me." They were talking about the English jumper, the Lady. He watched the other man walk slowly around the diagram, saw him pause as if to say something and then keep silent, as if he thought better of it. Eventually –

"Very well, I'll have the men start on the fixtures. How soon can we bring the horses in?"

He frowned. "Another month. Some of the varnishes, the paint—"

Elliot waved him off. "I want to get started. Now, about the rounding boards."

Luke walked over to his laptop and stabbed a few keys. No way he wanted those animals moved. Not yet. It was too soon and they were not yet fully dry. And while he brought up thumbnails of the images he'd been working on, he thought of ways to stop Elliot from ruining the past few months' work. "Here," he said. He brought up the first image.

"For the record," Elliot said after a few moments of study, "I never expressed any particular ideas."

"Nope." Luke folded his arms then quickly unfolded them, realized he was becoming defensive. He braced himself for an argument, but instead Black had a smile on his face. "Want me to slideshow them?" he asked.

"Yes. Please do."

Another few keystrokes and they watched as the display slowly shifted between one image and the next. Dark landscapes of purple and gray, occasional tube-like plants in the foreground; in the final image depressions glowed red like magma beneath a thin crust. They'd come at him in dreams, or in moments where he stared into space, when he was tired and taking a break from the horses, as if the images were always there, behind his eyes, waiting for a weak moment.

"Well?"

Elliot was rubbing his chin, staring at the screen. He nodded. "They'll do." He turned and left, leaving Luke glowering in his wake.

He closed up his laptop and went to stand in the center of the room once more. He closed his eyes and tried to imagine what it would be like once it was all put together. He'd been doing that a lot lately, and thankfully it no longer gave him a nosebleed. He still wasn't sure why it had happened in the beginning, but in the end he put it down to vertigo; the image of him spinning, surrounded by the horses and menagerie. It always felt so damned real. He looked down at his feet, they felt rooted and seemed unwilling to move, like they belonged here. It was odd because Emma hated this room and couldn't bear to be in it, and eventually, thoughts of Emma pulled him out of his trance, enabling him to break free and head back toward his workshop.

On arrival he checked his phone for messages and email. He found nothing and wondered if he should send something. It was weird. They'd begun their enforced separation with regular calls and text messages and they'd Skyped some evenings too, but gradually, as summer shifted into autumn it had all tailed off.

He knew she was back at college and that she'd settled in, and the last time they'd talked she'd seemed distant, tired, but hadn't given him anything to suggest their relationship was at risk. After all, it wouldn't be long now and he'd be finished here and back home, and they'd both agreed that would be a good thing.

Luke had recently checked his bank account. There was a substantial sum in it, more money than he'd ever had before in his life. Enough to make plans, enough to start a future, if she wanted...

He keyed her number, and when she didn't answer and it went to voicemail he hesitated. "Hey I'm just... give me a call?" He left it at that, and hoped he would remember to plug his phone into the charger.

He looked outside. It was getting dark. The nights were closing in now and he figured he'd better go in for dinner, despite not feeling particularly hungry. In all honesty he'd lost his appetite. He'd also stopped sleeping at the guesthouse. He bathed there, took care of his laundry, but that was about it. He no longer wanted to sleep in that bed, not after she had gone, in fact he'd dragged some bedding into his workshop weeks ago and was sleeping on the floor, alongside his work. It kept him focused, stopped him from brooding, and he figured he'd be okay providing he kept the place well ventilated.

As for leaving the grounds, he hadn't done much of that either. Now John had disappeared again there didn't seem to be any reason to leave, especially when Grace kept him fed and Elliot had all his supplies brought in. And despite the inherent loneliness he found the situation, the isolation, better for his work. For it was hard to explain to others just how deep he had to dig, how it felt as if he was stripping off layers of his own skin and using it to adorn his subjects until they became connected, a part of one another. It was one step away from mixing his own spit and blood into the paint and it was the only way he could work, and the long hours, the intensity, the obliteration of all else, it was all part of the deal.

He stepped outside, and listened. The usual twilight cacophony of insects was evident, but on some evenings lately he'd imagined he could hear voices, like a distant talk show playing on a radio. Another factor of his isolation he assumed, the beginnings of madness, but he wasn't particularly concerned. This job was driving him a little nuts, sure, but it was temporary. Only a few more weeks and he'd be back in California with Emma, and that would be that.

He caught the familiar scent of Grace's cooking and set off toward the kitchen. He smiled defiantly in the dark. Whispers or no, insanity hadn't claimed him yet.

"I saw him."

Luke stared at the screen, tried hard not to scowl. "Elliot." He watched her face, looked for signs of betrayal.

"Yeah. He has a friend at college, and I saw him on the quad—" She paused, and a slight frown appeared. She didn't appear to be hiding anything. More like she was having difficulty remembering. "Anyway, he bought me lunch."

"He did, huh?" The hair on the back of his neck bristled.

"Yes. And I kept asking him about you but he wouldn't go into any detail." Her frown deepened. "He just kept saying you were fine, and— well, are you?"

He offered her a tight nod. "Sure I'm fine." Especially now, after discovering Black had been wining and dining his girlfriend. He remembered the fancy Italian restaurant and her fingers splayed across the leather upholstery of that equally fancy car.

"It's just— Luke, I'm worried about you. Your face looks so thin and—"

"I'm fine. Really."

"Screw fine. I wish everyone would stop saying that."

He stayed silent, watched her on screen struggling with her temper while he wrestled with his own. He was being unreasonable, as usual, and his jealousy was conjuring up the usual demons, one of them brandishing a huge knife and making a big show of slitting Elliot Black's miserable throat.

"I don't want us to fight," she said after the silence became too much.

"I'm sorry. I'm being a jerk," he offered.

A smile broadened her features. Finally. "I wish I was there with you."

"Me, too." The sentiment tasted bitter on his tongue and he realized just how much he missed her.

"So... how much longer?"

"Maybe another month." He began to tell her about the rounding boards, how he'd already planned it out, laid down the initial artwork, and while he talked his eyes studied her face onscreen, her chin resting on the heel of her hand, and he took in the subtle changes; the slight shadows beneath her eyes, the remnants of a frown that simply refused to go away. Her face had grown lean, too, her cheekbones a little more angular. As for her eyes, they looked war torn, like she was going through an immense struggle of a kind that went beyond the rigors of a senior year at college. And just for a moment, someone had turned on that radio again and he could hear whispers.

When they finally signed off he leaned back in his seat and stared at the ceiling. He felt uneasy, as if there was something wrong beyond the petty jealousies that nipped at his heels and despite their mutual reassurances that everything was— that word again— fine.

In the end he stood up, made a deliberate effort to check all his electronic devices were plugged in, and he left the guesthouse, his intention to work through into the early hours and then fall on his face. He crossed the lawn; it was pitch dark, approaching midnight, and the whispering had followed him. It was still incoherent, like a foreign language, and it ebbed and flowed in volume and he wondered if Grace listened to the radio at night and kept her window open.

The chatter distracted him, his resolute stride became shorter, and in the end he changed direction and headed for the barn at the far side of the courtyard. He slipped through the door, switched on the light. The smell of drying paint and varnish greeted him and he breathed deep. He'd always liked that smell. It brought calm and resonated deep. He'd lived with that smell for as long as he could remember.

Before him were his subjects, balanced upright on their own merits or sat astride trestles, some of them completely dry, others still waiting for their final coats to oxidize. Polished black eyes stared at him. A slight turn of his head and they caught the light. It appeared as if some of them were winking at him, sharing a secret joke.

He began to pick them out, one by one, his mind's eye already placing them in their rows— the Lady to the outside, the military stander right behind her; the chariot was also on the outside but on the opposite side of the circle, while the hippocampus and the ostrich were side by side on the two inner rows. Once again he began to visualize how the final carousel would look, and a smile crept to his face as he closed his eyes.

When he opened them the creatures were still there, but they had moved forward and the surrounding walls of the barn had disappeared. He felt weightless, but confident he was simply caught up in his own creation, and he kept his eyes open, and let it roll.

The foreground was featureless, a mist that would swallow him if he chose to allow it. "Show me," he whispered, a little disappointed that his surroundings were so coy. He had to repeat the command before they crept forth. And when they did— "Don't be afraid." This was his dream, within the boundaries of his control, so when the ethereal, barely visible figures stepped closer, it was with a polite deference and hesitation.

One of them— a young man in torn, bloody clothes, his ruined face gained color, took on depth and dimension. "That's enough," Luke told him. There were others pressing in, eager to be a part of what he was creating. They drifted about him in a vague circle, and after a moment or two he began to connect each of them to a particular carousel animal. There was a resonance between them, a familiarity.

He returned to the boy— he was dead, Luke realized. They were all dead. They were ghosts, all belonging to the carousel. And yet, behind them were others, faint ciphers of humanity, here to witness. It made quite a composition and he hoped he could remember enough to lay it on canvas.

He felt the back of his neck prickle, and his eyes swept toward the Lady. The overhead light flattened her contours; she looked distinctly wooden, a carved animal provided solely for amusement. In this guise she was utterly silent.

Instead the specters had become three-dimensional. He began to see the frayed edges of collars, a string of pearls, the suppuration on the boy's wounds. He felt pressure behind his eyes, a mild sinus pain, while the image in front of him displayed willful reluctance to assume the correct depth of field.

One or two faces bore a slight twist of malevolence and the whispering grew louder. The carousel and its dark world now lay beyond them and the ghosts became a barrier. But that wasn't part of his vision, and so he refuted it.

He stared, faced them off. It took a moment but they began to recede and he let out a triumphant laugh. "You're mine," he hissed. Artist, puppet master, creator, this was one hell of a trip because he felt like God right now. He focused on the carousel, saw them restored while foreground became background and continued to fade. He licked his lips, tasted salt and iron. He brought his fingers up to his nostrils, and when he brought them away they were bright red. On the floor at his feet were a few drops of blood and yet more had stained his shirt.

He stiffened.

Someone was directly behind him. And now he couldn't move.

A hand locked into his hair and pulled. Luke would have fallen were he not braced against the shoulder of another. In his peripheral vision, two long, narrow points hovered close to his left eye. This was no vision. They were real, like needles, and cruelly sharp.

"You fool," Black hissed. "Had you been unable to control them, I would have had to kill you."

"Wait—" Luke struggled physically, fought mentally while blood still flowed. But it was useless, and raw fear clawed at his insides. "I don't understand," he gasped. He was disoriented, still coming out of his vision.

The sharp points disappeared.

And another object, blunt and just as real, slammed hard into his temple.

CHAPTER 23

EMMA

Life was a narrow path, her footsteps attuned to a hypnotic, metronomic beat. The future stretched ahead, mapped out, indelible, while her past folded behind her, obscured by a cloak of bland self-assurance. College was everything she had expected it to be, and having prepared over the summer, her studying was going well. Her father was also recovering, on a path that seemed much in tempo with her own while other aspects of her life followed suit. She ran circuits around campus every weekday morning; she went to the gym three times a week. She ate three meals a day, watched her favorite TV shows, called home once a week and met up with her girlfriends for lunch most Saturdays.

The only time the beat skipped was when she talked to Luke. Their conversations were fitful, awkward; they steered around subjects they'd never been leery of before as if they both had something to hide, and when they were done she was left with a terrible sense of wrong that upset her and pulled her sideways, away from her routine and off into sleepless nights and forgetfulness.

Thankfully, restoration arrived periodically in the form of Elliot Black. She spotted him occasionally on campus, always on his way to some meeting or other, and he always made time for her and gave her enough by way of reassurances. Luke was fine, he missed her, and it wouldn't be long now before he was back home and —

She looked up from the book she was pretending to read. Having attempted the same paragraph a dozen times she'd given up but had kept her head down while she sought out the latest source of her misery. And finally she had traced it down to a thin vein of anxiety that ran through every thought and every action since her conversation with Luke the night before. Something was wrong, his face was so lean and full of shadow. He wasn't eating, or sleeping. And what did that mean?

She stared out of the window of the library, frustrated at her lack of memory, of reasoning. She wanted to get angry and hurl her book across the floor, and she toyed with the idea, that maybe the act of throwing a tantrum right now would unblock the fog. Instead she placed the book in her bag, collected her jacket and left.

Outside the wind whipped at her hair and fallen leaves skittered in unruly streamers across the concrete and it became imperative to get back to the warmth and calm of her living room. And on the final approach to her apartment she stepped by a couple engaging in loud, animated conversation and passed a woman walking along the path aided by the use of a stick. Emma heard the resolute thud as the stick came down on the path and she quickened her pace, sympathetic to the woman's plight, and relieved she didn't shoulder a similar burden.

It was dark by the time she climbed the steps and opened her door, and once on the other side of it and out of the wind she let out a long sigh of relief. She flicked on the light, caught sight of her bedroom door and immediately she thought of Luke. Her gut twisted and abruptly she wanted to cry. She was missing him, so bad it felt as though someone had cut him out of her and the wound still bled.

She dropped her bag, paused for a moment as she heard a sound, until she identified it as the clunky elevator at the end of the block. Shaking her head and berating herself, she walked into the kitchen and switched on the coffee maker. And in the midst of staring into the freezer and trying to decide what to put in the microwave, there was a knock on the door.

Emma rolled her eyes. She'd already turned away a young man peddling magazine subscriptions this very morning, and while she headed back into the hallway she wondered what it might be this time. No way was she opening the door.

The knocking began again, loud, staccato— more like a hammer than a set of knuckles and she slowed her pace, became wary. She checked the door; the dead bolt was on, so was the safety chain, and so she tiptoed forward and looked through the peephole.

There was a woman standing there, leaning on a stick that, going off the noise, she had just used to rap against the door.

Emma frowned. "Yes?" She'd lowered her voice, attempted to sound authoritative.

"Emma? I need to speak with you." The voice came through the door, muffled, not entirely unpleasant.

She took another peek through the hole, remembered passing by a slender woman with a stick on her way home. Was this the same person? How did she know her name? "How can I help you?" She stood back a little, folded her arms.

"Please. It's about Luke."

Luke— a magic word that brushed aside her fears, awakened her curiosity and longing, and enabled her to slide back both the safety catch and the dead bolt and open the door. She stared at the other woman, young, maybe her age, her hair swept into a silk headscarf, her narrow frame wrapped in an overly large raincoat. And she was holding a pistol. It was pointed directly at Emma's stomach.

"I can shoot you faster than you can slam the door. Now, let me in."

Emma's mouth fell open. "You said this was about Luke." Her voice sounded muffled, far away; her eyes were mesmerized, locked onto the weapon.

"Yes. Now let me in. My leg is getting tired."

Her brain began to spin, parsing questions and answers, about Luke, about her own safety. If there was something wrong she wanted to know about it, the woman didn't look like a thief, or a rapist, but by the time she'd figured that she might well look like a killer she was over the threshold and the door was closed.

"Kitchen," the woman said. "Where I can see you," and motioned with the weapon.

Emma did as she was told. Meanwhile her brain had kicked into another gear. This woman had a physical disability. Could she take her? Maybe. She walked into the kitchen and looked for an opportunity.

"Stand over there."

She backed away, until she felt the edge of the cooker digging into the base of her spine. There was a knife block on the kitchen counter to her left. She wondered if she'd be able to reach it in time.

"Where's John?" The woman had cocked her head. Her voice had shifted, had become tight and angry.

"John?" Immediately she was confused.

"Yes. Where is he? When was the last time you saw him?"

"I don't—" She looked at the gun. Luke's brother. It had been weeks, months—

"Speak up."

"July," she spluttered. "I think that was the last time." Was it truth or lie? She couldn't remember. "Look, I'm sorry. I don't remember, and you said this was about Luke."

"I lied. And you'd better start remembering, pretty damned quick."

Emma narrowed her eyes. The fog was beginning to clear, blown aside by a growing anger. "Who the hell are you?"

"A friend of John's. One who happens to care very much that he's gone missing, so you'd better start talking."

"Missing? I don't—" She struggled to grasp threads of memory. A conversation. She seemed to remember a little of it. "I think I had lunch..."

The other woman hooked her stick on a drawer handle, reached into her pocket and brought out a small, brown glass bottle. She placed it on the counter between them. "Drink it."

"No way. What is it?"

"Drink it or I'll fucking shoot you." The voice carried a bitter fury. It was resolute, all too willing to carry out the threat.

Emma discovered her hands were trembling when she reached for the bottle. Her fingers grasped while she kept her eyes on her assailant. The tiny container felt cool and smooth to the touch. "I'm not drinking it until you tell me what it is."

The woman's mouth twisted. "Let's call it a nice, sharp dose of the truth. It'll make you see, make you remember."

"What, like a truth serum?"

"No. I think you've been hypnotized. It'll clear your head. Now, do it. I'm losing patience."

"I don't know what the f—"

"Drink it!"

The truth. Emma unscrewed the cap. "Fuck you," she said, and opened her mouth and swallowed the entire contents. She slammed the bottle hard on the counter like she'd just downed a tequila shot, and stared defiantly at the woman while her tongue and the back of her throat told her it tasted a little like aniseed, or maybe —

She convulsed, and bent double. She had no control

whatsoever. "Gonna puke," she grunted. And regardless of the gun, she swept past the woman and ran for the bathroom. She only just made it. And spent the next half hour on her knees, head poised over the toilet bowl, puking, sobbing, and puking some more.

The other woman was alongside her, offering encouragement, gripping her hair so it wouldn't be covered in vomit, and in between convulsions Emma heard her voice—"You're going to be okay," over and over.

By the time it was done the two women were both sitting on the bathroom floor facing one another. There was no sign of the gun. Maybe it had been left back on the kitchen counter. She stared across at her companion, saw that one of the woman's legs was distinctly crooked, and the set of her shoulders were unsymmetrical.

"What the hell did you just give me?"

The woman shrugged. "Poison. Let's leave it at that."

Emma wiped her hand across her mouth. Her throat felt raw, full of broken glass. "Are you going to tell me who you are?"

The woman smiled. She had an attractive face now it wasn't so intent on murder. "I'm Rhonda. I'd like to think I'm John's best friend, but being honest, and John being John, I couldn't tell for sure."

Emma raked her fingers through her hair. "He's in trouble. Same as Luke." She felt disoriented. A veil had been lifted and all the color and detail were pouring in.

"Yes. Any idea who did this to you?"

She barked out a laugh. "As a matter of fact, I do." She told Rhonda about all those reassuring conversations in the campus cafeteria with a certain Dr. Elliot Black.

"The antique dealer." Rhonda frowned. "John told me about him. But he said he was more concerned about you."

"What?" Emma stared at her.

The other woman shrugged. "I thought you might have

done him some harm, until I got a closer look at you. John told me you were sentient."

"Ha. I saw a ghost a couple of times." It sounded stupid and trite but she remembered. And that thin streak of anxiety she'd been carrying for months was now opening up, becoming a wide, treacherous delta that ran deep. As a defense mechanism she imagined herself wading against the current.

"Mind telling me how long you've had that?" Rhonda was pointing at her shoulder.

Emma looked down. Her shirt was gaping at the neck, revealing the gray and green trail, like a vine wandering idly across her sternum. She slipped her fingers inside her shirt in an unconscious effort to cover it up. "Since the summer." She smiled bitterly. "It doesn't hurt, but it keeps on growing."

"John and Luke's mother has something like it, too."

"Whoa, wait a second." She frowned, puzzled. Her scalp began to prickle. "Luke told me his mother was dead."

Rhonda shrugged and didn't elaborate.

The ensuing silence made her dizzy. "Look. I can't just sit here. Luke is in trouble and I need to get him the hell out of there." She shifted, and stood up nice and slow.

"Help me up?" Rhonda asked.

Emma did so; the woman felt gangly and weightless and for a moment they stood close, face to face. "Still going to shoot me?" This was a good time for assurances she decided, while she was in a good enough position to ram the woman's head down the toilet and drown her if need be.

"I'm sorry about that. Like I said, I had to be sure. But John comes first."

She made sure the girl could stand unaided before she let her go, and shook her head. "Last time I looked, John could take care of himself and we didn't exactly get along."

Rhonda laughed. “I know. He told me. And normally I would agree with you. But there’s a lot you don’t know.”

Emma stared at her. She was still wading, holding her own against the current, but it was getting stronger all the time. “Okay, here’s the deal. Don’t ask me to simply trust you. That won’t work with me. You start talking , I’ll listen. You explain everything. In the meantime—”

“I have a car outside. How soon can you be ready?”

“Give me fifteen minutes.”

She’d already called Luke twice and left an equal number of messages before Rhonda had asked her to stop lest they raise any unwanted suspicions, and worrying over the lack of communication had worn her down to the bone.

Rhonda had the vehicle adapted very well for her needs and had insisted on driving, and as they passed by endless, flat expanses of farmland they continued to exchange information, and in the end Emma didn’t know what to think, or whom to believe —

That Luke might have some kind of latent *gift*. That his elder brother was, like Rhonda, part of a group that had similar ‘talents’; that the world was fragile, had a propensity to split apart and occasionally allow the outside in, or the inside out, depending on your point of view, and that others with dire motives would do anything to make that happen. To hear Rhonda tell it there was some kind of war going on - good and evil, God versus the Devil, humans versus the grays - it was simplistic and ridiculous and yet —

More astonishing was the revelation that Luke’s mother was alive. A mother who hid purposefully from her child seemed inconceivable. And Emma had thought John was dysfunctional. It was all too much. Better to push it all away and concentrate on the figure of Elliot Black who, by some skillful sleight of hand had managed to trick her into forgetting anything strange had happened during her visit. There was a reckoning, a confrontation waiting between them, and this time she was determined she wouldn't be so easily deflected.

As for John, she had no idea what had happened to him. All she remembered was a rather odd, intense conversation between them; he'd been there when the ghost had appeared and seemed determined to help her. Right up until they'd arrived at the mansion.

Flat land was giving way to rolling hills and the sunlight was rapidly fading. "What if— what if Elliot did the same thing to John?" She was thinking aloud, and it took a moment for the other woman to catch on.

"Hypnotize him?" Rhonda flicked on the indicator and turned off the main highway at the junction with the gas station. It looked different in twilight, the canopy lit up, all shiny and inviting. "John knows to watch out for that and he's been trained to resist it. Black would have to be very strong, very persuasive."

Emma's lips twisted at the subtext, the suggestion of her being weak willed by comparison. She shrugged, covered up her annoyance. Her rancor was probably aimed more at John, anyway. And perhaps he wasn't as strong as Rhonda believed.

The car took the bends, the headlights giving Emma a good view of her former jogging route and eventually they arrived on Main Street. The lights in some of the stores were still on, and the local cafes and restaurants seemed busy.

"You said he had a store in town."

"Yes." She pointed. "That one, although it looks like it's closed."

Rhonda smiled and pulled into the side of the road. "Good. Let's take a look, shall we?"

They got out of the car and Rhonda hobbled immediately toward the shop doorway and stared beyond the closed sign into the dark interior. "No one inside," she whispered.

Emma was about to persuade her that night was closing in and they should try contacting Luke again when she saw the other woman reach forward and turn the door handle. There was an odd click, more like a crack, as if the wood had split apart, and the door swung open. Rhonda turned and winked, then stepped inside.

Emma followed, open mouthed, making sure to close the door carefully behind them. "How the—" Rhonda motioned for silence.

They began to move through the store toward the rear. Emma remembered her tour, the tables and chairs and the Tiffany lamps. Her heart was beginning to race, she was sure they'd be caught at any moment and that Elliot Black would appear. Instead it was the carved figure of Mr. Punch that made her gasp in surprise. He appeared in the gloom much sooner than she expected, his odd, staring eyes taking in every move. But Rhonda was beyond it, her stick tapping lightly on the polished wood floor, eventually coming to a halt in front of a pile of old trunks.

"This one."

Emma frowned, looked at the trunk at the bottom of the stack. It seemed familiar, and it was big— big enough to hold a body if you folded up the limbs. "You don't think—"

"We need to get it inside the car."

"You want us to steal it?"

"Think you can manage if I open the doors and bring the car around?" Rhonda didn't wait for an answer and stepped toward the back door. Emma remembered it led into the yard where she'd seen those men working on the carousel animals, and saw it open, too, just as easy as the other.

She let out a mild curse and tested the weight of a trunk that lay on top of the stack. It was empty and proved easy to move. The second one was a little heavier, but she managed to pull and push until it rested alongside the others, then she reached for the big trunk, simply to test its weight.

There were sounds coming from the yard, the outer gate opening. Her fingers touched the handle— and recoiled. She let out a gasp, remembered stumbling, not far from this very spot; she'd gotten dizzy. Oh, yeah. Something else Elliot Black had made her forget. "What's in there?" she'd asked. Images shifted in her memory, old and new, tying her stomach in knots and she stared, leery, like the trunk would snap open and swallow her up. The marks on her skin began to tingle and ache.

She heard the car out back. She shook her head and pulled off her jacket. And after wrapping the garment around the handle she began to drag it outside.

Rhonda had opened the trunk. "Quickly."

"I can barely touch it."

The woman grinned. "So, there is some life in you after all."

"What's inside?" It didn't feel all that heavy, in fact she was guessing it was empty, which made her question sound stupid.

"Not sure. Come on. In the trunk. I'd help, but—"

"Right." Emma hoped the look she gave her companion registered the correct amount of reproach as she began to haul the trunk into the rear of the car. It was too big to fit, and they ended up driving down the street with the object half protruding out of the back.

Rhonda headed out of town. "I called reinforcements," she announced, and when Emma had given her a withering stare, "Charlene is a good friend of John."

"Is she a good friend of Luke?"

Rhonda's fingers rapped along the rim of the steering wheel. "Look. You need to know things. If Luke is in as much trouble as you say, you'll need all the help you can get."

"Yes, but what kind of help—" She stopped. Rhonda was pulling into the side of the road just before the gas station. There was another vehicle already parked, and as they drew to a halt, the driver got out and approached. Emma saw a woman, middle aged, with shoulder length wavy hair, dressed in pale slacks and a floral T-shirt. The woman didn't stop. Instead she headed straight to the back of their vehicle and by the time Emma got out she was standing and staring at the trunk, her fingers trailing along one of its edges.

"This what I think it is?" The accent was a gentle southern drawl.

Emma stared, her temper on the rise. Rhonda was still struggling to get out of the car.

"My manners," the woman continued. She held out her hand. "I'm Charlene. I'm guessing you're Luke's girlfriend? Emma?" And after they'd shaken hands. "You're pretty. He has good taste."

"Thanks." It came out petulant and dour, but she couldn't help it.

"Let's get this out of the car before it gets dark for real."

She looked around for her jacket. "I can't touch it— not directly."

"Sure you can." Charlene smiled. "You'll get used to it." She started pulling at one of the handles.

Emma chewed on her lip for a moment, and stepped forward. Breath hissed through her teeth. "It feels— weird."

"Yes. It does."

No more explanation was offered, and once again, in a bid not to feel weak and outclassed, Emma said nothing more and helped the other woman half-carry half-drag the trunk they'd stolen from Black's shop away from the road. Contact with the thing made her skin crawl, and now both sets of car headlights were extinguished she realized twilight was done for the evening, and with the exception of Rhonda's skittering flashlight it was becoming too dark for comfort.

She stood aside as both women greeted one another with a warm embrace. She felt sidelined, awkward, and she wanted to call Luke more than ever.

"Well?" Rhonda said.

"Won't know for sure till we open her up."

Emma took an involuntary step back as Charlene pulled at the buckles and threw back the lid. Her hand clamped over her mouth. "Oh God."

The women stared at her for a moment, then looked at one another as if she was behaving entirely as expected. She wanted to scream at them, but ultimately it was the open trunk that drew her attention; she was both mesmerized and repulsed.

Her perception offered her the view of a deep, dark hole, despite the layer of fine sand, or dust, lining the base. She could see beyond it, below it. Odd, too, how the sand hadn't all collected at one end of the trunk after all the pushing and pulling. It looked smooth, flat, as if someone had carefully raked the surface, and after the initial shock, curiosity got the better of her and she stepped a little closer.

"That's quite the illusion," Charlene said. "You'd need to be a true Adept to build something like that, and I'm beginning to wonder why this Doctor Black isn't already on our watch list."

Rhonda shrugged. "Think you can keep it stable? Handle the dead?"

"Honey, you're not suggesting—"

"Yes."

"And if it's a one way deal?"

"Then we find another way out."

Emma looked on as Rhonda handed Charlene the flashlight, dropped her stick, sat on the ground and started pulling off her shoes. "What's happening?" she asked.

"It'll be safer for you if you take those off," Charlene said, pointing at her sandals.

"Oh, no, I don't think so." She began to back away again, resolutely shaking her head. The sides of the trunk were becoming distorted. Gray tendrils were beginning to creep forth, extending out along the grass.

"John's in there." Rhonda pointed an accusing finger toward her. "You know he is."

She stared at the open trunk. The sand was shifting, moving, as if there was something buried beneath its surface. Her scalp prickled, and her guts writhed inside her abdomen. "I'm scared."

Both women nodded. Terror was a given, by all accounts.

"I'll go first," Rhonda said.

Small consolation. Emma bit her lip. She looked toward the thin halo of light hanging over the town in the distance. She wanted to run in that direction and never look back. She began to pull off her sandals. "Soon as we get John out of there, we go after Luke," she demanded. She stared at them, and didn't make another move until they'd acquiesced.

Her trembling fingers struggled with the buckles at her ankles. This was stupid. This was dangerous. It made absolutely no sense. And yet it did. The tattoo-like markings on her skin tingled with anticipation, in direction contrast with a brain that was trying hard to be rational and why the hell did she need to be barefoot?

But in the end it didn't matter. Rhonda was right. Dancing amidst the wonder and revulsion, just one look inside that trunk had given her John's distress, had illustrated the terrible certainty and terror he'd felt on being shut inside. He'd thought he was going to die; that he was about to be murdered, by the indomitable, indifferent figure of Elliot Black. And wherever he was right now, she and Rhonda were about to join him.

CHAPTER 24

JOHN

Use your wits.

Strings of bones, like giant necklaces; rows of skulls, a ribcage surrounded by a splay of femurs; they were just a few examples of a display both horrific and repulsive. It was nevertheless artful, and suggested an exploration of aesthetics that went beyond the hardwired basics of sustenance and had finally given him the notion that he might, by the barest skin of his teeth, get out of the plant's clutches alive. Nothing more than guesswork on his part, but considering his life was at stake he'd taken a leap of faith, assumed some manner of intelligence in the thing about to consume him, and had therefore tried to reason with it.

And while it had continued to bombard him with pheromones he had, in rare moments of clarity, fed it wave after wave of suggestion in return. He'd offered up a form of symbiosis. Repair me, cut me loose, and I'll bring you more; he had appealed to its greed, its appetite. He'd kept it up for hours, days, praying the thing was neither too stupid to understand, or too clever to see through the ruse. He'd begged and pleaded and seduced and when he'd finally realized that it was useless, when he was sobbing and at his lowest ebb, he'd become aware of his taste buds telling him that something had changed and that fat, obscene tendril forced down his throat was feeding him an entirely different cocktail.

When it finally released him he'd fallen hard onto a shallow bed of voracious, nasty, and thankfully tiny abominations that were the direct result of feeding from the offal of previous victims. They'd nipped at his flesh as he'd attempted to get his atrophied muscles to work, and blood had flowed from a hundred tiny cuts as he'd crawled out of their reach.

The initial wave of euphoria, at having escaped, had proved fleeting. Such a prolonged ordeal had left him wretched and weak, every one of his orifices had sang with pain, and he had been unable to string two coherent thoughts together after being constantly, sexually overstimulated. He'd felt like giving up, curling up, and dying right then and there. Instead he'd continued to crawl until the ground felt soft and the air brushed moisture against his naked skin and he'd realized the dusty ground he'd escaped from had given way to the jungle of Bower's Fall.

Use your wits.

He'd remembered. He'd also remembered this was familiar territory, lavender moss beneath his knees and the gentle buzz of insects. And, if he could shake off his despair and misery, and find shelter and food, it was time to entertain the notion that Llennendhrad just might have wanted him to stay alive.

Hours, days, weeks later, it was difficult to tell, he still hadn't figured a way out and despair had a stronger grip on him than ever. No one had come for him— not Doc, nor any of the others. He'd been written off and forgotten and it had become harder and harder to celebrate the fact that he was alive and fully healed.

Physically he felt damn near super human after such a long period spent in the Fall— chewing on it, drinking from it, breathing it in. But it was a mask. The truth was, he was overexposed and slowly starving to death.

He sat on a mat he'd tightly woven from strips of dark gray vegetation, the kind that wasn't about to blossom forth and attempt to consume him. Beneath it was bare, gray dust. He was far safer on the ground, where the surrounding flora were smaller and more easily controlled, as opposed to being up amongst the trees and vines where it most certainly wasn't. He couldn't be sure, especially beneath the dour hue of the clouded sky, but it seemed as if his skin had taken on a gray tint, one he sincerely hoped was an optical illusion. There was no telling what such prolonged exposure would do to him, but he harbored firm hopes that whatever it was, if he ever got back home, he'd be able to shrug it off like an old coat.

Geographically he was roughly at equal distance between Llennendhrad's harvester horror, and the ruins. He still had no clothing to call his own, but he'd long gotten over his sense of vulnerability on that score, and what he did have was weapons— spikes of various lengths, the longest of which had come in handy a few hours ago when a bulky, tubular harvester pod had come foraging, singing its merry, alluring song. He dearly hoped it hadn't come from the plant he'd lied to, preferring to think it had forgotten all about him and that it wasn't hunting him, but there was no telling for sure.

As for food and water, he'd struggled at first until he'd found a ready supply of fruit that went a long way toward satisfying both requirements. He was malnourished, but so far his teeth hadn't fallen out, and he hadn't starved to the point of extinction. And for the most part, except for regular, secretive forays into the outskirts of the city in an attempt to discover another gateway, he'd kept his head down and stayed out of trouble. Physically, he was surviving. Mentally, it was a whole different ball game.

He peered out from his little hiding place and realized he shouldn't have left it so late in the day, or night, to go hunting for food. Hunger made him weak, made him take risks, but he'd been wandering through the halls of despair, struggling with bouts of loneliness that lay hard and heavy on his shoulders, a battle that kept him fully engaged and curled up in his little woven sanctuary while he fought it out.

Not to be outdone, guilt had come a calling, too, and the real reason he'd shot that old guy in his laundry room was stabbing a hard finger of accusation and hypocrisy at his chest. With just a little of a man's sperm the plants here were able to create monsters; they were good at it, they were inventive. Better to kill whoever might land in their clutches than give them the opportunity— and yet there he'd hung, for days, weeks, contributing enthusiastically to the evolutionary cause. He considered that Hell wasn't all that far off, and was beginning to wonder if he should just set off in that direction, get there early and get it over with.

Such thoughts stayed with him and refused to leave. And so burdened, he left his tiny cocoon, the body intent on feeding even if the mind wasn't particularly interested.

He looked up. There was, he'd been told, an open sky up there somewhere, one that might, given the opportunity, inspire the diurnal and nocturnal cycles he was usually familiar with. Some of the local plants however had had other ideas and considered it was better for them if the lights were on all the time. The resulting dull lavender haze was a product of the light they exuded that, as an extra bonus, bounced gently back at them from a perpetually clouded sky. They had light, sure, but now nobody knew what time it was and whether it was day or night. Neither were there any variants in temperature that would offer any further clues. Rain, when it came, felt like a gentle, warm bath.

Of course the locals had given themselves time to adapt, whereas John hadn't. It was part of the reason why he'd built his little shelter, simply to lock out that perpetual twilight, just for a little while, until hunger, and more urgently thirst, brought him back out again.

He picked up the shoulder height spear and a spike he'd fashioned into a dagger and set off along a narrow path that led toward the ruin. There were pitcher plants along the route; he could drink there, and a little further on were squat, wide shrubs that provided fleshy fruit that either tasted like eggplant or old, sodden library books, he couldn't quite make up his mind.

A short while later, his stomach assuaged if not entirely satisfied of its cravings, he decided to venture further and continue his quest to find a gateway. An easy enough task if he'd had the perception of either Rachel or Rhonda. Alas...

Up ahead he caught sight of a wall, a pale flat plane totally at odds with its surroundings. It heralded the beginnings of the city, its shattered remains providing shelter and feeding grounds for the surrounding insects and plant life. It reminded him of some of the artificial reefs created from old sunken battleships. He'd read about those in airline magazines, and like the ships, and despite not belonging, the city was welcomed anyway and made full use of.

When he reached the wall, he stopped and looked down. The view stretched out before him was magnificent.

Back at the house, theories abounded; that Bower's Fall was complete, distinct, a legitimate ecology, separated from his own world by some inter-planer chicanery that made John's eyes glaze over whenever anyone tried to explain it. Or, alternatively, it was a dumping ground, where slivers of existence had been thrown, or had squeezed ignominiously through various cracks, and had been given no other choice but to try and coexist. It's geographically corrupt and there's too much variation he'd been told, too many evolutionary gaps.

But they were guessing, theorizing; most of those engaged in supposition hadn't set one foot in this place; neither had anyone mapped it out successfully or knew how big it was. Also, if that latter theory proved true, he reckoned life here was managing to coexist quite well, thank you very much. It was evident beneath the feet, in the air, and amongst the riotous growth— an established rhythm, a subconscious beat that signified this place was both alive and thriving.

Bower's Fall was wondrous and beautiful, and utterly deadly. It made the Amazon jungle look like a theme park and well, if that wasn't enough for some folks, Hell itself was only a few days hike away.

As for what lay in between his world and this one— no one knew why so many of the dead ended up there, trapped in that dark ribbon of nothingness. But they sometimes congregated at the gates, the breaches, hungry, scared, pleading. A few of them even managed to escape. Into his world, or the Fall, and maybe even Hell. Every destination appeared preferable to that dark gap. He'd seen it in their eyes, and they all wanted the heck out of there.

He stood for a while, looking down into the ruins. Rachel had told him once there was a gateway down there, right at the very bottom, but for a man, it was particularly hard to get to. The mere suggestion hung there like it had done for days now, a promise, a lure that would draw him down into streets and alleys choked with vines that sprouted flowers with steel trap mouths that were tended by swarms of black wasps with stingers the size of veterinary hypodermics. It was pure madness to even think about going down there, although in his current state of mind —

"The hell with it," he muttered. He hefted his short spear, checked his balance, and began to descend. His black mood hadn't lifted and right now he considered it never would. Day upon day of searching for another gate and finding nothing; he was down to skin and bone, no one was coming to rescue him and it was time to do something before he gave himself back to Llennendhrad's harvester in despair.

The first few steps were easy, until he encountered a fat shrub whose flowers lashed out toward him with narrow, hungry tongues. He lost his footing and almost pitched over a ledge; it was the spear that saved him, its point digging into the loam beneath his feet. He was off to a great start and it didn't get any better during the remaining descent.

Further down and the already poor light began to dwindle. Flowers and foliage gave way to vines like thick rope, some of them twisting about one another until they were the width of tree trunks. Shifts in his peripheral vision gave him a start and made his flesh twitch. Right now it was only in the darkest corners, in the deepest shadows that the dead lurked. As much in alien territory as he was, they'd stumbled in here through breaches in the gates, and now they clung to what they knew— buildings, civilization, however decrepit— and the dark— despite wanting to be free of it. And he wondered if the relentless, continual glow was driving them crazy, too. All the more reason to stay away from those dark corners. Unfortunately, the further he descended, the more the shadows grew.

At the very bottom, after enduring far too many

treacherous slips and scrapes, he reached a wide avenue. Building shells rose on either side, their innards rotted, their roofs torn down by exuberant foliage. He'd never got this far down before, never figured he'd be able to on his own. The thought brought a chill to his spine. He felt it crawl there like a snake, back and forth, rattling his vertebrae and bringing his bones alive, enabling them to remonstrate. One more step and you're going to kill yourself they told him. He let out a sigh, took note, and kept on going.

Ahead of him, a taller building rose out of the choking tangle. It looked like a cathedral, or maybe one of those high tech modernist towers, once again something he'd only ever seen courtesy of the ubiquitous in-flight magazine, and right now the tower appeared to be in the midst of a mighty tug of war. Vines were anchored in the ground and were crawling up the sides of the structure, their thick lengths dark and muscular; just illusion but one slight flex and they'd break the tower completely in two.

He advanced, awestruck, his maligned sense of self-preservation jumping up and down in the background, hoping there was a purpose behind the building's attraction, that it heralded the entrance to a gateway, an escape, and not his immediate doom. A little closer and he could see more detail; not bricks or concrete— the walls looked woven and knotted, a series of strands put together like lace but of a design strong enough to remain erect and a worthy opponent of the vines that covered it. The roof had gone, like every other dwelling in the city, but even like this it was beautiful and it made him wonder who might have constructed such a thing.

He heard a buzzing noise.

He ducked, wheeled, brought the spear and dagger to bear, and saw nothing. Shadows shifted as wings descended, blocking out some of the light from above and so he made a run for the nearest shelter. A vague, cluttered arch led him into the tall building's interior, and for a moment he thought it was empty inside, just a shell, like the others, until the walls came alive.

His arrival had frightened them and abruptly there were so many of them aloft they completely blocked out the light. He couldn't even see the way out. A blunt edge hit him on the shoulder, another smacked him hard in the face and he went down. He rolled, lay on his stomach and remained there, not moving despite every muscle and tendon straining at the leash, wanting to pick him up and make a run for it. The noise was deafening and left his ears ringing for long moments after it had abated and the startled, winged residents were back in their roost.

The light had returned, thin shafts from above that highlighted spots on the floor. Slowly he extended his arm and let his fingers trail across the ground in an attempt to find his weapons. Directly ahead of him, something crawled into one of the pools of light. Its face was dark with rot; gray, spoiled skin that barely covered the skull beneath it. John almost yelled out loud. He froze, but it was too late. The thing grinned and continued to haul itself toward him. And it wasn't alone. More of the dead were creeping forth, some more substantial, able to approach with a controlled level of caution, while others, like the crawler, shambled along as best they could.

Heart hammering he considered his next move. Silence was crucial, otherwise he'd disturb whatever winged creatures hung above him and right now, not knowing exactly what they were, he didn't want to risk it. He could feel the weight of them bearing down, as if they floated en masse, directly above him only inches away. It was a horrible feeling that made his skin crawl. However, despite their apparent lack of corporeality, he didn't want the advancing ghosts any closer, either. Chances were they couldn't touch him, but then again, he'd already been witness to a kinetic event when he'd been sat in the diner with his brother's girlfriend. If just one of them could push like that, things were about to get a little too exciting for comfort.

Off to his left he saw the doorway he'd so recently dashed through and he figured he was better off taking his chances outside. He found his dagger tucked close by his side, and his fingers traced the smooth length of the spear at the end of his outstretched hand. It had rolled away a little, but not so he couldn't reach it.

His head began to throb where he'd been hit, but right now that couldn't be helped. He ignored it and ever so slowly he began to rise, pushing his shoulders off the ground, into a position where he could crawl, then one leg beneath him, nice and slow.

One of the ghosts had got to within five feet of him. It was an elderly man in a gray 1940s suit; he looked fine but for the odd cant of his head. Above his collar the flesh of his throat was red raw and flapped slightly as he stepped forward. John could only imagine what had happened to him. He tried to ignore the figure and concentrated on regaining his feet.

"Careful," the man whispered.

John froze. He saw the man's eyes lift as if looking at something, but he didn't figure it out at first; he was too overwhelmed by the notion of one of these spooks actually talking to him. And if it could talk then maybe it could –

The bearing down feeling he'd experienced moments ago wasn't getting any better. His hackles were rising, the throbbing on his skull had stopped completely. Forget the pain, stupid. You're in danger.

He looked up.

She must have come down through the open interior and landed silently behind him. All his senses had been screaming at him, begging him to pay attention, but he'd been distracted by the approaching horde of ghosts.

And he'd always thought, if he ever got the chance to see a creature like this up close, that he'd be repulsed. He'd seen magnified pictures of insects, all hairy faces and giant compound eyes and pincers, but this —

She looked plastic, or ceramic, her polished face like the front end of a Boeing 737 painted iridescent blue. He'd caught a glimpse of wings as he'd made a run for it earlier, but they were tucked away now, behind three pairs of legs that had to be fifteen feet tall. His fingers curled hard and desperate around the shaft of his spear, but he couldn't kill her; couldn't touch her. Not here. Not in Bower's Fall. Not ever.

There was a moment of stillness, of silence, until she rammed a proboscis the length of a pike through his shoulder. In his current state of abject fear, he thought his body might spare him the pain. It didn't, and he let out his first desperate scream.

CHAPTER 25

LUKE

The crowd overwhelmed him.

Once he'd discovered they were real he'd lost his grip and a mass of bodies had surged forth, pushing and pulling, whispering their pleas and demands, their awful faces upturned, their eyes staring at him. He kept telling himself they were simply ghosts, that they couldn't touch him. But after a while he could feel their slender, bony, rotten fingers, sliding along his thighs, and combing through his hair. He felt their bodies pressing in, blocking out the light; he couldn't breathe and he started to panic; he struggled but he couldn't get free. His skin shivered with revulsion and he let out a scream but still they wouldn't let go. He felt the neck of his T-shirt pulling hard against his throat, felt it give and heard the fabric tear. One of them hit him hard in the chest and knocked the breath out of him. Take us. Take us with you. And in the end he had to strike a bargain, make a promise...

He grunted, spat blood out of his mouth. He felt punch drunk and disoriented while his peripheral vision offered up a crowd of hideous dead against a backdrop of purple and gray. It was all mixed in. The land of his dreams and nightmares, and his lost, hopeful, demanding herd...

"Again," Elliot told him.

"I can't." The sinus pressure was unbearable, like he'd been hit between the eyes with a hammer. Or maybe it was the after effects of the beating Elliot had given him. Now he'd finally managed to overcome Black's pervasive mental onslaught it was down to the basics— threats, promises, and the obligatory strong-arm stuff.

"You can. And you will. You must learn to separate the two. Control one, and in doing so control the other."

Luke let his head roll forward. He didn't want to swallow any more blood. Didn't want Black to hit him again and he certainly didn't want to conjure up another wall of ghosts or poke holes in the fabric of existence or any other of that impossible sounding, skin crawling crap.

He could barely move. Black had bound him tightly to the Lady. "She'll help you focus," he'd said, and in the end, foolish as ever, Luke hadn't put up much of a fight at all. And it wasn't because he was an eager participant in these repeated forays into a waking nightmare. And it wasn't because Black had threatened to harm Emma— that was a separate issue and would be duly dealt with. It was because John, his only brother, the only real family he possessed, had lied to him. That reason alone burned like coal in his gut, heating up a nice hot kettle of rage.

If just a fraction of what Luke had already seen was legitimate, and not the result of drugs, of psychosis or some other mental breakdown, and if Elliot was right and his brother was already aware of all this and what Luke was capable of...

He coughed, spat again, and watched flecks of blood land on the Lady's silver mane. "Sorry," he whispered. The nosebleeds were a problem but they were thankfully beginning to wane. Just a little blood spilled for that last attempt. He felt like he was appeasing some dark god. Maybe he was.

He shifted, tried to get comfortable. He was facing forward astride the carousel horse, Elliot's men had bolted her in her rightful place, and Luke's arms were drawn behind him, his wrists tied firmly together. Rope circled his torso several times, binding him securely to the center pole, while his ankles were looped together beneath him, in between the Lady's front and back legs. Being bound like that had left him extremely vulnerable. It meant he wasn't going anywhere despite being scared out of his wits and the arrangement had left him no choice but to deal with the crowd he'd drawn.

He could still feel their fingers, their arms, pulling at him, tearing at this shirt and trying to drag him down, and that desperate sea of faces, some of them so rotten and horrific —

But he could control it. He could. He just had to get over the fear of it. Maybe pretend it wasn't real. Like the first time in the barn. There he'd done just fine.

Black was hovering, a faint smile on his face. "One more attempt and I'll let you go back to your studio."

Luke gave him a mean look and then turned his head, and closed his eyes. It became almost too easy to slip away, to let the room disappear, and on this occasion it proved no different from the last. The dead were still there, hundreds of them, and downstairs there were more, including some tied to the vertical poles within the circle of the carousel.

They'd come here, young and old, drawn by an antique wooden construction designed for some terrible purpose and now here he was, the tin hat, the cherry on the cake, the guy with all the keys to their salvation.

"Don't forget, in the end they'll do exactly what you want," Elliot reminded him. "Because of what you are."

He was a Rook; he could take them out of that dark purgatory, he could take them home. But for now he had to keep them gathered here, for without them Elliot Black's scheme wouldn't work.

He kept his breath slow and even, regarded the faces at the edge of the circle. They were mostly polite, hopeful.

Only a few in the crowd seemed to know what the game was, that this was a ruse, a trick, but even they appeared reluctant to call him on it, as if there was still a chance he would take them with him, because after all he *had* promised. He began to believe, that after the initial frenzied attempts at getting his attention, they were as resigned to the game as he was.

"Excellent," Black whispered alongside him. This time there was no evidence of that dark gray and lavender landscape, a place his brother had visited on more than one occasion; a place John had hidden from him and lied about. A dream that wasn't a dream at all.

"Let the ones downstairs go," he said, his eyes still closed. "They're not going to give you any more trouble."

"You sure?"

He nodded. Black had an ability to control the deceased, but it had its limits. Luke shifted focus, went back to the crowd. A solid wall of horror now surrounded the near empty carousel, row after row after row; sentinels, unwitting guardians, gathered there to control the chaos Elliot Black was about to unleash. Their presence made him shiver, they made his gut crawl, and he berated himself. Toughen up. Get used to it. It became a mantra, over and over. Get used to it.

He felt the Lady beneath him, resting against his aching thighs. He'd brought her to life, spread his vision across her flanks, instilled his dreams into the shadows painted so carefully beneath her eyes. The crowd of ghosts had told him she was a killer, had let two children slip from her saddle and crack their skulls. Her fault purely by design of course, nevertheless the stain of death, the resonance was there and she, like the others, had been specifically chosen; a fairground attraction still.

Another sharp moment of concentration, that sinus pain again, and he opened his eyes, saw Elliot alongside him, and he imagined grabbing a stick and beating the man to death with it. Pity this psychic awakening didn't extend to childish expressions of malice and revenge. "I think this is as good as it's going to get," he told the man. He'd drawn and cowed his congregation, created the necessary barrier, easy as pie now he'd struck a bargain. "How about we do it again and pay a visit to the other place." He was lightheaded, getting his second wind; he wanted to go there, see what his brother had seen and experience it for himself.

Black shook his head. "No. You've done enough for tonight, and you have the rounding boards to finish." He reached forward, pulled at the rope holding Luke's feet together.

Luke let out a gasp of relief. When he was finally able to slip from the saddle he almost fell to his knees. He rubbed his wrists, slid a hand under his torn shirt and discovered abrasions on his torso. He must have fought quite a lot in the beginning; tried like hell to get loose. His fingers hit a patch of grazed skin and he winced.

"I apologize for that. But it did improve your concentration, yes?"

Luke scowled at him. "Let me get back to work."

He stood in the center of his workshop, his eyes focused on nothing, the scent of paint and solvent a part of every breath he took.

What was he doing here? Why wasn't he making a break for it, just taking off, climbing over the gate and running all the way into town? He could call Emma, hitch a ride, get a taxi, call the cops...

Questions circled around him lazily as he shifted his attention to the boards— propped up and leaning against every available surface. All the rounding boards shared the same basic landscape and both background and under painting had taken him no time at all. As for the details, the middle and foreground, he began to wonder if he simply closed his eyes and concentrated, maybe he could see...

But no. Not yet. He shook his head and frowned while questions wheeled like buzzards. Why wasn't he running?

And why wasn't he kicking Elliot Black's ass? He looked around at his workshop, and then at his hands, the long-fingered tools of his trade. What magic had he already created with them? All the work he'd ever done— how much of that secret life had he imbued onto the surface of the canvas with just a dab of paint and the twist of a brush?

Now he didn't have Elliot Black breathing down his neck, he let the thrill of it get to him and allowed himself a little shiver of excitement. It was like a switch had been thrown and he'd discovered hardwired capabilities he never knew he'd possessed. He was eager to try them out, too, and it didn't take him long to realize they were seducing him, drawing him into mystery and danger and to hell with consequence and all of its cousins.

His eyes moved toward the windows and the barn across the yard containing the carved horses and their kin. No longer a rich antique collector's fancy, they had a purpose, one in which he had a major part to play, one that would offer answers, that would draw him toward a destiny that had been hidden from him.

And there another question emerged. Why the secrecy? It implied a great deal, raised other questions he really didn't want answers to, about his father for instance. But it was his brother's lack of trust that dug in like a hook, made his mouth twist and stuck in his craw the most. Why hadn't John confided in him?

Of course, he only had Elliot's word, but...

He stared at his hands once more. Father had thrust a knife in his abdomen. He'd tried to kill him. Maybe he'd had a reason. And maybe that's why John couldn't trust him...

He shook off the self-pity. It was time to concentrate, get the job done. Get this over with. And so he began. He didn't need the designs stored on the laptop, he remembered them well enough; they'd come from a deep well of dreams, easily accessed and so he began to recreate them—partially unfurled flowers amongst a tangle of thick, fleshy vines; a string of bones and a pink-tinged skull, inexplicably strung together against a sandscape that faded gradually toward a red and black horizon. That particular board reminded him of a 1970s rock band album cover—retro, surreal and it made him smile. His work pulled him deep into the zone, and by the time he'd taken a step back and become aware of his chilled surroundings he was looking at a different subject altogether.

He'd switched, given up on the boards and continued work on his latest portrait of Emma. It didn't come as a complete surprise. Lately he'd always finished with Emma, right before curling up to sleep in his little nest of blankets in the corner. But to become aware of her, looking at him like that, brought a lump to his throat and reminded him all over again that he missed her and that he was lonely and a little scared and he'd even welcome a visit from his lying bastard brother right now.

He stood back, wiped his brush while taking in the sweep of her hip and the defiant turn of her chin. He'd incorporated the latest changes, the cheekbones, those weary eyes, and right now, on canvas, she appeared to be a little angry. With him? He hoped not and the smile crept back on his face. She looked magnificent, standing in the center of the portrait, surrounded by lush, variegated leaves. He'd painted marks on her skin— the swirl of a tendril on her throat, a stalk easing its way over her shoulder; that play of deep green on her flesh seemed inevitable, a natural part of her. They resembled the marks on her skin and of course, why wouldn't he make use of them, incorporate them into his art?

Even so, the more he mulled over it the more it tugged and nagged at him until he walked over to the corner and pulled out the very first acrylic he'd done of her before the marks had appeared. He swept away a pile of rags and propped it in a position from where he could stand back and take a good look. A mild twist of self-assurance lay at the corner of his mouth as he prepared to say I told you so. That his depiction was merely a representation of what was already there, that the shadows on her skin had arrived well before he'd taken brush to canvas.

He stared. Looked again. "Oh, shit."

Her shoulder on this particular piece was in shadow, so it was that within the contour at her hip and groin he saw first. Ever so faint, barely noticeable. The lines were there nonetheless. His eyes shifted toward her ankle and he let out another curse. He couldn't understand it, why he hadn't seen it before and why he hadn't connected it all together.

He stepped up to the bench, close enough that he could see the brushwork. His hair rose at the back of his neck as he considered the implications. Rationality beat him about the head, telling him that he'd probably noticed the markings before he'd done the painting and that had to be the only explanation. But now he couldn't remember; he couldn't.

He cleared away another section of the bench; a jar crammed full of brushes dropped on the floor, it rolled and the brushes splayed out over the concrete. Luke didn't care. He pulled out another canvas, and another, and placed them both next to the first.

Revelation arrived with a healthy side dish of guilt. He'd lied to her, feigned ignorance, when all along...

"What have I done to you?" He raised his hands, looked at them as if they belonged to someone else. He tried not to panic, thought maybe if he'd painted the designs onto her skin in the picture, then he could paint them right out again.

After a few moments he felt dizzy and had to walk outside. He dropped to his knees on the gravel. His surroundings curved toward him, sank into his skin. This new vision, this perception, the power in his hands, everything Elliot had suggested he was capable of; he was changing her, defiling her flesh, he was becoming a manipulator, a monster...

"Help me," he whispered. The plea drifted away unheard. He was alone in this, same as he'd always been and stupid to think otherwise. His world had shifted, changed, become something new and he'd have to deal with it as best he could.

Eventually he stood up, brushed specks of gravel from his knees and re-entered the workshop. He stood before the latest painting, ready to wipe off the latest intricate design that decorated her skin. It would be the right thing to do. Or at least it would if he'd painted her in a different environment. As it was, it looked natural on her, like it belonged. It seemed to enhance her limbs, give them beauty and strength. Also, the act of removing it would change the scene, re- create her as something vulnerable in the midst of all that dark, fleshy foliage.

And so he made a decision. Apprehension, rationality, fear born of the unknown— they railed at him, told him it was the wrong one. But in the end he reasoned it was down to an understanding between an artist and his muse. It was nothing more, nothing less than an act of worship, one that demanded the ultimate bond; he was locked in, a slave, and would do anything to bring forth her true spirit. What lay on the canvas was truth, and to despoil it meant abject, despicable betrayal. No, the marks would stay.

Breath clouded in front of him. Resolve calmed him, lowered his shoulders. He was the artist, the Rook, the opener of doors and the caretaker of the dead, and it was time to get back to work.

CHAPTER 26

EMMA

The first scream shocked her and brought her to a standstill. It echoed through the ruins, easily recognized as human, and male. It made the hair on the back of her neck stand on end and froze every single major muscle. Her eyes flitted toward her companion. "What the hell—"

Another scream, longer but not quite so loud as the first, and she pitched forward into a flat out run before Rhonda could answer her. She covered the ground quickly and was soon swallowed up in the dark shadow cast by the tall building directly ahead. Thick trunks pushed upward on either side of an immense doorway, erupting in a tangle of sturdy vines higher up. But she didn't pay too much attention to what lay above her head; there was movement up there, giant moths flitting back and forth across a fractured skyline while on either side, the surroundings seethed with movement of a different kind— ethereal and faint— ghosts, eager as she was to get to the source of the trouble.

She ignored it all, brought to bear her makeshift spear— a large plant spike Rhonda had procured— and entered the lattice-walled tower.

"Hey!" she yelled.

The interior was huge, a partially vaulted cathedral, and the walls were crawling with bugs the size of cars. She kept it all in her peripheral vision. No need to see too much, she was already regretting her headlong dash. Directly ahead were huge eyes, as smooth as glass and staring right at her, and below them, a long spike dipped generously in blood that hung menacingly over a flesh colored, shapeless bundle.

Emma remembered something her father had told her once, when they were caught walking through a field full of feisty horses that came charging toward them. Just make yourself appear larger, he'd said, and they'll think twice, and so she did that now, and she waved her arms, made an arc with her spear. "Over here!" She started to move, saw the head swivel and follow her. She heard Rhonda coming up behind, breathless, but couldn't take her eyes off the monster in front of her. The flutter of wings grew louder above but she refused to be distracted. More bodies, more ghosts were crowding in as if they'd all bought ringside tickets to a Vegas prizefight. She could hear some of them whispering, but it was the giant insect— a butterfly, a moth, she couldn't be sure— that had her attention. She began to back away, hoping the creature would follow.

But it didn't. It simply canted its head and watched her.

Rhonda was edging toward the body on the ground, so Emma kept up her waving and yelling, although she doubted the other woman would be able to drag John quickly away from harm, if indeed that was John lying there, oh so very still. After the second scream she hadn't heard anything, and there was an awful lot of blood on that proboscis.

In desperation she tried something different. She stepped forward, advanced on the thing. It was utter madness and her next few exclamations were directed toward herself. All this, for a guy she didn't even like very much, and here she was, her shirt ripped, revealing her bra and the winding skin discoloration on her shoulder, brandishing an overblown cactus spine at an equally overblown lepidopteron. Maybe the only reason she kept moving forward was because she still considered this part of a ridiculous, vivid, tactile nightmare.

"Get away from him," she growled. She jabbed forward with her spear, almost came in physical contact with the wicked, narrow extrusion angled toward her from the base of the creature's head. Right now it was all she could see. Rhonda, John, the ghosts and whatever might be fluttering above and attempting to ambush her— they had all disappeared. It was just Emma, and the creature. Another female, she realized. This was a standoff between two rare commodities in this awful, dark, ruined and overgrown place. Females are scarce here, Rhonda had told her, part of a lengthy pep talk as they'd struggled to get here.

She frowned. This was as close as she dared.

The creature startled her, it shifted its stance and made her duck as it crouched slightly and then leapt into the air. It came to rest about a hundred feet up, those long legs clinging easily to the filigree walls. Wings fanned out, shell pink and magnificent.

"Quickly!" Rhonda was beckoning, her own limbs trembling, her body almost bent double.

Emma dashed over. "Are we too late?" She looked down at John. Blood oozed from a swelling wound on his shoulder. Already he looked pale and gray. Dead and gone.

"No." Rhonda had grabbed an arm. "Help me before Madam changes her mind."

They began to drag his lifeless form toward one of the walls. Emma could see the beginnings of a stairwell, going down. It made sense. If they went outside they'd still be moth bait.

They worked quickly, dragging and pulling; it was hardly the careful EMT response she'd seen on the TV news, and they stumbled and slid down the curved half-ramp, half-stairwell until they couldn't see the upper floor any more.

"Can you feel it?" Rhonda asked.

Adrenalin was pumping hard and heavy; consequently she wasn't in the best of moods. "Stop asking me that," she said. The woman had been beating her to death with that question all the time they had been here, and she still didn't know what she was getting at.

After a long, overly patient sigh, "There's a gate down here," Rhonda said. "I think that's where he was headed."

"Now you're talking." Emma tried to calm down. So far there had been no attempt at pursuit, and thankfully it wasn't completely dark down here. The walls contained growth; long fuzzy strands that oozed pink light, enough to pick out the floor and walls ahead of them, and certainly enough to tell her that John was in a bad way. He gave no sign that he was breathing and his shoulder wound looked ugly and rotten.

"What are we going to do?"

"Just a little further," Rhonda told her, "while I'm strong enough. I can feel the sap beginning to wear off."

Emma nodded. Up until now there had been no need to worry about the woman's mobility, having watched with bated breath while her companion climbed down from the higher boughs of that horrific tree full of bones. "It's designed to make its victims live longer," Rhonda had explained, in between drinking from a small tendril the tree had generously and graciously proffered on the way down, "and it works wonders on my joints." Descending into the city hadn't been a problem for Rhonda either, in fact Emma had had trouble keeping up. The woman had been incorrigible, both chiding and encouraging, while Emma was still very much in shock, every one of her senses overloaded, whited out, scrubbed clean. And as if to compensate, her surroundings had turned up the dial. The air was full of noise, the buzzing of insects, the rustling of leaves; everything was a threat.

They continued to drag the fallen man down the

remaining shallow steps and along a passageway built of pale stone. The light continued to shine, its strength dependent on the varying profusion of plants that dangled from the walls, until Rhonda was very clearly exhausted and in pain. Some of the dead had followed them, curious, or perhaps unwilling to be left up there in that giant hall of bugs.

"I think— if we're to save the day, we need to split up," Rhonda began, her breath coming in raw gasps.

Emma shook her head vigorously. "No. I don't know my way around here."

"You think I do? I need to find the gate, get help. You need to extract the poison and heal him."

It all sounded so simple, like they were at summer camp and one of their colleagues had suffered a bee sting. She shook her head. "No. I don't—"

"Place your hand close to the wound. Close your eyes and breathe."

Some of the dead were nodding as if they agreed it was the best course. She wondered if Rhonda could see them, and realized she hadn't asked. There were a lot of other things she wanted to ask, too, and all of a sudden it appeared to be too late.

"It's okay," the woman whispered. "You'd be surprised at what you're capable of here." She took Emma's hand and placed the palm flat on John's ribcage. He felt as cold as a grave.

"I— I don't know what to do," she stuttered. Her own shoulder began to ache. She could feel those marks on her skin, pulling against every beat of her heart. The palm of her hand felt warm.

"Now. Closer to the wound."

Emma let her fingers crawl up the fallen man's pale flesh, until her hand was directly alongside the puncture. There, her hand grew hot, and abruptly her head filled with images. She was aloft, way above the trees, searching. It was the poison. A connection. "I can feel her," she whispered.

Rhonda nodded. "Don't let it go too far. I'll be back as soon as I can." She rose to her feet with a sharp hiss of pain.

Emma watched her go, saw her disappear around a sweeping curve in the passage. She wanted to shout— don't go. Instead she looked down and pushed a dark lock of hair from John's forehead. Like this, his face so thin, facial hair covering that square jaw, he looked so much like Luke it was scary, and she wondered what had happened to him in the weeks after he'd disappeared. Rhonda had told her some pretty horrific tales, about what it was like in this place, and so far she hadn't seen anything to refute the woman's claims.

She shifted, pulled off her torn shirt and made herself comfortable. The ground felt solid beneath her bare feet; it underpinned the reality of the situation and denied her hitherto escape to sanity clause, that this was a dream, that it wasn't real. But contact was important and she understood now why Charlene had told her to remove her sandals.

John's chest was beginning to rise and fall slightly; his head rolled to one side. She could feel him coming alive beneath her fingers, underground in a ruined city wrapped in vines as thick as trees that moved like snakes; where huge flowers sprang open like umbrellas, plying their scents and flaunting their lewd stamens, their intent so bawdy and blatant; where trees sought fit to decorate their boughs with the bones of their victims; where tiny shrubs turned petal- less heads in her direction. They had made her skin crawl, as if they were watching her, and waiting to take a bite if she grew careless. But no, that wasn't right.

"They eat people," she had remarked during the beginning of their journey, disgusted by the display of bones.

"Only the men," Rhonda had reminded her.

Only the men.

"How did you survive?" she whispered.

She stroked his hair. He no longer looked like the city— ruined, opened up and shattered. The wound was puckering, drying up. He stirred and her hand felt as if it was burning. But she didn't take it away. Not yet. She looked along the passage for signs of life, but it was too soon. She knew that, knew it in her gut. They'd have to wait, be patient and wait it out. But that was okay, he was getting stronger, she could feel him beneath her hands, his chest rising and falling, no longer the troublesome acquaintance, or the disapproving, elder brother. Their relationship had shifted. Likewise the song of blood and poison from the big female swirling through her, telling of a similar bond between her flock of tiny males, numbering in their hundreds; her children, her lovers, their miniature beauty giving her such joy.

Sometime later she began to pull off more of her clothing. Contact. The act of healing required more. John sighed beneath her like he was caught in a dream and she reached forward and cradled his head. His eyes were closed but she remembered them well enough, guarded, and judging. She smiled. So vulnerable now in her hands, his life bloomed at the tips of her fingers, and in her mind's eye she had wings and was soaring...

She closed her eyes, let her head fall forward.

And in the ensuing silence the dead kept watch.

CHAPTER 27

JOHN

He wasn't sure how long he sat there while she slept in his arms. But he wanted to make sure she had enough time to recover before he disturbed her. He'd been through this many times before with his mother, knew what patching him up entailed, and he remembered well enough that cruel spike slamming into his shoulder and the pain that followed it. On awakening he had sat up, rolled his shoulder and marveled at the woman lying alongside him, her eyes closed, her skin so pale, those marks on her body in defiant relief— pulsing, feeding her, bringing her back so much faster than Rachel.

She was his brother's girlfriend; she belonged to Luke. But it was no use pretending there was nothing between them any longer. His weeks crucified on the harvester had stripped away all his bravado, his protection, had called his bluff again and again until he'd begged for mercy. So now he was in quite the predicament, wasn't he.

He stroked her hair, listened to her breathing. In his peripheral vision he caught the occasional glimpse of movement. Not so many of them, now all the excitement had gone. These particular dead had gathered out of curiosity he assumed, unless, like him, they were here for her.

"What do I do?" he asked them, and received nothing by way of reply. But it was okay. In their shoes he wouldn't have been able to come up with a viable solution either.

And in truth he already knew what he needed to do. He'd have to rebuild the wall, step back, grow as distant as he had before, and nurture that thoroughly fabricated dislike.

He leaned back a little, shifted his weight. His shoulders ached. He'd awoken on smooth, bare rock, while alongside him, moss had sprouted and pushed beneath Emma, cradling and insulating her from the same; so typical of this place, everything for the female.

Another few minutes and she began to stir. Nervous, he raked a hand through unkempt hair and waited. A moment later and her eyes flicked open. She didn't flinch or pull away, she simply stared.

"Hey," he whispered, and offered her a smile. It was reciprocated, in a manner that brought such relief and joy that he threw all caution to the wind. He leaned in and kissed her brow. He felt her fingers slide along his beard until she had reached his chin. And there she pushed, redirected him until he was kissing her on the mouth, his lips tentative and light, waiting for her, daring her to make the next move.

When it came he wrapped his arms around her, brought her up into a tight embrace. Her skin felt so smooth and soft, it was just as he imagined it would be, how the tree had told him it would be. He grew bolder, placed his hand on the flat of her belly, and when her thighs opened up he let it sink further, let it search for that narrow cleft that he'd dreamed of over and over.

In the meantime her mouth was greedy for him, her tongue sliding in between his teeth while her fingers explored him, pressing into the lean, freshly repaired muscle on his shoulders and upper torso, and traveling lower across his abdomen. I'm going to burn for this, he thought. It was the worst kind of betrayal but there seemed to be nothing to stop either of them. They were two people caught in the Fall. His mother and Charlene were always telling him of the strange consequences after stepping into a place such as this and up until now, apart from the obvious dangers he'd never truly known what that had meant.

He gasped as her hand, proprietary and sure of itself, encircled the base of his cock. It was ramrod straight, all ready to go and eager to perform. His fingers continued to work on her, already slick, her body responding beautifully, her hips rocking slightly back and forth. Until —

"Do it," she whispered.

He pushed her down onto that dark, mossy bed, and for a moment he hovered above her, watched her lying there, looking up at him with her hair splayed out like a halo. Her skin looked gray in the light and the markings on her flesh had taken on the same hue as the tiny plants beneath her. Somehow she had become part of this place, and he realized just how much he was at its mercy and how little he cared. He was lost. So be it.

He kissed her again, hungry, and entered her, hungrier still. He pushed, gasped as she engulfed him, until they were fully connected. Up on his hands he began to drive into her, slow at first, rocking her hips until she moaned, and as he built up speed her legs rose up and wrapped around him, imprisoning him, locking them together. She let out a low growl as he powered into her, raked his flesh with her nails during the final throes. And afterwards, as they both gasped for air, her eyes were back, staring at him, her face a mask.

He leaned in, brushed her throat with his lips. "I love you," he whispered. It was barely audible and yet it escaped him, he'd said it, and there was no more pretending. He took her ensuing silence on the chin; he'd been prepared for that.

In the space of a few more breaths the moment had gone. She wriggled from under him, pushed him aside. "How long have we been here?"

"I don't know," he answered honestly. "A little while."

"Rhonda should have been back by now."

"Rhonda?"

"We came to rescue you. She went to find the gate, to get help."

Suddenly he felt embarrassed. He cleared his throat. "We should go. Are you okay?"

She nodded, reached out, slid her fingers across his chest while her eyes examined the healed flesh. "I didn't know I could do that. I thought you were dead."

"I might have been, had you not turned up." He helped her to her feet, tried not to linger too long on the sight of her breasts and he fought hard to push away what they'd just been through and what he'd just said. Fears for Rhonda's safety began to prick at him and admonishment quickly followed.

Emma had pulled on her underwear and was staring down a tunnel partially decorated in pink gray light, its edges blurred. The ghosts were still there, were still witness. She held out a hand. "After you."

"Yes, ma'am." He set off, treading carefully.

"I wonder why she didn't stop us?"

He looked over his shoulder. "Who?"

"The moth. She could have— I don't know. Rhonda and I— we didn't seem that much of a threat."

He remembered that giant face. The twitching pectoral muscle on his left side remembered it, too. He carried on walking. "I never thanked you, for patching me up."

"Oh, really? You didn't?" Her eyebrows were raised.

He barked out a laugh and shook his head. Dangerous territory, he decided. Far too dangerous. Ahead the passageway curved and began to spiral down. He quickened his pace after making sure she was keeping up, and eventually they emerged into a wider space that offered a double fork. Now they had four choices.

"That one," she said. She was pointing to the extreme left, a narrow pathway, darker than the others. She pushed past him. "I hope she's okay. The sap she drank was wearing off."

"How did you get here?" He had to duck slightly as he followed in her wake.

"The same way you did. We stole that stupid trunk, climbed down that ridiculous tree. Rhonda said if you were caught, it must have taken some ingenuity for you to escape."

"You have no idea."

She shrugged and continued ahead. He didn't say anything else; didn't want to be reminded. They reached another fork and Emma once again took the left passage. Right now he didn't have a clue and so he followed, placing his trust in her senses. Once in a while he looked back and spotted the occasional face, barely coherent, a suggestion of humanity, but it was enough to tell him the dead were still following.

Abruptly he had to pull up short. Emma had stopped in front of him and was staring at the wall on the left hand side of the passageway.

"Damn," she said.

He followed her eyes and for a moment saw nothing untoward, until –

It was well hidden. Under normal circumstances he would have walked straight past. Having been given the necessary clues, the dead crowded in. John tried desperately not to flinch. He placed his hand against the wall. It felt solid, impassable.

"Okay, so how do we do this?"

"Faith, trust," he told her. "Well, partially..."

Emma gave him a confounded look. "Where does it lead to?" She made a fist and started hammering against the stone. "Hey!"

"The house. Maybe. But I don't think it works like that—"

"Just give me some help, here."

Rachel had told him all the gates were different, and he'd never tried to get through this one before. But it seemed odd to start knocking, as if someone was simply on the other side and might hear them. He was about to raise an objection, citing the dangers of drawing unwanted attention, when a hand appeared, grabbed hold of Emma's wrist, and pulled.

A quick shower, as ordered, but he didn't have time to shave, didn't trust his hands right now in any case. He pulled on clothes quickly and distractedly, with no care if his T-shirt was on backwards or whether his shoelaces needed tying. Back in the main salon some of the others were gathered and they offered him guarded expressions of distress.

"Where is she?"

One of the younger Adepts gestured toward the library. "Rachel's with her. John, I think it might be—"

He ignored them, swept past, and entered the room directly ahead. He expected more of the others to be in there, paying their respects, but in the end it was only Rachel who knelt alongside his fallen best friend.

He stopped short. Rhonda looked as if she was simply asleep, and not dead at all. Breath caught in his lungs, and when he swallowed he nearly choked on a tongue that had the consistency of concrete. "Oh, God..."

Rachel beckoned, held out her hand. She didn't say anything at that moment, but she had been weeping, he could tell that much. He took her hand in his own; it gave him strength, enabled him to breathe.

"Was it Ralt? Was it Llennendhrad? Elliot Black?" So far no one had been able to give him any answers. Announcing that someone so formidable as Llennendhrad was at large had been a mistake; it had simply brought up a high wall of shock, disbelief and mistrust. They'd shut him out, shut him down, stuffed their collective heads firmly in the sand.

She shrugged. "This is all my fault."

"Rachel—"

"No." She let go of him and stood up.

Dread, sorrow, loss, intolerable anger, it began to well up inside him. There were questions he wanted to ask, but this didn't seem to be the place because he knew he'd raise his voice, get angry, and he couldn't do that to Rhonda, who'd come to rescue him, who had found her way back, and who'd been shot in the stomach out on the driveway and had bled to death.

Rachel was staring at him, reading every twitch on his face. In contrast she appeared to have re-established some of her equilibrium. "You'll go and find who did this. And it seems you already have the help you need," she said.

He nodded, turned and stepped back outside. Others had gathered, one of them— Gabriel, a tall, thin man in a black cashmere sweater— approached.

"We've sealed the gateway, but it'll be a long while before it's stable and ready for use once again. The woman brought quite a few of the dead with her and— "

"What *woman* are you talking about?" He really wasn't in the mood for a lecture from one of his so-called betters. "The one lying dead in that room, or—"

"No. The stranger. The one you brought with you."

"Emma. She has a name." He looked around. There was no sign of her.

The man shrugged. "John, I know you're upset, and angry. We all are. Rhonda was—"

He stabbed a finger. "How the hell did it happen? Who did it? Who killed her?" He'd already asked these questions and had yet to receive a satisfactory answer. And he must have been pressing, had evolved into a threat, because all of a sudden Gabriel had back up.

"We don't know." It was Shirley, one of the older Adepts.

The look on her face told him he'd better get a grip on his temper, Rachel's son or no. "Doc has gone out to investigate. He told us we were safe, and not to worry."

"Doc, huh?" He frowned, felt his stomach curdle with unease. He was starting to see the enemy everywhere, even in the father figure of Doc, who was out there right now, trying to help. He realized they were all looking at him now, their expressions ranging from mild distaste to a barely concealed horror that he might blow up in their faces. He wouldn't put it past them to wonder if, by some sleight of hand, it was him that had pulled the trigger, who had murdered his best friend. They were so remote, detached and insular, he wanted to spit in their faces.

And like a switch had been thrown, he abruptly became non-existent.

Emma was standing by the door, hesitant to enter this den of silent snakes. They were staring at her, unrelenting and curious. He saw her raise her chin and meet their scrutiny, and he smiled. Good for you, he thought. She was dressed in a borrowed sweatshirt and jeans, and her hair was still wet, slicked back from her brow into a ponytail. As soon as she saw him she approached. Eyes followed her in silence.

"Is Rhonda still here?" she whispered.

He nodded, pointed toward the closed library door.

Her lips grew tight and thin as she struggled for composure. "I'd like to pay my respects, and then— " she looked over her shoulder briefly. "I don't know who these people are, but we need to leave. This isn't over and I'm worried about Luke."

"I know." He watched her enter the library, where she would come face to face with his mother. He let out a sigh, pushed all thoughts of that confrontation out of his head and he attempted to come up with a plan. They'd need transport. Guns...

He placed his cell phone back in his pocket after talking to Charlene. She was going to rendezvous with Helen and Henry in Texas, get him the supplies he needed, and they'd all meet up with Doc. Luke first, and then they'd go after whomever had killed Rhonda.

"Here she comes." Jim pointed toward the door where Emma was emerging. He'd brought out one of the vehicles, ready to take them to the airport. John knew the old guy was looking at him, watching his reaction, wondering what relationship lay between them and so he kept his face blank, tried not to register the pleasure he felt at the sight of her.

Emma was equally poker faced. When Jim opened the rear door of the car she thanked him quietly and slid inside without another word. The man shrugged. "You getting in or riding up front?" he asked.

John chose to ride shotgun. He didn't trust himself; he despised himself. Rhonda dead and yet all he could think about was being in the back of that car.

"I'm sorry," Jim told him after a long silence, when they were on the approach to the airport. "And I hope you and Doc find who's responsible, you hear?" The old man's hands were trembling on the steering wheel. He'd thought a lot of Rhonda, too. They all had, and John suspected he'd been a little disingenuous earlier, in considering they didn't care.

He nodded. "Don't worry. When we find them, they'll pay." He swallowed. His throat was getting knotted up again. Oh, they'd pay all right. Anger was like a strait jacket, pulling him tight, and in an attempt to shrug it off he turned and looked over his shoulder. "You okay?" They were the first words he'd said to her in the car.

Emma shrugged. For a moment she looked vulnerable, in shock. It was quickly covered over with a layer of defiance; that chin, just a slight tilt upward. She was worried about Luke, he knew that, and he wanted to reach out, reassure her, but in the end he decided against it. Just touching her would bring it all back, the feel of her skin in that tunnel, what they'd done...

It was cold when they got out of the car. He could see the mountains, snowcapped; the sight made their surroundings seem colder. John said his goodbyes and shook Jim's hand while Emma stood and watched. He led her into the airport terminal, where they breezed through First Class check in and security, and were on board their flight not long after.

It felt odd and quite pleasant to have a companion on the trip. It was only a two-hour flight, but he almost always had to travel alone and having Emma sitting in the next seat brought a smile to his face despite the dire circumstances. Her hand was resting on the partition between them and he risked lying his own on top of it.

He watched her look down at the physical connection, and figured she'd pull her hand away, but she didn't. She spread her fingers, wove them in between his own, and there they remained. Would it have been wrong to admit he was a happy man at that particular moment? Yes, he expected it would. A dear friend had been murdered; he'd almost died, and they were on their way to rescue his little brother and oh by the way Luke I just stole your girlfriend. Just something else to beat himself up with later. But he'd bear it. Right now he felt wanted, needed, a part of something he'd never felt before. And all the fires of Hell could wait.

CHAPTER 28

LUKE

The afternoon sun poured heat into the yard and shone down so bright that Luke's eyes were two narrow slits. Nevertheless he felt cold and couldn't stop shivering as he watched Elliot Black's men, including a stranger he hadn't seen before, carry the rounding boards over to the carriage house. He'd complained, that he wasn't quite finished, that they were still wet and he'd tried desperately to hold on to them a little longer. But in the end, as with all his work, he'd had to let them go.

He felt sick, and weak. He was thirsty and starving and there was a half-eaten sandwich on a plate nearby and he'd tried to force it down past his teeth and tongue but in the end it had become a Herculean feat and he had given up. His stomach had shrunk to nothing. Just a couple of bites and it had felt like the aftermath of a Thanksgiving dinner two times over.

He looked at the pitcher of lemonade alongside the plate, melting ice on the inside and condensation on the outside, running down and staining the bench it was sitting on, and he still couldn't stop shivering and he wondered if Grace would make him some hot tea instead like Emma used to when it was cold outside and she had a blue tea pot and tiny cups and she always put the timer on for five minutes to ensure it brewed long enough...

He coughed, leaned on the door frame, the world spun

and it became a matter of urgency to find somewhere he could puke up his guts discreetly and without embarrassing himself. Outside, beneath one of the workshop windows, he leaned over a squat, pink-headed hydrangea and threw up the two bites of sandwich and a string of bile.

"Performance anxiety?"

Luke groaned, wiped his nose on his sleeve. "Fuck you."

Elliot was watching him, eyes predatory and unblinking. "You did what I asked, for— what has it been now— forty eight hours straight? Now it's time for a little sustenance, and some rest." He pulled Luke upright, began to march him toward the main house kitchen. "Come, we have a big night ahead of us."

"So this is it?" He tried not to slur but every word seemed intent on rear-ending the one before it.

"Yes. Watch your step."

Elliot led him along the path and around to the kitchen, and once inside, Grace took over, cleaning him up, sitting him down, and feeding him broth as if he was a child. He wanted to kill them both but he didn't have the strength. He wondered if Grace knew he was a prisoner. Now Emma was gone she never said anything other than the usual daily mundane courtesies, and even if she *did* know of his predicament, it wasn't as if she'd caught him continually trying to climb over the front gate. The matter appeared of no consequence or importance to either of them. Like the men in the yard, they were here to do Elliot Black's bidding, and that was that.

He drank more of the broth. It was certainly easier on his stomach and after a little while he began to feel better. And Elliot was right. He did need sleep, and he wanted to be in reasonable shape, especially for the unveiling of the carousel. He'd seen it in his mind's eye often enough, but to see it for real...

Grace brought pillows and sheets. She knew of his

aversion to sleeping in the guesthouse and so she made up a bed on the couch in the adjoining living room, all the better to keep an eye on him, he suspected.

When he lay down he could hear Elliot's voice outside. They were installing the remainder of his animals, setting everything up. A few more hours, everything would be ready, and it would be time to discover the truth and what he was truly capable of. It would be time to rock and roll.

He wasn't afraid. This was his birthright, his destiny. And when he closed his eyes he saw his dead audience; everyone had turned out— the little kids, the shambling wraiths, they were here to do their part, same as he was. And that settled, he slept.

Feet planted in loam, arms spread out, content. And yet —

In the end he had no choice; he had to see for himself. He burrowed like a worm and tasted the earth, felt a moment of suffocation, of terror, until finally he broke the surface and there she was.

Beneath her the whole city was aflame. Heat was rising, the air so hot that every intake of breath tore at his lungs and he knew he'd have to dive down below again lest he share the same fate as the others. The dead were everywhere, and those still alive were screaming— their flesh crackling, their eyes bursting and the stench wafted upward with the heat, caressing, buffeting her magnificent wings and he saw them flex and fan out like a hawk's tail in flight. This was easy, she lived for this and had done it many times before, and right there he realized the horror of what he was about to set free.

Flames were rolling up the hill, consuming everything

in their path and any moment now he'd be destroyed like the rest —

"It's time, young man."

He opened his eyes. "She flies," he said. The words stumbled out before he could stop them.

The stranger was smiling at him, his expression one of mild curiosity. "Yes." He nodded. "She does."

Luke sat up, rubbed his eyes. He thought that might do the trick, but no, she was still with him, her wings a bold, fluttering banner of destruction. "Who the hell are you?"

The man shrugged. "A family friend. You can call me Doc." That smile again, his voice so light and easy it slipped through Luke like strands of silk thread, becoming sticky like a spider web once they'd penetrated. "And I have to tell you," the man continued, "I'm very impressed."

Luke stood up, ran fingers through unkempt hair and faced the man. "You are, huh?" He frowned. It became hard, took effort, to deliver his usual belligerence.

"Yes. The artwork is breathtaking. But it's what lies beneath, the architecture. Tell me, did you really know what you were about, when you started? Or did your skills evolve over the duration? I'm curious."

Luke was in no mood for answering questions. Not until he'd gotten some answers. "How come I haven't seen you before?" He was searching his memory and coming up short, and those sticky strands had become stronger, like needles picking through his brain. It was uncomfortable, making him feel dizzy all over again.

Doc shrugged. "We've met. But you were very young and I'm sure you won't remember. You were staying with Matthew and Lola at the time."

He stared at the man, old, early sixties maybe, oozing self-assurance like he was used to calling the shots. Just the kind of guy he didn't want to butt heads with right now. The back of his neck was bristling like a porcupine, issuing a warning, and a moment later he knew why. “Hey. Get the fuck out of my head.” The man blinked, faltered, it was barely perceptible but Luke chalked up the victory nonetheless. And while he was on a roll, “And if you think I’m going to do what you want, you’re out of your mind. Screw you, I’m not doing it.”

“My dear boy, you don’t have a choice.”

He saw the man pull a gun. The sight of it was mesmerizing, but the threat— it wasn’t enough. “I’m not doing it,” he repeated. “I let her out— she’ll kill us all.” He remembered the heat, the smell, stamped so hard behind his eyes it was difficult to think of anything else.

“Now, why would you think that?”

He barked out a laugh. “Because it’s what she does and I’m not going to be held responsible for that.”

The man’s expression had grown glassy and hard. “I expected you to be stubborn.” He glanced down at his weapon. “You think I won’t carry out my threat?”

“If I do this, everyone’s dead anyway. Go to hell.” It was okay. He didn’t matter, and he was the only one in danger. Emma was hundreds of miles away.

The other man nodded. “Grace, would you come in here, please.”

Grace.

“Hey wait—” Luke saw movement by the door. He leaned forward. He thought he had time. “Grace don’t—”

The noise— deafening, horrific— stopped him dead. He watched the woman fall in slow motion. There should be red, he thought, his mind analytical, searching, busy with composition in the midst of the trauma.

The man called Doc punched him hard in the face, so hard he fell backwards and hit the floor and for a long moment he thought he could hear the sea, like a wave breaking at the shore.

Elliot swam above him, hazy and out of focus. He

floundered, couldn't breathe. Did the punch knock him out?

Where was the other guy? He felt something hard and pointed like a dagger, jammed against his jaw. "See what you did?" Elliot's voice was a mild hiss amongst the roar of the ocean.

Red, a familiar taste in his mouth. Pain arrived and his face began to throb. He shifted his head. And there was Grace, lying on the floor, same as he was. Still no sign of the guy with the gun. He began to gag on the blood pouring down his throat. Black rolled him over onto his stomach. As he did so, Luke caught sight the other man's fingers. The view stilled him, silenced the noise in his head.

"See what happens? Grace is dead, and you have a broken nose. Both a direct consequence of you not doing as you're told."

He tried to speak, to explain. He gurgled and coughed instead. He extended his arms and attempted to crawl. Directly ahead of him, dark spikes came down like a portcullis— extensions from one of Elliot Black's hands. He froze. Thorns, he thought. They look like thorns. As deadly as the other man's gun.

He found his voice. "Why set her free? She'll destroy everything."

Black grabbed his collar and shook him, an angry gesture, at odds with the tone of his voice. "Because she doesn't belong in there. And do not assume that you know everything about her."

It hurt to draw breath, to get his heart rate to the point where he could speak without babbling. "Think I'm going to take your word? You're not even fucking human."

Laughter descended from somewhere close. "Oh, Luke. And you think *you* are?"

Black hauled him to his feet. The room was spinning, offering the occasional glimpse of the red he'd sought earlier. It was there, through the doorway, splattered on the side of the kitchen counter. He breathed, fought dizziness and room spin. He had to get a grip. He had to think.

But those hands...

Elliot was still with him, was holding him up. "Now—shall we?"

They had to step over Grace's body and go through the kitchen. Luke had never seen so much blood before. The cupboards were spattered with it, and a large pool of it was expanding slowly outward across the tiles, the outer edges beginning to flow along the crisscross runnels of grout. He kept his eyes averted and felt like an abject coward for doing so. But he couldn't afford to go into shock. He had to keep his head clear and come up with a plan. If he could just get to his workshop —

"You're wrong, you know," Elliot told him as they crossed the yard. "About her?"

"No I'm not."

"Then we'll beg to differ."

Luke kept walking, kept breathing. All the lights were on in the yard. The barn doors were wide open and he could see inside. Once full of his carousel horses, the place was now empty. It looked cavernous— a yawning, empty mouth. They passed wide of his workshop door and he could see inside there, too. Pots bristling with brushes, cans of turpentine...

The side door of the carriage house opened and Doc emerged. Luke stopped, wary, until Black gave him a shove forward. The other man approached and smiled. A family friend. He was betting John knew exactly who this guy was. And speaking of John where the hell was he right now? He frowned. Maybe his brother was in on it, too. And once again it became difficult to know whom to trust.

"Well, we're all ready for you," the man said, that smile back on his face.

Luke didn't know what to say, and so he simply stared. At least the guy had stopped trying to get inside his head. That ploy obviously wasn't working. It made him wonder when they'd get down to bullets again, or maybe they'd just keep beating on him. He was glad Emma wasn't here.

"We're wasting time," Elliot said behind him, and gave him another push.

The man called Doc accompanied them back to the carriage house. "You're not going to be difficult, are you, Luke?"

He smiled, defiant. Yeah and fuck you, too, buddy. He kept his mouth shut, stayed on the move, until Elliot propelled him through the carriage house door where he stumbled through— and stopped in his tracks.

The carousel. It had finally come together, filling the room, lending the air a whiff of varnish and still drying paint. Mesmerized, he forgot all about Grace reduced to a bloody mess on the kitchen floor, and Black and his cohort pushing him around, and he stepped forward, drawn inexorably, and began to walk around the perimeter of the magic circle. His mind was already busy, going through the layout. All his creations were standing in their proper places. In this respect Elliot had obeyed him to the letter.

He shivered, and this time not from the cold. He caught sight of the Lady, her martial protector right behind her; he saw the fish tail of the hippocampus, the long neck of the ostrich. He looked up and frowned, slightly puzzled. A quick glance toward the other two men, who seemed content to let him roam now he was here, and he stepped over the line, past an outside stander with a glossy black mane, another jumper similar to the Lady in the center and a boar that he'd painted jet black on the inside of the row, until he stood at the very center of the carousel.

Here was a clear, circular space of about twelve feet, just bare, polished boards, and from here he could see out toward the perimeter and the rounding boards. They'd been hung in a non-traditional manner, with the design on the inside, just outside the circle. When the carousel began to move, they'd stay still, and from here —

He returned his attention to the carved carousel animals. He was surrounded by his work and their macabre history, and in painting them he had woven the two together— the realm of the dead and that terrible, voracious land beyond. Both were now interlocked around the center clearing, neither one able to impede on the other. The gate, once manifest, would be quite stable.

He looked beyond the lines of horses toward the two men watching him. Both were standing beyond the circle; Doc appeared wary, and Luke's lip curled derisively. "Clever," he said, looking toward Elliot. "You made good use of me."

The man shrugged. The smile on his face suggested he was mildly flattered. Doc was regarding Luke with a watchful eye that suggested he knew what he was thinking. But that didn't matter. Both men had made the mistake of letting him walk into the center unattended. For already the dead were arriving.

Those accidentally killed by the carousel stepped forward and straddled the ride that had murdered them. Their presence mingled with the dark beauty of Luke's artistry, further underpinning the overall effect. He was pleased to see the Lady was passenger-less; at least her particular charges had made it through to the afterlife— Heaven, Hell, or wherever they were supposed to be.

He rolled his shoulders. He could feel the connection beneath his feet, the mechanics of the thing, the center pole and its branches, utterly alien, its life throbbing within the carved wood. There was quite a crowd down there too, robust figures, shuffling shapes, all of them standing at the perimeter of the circle. They all knew what was expected of them.

"Are you ready?" Elliot asked him.

He nodded, sucked in a breath, blew it out. The tree below him affirmed what power he had. He wondered if those two guys knew exactly how much.

Elliot disappeared for a moment. When he returned Luke could hear the low hum of a generator, and then slowly, the carousel began to move. As it gathered speed he shifted his weight, spread his feet a little further apart. The twisted landscapes he'd painted on the rounding boards began to sweep past. To the left of him was the Lady and he turned in that direction, used her to ground his vision, to stop him from getting dizzy. Guide me, he implored.

The carousel moved smoothly beneath him on its axis, and hardly made a sound at all. And after a little while, satisfied, he closed his eyes, and sank to one knee.

He remembered that time in the barn, when his creations had shifted a little closer. An optical illusion, but this time he could feel it. They were crowded in on him, as if the carousel was beginning to fold toward him. Further and further until he could hear the distant buzzing of insects, the air felt humid and carried a strong floral scent and he wondered if he could now open his eyes and take a look at his new surroundings, a place he'd dreamed of for as long as he could remember.

And when he did— the landscape changed, caught him by surprise. He could see buildings to the left and right. Just a glance— a wall here, fully intact, and then another partially ruined, its edges choked with weeds. There were things in the air, insects of some kind. They looked big, too. But now the light was beginning to dim as the city closed in. He looked left and right, attempted to recognize the skyline, New York perhaps, or Chicago, but it wasn't anything he remembered.

Alongside was a tower, sticking up like a jagged, broken finger, its roof gone and the interior open to the elements. The light dimmed significantly and when he looked up he saw her crawling out, all legs, a body the size of a railroad car and giant sail wings slung on her back. He hadn't expected her. Not so soon. "Shit," he muttered. "Ah, shit..."

His skin crawled and he fought for calm. He tried to remember how this was going to play out. But he had to shut out the sight of her. Terrifying, yes. But she was also beautiful. So magnificent he knew if he stared long enough, he was gone.

Resolute, he concentrated, began to whisper. He began to call for the dead.

CHAPTER 29

EMMA

"Oh, darlin' I'm so sorry."

Emma stood back and watched John withstand Charlene's bear hug embrace. News of Rhonda's murder had brought a look into the woman's eye that promised something nasty to the culprit if she ever caught him, or her.

"What did you do with the trunk?" John asked once he was free of her grip.

"Destroyed it. Took some doing, too. Although now I know who created it— are you sure he killed Rhonda? I just don't see a creature like Llennendhrad killing a woman. A man, sure," she added with a shrug.

"Maybe it was someone at the house?" Emma offered. It seemed obvious. But they both stared at her, uncomprehending, and in the end she threw up her hands and backed off.

Still the outsider. What she had suggested was obviously impossible. But she hadn't liked the atmosphere at that place in the mountain foothills. The people were strange, otherworldly, Luke's mother Rachel most of all. In fact the woman had flat out given her the creeps.

She approached Henry and Helen who were loading up one of the vehicles. These two she had taken a liking to immediately, while her opinion of the formidable Charlene was still on the back burner, as yet unresolved.

Henry smiled at her. He appeared a quiet man, and like John he carried a lot of hurt in his eyes. She was beginning to understand a little more why Luke had been kept at arm's length, why John's visits had been so infrequent, why his mother appeared to have abandoned him altogether. She had never thought ignorance was a gift— until now.

She grabbed one end of a wooden case and helped Henry load it into the trunk of the SUV. "Is this it?"

He nodded. "And remember, young lady, when we get there, you stay by me, where you'll be safe. Don't want you getting all shot up or worse."

"I'll try," she said. It was a lie and he appeared to see through it well enough. He was about to say something else but John arrived.

"You okay?" He stood close, gave her the kind of smile a lover would, warm and full of shared secrets. "I need to ride with you guys. Henry and I need to—"

"Then I'll ride with Charlene," she said.

He blinked. "You sure?"

"Yes." She gave him a look that told him she wasn't about to change her mind, and as she walked away she blew a quiet sigh of relief. She understood his attentiveness, the looks he gave her, and it was breaking her heart.

In the passenger seat of Charlene's car she sat in silence, while her head turned over and over and she considered the mess she had gotten herself into. Her companion didn't say anything as they set off, but as soon as they were out on the road —

"I'm guessing something happened between you two."

Emma nodded, decided she might as well get this obligatory conversation over with. "Yes. Down in that ... place." She steeled herself, expected to be on the receiving end of a stern lecture. Instead —

"Don't beat yourself up, hon.' It's not your fault. It's not his either. Bower's Fall changes everything and everyone it touches."

She stared at the woman, surprised. "I don't know what I'm supposed to do."

Charlene flashed her a smile. "Well, you'll figure it out, one way or another."

Emma looked out of the window. The other vehicle was ahead of them on the road, its tail lights plain and bright in the dark while the rest of the world swept by like gray curtains on either side. "Have you ever been in there?"

"Yes I have, and thankfully not for too long. The men think they have the worst of it. But with us the changes are deeper, more profound..." Charlene hesitated for a moment. "Isn't that right?"

Emma shuddered, couldn't help it. "I'm scared."

"I know. But you'll do fine."

She considered the woman was simply being reassuring, making the right noises so that her passenger wouldn't go bat shit crazy, and so she decided to change the subject. "Who's this Doc guy we're meeting?"

Charlene wrinkled her nose. "One of the Adepts."

"You don't like him."

"Let's make that plural." She waited until after they'd slowed for a junction and taken a left before continuing. "They're a little too authoritarian for my liking. Seems like they have all the answers, which sounds like bullshit to me if you'll pardon my language. Not to mention some of them have spent far too long in Hell."

Hell.

Emma started chewing on one of her fingernails then made a deliberate effort to place both hands in her lap. "Those people there..."

"They're an odd bunch for sure, but—" they took a right this time, "—this is an odd business wouldn't you say?"

She nodded, left her fingernails alone, chewed her lip

instead. "I just want to get Luke out of there."

"Well, that's the plan. Of course if they've managed to open up a gate and create a breach, then that'll change things, and that's where I'll need to get directly involved."

"Oh?"

"Yep. I'm real good at closing gates."

Lights on the side of the road. It was the gas station. But it was too soon and she wanted to leap out of the car and make a run for it, to anywhere other than here and the sudden need for escape brought back a recent memory. Same place, same company and it made her want to cry. Instead she rubbed the sweating palms of her hands on her thighs and tried desperately to stop her heart from hammering. Focus on Luke, whom she'd betrayed with his brother...

They parked the vehicles just around the corner from the end of Main Street. It was 2 a.m. and all the cafes and stores were closed and there wasn't a soul around, including the man called Doc who was supposed to meet them near the house. She'd already told the others that Luke was probably still awake, would no doubt be in his workshop and it seemed like a simple thing as far as she was concerned. Just open the gate, slip in there, get a hold of her boyfriend and get out as fast they could.

But there had also been talk of destroying his work—the carousel animals, any paintings he might have done. She didn't quite understand that part of the plan, and she knew exactly how Luke would feel about that. And right there any notion of a simple rescue had flown right out of the window.

There was also a question of how strong Elliot Black's

hold on him was, too. She still burned with anger every time she considered how easily she had been duped and manipulated. Her Dad's heart attack hadn't helped, of course, but...

She pushed it aside, the thought of how it had happened at such a convenient time. She was becoming suspicious of everything, letting it tie her up in knots, and she couldn't afford to indulge in thoughts like that right now. She had to focus on Luke. Nothing else mattered. Everything else could wait.

A dark shape emerged from around the bend in the road. It was John.

"He's got someone posted outside the gate. Looks like it's on."

Charlene clicked her tongue. "Looks like I might need to go in there after all. And I might need some help, ladies."

A gate, a breach, maybe a whole lot bigger than those Emma had already traversed, and she hadn't the first idea on what it might take to shut one down. She remembered a conversation she'd had with Rhonda while they were pushing their way through fern fronds and libidinous flowers, about the basement workings of the carousel and how it had looked in her mind's eye. Makes you wonder where the timber came from, the other girl had said. Indeed. And thinking about Rhonda made her feel sick all of a sudden. There had been the beginnings of a friendship there, all gone now.

The others had gathered in a little clutch and were whispering amongst themselves. Her exclusion, that they continued to keep her at arm's length, brought forth more feelings of disquiet. Those marks on her skin were dug in and felt like steel bands; they made her feel as if she was no longer human.

Determined to be proactive she approached, her hands in her pockets so they couldn't see they were shaking. "I'll go up there. Distract whoever it is," she said. She was sick of waiting, of the others shielding her, or maybe shielding themselves. As she saw it getting Luke out of there was her priority and to hell with everything else. And before they could stop her she set off, rounded the corner and strode up the narrow road that led to Elliot Black's mansion.

There was indeed someone standing outside the gate. A little closer and she recognized the older man who worked in the back of the store preparing the carousel horses. He was holding something— a rifle, a shotgun. She slowed her pace, kept her hands rammed in her pockets, smiled and tried to look casual.

"Hey, is it okay if I go in?" Surely he recognized her. She attempted to walk past him toward the far pillar of the gate, so she could enter the number on the keypad. Almost there and he brought the weapon to bear. Two barrels. Two black holes pointed right at her. Shotgun. She stared at it.

"Sorry, ma'am. You need to head right back into town."

"But I need to see Luke. It's urgent." She took another step toward the pillar, saw him make a half turn toward her. She kept her eyes on him, regardless of the shadows that played behind him. Another second and John was alongside the man and it appeared as if he'd grabbed hold of the gun barrel and flipped it backward, but it happened so fast she couldn't be sure. Only a moment later and both men were on the ground struggling.

Helen and Charlene appeared.

"The gate," Charlene hissed.

Emma dashed over to the keypad. Her fingers trembled as she pushed the keys. If Elliot had changed the combination —

The gate began to swing open, just as John regained his feet. Dark, but she could still make out the deep frown on his face. "Emma, damn it—"

She shrugged, ducked through the gate opening. There was movement up ahead and so she dived quickly into a line of thick shrubs that ran up the left hand side of the driveway. She heard a sound, a sharp zip followed very closely by a loud crack.

"Get back!"

Emma ducked low, ignored Henry's plea and pushed her way through the shrubs until she could see the front lawn. From here, so long as she was careful and there was no one guarding the front door, she could make her way undetected around the far side of the house.

A few steps and someone called out John's name.

She froze.

"Stay right there," a male voice called out.

"What in God's name is going on?" That was Charlene. She sounded pissed.

Emma willed her feet to move. Whoever was on the approach had just fired their weapon and might do so again. She scuttled like a crab, sticking to the wall of the main house. None of the lights were on in the front rooms, but she kept low and hugged the shadows whenever she could.

Around the far side was a tall, solid gate that led toward the kitchen, the pool house, and out back toward the rear yard and the guesthouse. Slowly, carefully, she tried the latch. Through a gap she could see the kitchen light was on and despite the fact it was so late it was entirely possible she might run into Grace on her way around the back. She wondered briefly if Grace would have a gun too, while she slowly pushed open the gate and crept along.

She risked a glance through the kitchen window. No movement, but —

"Oh, no." Her voice escaped in a soft hiss, pushed out weakly as she saw the red, gory mess on the tiled floor. There was a shape, like a discarded pile of laundry over by the far doorway, only it wasn't a pile of laundry at all. And abruptly she felt ice cold and her stomach twisted.

She pushed open the kitchen door, stepped inside and looked down, even though she didn't want to, for the blood had traveled along the tiles, a huge puddle of it. She'd never seen so much, and beyond the kitchen table, where she'd sat with Luke, and Grace, and Elliot for dinner —

She wanted to scream and her hand came up and clamped hard over her mouth. Grace's head was disfigured; it was a floppy, odd shape and blood had flowed from it like a stream of crimson hair and had spread out, taking up nearly a quarter of the kitchen floor. As for the smell, it wasn't particularly cloying, but it was poignant enough to rip away all that reminded her of the recent past. Just one look, and all fond memories were gone.

Emma stumbled and backed up, one step, and then another, and her thoughts ran to Luke. She knew exactly what he'd be like if he was pushed. He'd be stubborn, he'd mouth off and dig in his heels, and maybe he was dead too, and lying in a similar pool of blood, in his workshop, or over at the guesthouse.

In a hurry to get out she scraped her arm painfully on the kitchen doorframe. She cursed and broke into a run, not caring any longer if she was discovered or not. At that moment, if Luke was dead then it didn't matter. Her life. John. The carousel. None of it.

There were no lights on over at the guesthouse. The barn was wide open, and empty. She saw a light on in his workshop and so she headed straight for it and blew a sigh of relief when she saw he wasn't inside, lying on the floor. She heard another shot fired, and another and another. A gunfight. Over by the front gate. But she couldn't stop.

A shape appeared in her peripheral vision. She risked a glance and saw it was a man standing in the middle of the yard. The carriage house lights shone through his shoulders and he was pointing back in that direction, his wide sleeved shirt fluttering in some terrible wind.

She nodded. All this time and he'd tried to warn her. She felt him behind her, accompanying her as she ran headlong across the yard, past the BMW, and through the partially open door, and as soon as she had both feet planted inside the building, everything changed.

There was light in the center of the room but it was softened, filtered through a thick fog of the assembled dead, and for a moment she simply stood there, transfixed. A few heads turned, a couple of them even nodded. Oh, it's you. Beyond them the light drew her in. She could see movement, vague shapes, like horses in mist. It was the carousel, and at the edge of it, with his back turned —

"Elliot." Anger rose within her, ran through every artery, every vein and every new line carved into her flesh. She began to push her way through the ghostly crowd, an easy enough matter while she pulsed with fury. "Where is he?"

The man barely turned to acknowledge her as she came alongside. "Where do you think?"

Having got through the crowd, Emma could just make out the carousel. It was enveloped in mist, and the air here was moist and fragrant and she remembered it well. But beyond the slow travel of horses and menagerie she could see nothing but a lavender glow.

The hypnotic scent began to beckon, to draw her in. She shifted her weight, was about to take a step forward when the light at the center began to distort and something dark emerged. There was a flutter of huge wings followed by a dull thud. When she looked up she saw a giant, moth-like insect, its body maybe four feet long, clinging to the canopy ceiling. A few days ago she would have screamed and cowered at the sight of it, but it was familiar now, and she had already faced off something far bigger, and it came to her then.

"It's her," she said. "It's always been about her. You want to let her out."

"Of course."

She remembered John, lying on the ground, full of holes and poison, echoes of the latter still lingering, telling her the creature would unlikely be any more merciful to the one who'd opened the way. "I'm getting him out," she muttered. She stepped onto the moving carousel, reached out and grasped the carved wooden mane of one of the horses. Her body lurched and she was drawn sharply to her right.

"No," he said. He'd reached out with extraordinarily long fingers and missed, and now he was stepping aboard, following her.

Emma swung beneath the head of the horse and approached the next one, still getting her balance on the moving ride. This one, a rabbit, or a hare, dark gray with the blackest eyes it seemed as though Luke was staring through them. Its neck felt tacky, not quite dry and it plucked at her fingers as she continued on to the inner row. Another horse, and there was a male child astride this one, watching her with bland disinterest, as ragged and as gray as the creature he rode.

Sharp points bit into her shoulder.

"No," Elliot growled. Less self-assurance this time, he sounded desperate, as if she might actually do some harm.

She turned around. She wasn't afraid. She grabbed that arm and its hand littered with thorns, and pulled him toward her with consummate ease. But then she wasn't just a woman, not here, not while she was bathed in this pink blue light. "You can't stop me," she said.

He tried to pull away but the momentum was already carrying them toward the center where the mists were at their thickest. Another step back and she was falling and Elliot was falling with her, and she held him in arms as strong as steel, as indomitable as the earth. It must have only taken a second to fall to the ground, to the center planks that lined the floor of the carousel, but during that time she saw the ruined tower with its burden of thick vines, and dozens and dozens of flashing wings.

On landing she pushed and rolled until she was astride him. The sense of wellbeing she felt was near overwhelming;

it was like coming back home, a strange thing to feel when she could see the commotion off to her right. She looked down at Elliot, bared her teeth in a grin.

"What have you become?" he whispered. His skin had shifted pallor; she could see it above the neck of his shirt, flesh pale and mottled like one of Luke's dappled horses.

"Like you," she said.

She stood up. The insects were everywhere, aloft— agitated and erratic. They fought for her attention while the burgeoning figure of their mother continued her struggle. One of her wings was pinned, was beginning to tear, while below her was a flurry of activity— a knot of ghosts and shifting shadow, fending off a continual assault by the huge lepidopteron's smaller but still considerable sons.

Emma looked down. Black was up on his elbows attempting to crawl from beneath her then he could stand.

"No," she said.

And from the ground, spiked tendrils sprouted. They lassoed his throat, and pinned his thighs. The rest was easy, and he yelled and thrashed until he was firmly tied down and his mouth was plugged.

But there was no time to gloat. She stepped away, switched her attention to the chaos beneath the giant female. "Luke!"

Winged creatures hovered above her, but they dared not touch. Instead they floated en masse like the canopies of great trees, knocking out the light.

The shadows fleshed out the dead, giving them corporeality until her immediate surroundings became a crowded war zone. "Luke!" She thought she could see something in amongst the mass of bodies. Were they protecting him? It was so hard to see anything as she ran into their midst. She could feel them, an arm, a shoulder, fingers grabbing at her knee, pulling at her hair. She began to despair.

"Luke!"

A bloody foot. She pushed, jabbed with her elbows

until she was able to reach him. And her worst fears were realized. Just like John he was on the ground, crumpled, gray; the only difference, his limbs were shivering— he was conscious.

"Can't let her go, Em. Can't let her go."

He felt cold to her touch, like a fish packed in ice. She could see past clothes reduced to rags, to the punctures on his skin. He'd been hit— multiple times, small jabs, but there were a couple of deep, dark gouges, too. No need to wonder where they had come from.

She was aware of the big female somewhere close by. Luke had trapped her somehow, and now her attentions were on freeing herself rather than wielding that huge protruding bayonet. Emma figured she was in with a chance. She looked past her left shoulder and saw the fair-haired ghost crouched alongside. He'd followed her in.

"Help me," she said.

Luke still shivered and chattered during the pull and push. "Can't let her go, can't—"

He was dying and she'd have to heal him, the same as she had with John, and she would fade, be reduced, and the poison...

She couldn't see Elliot Black any more, so there was no telling if he was still tightly bound or whether he was now free to do his mischief. No telling how long it would take to heal Luke either. She couldn't remember what happened before, only the aftermath.

There was a tearing sound, like rent fabric. A high-pitched cry burst inside her head— frustration and pain from the other female. She wouldn't have much time.

CHAPTER 30

JOHN

Helen was a few paces behind him, crouched on her knees, her hands pressed firmly on the wounds suffered by her husband while Charlene was on the opposite side of the gate, hunkered down, making full use of shadow and the tall brick gatepost.

"Why don't you put the gun down, come out, and we can talk this through?" Doc's voice, from somewhere beyond the gate, it sounded confidant and assured, effectively scattering seeds of doubt in amongst John's resolve.

Inside he felt bitter and confused, unwilling to swallow the betrayal, the realization that one of his most cherished and respected mentors had just tried to shoot him. Someone at the house, Emma had suggested. Doc had killed Rhonda. It fit, didn't it? A whole lot better than Llennendhrad, or one of Ralt's crew popping in and out like a magic rabbit.

"And why don't you do the same thing?" he shot back. He afforded another glance toward Henry, hurt and bleeding. It was enough for John to dispense with any lingering respect and stoke the dull anger that burned in his stomach, born of his own stupidity, his gullibility...

"Come on, John. We don't have to do this."

From his side of the gate, "Oh yes we freakin' well do." Charlene's harsh whisper barely made it across from her position. "Keep him busy."

He watched her back away and disappear into the shadows along the wall. She had the rifle; he was more geared up for close quarters. He had a 9 mm pistol in his right hand, another stuffed behind him in the waistband of his jeans that Doc didn't need to know about.

He heard Henry cough and follow it up with an awful gurgling sound. He looked down at Helen. Don't, her eyes were telling him, but it was too late, now. They had to finish this. The gate was fully open and for a moment he thought about the dogs— still no sign of them, another of Llennendhrad's mental tricks.

He cursed under his breath and stepped out, his hands in the air, his gun held between thumb and forefinger. He leaned forward, bent his knees, placed it carefully on the ground and stood up nice and slow. He took a few paces forward, beyond the gate. "I don't understand, sir," he said. He stared ahead, the same dumb, do as he was told John that Doc was familiar with. He could feel the tendrils of persuasion tickling his scalp, sliding down his throat. The effect brought to mind a recent, horrible memory, one that made a particularly effective shield.

The other man was a little ways up the drive. There was a pickup truck parked there. It made good cover, but the driveway was partially lit and he could see well enough. Doc had a pistol too, the business end pointed right at him. John wondered if he'd used it on Rhonda.

"John, I want you to trust me."

"What about Luke?"

"Luke will be fine. I promise."

"Rachel didn't want him to get involved. With any of this."

"I know, but he has talent, John, the likes of which you and I can only dream about. Now, enough talk. Step past the truck. Where are the others?"

His voice cracked. "All shot up barring Helen, and she's trying to stop Henry from bleeding to death."

"Charlene?"

He swallowed. "Down."

Doc stepped out from behind the truck, the gun still pointing ahead at shoulder level. "All right. No other weapons?"

"No, sir." Doc hadn't mentioned Emma. John hoped she was hiding some place and not doing anything stupid, or hadn't got in the path of one of those bullets. He had to step over a body of a younger man and he had no idea if he'd taken him down or whether it was Charlene. Probably Charlene. She was always the better shot. He kept his eyes on Doc as he advanced, watched for body language that right now told him he was simply lining himself up to get killed. His former mentor wasn't buying it. Not in the slightest.

Beyond the driveway, from the direction of the yard, came a rattling, scratching sound. Both men kept their places. The scratching softened, became a soft, reverberating purr. A patch of night above their heads abruptly became darker.

John dived away just as Doc's gun went off. The bullet sounded as if it had hit the truck but there was no guarantee the next one wouldn't end up in his chest. He rolled, crouched, fumbled for his other weapon, heard another shot, saw something big, the size and color of a trashcan, drop on the driveway. Another shot from some distance away and a hand grabbed his collar and warm metal jabbed hard, just below his ear.

"Put it down, John."

"Or what? You're going to shoot me anyway." God damn it Charlene where are you?

"I thought you might still be armed. And now that we've established that, and you're blocking Charlene's considerable aim, maybe you're more useful to me alive for the moment. You lied to me."

No shit. John let the gun slide through his fingers, and

stared ahead at the thing on the driveway. "What's going on, Doc? You always told me nothing good came out of the Fall." Blood like oil was seeping from the dead creature, staining the interlocked paving stones. He wondered if Charlene would take her shot despite the risk, and hit him by mistake.

"True, but Llennendhrad, it turns out, is quite persuasive and— we reached an agreement." Doc's voice lowered to a bare whisper, became covert. "John— I know where Lucifer is."

The words floated past, flung out hooks that sought to snare him and carry him off. But it was a lie. It had to be. "Doc—"

"Enough." The man shook him. "Now, stand up, nice and slow, we'll do it together."

He tested Doc's grip by leaning forward a little more than he needed to. But it was rock solid. His gun lay on the ground, about a yard away. It taunted him— a solid, matte shape in the dark— go on, lunge and you can make it. He stood up, and Doc's hand grasped the rear of his jacket.

"Very good, now start backing up and to your right, easy now."

He took one step, and another. He felt the bullet like a hot wind and all of a sudden that grip on his jacket wasn't there any more and something hard clattered to the ground. Maybe he'd heard the shot, but right now there was too much input.

Damn it, Charlene. He fell forward, scrambled for his weapon. Doc was immediately on top of him, surprisingly strong, and they began to wrestle for leverage.

Behind them a battering ram was trying to burst open the carriage house doors from the inside. Wood began to creak and groan under stress and he could feel Doc's arm trying to get around him for a chokehold.

John slithered away. He couldn't see his weapon. Maybe they'd kicked it away in the struggle. Doc pinned his legs and there was another shot but this one must have missed completely because his former mentor, strong as a bull, kept on coming.

John managed to flip onto his back; he curled up and head butted the guy. He could see a weapon— his, Doc's, he didn't know but it was there on the ground while whatever was trapped inside the carriage house continued to lay down a heavy beat against the doors. Something was coming out. Something big.

Doc's weight was still on him but this time he was able to crawl out from beneath him. He leapt for the gun, scraped his elbows and ribs on the hard ground. He was able to connect but his fingers felt like fat slugs and he had to adjust his grip. He rolled onto his back once more and took aim, his turn to make all the threats, but Doc was already bringing up his own weapon and so John fired. He fired again, and again, from an awkward angle while muzzle flash drew blots across his eyes and his mind screamed a litany of anguish.

A loud crack, and flying pieces of wood. Another creature took to the sky and disappeared in the dark.

Footsteps.

He rolled, brought up the weapon, saw a pair of Keds and bare ankles. "Jesus, Charlene I nearly shot you."

She ignored him, went to the fallen figure of Doc. After a moment, "Dead," she pronounced. "Good job." Her eyes searched the sky. "Go get your brother. I'll try and find that fool girl and handle the breach."

He scrambled to his feet, checked his weapon. "And Llennendhrad?"

"If I see him, I'll shoot that son of a bitch. You do the same. We need to wrap this up before the cops get here."

He stared at her as she walked away, her eyes on the night sky, still looking for the escaped bug, then he shook his head and looked back toward the fallen figure of Doc. He felt stunned, knowing what he'd just done and realized he'd have to pay for it at some point. But he couldn't think about that now. He had to get Luke out of there and where the heck had Emma got to? He took a guess. It got him rummaging real quick for Doc's pistol and some spare ammo that he shoved in his jacket pocket.

He approached the carriage house. There was an odd light seeping through the broken door, shifting shadow and hinting at movement within. Closer still and he saw the dead, crowded in there as if it was free beer night and a band was playing. No sign of Elliot Black, or rather the creature Llennendhrad who, John assumed, had managed to crack Doc's tough facade, had got into his head and had spun a web of lies. Llennendhrad's fault then, that John had had to shoot his mentor. Right or wrong, at this particular moment it was the only explanation he could stomach.

He entered, became enveloped in bodies and mist. Heads turned, regarded him with a momentary interest that soon waned. A break in the crowd and he saw the carousel— it was moving, slow and smooth the horses drifted past. No sign of Luke, or Black.

He kept his pistol to the fore and began a slow circuit, all the while looking for something more substantial than the current crowd. One full circuit and he risked a call out. "Luke!"

The center of the carousel darkened, and a thing way too big to be human slapped hard against the canopy. John ducked. Another insect. It crawled upside down toward him. And at once he remembered her children in that giant, ruined cathedral. They had been frightened, and in jostling him hadn't meant him any harm. He gave it a nod. Pass by, little brother. He lowered his weapon and the creature scuttled quickly toward the broken door.

No time to understand what he'd just done, he focused once more on the center of the carousel. The light flickered there, promised another arrival. So close now, he felt the pull; he was part of the fabric, one of the threads alongside the dead, who for a moment solidified en masse.

The blow, when it came, threw him backward and toppled him like a bowling pin. Both canopy and the ceiling above it exploded as she rose quickly, her momentum carrying her up and through. An instant of being crowded out, of being partially crushed, he couldn't breathe and then she was out, taking the roof along with her. She was accompanied, too. One, two, maybe three of her young. He still had the gun and he scrambled to his feet and raised it, tracked the giant black shape in the night sky, but in the end...

The carousel was still spinning, and staggering like a drunk he approached. He stepped onto the moving platform and hooked onto a jet-black horse with flared nostrils. Its eyes looked utterly real. Why didn't you take a shot? The question was writ on its features. He frowned, made sure he had his balance and then began to work his way into the center.

Beyond the inner line the floor had dissolved and a familiar scent wrapped around him, prodded his memory and made his left shoulder ache. A thud against the toe of his boot; he looked down. Floorboards. Two bodies lying there at the center. He took a tentative step toward them and the one beneath the other crawled out toward him.

"...too fucking late and the others are going to break through."

A hand reached out, grabbed his ankle, made him jump. "Luke. Holy shit." He had both feet on the center floorboards now and something heavy hammered hard from below. He felt the abrupt, shocking reverberation. Felt it again. More children, wanting to join the Mother.

Luke was moving like a crab, his clothes trailing in rags behind him. He exhibited the hard shadows of puncture wounds on his back. A recent heal and still a work in progress by the looks of it. John looked to the other figure and for a long, stupid moment he thought he was looking at Rachel.

Her skin looked like paper, all her energy gone, she rolled drunkenly onto her back and shuddered as something particularly heavy butted against the barrier beneath them. Luke was already crawling past one of the horses. "Fire," he said. "Burn it down."

John holstered his weapon and dashed over to the very middle of the carousel floor. "Emma," he whispered. He scooped her up, she felt too light to be human, nothing but a mannequin of wire and paper. Her eyelids flitted, her head rolled. Her skin appeared to be adorned with slender, decorative strings of vines; they were part of her now, and when her eyes came open they were the color of pale jade. She had a shadow alongside her, too, the ghost from the diner. Whatever had happened, he'd been with her all the way.

Luke had gone, and with the continuing hammering beneath him, so hard it rattled his teeth, he figured he'd better do the same and get Emma to safety. He cradled her flimsy frame, weaved his precious cargo in between the carousel horses and pushed resolutely through the dead mob. Part way through he looked back, and the center floor was becoming thin. He could see woolly insect heads, all pressed in, and a face among them...

Outside, the yard was littered with fragments of timber and parts of the carriage house roof. No sign of the cops.

It seemed a miracle that the building wasn't surrounded with flashing blue and red lights. Maybe they were out there somewhere beyond the outer gate, Henry and Helen already in custody.

"Is he out?"

He looked down at her, a long bundle of ancient, crumbling newspaper. "Yes," he told her. "Now, you need to rest."

"Too late," she croaked. "Too late."

"Shh." He had to be content with his knowledge of Rachel, in similar situations, how she'd always bounced back. It would be no different with Emma. Get some food down her —

Charlene appeared alongside him. "Darned thing was the size of a school bus."

"Did you get a shot at her?"

"That was her? Oh, dear, sweet Jesus. Where's your brother?"

Sounds coming from the workshop. Luke emerged, staggering, weak, but he was carrying two large metal cans. "Quickly," he rasped. "We need to destroy it."

Charlene was staring at the cans. "Well, that'll do it." She reached for Emma. "Go help him. I'll mop up if there are any remnants."

John released Emma carefully into Charlene's arms, as if she might break in two. A pang of regret, at having to leave her with the other woman, and then he dashed after his brother who had already reached the carriage house, or what was left of it. The dead were still there, packed like sardines, their heads turning toward Luke as if they were expecting something.

"Shut the power down." Luke pointed toward the stairs. He began to push his way through the throng. Hands reached out and touched him, dozens of them, feverish and desperate, like he was their messiah.

John dashed down the steps, found the switch soon enough. The soft, underlying hum dimmed and the lights down there flickered a little brighter. More dead down here, looking up, rotten eyes brimming and full of worship, of hope. At the center of the room an illusion flickered. The thick pole support— in his peripheral vision it appeared darker, its lines uneven; it promised him endless hours of torment before his eventual evisceration. He swayed on the bottom step. He'd never forget that for as long as he lived.

Hammering akin to a giant's fist on heavy oak brought him up and out of the cloying pit. He ran back up the steps to where various inhabitants of the Fall were still trying to get out and the dead were waiting. He smelled paint thinners, turpentine. Luke had opened one of the cans and was sloshing it all over his painted horses.

"Get the other can. Quickly."

John didn't need telling twice. He unscrewed the cap and got to work. When he was done and the can was empty and the surroundings reeked of solvent he looked for his brother. They'd need a match, a spark.

The dead were pushing close. He could feel some of them, their shoulders and arms jostling, wanting to get closer to the pyre, and scrambling toward the very center of it all —

"Luke!" His brother had something in his hand, long and narrow like a short wand. It was a thin, butane kitchen lighter. "Luke! This way or you'll burn—"

His brother turned, and smiled.

CHAPTER 31

LUKE

Murder.

He was going to murder them, the Lady and her kin, bathe them in fire, consign them to oblivion in a boiling wall of flame; that's all it would take to reduce them to ruin. But he was ready, prepared, and the dead were waiting.

"Luke, for God's sake!"

"If you don't want to burn, big brother, I suggest you stand back." He brandished the lighter and saw John hesitate at the edge of the inner circle.

"Look, I know this is your work, but—"

"And you know *exactly* what my work can do. Why didn't you tell me?" He saw his brother's shoulders sag.

"It was for your own good. You don't know—"

"My own good? You fucking lied to me and for how long? Years. My entire life." There was a heavy jolt from below, like they'd found something more solid and were using it as a battering ram. He almost lost his balance.

John had grabbed onto one of the horses, a paler gray than the rest. Funny— Luke had given it his eyes. "Not here, Luke. And not now. I'll try and explain things but you need to step out of that circle."

"And then what? This needs to end. Right now." He examined the lighter. Saw the button he needed to depress.

"And what about Emma? What about your girlfriend? Think she'll understand?"

He looked up from his examination, saw John through a veil of rat-tailed hair. “She’s safe?”

“Yes. She’s safe.”

“Then that’s good enough. I can’t stay with her. Those marks, John, I’m killing her.”

“That isn’t you. It’s Bower’s Fall. It does things, to them, to our women. Stop this. Come out of there and let’s talk.”

Bower’s Fall. The place even had a name. He shook his head. It was becoming too late for words, and he could see through the floor. Another few attempts and they’d be through. “Dad knew, didn’t he. He knew how bad I was. That’s why he stuck a knife in me.”

“Luke, we can put this right. We can go after her.”

“No. You won’t catch her. She’s a monster and she’ll burn everything. And God only knows what else is down there.” His hands were shaking. Any more and he’d drop the lighter on the floor. He gripped harder, became resolute. He smiled at his brother. “And anyway. I made a deal with the dead. I promised when I died I take them with me. I can do that, don’t you know? I can take them home.”

“Luke. Please...”

He clicked on the button, hard and deliberate. A tiny flame appeared and he threw it toward the black and silver tiger, on the opposite side of the carousel from where his brother was standing. I’m sorry, he thought. I’m so sorry. And for a short moment he was bathed in silence and regret. But he had apologized to them, and he could do no more.

Decision made he felt relieved, and he lowered his shoulders, let out a breath. He was death. He would go forth with his lost flock, and he would open up his last gate –

And immediately his face was full of flame and heat as the rising fumes ignited. He was knocked flat. The fire waved like a banner above his head and his foot became caught; he was being dragged. He couldn’t breathe. He twisted and turned. The heat was incredible. He lost his bearings, felt his naked ribs scraping on the ground, and a little ways ahead he saw the Lady. Fresh paint and varnish cracked like tiny gunshot. She was enveloped immediately.

He blacked out for a second. When he came to he rolled over, drew in a breath. His lungs hurt but he wasn't burning. Nearby John was beating himself down with the help of a woman he hadn't seen before. He'd been dragged out. His brother had saved him from the inferno.

"Son of a bitch I should kill you myself."

Still alive. He stared at the remains of the carriage house, watched his animals go up in flames. He felt gutted, like he was still right there with them, already reduced to bones. But was the gate still open? He didn't think so. The hammering had stopped as soon as the carousel had ignited, and now the flames and heat had started their journey to the lower floor, greedy for fuel. They were safe, he considered. For now. And yet he could paint another carousel, couldn't he? And another, and another. Hell, he didn't even have to go that far. Just one trip down there was all he'd needed to get acclimated and now all he required was canvas and —

He climbed to his knees, stared at his hands. While John was still busy he stood up and set off for the kitchen. This had to end. He'd made a mess of things. He'd thought he could control it all— control her, just like he could control the dead but it wasn't like that. It wasn't like that at all. She'd called to him through the Lady months ago, and he had been such a willing, stupid, unknowing accomplice.

He paused at the kitchen door, remembered what had happened in there. His fault. All his fault. He could feel some of the dead alongside him, hear their whispers, curious, disappointed or simply chattering amongst themselves about this night's events. Well, the show wasn't over yet.

He stepped inside, looked at all the blood on the floor. It had shifted color, become darker. His artist's eye took in the changes, preferring that particular hue to the more vibrant, earlier version.

Grace was still lying where she had fallen at the far side

of the kitchen. His fault.

"Luke?" It was John, outside, no doubt looking for him. "Luke!"

He didn't have much time. He stepped past the kitchen dining table, brushed past a chair; it clattered over onto the tiled floor. Some of the blood had crawled along the grout, spilled over and flowed across his path. He slid across the slick surface, almost fell before regaining his balance.

"Luke, what the hell—"

The drawer. He gripped the handle, pulled it open. He couldn't see what he was looking for and so he moved to the next one. There. The handle felt cold, the utensil was solid and heavy in his hand. But not this hand, no, he'd have to switch.

"No. Don't—"

Left hand. On the counter top. The bad hand; the one that held all the magic. And now time had slowed. John had his arm outstretched. Luke raised the cleaver in a high arc and brought it down.

He thought it might bounce, that he'd have to do it again and again; keep hacking and chopping until there was nothing left. But he must have picked the right spot and hit true. Pain arrived once the blood began to spurt. Back to bright red. Back to seeing what should not be seen. He took in a breath, felt his lungs expand. And when the scream arrived it was glorious.

His surroundings were pale gray and white. Flat walls provided a blank canvas. The few dead who had stuck with him hung at the edges of the room, their features easy to pick out.

It was too hot, stifling in fact. He was sitting partially upright in bed, he wore a gown, the stump at the end of his left arm was bandaged and there was a needle in the other. There was a window to his right and he could see out into a corridor. People walked past, on their way to see others more deserving of the company of the living.

He closed his eyes. The dead remained, silent and emotionless, retreated into their own thoughts, like people waiting for a bus. He wondered if there would be any visitors; wondered maybe if he'd be better off left alone. He could feel his left hand, even though it wasn't there any more. He wanted to reach over and scratch the tingling knuckles. It was an odd feeling that ultimately became a wave of nausea and so he opened his eyes in an effort to distract himself.

Emma was standing in the doorway. Her appearance brought forth a heady mixture of shame and relief.

She smiled, stepped forward, ignored his ethereal companions. When she leaned across to kiss him, he caught the scent of flowers. It was only her perfume but it reminded him of that place, of Bower's Fall.

"How are you?" She took a seat in the chair next to the bed, and held on to his right hand, the one with the needle in it.

He shrugged. "Better now you're here."

"Doctor says you can come home tomorrow."

"Home."

She nodded. "I went to look at the place today. That's why I'm late."

"Not home though, is it."

"We'll see. If we don't like it, we'll move."

It became a matter of urgency. "Emma, I don't want this. I don't want them..."

"I know, I know." She let out a sigh. "But right now I don't know what else we can do."

"The police."

"Yes. John says it'll get straightened out. But until it does—" She let go of his hand, leaned forward and rested her head on his shoulder.

"I'm sorry," he said.

"Don't be. It's not your fault."

He clenched his jaw, knew it was pointless arguing over it, and that he'd already attempted to pay for his sins. The fingers of his missing left hand tingled and agreed. He stared at the ceiling. "They tell me Mom is still alive."

"I've met her."

He sat up a little further, stared at her. "What?"

Emma turned her head, looked up at him with her strange, altered eyes. "I'm not going to lie. She's... odd. I don't like her."

He wanted to laugh, but he knew how it would sound, so instead he simply breathed in and out for a while. His mother. He wondered if she'd try and stab him with a knife, too. "I want you to promise me something."

"Anything." The look on her face told him she meant it.

"We disappear. The very first chance we get."

She was sitting up now, staring at him. He watched her deliberate, chew over the consequences. And after a long moment, "Sure."

"What is he?" His brother visibly squirmed, but Luke reckoned he deserved it.

In the end John shrugged. "Part Hell, part Fall." His eyes hardened. "He's a demon. But the real question is whether or not he escaped."

A face among those crowded heads pressed close beneath his feet. No, Llennendhrad hadn't gotten out, but he would, given time.

Luke turned away. He couldn't face his brother, his final visitor in this antiseptic prison. One more night to check his progress, and then he'd be out, with Emma, in an unfamiliar bolt-hole somewhere on the coast. And then what? His left hand, his artist's hand, was gone...

"Luke." The voice had lost its razor edge. "I'm having a tough time with this, too, okay? I knew we'd get to this. Just... not so soon, and in better circumstances."

He swallowed. "Do I get to see our mother?"

"If you want to. She's leaving the choice up to you."

"How could she just—?"

"Stop it. Just stop." The words cracked like a whip. "She was protecting you, so enough of this self-indulgent bullshit. You're not the only one getting fucked over by all of this, you hear me?"

He slammed his eyes shut, couldn't look at John any more. But he heard the chair scrape back. He was cutting out, he was going to leave him. Maybe that was deserved, too. His brother's eyes had taken on another dimension, deeper, darker; he hadn't thought it was possible and the observer, the artist wanted to remember, then he could paint... "Wait," he said. One more thing. Just one more thing.

"Look, we'll talk when you're out of the hospital, okay? We'll get through this, Luke. Just give it time."

One more thing. He opened his eyes. John had almost made it to the door. "Wait. Llennendhrad said—" The idea choked him, he could barely get the words out. "He suggested I wasn't human."

John's face took on the pallor of the walls. Slowly, deliberately, he shook his head, and kept on walking.

"Well? Is it true?" Luke's voice rose. Fear and outrage powered it out through the doorway in the wake of his brother. He sat upright. His left arm began to throb. The scream tore at his throat.

"Is it true?"

WINTER

CHAPTER 32

EMMA

"No, it's okay. I've filled in all the paperwork, and I'll go back next semester. Sure. No, I'm fine, really. I know. I should have told you. So, how's Dad?" She listened, tapped her foot against one of the cafe dining table legs. Calling home. On a practical level, not as easy as it used to be, emotionally it was devastating. And when the call came to an end it left her with an empty feeling in her stomach, after the lies she'd told, and having had a glimpse of a life she was no longer a part of. She handed the phone back to John. "You sure this isn't traceable?"

He nodded, slipped the phone in his pocket. His silence was both sword and shield and was very effectively wearing her down. She observed him as he stared off into middle distance. He looked good. He'd filled out a little. He'd cut his hair, kept his beard although he'd trimmed it considerably. The look suited him, pulled attention away from those devastating eyes and made her envious that she couldn't employ similar, visual sleight of hand.

She wanted to talk— anything from shooting the breeze to discovering more about this mysterious group she was now a part of; how he felt about what happened those few weeks ago; how he'd managed to keep both her and Luke off the radar once the authorities had swarmed in on a burning house and four dead bodies. She'd had to give an interview to the police, about how she and Luke had split over the summer and she hadn't seen him...

She drank her coffee.

When she was done, "I'm ready."

He stood up; he came around and pulled back her chair as she rose, and when they reached the car he opened up the passenger door, ever the attentive companion. She wanted to punch him in the face. Instead, while they were this close —

"John—" He turned his head away like she'd slapped him, but she didn't move, and kept her eyes on him until he melted.

"I'm trying to be polite," he said. "I don't know what else you want."

"This silence, is polite?"

He gave her a helpless, utterly humorless smile. "Better that, than—"

"Than what?"

They were standing so close together it was easy for his hand to slip around her waist, to reel her in and brush his lips so lightly against her forehead, and against her temple, and against the side of her jaw until they finally came to rest on her mouth, soft and tentative, waiting until she responded because she couldn't help it. She still remembered that moment in Bower's Fall like it was yesterday. She could taste it on him, feel it resonate through physical contact that made her flesh tingle, especially within those curling trails tattooed on and beneath her skin.

"Better than this," he whispered when he finally pulled away, "where you tell me, despite knowing how I feel about you, that we can't do this because you love my brother and you need to take care of him."

Straight to the heart of the matter. Typical John De Grasse. She gave up. "Not even a truce?"

He toyed with a strand of her hair and then let her go. "No. Get in the car."

Her first view of the sea arrived after John turned off the Pacific Coast Highway and swept the vehicle beyond the trees. Her new home was quite the consolation prize, and despite the ominous upcoming meeting, the sight of the ocean brought a faint smile to her face. She wound down the window, closed her eyes and breathed deep while her taciturn companion took the car around the remaining twists and turns, slowing for the last hundred yards as they drove past the high walls and tall wooden gates of their neighbors. The houses were packed tight in this little enclave next to the sea, but the people who lived there didn't seem to show any interest in getting to know their neighbors, which was just fine as far as Emma was concerned. Nearly half of the houses seemed empty during the week anyway.

John stopped the car outside a teal-colored garage door and activated the opener. He nodded toward a silver Mercedes, parked nearby. "She's already here," he said.

Emma stared at him. "Oh, no. I told Luke I'd be here when she arrived."

He grinned by way of reply, drove the car inside. "I'm betting he ran down to the beach as soon as he heard the doorbell." He got out, opened her passenger door.

She got out of the car. "Assuming I had a key, I wouldn't have used the doorbell."

He nodded. "You're getting more like her every day."

He was saying it to rankle her, but seeing as it was the most conversation she'd got out of him all day she counted her blessings.

Inside there was no sign of Rachel. But she was here, Emma could tell.

John strode on ahead toward the rear of the house.

Emma hung back. There'd be no yes ma'am and bowing and scraping from her. She went to the bathroom, freshened up, straightened her hair and then stopped herself, fearing she was doing it to pass muster. She adjusted the collar of her shirt, fastened another button, and walked out to join the others.

Across a huge, polished wood floored living room toward tall windows that looked right out to sea. There'd been a storm out there a few nights ago, and she and Luke had stood at the windows and watched the lightning flash. Down past the pool, by the fence, John and his mother were looking down toward the beach.

No sign of Luke. Instead, a stranger hovered just outside the door. He nodded politely. Emma attempted a smile. Their new bodyguard. Rachel had brought him. After everything had happened, there was fear that the newly awakened Luke might be kidnapped. By whom, she still wasn't exactly sure.

She stepped outside, skirted the pool. She'd left her beach towel out here, and a book she'd been reading, and she made a note to collect them on her way back, just another little distraction to keep her mind off the main event.

Rachel turned and smiled as she approached. "John, would you go and join your brother?"

"Yes ma'am."

Emma watched him walk to the steps and disappear from view. It hurt that he didn't even glance her way before leaving her in the clutches of his formidable mother. And when he was out of earshot —

"You have both my sons, it seems."

They were off to a good start. She felt her hackles rising immediately. "John—" She stopped, didn't know what to say.

"Keep leaning on him, make him feel as if he is needed,

then he'll keep coming back to you." Rachel shrugged. "It's how he is."

Emma felt her cheeks burning. "I'm not trying to torment him. I didn't want this to happen."

"The Fall. I understand." The other woman's eyes were implacable, eerily similar to her own these days. She had looked beautiful the last time Emma had seen her but on this occasion she appeared younger too, by about ten years. Not quite Emma's age, but still, early thirties maybe. It appeared as if she'd found the magic bullet, a way to regress. No doubt everyone woman on the planet would want to know the secret, until they considered the implications.

Luke had been having nightmares ever since the night of the burning carousel and they'd torn and pushed through her own attempts at distance, and no matter how hard she'd tried to dismiss what had happened, had tried so hard to forget, he reminded her of it every time he cried out and sat up in bed surrounded by a crowd of the dead, sweat drenched, delirious and shivering and telling her he wasn't human. As if her odd eyes and the vines still snaking across her skin weren't unsettling enough. His wicked, merciless dreams had made them both doubt their claims to humanity.

She watched Rachel look over the fence, and so she stepped forward and shared her view of the two men at the water's edge, their backs turned, looking out to sea; one slightly taller and narrower than the other, his arms self-consciously wrapped about himself, the other with shorter hair, his shoulders set square and determined, built to carry the world.

"Mind if we go back inside?" Rachel asked. "I'm a hot house flower and this open air is a little too much."

Emma nodded, tried not to feel uneasy with the metaphor. She followed the woman inside, nodded at the sentinel at the door. Rachel seemed to be at home, or at least gave the impression she'd been here before. Maybe it was her house, who knew? Emma still didn't know all that much about her new benefactors, every one of them still a stranger, and it made her miss Rhonda and the beginnings of their friendship and damn that horrible man who had taken her life. Had he lived, Doc was going to abscond with Luke, too, just as soon as Elliot Black had got what he wanted; he was going to steal him away, and use him...

They took seats on adjacent couches, wary as cats, and she fought hard not to compare— the eye color, and faint markings on the other woman's arms that were so similar to her own. What did it mean? She discovered she didn't want to know and she sat there silently, willing this audience to be over as soon as possible.

"So. How is he?"

"Did you talk to him?"

Rachel shrugged. "A few words. Not enough. He's angry with me, of course."

Emma wondered what she should say; what he'd want his mother to know. She decided to stick with the basics. "His arm is healing up well. But he won't let me do anything, and he shuts down all mention of prosthetics."

"He's aware you can give it back to him?"

"He's aware of a lot of things these days."

"I can imagine." The woman had shrunk back a little into her seat. Her mind seemed elsewhere. Something was coming. But not yet. Trust had still to be established between them, and Emma was beginning to feel it might never happen. "I'll make sure the house doesn't intrude too much," Rachel said eventually.

Emma frowned. "They're afraid of him. Of what he can do."

"And, what might happen if he were to get into the wrong hands. They'd prefer to render him... safe." Rachel laced her fingers, and her lips became a thin line.

"They'll destroy him."

"More or less."

"It's not going to happen. Have they done anything to John?"

"No." The woman's smile was cold.

Emma tried to remain composed. Her muscles twitched; she wanted desperately to make a run for it, and inside she railed at her timidity. She should be used to this by now, of that world that assailed her consciousness and refused to dissipate whether her eyes were open or shut; a scent-filled backdrop that waxed and waned, back and forth like a flag in a lazy breeze while in the foreground, even more out of focus, the occasional dead thing drifted, including her new, near constant companion, the fair haired ghost from the carousel. It was enough to drive a person crazy. More than enough.

"And what about *her*?" The moth. A subject that overshadowed everything.

"Your responsibility is Luke. You know what's at stake. Leave her to John and the others."

"Will they ever find her?"

Rachel's eyes narrowed. "What do your insides tell you? You're more a part of her than I."

Poison.

Emma could see her. Massive, soaring, letting the wind carry her while her offspring struggled to keep up; but she wouldn't remain that way for long. She'd adapt like she always did, until the day of reckoning came and it was time to feed...

Luke had whispered to her in moments of confession, about Llennendhrad, how the man refused to believe the threat she so obviously was. And now Rachel was giving her an odd look and she wondered how long she'd drifted off and let her thoughts run.

Your responsibility is Luke.

She took in a breath, let it out, and stood up. Admirably her legs remained strong and held her steady. "I need some air."

The other woman smiled and rose like a cobra from a basket. "Very well. Let's go back outside."

It became hard not to bolt. And in the end she gave into it because she needed the distance. Outside, she headed straight for the narrow wooden staircase that led down to the beach, and became immensely relieved when Rachel didn't follow and chose to remain at the railing. When she reached the bottom she ploughed resolutely through dry sand. Luke and John were still at the water's edge. She saw John turn, say something to his brother and then start toward her. They passed by one another with barely a glance.

Luke held out his hand when she arrived alongside him; held on to her as if to stop himself from sinking in the wet sand. Some of his ethereal followers were evident, broad, faint strokes, dancing atop the incoming tide. She looked back, saw John climbing the stairs, and Rachel still there at the rail, and wondered if they knew she and Luke were going to run, the very first chance they got.

CHAPTER 33

JOHN

He tried to remain above it, to regard the pair standing at the shore with some manner of dignity and objectivity, and not descend into a pit of jealousy and anguish.

"Hard to be magnanimous, but your brother needs her right now." Rachel was alongside him, her arms folded as if she was cold out here on the border between continent and ocean. No need to read his mind, he guessed the look on his face was enough.

He nodded. "He's not as strong as his bullshit wants me to believe."

"Always the same with you two." She was smiling now. "How soon do you think, before he starts painting with his right hand?"

He looked down toward Luke, who now had his good arm thrown around Emma's shoulder. John shook his head. "I'd be surprised if he hadn't already started." It felt vindictive perhaps to say that, but it was the truth as he saw it.

He turned away, couldn't face the sight of them. He was, a grown man, beginning to act like a sulky teenager in front of his mother and he needed some space. It was time to run, he supposed. Now he'd done his duty and his younger sibling was settled in and away from prying eyes, it was time to do a little disappearing act of his own, before the house got their hooks in him. Time to drift, survive, until someone figured out where the moth had got to, and he became useful once more. Someone had gone to great pains to lock her up in that lush gray prison, and now she was out.

"I want you to drive me back," Rachel said.

Her words came as a shock. So. He wouldn't be allowed to pull an escape act of his own. His heart shrank back and fear crept into the gap. He'd shot and killed Doc. Despite the man being a murderer and a traitor, he had been one of the house Adepts. There would be a price to pay and even his own mother wasn't about to let him run from it. He closed his eyes, lowered his head. His mouth tasted bitter.

"It isn't what you think," she said. "You've changed, evolved since this latest event, everyone can see that."

He wondered what she meant; evolved as in becoming more trigger happy, or after that stint on the tree, had devolved into an addict, a victim of his perversions? But no, the guns he was used to and his encounter with Emma made him believe he wasn't cast adrift on that score either.

He remembered Llennendhrad and that nasty little conversation they'd had about his father and the scars on his back and how it had made him tougher. Was that it, then? This latest experience had thrown yet another protective layer around his hide? Pity that didn't apply to his heart. He stepped away from the rail, determined not to look down toward the shoreline again. He gave Rachel a look that said he didn't necessarily understand. She continued regardless.

"With Doc gone, we need someone to take his place, a leader, someone who can inspire us. Our immediate future is likely to prove difficult, not to mention dangerous." She smiled at him like it was his birthday and she had brought him a gift, which under normal circumstances she never did. "I recommended that person should be you. I received no objections."

John stared at her. Difficult and dangerous. He barked out a laugh, he couldn't help it. Sure, now the shit had hit the fan they'd bring one of the grunts to the fore, let them take all the responsibility, along with the rap when things started to head south. There was no choice, of course. He'd do as he was told, just as he always had. Good old dependable John.

"If I'm—" He struggled with the concept. "If I'm to be their leader, there'll need to be some changes."

"Of course." Rachel's smile grew only more delighted. Which worried him even more.

They left quietly. Rachel gave her Mercedes keys to Luke and Emma's new bodyguard. John brought his vehicle out of the garage, and opened the rear passenger door.

"I'll sit up front," she said

He kept silent and drove. What else could he do? His future lay ahead, mapped out by his dear mother. And again he recalled that conversation, about Rachel standing by while his father laid into him, again and again. But in the end, no matter what she said, it came down to trust. And unlike the house he wasn't afraid of his younger brother and his newly awakened talents. And unlike his mother he wasn't afraid of Emma. He'd noted the changes; her eyes and skin only gave away a part of it.

Rachel had lowered the back of her seat. Her head was turned away, her attempts at youthful energy had worn her out and she was already napping.

The lights changed, and he shifted gears and headed inland toward the nearest Interstate. A quick glance over his shoulder, back toward the coast, and a bitter smile appeared on his face. After all the events surrounding the carousel, everything had changed and the world had become a more dangerous place. They were heading into a storm, and he hoped those two back there would be ready.

About the Author

Janet Joyce Holden was born in the North of England, a land of boisterous winds and persistent rain, and currently lives in Southern California where the air is dry, the winds are hot and precipitation is a rare but mostly benevolent gift. She is a writer of dark, supernatural fiction, is the author of Carousel and a number of short stories published in various anthologies. Other activities include photography, mixed media art and dallying with sharp objects: sewing, embroidery, the study of historical European fencing, and the custodianship of twenty or so feisty and decidedly prickly rose shrubs.

You can find her on:
Facebook https://www.facebook.com/janetj.holden
Website: janetjoyceholden.com

Acknowledgements

I want to thank Bob Booth, Matt Bechtel, Dan Booth and Kelli Jones at Necon E-Books, for having so much faith in me, particularly Bob, who offered such kind words, and Matt who has been such an amazing cheerleader and source of inspiration throughout. I want to thank Kate Jonez at Omnium Gatherum for allowing my painted horses into her stable and into print. I want to thank Christopher Jones for his painstaking efforts in trawling through an earlier copy of the manuscript, offering the needed critique and helping me make this a better book, and the inimitable, amazing gang at Horror World for their camaraderie and inspiration. I also want to thank David Smithson, Tony Tremblay, Cheryl Jones and David Dodd, for valiantly reading through some of my other works and making me believe I could actually do this. And last but not least, I want to thank my husband Tony for all his support, and who puts up with my writer nonsense without complaint.

29711525R00192

Made in the USA
Charleston, SC
20 May 2014